Fat
Fridays

BOOKS BY JUDITH KEIM

THE HARTWELL WOMEN
The Talking Tree
Sweet Talk
Straight Talk
Baby Talk

FAT FRIDAYS GROUP
Fat Fridays
Sassy Saturdays

THE BEACH HOUSE HOTEL
Breakfast at the Beach House Hotel
Lunch at the Beach House Hotel

Winning Big

CHILDREN'S BOOKS BY J. S. KEIM

THE HIDDEN MOON SERIES
The Hidden Moon
Return to the Hidden Moon
Trouble on the Hidden Moon

Kermit Greene's World

Fat Fridays

A Novel

Judith Keim

LAKE UNION
PUBLISHING

Text copyright © 2016 Judith Keim

Published by Lake Union Publishing, Seattle

www.apub.com

Amazon, the Amazon logo, and Lake Union Publishing are trademarks of Amazon.com, Inc., or its affiliates.

ISBN-13: 9781503940666
ISBN-10: 1503940667

Cover design by Danielle Christopher

Printed in the United States of America

For all the women whose friendships
have meant so much to me . . .
Love you!

CHAPTER ONE
SUKIE

Life was good, Sukie Skidmore thought, as she returned home from an early Christmas shopping day in Atlanta. Her daughter was doing well in college and her son and daughter-in-law would present her with a grandchild in the next few months. Ted, her husband, hated the idea of becoming a grandfather, but Sukie, even as young as she was, loved the idea of a little one in the family.

Surprised to see her husband's BMW in the driveway, Sukie hurried inside and up the hallway stairs to see if he was all right. He'd complained earlier that he was coming down with a cold. The door to their bedroom was closed. She stepped closer. At the noises she heard from inside the room, she realized something was wrong. Very wrong.

She flung open the door.

Ted's bare bottom was moving rhythmically on top of Emmy Lou Rogers, her Pilates instructor. Seeing Sukie, Emmy Lou shrieked, pushed Ted away, and scrambled to her feet. Taking itty-bitty steps that bobbed her ample breasts up and down in a comic dance, Emmy Lou hurried to reach her clothes strewn on the floor.

Ted faced Sukie, his manhood standing tall. "Get out of here!"

His snarling words shredded Sukie's attempt at composure. She let out a howl, reached for Emmy Lou—who was trying to edge her way out of the room—threw her to the floor, and pinned her down.

"Your boyfriend, the one you talk about in class, is my *husband*?" she shrieked at Emmy Lou.

"Stop it!" Ted grabbed hold of Sukie and pulled her off Emmy Lou.

Outraged, Sukie fought him with all her might. She didn't realize that while she and Ted were scuffling, Emmy Lou was calling the police.

◆ ◆ ◆

Now, sitting in her car outside of Anthony's Pizzeria, remembering the humiliation of facing the police chief in such mortifying circumstances, Sukie felt her body hum with indignation. During the past few months, her personal situation had become even more of a public nightmare as Emmy Lou eagerly spread her version of the sleazy details, making Sukie seem a pathetic woman who couldn't keep her husband happy.

Sukie let out a sigh. She'd promised to meet a friend for lunch, and though she hated the thought of being out in the community, she couldn't let Ted and Emmy Lou's actions force her to continue hiding in her house. No more, she vowed, climbing out of her car. But crossing the parking lot toward the popular restaurant, she felt as if she'd swallowed a whole colony of ants. Anthony's was one of the busiest places in town, and she despised being the cause of small-town gossip in Williston, Georgia.

She entered the restaurant and then paused. Trying to ignore the stares and whispers cast in her direction, she searched for Betsy Wilson's friendly face. The delicious aroma of garlic and tomato wafted around her. Anthony's wasn't fancy, but it was known as the best place in town for pizza.

Sukie followed the sound of Betsy's distinctive laugh to a back booth, where Betsy sat with three other women. Seeing her, Betsy smiled and patted the empty space beside her. Sukie gratefully slid into the oversized booth onto the soft, red, plastic-covered seat.

"I'm so glad you came!" Betsy gave her a grin that eased some of the tension from Sukie's shoulders. "I want you to meet my friends. And this, dear ladies, is Sukie Skidmore."

Curious about Betsy's companions from work, Sukie nodded to each woman as introductions were made.

Lynn Hodges reached across the table to offer Sukie her hand.

Studying her, Sukie shook it. Lynn was as well-padded as Betsy. Her short, no-nonsense haircut showed signs of gray, making her the oldest of Betsy's three friends. Intimidated by Lynn's frank, blue-eyed stare, Sukie picked up a menu.

Betsy turned to the others. "I told Sukie, 'Be there or be square.'"

Sukie couldn't help rolling her eyes, and everyone laughed.

"There's no stoppin' her." Lynn's features softened with affection, momentarily erasing the deep worry lines etched across her brow. "But it's great, us, getting together every Friday, taking an extra-long lunch hour from work."

"We order anything we want—no calories counted," Betsy explained. "That's why we call them Fat Fridays. Right, girls?" She winked, and Sukie laughed. It was another of Betsy's fun ideas.

"Yeah, and when Betsy brings her famous cupcakes to work, it's even better," said Lynn.

Carol Ann Mobley smiled at Betsy. "I love the strawberry the best. The ones with the pink icing and hearts." Clasping her hands primly in front of her, Carol Ann turned to Sukie. "So, how do you know Betsy? She told us you're old friends, but you don't look so old to me." Carol Ann's eyes widened. "Oh, Betsy, I'm sorry . . . I didn't mean . . ."

"No problem, hon." Betsy gave Carol Ann a good-natured smile. "While Sukie and I have sons the same age, she started her family much younger than I. We've been friends ever since she moved into the neighborhood several years ago."

"We've already ordered the pizza—sausage and peppers," said Tiffany Wright. Her face was baby-doll beautiful, and she had blond hair and a body that wouldn't quit, as Sukie's son Rob would say. Her dark brown eyes held a vulnerability Sukie found intriguing.

"Is that okay, Sukie? I mean, the pizza choice?" Carol Ann's gaze darted uncertainly from her to the others.

Sukie gave her a reassuring nod. "It's more than okay." She struggled to temper the bitter edge that crept into her voice. "It's time for me to have a little fun."

Betsy gave her a sympathetic look, but Sukie vowed not to feel sorry for herself. She didn't want to stay stuck on that pitiful merry-go-round. Ted Skidmore wasn't worth it.

"Heard about your divorce. Been there, done that." Lynn's gravelly voice matched her brusque manner. "Best thing that ever happened to me. My husband, the son of a bitch, was a real asshole."

Sukie's breath caught with surprise. She'd thought those things of Ted plenty of times, but she'd never voiced them in front of people she didn't know. But it didn't seem to bother Lynn one bit. Or else these women were closer than Sukie had first thought.

"Well, y'all, I don't care what you say, I'd sure like to be married someday," Carol Ann said. "But I haven't met the right man. I want someone handsome and rich." She nudged Tiffany. "Like Beau."

Annoyance flashed across Tiffany's face and disappeared just as quickly. Her cheeks turned a pretty pink. "He *is* cute, isn't he?" Her lips curved, but Sukie knew Carol Ann's remarks had bothered Tiffany, and she wondered why.

The pizza arrived. Betsy slid a large, crisp slice onto each plastic plate and handed them out. "Okay, ladies, enjoy! Here's to another Fat Friday!"

"Hear, hear!" Lynn took a large bite of pizza, and murmured her satisfaction as she swallowed.

Sukie's first bite of pizza was wonderful—cheesy and warm, almost sinful. Since the divorce, she'd studied her image in the mirror, forcing herself to acknowledge every flaw, every bulge. Truthfully, for a woman in her early forties, she wasn't in bad shape. More than that, she'd been a good wife and a good mother. That had to count for something more than having a voluptuous figure.

"You doing okay?" Betsy's voice startled Sukie out of her thoughts.

Sukie nodded. "I'm learning how to operate all the equipment around the house—things I'd ignored before. The lawn mower gave me some problems, but I finally got it started. It's a whole new thing for me. That, and handling all the financial stuff Ted used to *insist* upon doing himself."

"Is your ex a know-it-all, control freak like mine?" Lynn said. "Bet he thought of you as the little lady or somethin' like that, huh?"

Sukie started to shake her head and stopped. Ted had sometimes wanted to know every moment of her day and had often quizzed her on how she'd spent each penny. He'd stated that his need to know was merely part of his banking persona. What a load of B.S.!

Lynn gave her a satisfied smile. "You're gonna surprise yourself by takin' hold of your life. I swear it's gonna make you happier than you've ever been." There was no judgment in her rough voice, just encouragement.

"Hey, Sukie," said Tiffany, "we've wanted to add to our group." Her dark eyes shone. "Why don't you see if you can get a job at MacTel? They need another admin."

"Admin?"

"Yeah, you know, an administrative assistant. A secretarial type, like us," interjected Carol Ann. "Any friend of Betsy's is a friend of ours. Right, y'all?"

After having so many of her so-called friends drop her socially, Sukie's heart warmed at their easy acceptance. "My daughter, Elizabeth, has been after me to take computer courses, but I told her I need to have time to pull myself together emotionally. I'm going to have to earn money, though."

Tiffany nodded. "Maybe later, when you have more training, something will open up. We'll keep an eye out for job postings."

"In the meantime," said Betsy, glancing around the table, "let's vote Sukie into the Fat Fridays group. What do you say, girls?"

Tossing her blond hair over her shoulder, Tiffany gave Sukie a thumbs-up sign.

"You betcha," Lynn added.

Carol Ann clasped her hands together and smiled shyly at her. "Of course!"

"You in?" Betsy pinned her with a steely gaze that made Sukie squirm.

Feeling as if she'd just been accepted into the most popular sorority on campus, not a group of relative strangers, Sukie embraced the idea. "Why not? It's the best offer I've had in a long, long time."

Sukie answered the questions the others had about her and her family, happy to discuss her children and the grandchild on the way.

"You're much too young to have a grandchild," said Carol Ann, leaning over for a closer look. "And so pretty."

Sukie remained quiet. She might never have married Ted if she hadn't gotten pregnant during her freshman year of college.

After enjoying a bite of Lynn's shared dessert, Sukie left the other women feeling more upbeat than she had in some time. It was a diverse group, but she felt freer with them than she did with her old friends, who knew or had imagined every wretched detail of her humiliating situation.

She climbed into her Camry and headed over to the local World Foods store. Turning on the car radio for the first time in months, she thought about the group she'd just joined. Betsy was a fairly recent widow, Tiffany a young beauty, Carol Ann, an unsophisticated sweetie, and Lynn? Lynn was a tough puzzle. Sukie wondered about their stories. Everyone had one.

Sukie's hands tightened on the steering wheel as she pulled into the World Foods parking lot. Everyone in the neighborhood shopped there on Fridays. She drew a couple of deep breaths and parked the car. She had no choice but to go inside. Her refrigerator was empty and she was tired of sneaking into the store during off-hours.

She grabbed her purse. It was now or never, she told herself, even as that old feeling of inadequacy threatened to overwhelm her. Ted's betrayal had made her feel so ugly, so unlovable, so . . . so . . . stupid!

Like a frightened child on her first day of kindergarten, Sukie timidly entered the store. Fresh strawberries, straight from Florida, greeted her in a rosy display. She picked up a small basket of them and walked into the produce department, bypassing the colorful flowers that seemed to shiver each time the front doors opened, blasting cold February air over them.

She was evaluating the freshness of the romaine lettuce when a familiar voice rang out behind her.

"Sukie, bless your heart, how are you? I haven't seen you in a dog's age."

Her blood turned cold. She turned to face Katy Hartmann, the president of the neighborhood women's association. Katy thrived on a steady diet of gossip, no matter who or what the occasion.

Sukie forced a smile. "Hi, Katy. I'm fine, thank you." She crossed her fingers at the white lie. "Just stocking up on my fruits and veggies."

Katy's overly bright smile faded into an exaggerated show of sympathy. "I'm so sorry about you and Ted. Not that I was surprised, mind you. He was forever flirting with me. And, Emmy Lou? Obviously she did a whole lot more than coach at the local gym." Fishing for more information, she leaned toward Sukie eagerly. "I had no idea you had such a temper, Sukie. I say, good for you. We women need to stand up to our naughty men!"

Hiding a shudder, Sukie stepped back. "How was the Valentine Party? Betsy Wilson told me the club did a beautiful job with the luncheon."

Katy shook her head. "That Betsy. She's such a character. You should have seen her tackle her food."

Staring at Katy's rail-thin body, anger built inside Sukie. "It's nice to know *she's* secure enough to eat what she wants."

At Sukie's sharp tone, Katy's eyes rounded. "Well, that's one way to put it." She wiggled her fingers hello as a woman came into the store. "Oh, I've got to go! Debbi is in charge of our next meeting, and I need to talk to her." Katy's smile wavered. "Are you going to be able to attend this one, Sukie?"

Sukie shook her head, struggling to come up with an excuse. "Probably not. I'm taking courses at the library."

"Courses?" Katy perked up. "Why, bless your heart, that's wonderful! Which ones?"

"Computer courses," Sukie blurted uneasily, caught in another white lie.

"Good luck. I'll tell the others." Katy all but flew to Debbi's side.

"You'll tell everyone," Sukie muttered, grinding her teeth together. *Bless her heart!*

Sukie carried the groceries inside her house and set them down on the kitchen counter. It hadn't been that long ago when doing so would have brought her a great deal of satisfaction. But cooking for one had taken the joy out of creating meals her husband had once loved.

She set to work putting away the groceries. She'd heard Ted and Emmy Lou ate out together every night. In a small but growing suburban town like Williston, with just six local restaurants, including the Dairy Queen, that meant strutting their stuff all over town. Back when Sukie had attended Pilates class, Emmy Lou had bragged about not being able to cook. Sukie shook her head. After all her sumptuous meals Ted had loved so much, he'd taken up with a bimbo who couldn't even put together a simple supper.

Sukie opened the cupboard where she'd hidden the chocolates she'd gorged on through the tough times and tossed the few remaining pieces into the garbage. No more self-indulgence for her! She stopped, retrieved one oversized chocolate bar, and tucked it behind the vinegar. An emergency might come up. Better safe than sorry.

Outside, blue sky and bright sunshine beckoned. Sukie grabbed her coat and headed out the door. It had been ages since she'd walked the neighborhood. Spring—her favorite time of year—was on its way, about to nudge winter from the scene in a few weeks.

She stood a moment, admiring her surroundings, so full of promise. Plantings of various sizes and shapes filled the landscaped spaces between the large houses and served as a playground for the birds flitting among the budding branches. The trees would soon leaf out in pale green glory. Bradford pear trees were about to blossom, and then their white flowers would coat the branches like fallen snow. Redbud trees would soon add patches of brilliant pink, making the world seem a fairyland of spring colors.

Sukie drew in a breath of fresh air and vowed to make a fresh start too.

Walking along, she noticed a Sold sign in front of a house in the cul-de-sac at the end of her street. She idly wondered if it meant more children in the neighborhood. She hoped so. It seemed like yesterday her Rob and Elizabeth had been running through the neighborhood. The sounds of active children playing, calling to one another, reminded her of the satisfying years when her own children's activities had filled her busy days.

As she drew closer to the newly sold house, a golden retriever galloped across the lawn toward her. Sukie stopped and waited for him to approach. He came to a halt, sniffed her palm, and wagged his tail.

A low male voice called from the direction of the garage, "Prince, come."

"I'll get him! Let me!" came a high, sweet voice from the same area. A little girl with blond ringlets ran toward Sukie, her hair flying behind her like a falling crown of gold. The lawn dipped in front of the child. She tripped and tumbled to the ground with a high-pitched yelp.

Sukie reached her just as a man, whom she assumed was her father, joined her and lifted the sobbing child into his arms. Sukie studied the little girl. She appeared to be about three years old and was among the prettiest Sukie had ever seen.

"I've got her, but thanks," the man said above the noise of the child's cries. "Come, Prince."

As they walked away, Sukie wondered what her own grandchild would look like—perhaps, a dainty little girl, all pink and white, with honey-colored curls, or a broad-shouldered, lusty-voiced boy like Rob.

The man stopped and turned. The sniffling little girl in his arms laid her head against his shoulder and stared at Sukie. She saw now that the girl had her father's refined features. His blue-eyed gaze settled on Sukie. They stood, studying each other.

She couldn't pull her eyes away. He was a very intriguing man—sexy and masculine, yet sweet and gentle with his daughter. As handsome a man as she'd ever seen. A real hottie as Elizabeth would say. The rest of the world disappeared in a haze of keen mutual awareness and a quiet seemed to settle around them, like something she'd read about in romance novels.

He shot Sukie another admiring glance that lingered. Heat spread in delicious pulses to every part of her body, reminding her how it'd once felt to be sexy. As if he knew her thoughts, he smiled.

Sukie's cheeks flamed with teenlike embarrassment. She forced herself to mind her manners. "I'm Sukie Skidmore, your neighbor from down the street. Tell your wife I'll stop by sometime next week. In the past, I've tried to welcome everyone to the neighborhood."

"Thanks." He nodded. "I'm Cameron Taylor."

With a quick wave to her, he disappeared into the garage, and Sukie went on her way. Overwhelmed by the instant attraction she'd felt toward a complete stranger, she took deep breaths to calm her racing heart. His wife, she thought, was one lucky woman.

When Sukie entered the house, the phone was ringing. She checked caller ID, happily picked up the phone, and took a seat at the kitchen table. A call from Elizabeth, attending college in New York, was a rare opportunity for a mother-daughter conversation. Though Sukie missed her, she was glad Elizabeth wasn't around to witness all the crap with her father.

"How are you, Mom?" Elizabeth asked. A note of worry wavered in her voice.

"Holding on. Betsy Wilson called me earlier this week. I met her and a few of her coworkers for lunch today. She calls it Fat Fridays because no calories are counted."

Elizabeth laughed. "I've always liked Betsy. But, Mom, be careful how you soothe your sorrows, so to speak."

"I am. As a matter of fact, I'm losing weight. I can't decide if it's worry or anger."

"Probably both. I hate that Dad did that to you." After a pause Elizabeth continued. "Guess what? My friend Laurie and I went to an off-Broadway play last night, and afterwards we went to this great little Italian place for dinner. And, Mom, I met this really hot guy. I love living in the city."

"I'm glad." Sukie said, meaning it. Elizabeth was living the kind of life she herself had dreamed of as a young student—a life that was productive, independent, and full of fun. Somewhere along the way, she'd lost it all. But, no more! She'd crossed the bridge from depression to determination and she was going to enjoy her new status.

After they hung up, Sukie stared out the French doors of the kitchen and clutched her cold fingers. She'd lied to Katy Hartmann and had to make it right.

Her mouth grew dry at the thought of what she was about to do, but she went ahead and punched in the number.

"Williston Public Library," a voice answered cheerfully.

Sukie took a deep breath. "Is it too late to sign up for the computer course?"

CHAPTER TWO
BETSY

Betsy Wilson returned to the office, pleased Sukie had joined her and the others for lunch. In many ways, theirs was an odd group of women, but they'd become good friends in a short time. Working together on the top floor of MacTel Communications, where tempers ran high from execs under stress, it was good to have a buddy or two or three on your side. Funny, Betsy thought, how you meet some women and there's an instant connection, a willingness to help one another get through the ups and downs of another day. She'd always treasured that about women.

Betsy leaned back in her desk chair and gazed at the framed photograph of Caitlin and Garrett, her two grandchildren. She'd placed their picture on the corner of her desk where everyone could see them. Studying their sweet little features, her heart swelled with love. She felt so lucky to have them in her life. Lifting the tiny bottle of perfume they'd bought her at the dollar store for Valentine's Day, she opened it, inhaled the flowery aroma, and dabbed a little behind her ears.

Her grandchildren were the frosting on a cake, the sugar in her coffee, whatever cute saying she could come up with. She loved them like crazy.

Their mother? Not so much.

Betsy's thoughts turned to Sukie. She had a heart of gold. They'd been neighbors a long time, friends from the first day they'd met, back when their boys were young. Growing up, Richie had spent a lot of time at Sukie's house. Betsy had always admired her.

Her husband? Another story.

Betsy's boss handed a folder to her. "I need this done right away. Think you can do it?"

"Sure." Betsy smiled, but wondered why he always waited until the last minute to land a new project on her desk. Setting aside her personal thoughts, Betsy focused on her work.

The afternoon sped by as she put together an agenda and a PowerPoint presentation for a sales meeting. She'd tell anyone who asked that she was no techie, but she loved being part of the scene at MacTel Communications. All those crazy scripts and programs everyone talked about meant little to her. It was the admin work she enjoyed. She edited the presentation one last time, emailed it, and printed off a hard copy for her boss.

"Night, Betsy." Carol Ann waved and headed for the elevator.

Surprised at the late hour, Betsy gathered her things. It had been a hectic week and she was tired. But she would take the time to stop by Sukie's to make sure she was really on board for Fat Fridays.

Betsy drove into the neighborhood and pulled up to Sukie's house, one of the bigger ones in the area. Betsy remembered how Ted used to brag about that. Funny, she thought, how some couples seem so out of kilter—Sukie, so genuine, and Ted, so full of himself. Lately, Betsy had pushed hard to force Sukie out of the house. She figured once Sukie began to show herself around town, all that nasty gossipy stuff would die down. Small towns could be mighty difficult. Small Southern towns, even worse.

Sukie answered the door with a smile that lit up her face. Returning her smile, Betsy thought it unbelievable that Ted had left Sukie for someone who looked and dressed like a slut and didn't seem to have much going on in the brains department.

"Come on in." Sukie tugged her inside. "How about a glass of wine? After lunch today, I went grocery shopping and took a long walk in the neighborhood."

"Congratulations, hon! It's a beginning, right?" Betsy was glad her campaign had done some good.

Sukie nodded, blushing prettily. "I talked to Elizabeth. She was pleased I'm joining your Fat Fridays group. She's always liked you, Betsy."

"Elizabeth is a great gal. If I'd had a daughter, I would've wanted her to be like Elizabeth—smart, kind, pretty."

While Sukie poured two glasses of white wine, Betsy took a seat on one of the black leather stools lining the gray granite counter at the kitchen bar. They clicked glasses in a tinkling salute and sipped. The cool liquid slid down Betsy's throat easily and warmed her stomach.

"So, how are you doing—really?" she asked Sukie, taking another soothing sip of wine.

Sukie shrugged. "I'm getting by, though I'm still trying to figure out my finances. I got the house and I'm getting some alimony. It surprised me that Ted agreed to it so quickly, but I don't trust him. You know how he is. He'll find a way to make my life miserable. He betrayed me once, who's to say he won't again?"

"Is there a catch somewhere? Ted isn't exactly known as being easy to deal with."

"I know. I'm pretty sure this so-called generosity of his won't last. No doubt, we'll end up in court with him trying to pay me less after the glow of being with that . . . that . . . woman wears off." Sukie caught her lip with her teeth and frowned. "I don't think Emmy Lou was the first. You know how he was at our neighborhood parties—he always had his arm around one of the women. Remember?"

Betsy was quiet a moment. "Well, I wasn't going to say anything to you, but he even hit on me one time."

Sukie's eyes rounded. "You? Why didn't you tell me?"

"I thought it was a crude joke at the time, nothing more. You know how nasty he could be when he'd had too many drinks. God knows, at my age and with my body, I'm not exactly a sex goddess."

Sukie grimaced. "I'm sorry he did that to you. I didn't know. I was so stupid."

"Oh, hon, it's just that you're so nice, it probably never occurred to you that your husband was such a lyin', cheatin' . . ."

"Bastard," Sukie finished. Her nostrils flared. "I was such a fool . . ."

Betsy shrugged. "Well, life has some hard lessons for all of us. Believe me, I know. What is it Lily Tomlin said? 'Things are going to get a lot worse before they get worse.' I know it seems like life sucks right now, but this whole thing may turn out to be a good thing. You couldn't have been that happy with Ted. Not really."

"What do you mean?"

"Never mind," Betsy said, wishing she hadn't been so blunt. "I'm way outta line here. We'll talk about it some other time."

Silence filled the room as they each took another sip of wine.

Sukie broke into the quiet. "So, tell me, how are you doing since Rich died? It's been almost two years. How have you managed? I need to hear the gritty truth from someone who's gone through the process of learning to live on her own."

How am I doing? I'm doing, well . . . great. Betsy stirred in her seat, trying to find the right words. "This may sound strange, but I feel younger, and in some ways, happier. Living with Rich wasn't what I'd expected." She held up a hand. "Don't get me wrong. He was nice enough, but as bland as unsalted and unbuttered grits. I miss having someone else in the house, of course, though I don't feel totally alone. Richie and Sarah and the kids are only forty minutes away."

"I didn't realize . . ."

Betsy cut her off. "Rich was a good man. He didn't boss me around or abuse me or purposely do anything at all to make me unhappy."

"But . . . ?" Sukie gave her a steady look.

Betsy took a deep breath, wishing she hadn't opened her mouth. "There was no real spark between us. It was just the state of our union," she ended, hoping for humor.

"I'm sorry." Sukie's voice held a note of concern that made Betsy's stomach curl inside at what she'd revealed.

"Good God! I've never told another soul about the way it was with Rich and me. It must be the wine."

Sukie clasped her hand. "I'm glad we can totally level with one another."

Betsy nodded, though she felt guilty for badmouthing Rich. It wasn't his fault that he never truly made her happy. It was hers.

"Did you ever consider divorce?" Sukie asked.

"From Rich? Never. That wasn't an option for conservative, churchgoing people like us. I went ahead with my daily routines and kept busy with Richie, even though I sometimes felt like I was drowning." Betsy set her wine glass down. She'd had enough wine and enough confessing.

"We all have problems of one kind or another, Betsy," Sukie assured her, then smiled. "On a more pleasant note, how are Garrett and Caitlin?"

Betsy smiled happily. "Garrett is proud to be in first grade, old enough to take the bus. Caitlin looks so grown up. She just had her ears pierced for her eighth birthday. I love them both dearly."

As if on cue, Betsy's cell phone rang. She knew without looking at caller ID who it was. She pinched her lips together. "It's Richie's Sarah. Bets on whether she asks me to babysit? It's happening every weekend."

Sukie clucked her tongue sympathetically.

Sarah greeted Betsy in a rush, her voice high and demanding. "Betsy, I really need your help! It's been a busy week and the kids are driving me crazy. I need to get away and have a break from them and from everything."

In Betsy's opinion, Sarah didn't know what busy or hard work meant, unless it was trying to keep up with the neighbors in the high-priced neighborhood in which Sarah had insisted she and Richie live. Sarah was never satisfied with anything. She constantly shopped to make things "nicer."

Betsy sighed. "So, what do you want me to do this time?"

"Take the kids for the whole weekend. Richie can drop them off in an hour. He's agreed to take me to the Biltmore Estate for a weekend of rest and pampering. Isn't he a doll?"

More like a puppet, Betsy thought grimly.

"So, can you do it for me? Please?"

Betsy sighed. "Okay. It's the third weekend in a row, but you know how much I love the kids."

"Great. I have their overnight bags packed and ready to go. Oh, by the way, how are you?"

Betsy rolled her eyes at the afterthought. "I'm fine. Busy. Make sure the kids bring one of their movies. It's been a hectic week."

"Okay. See you Sunday afternoon when we pick them up. Thanks."

"You're welcome, Sarah." Betsy disconnected the phone and turned to Sukie. "Another weekend Sarah has to get away from the kids. I swear I don't know how Richie puts up with her. But, believe me, as the wicked mother-in-law, I don't say a word. I tried it once and it caused a huge fight between us." At the memory of Sarah's wounding words, tears stung Betsy's eyes.

"A difficult situation," Sukie said, commiserating with her. "I can't wait for my little one. Madeleine and Rob are beside themselves with joy over their first baby. They've been reading books and attending birthing classes together. Ted went into a tailspin when he heard he was about to become a grandfather. I sometimes think that's what started the whole break between us. Pathetic, huh?" Sukie lowered her gaze.

Betsy tried to think of one of her cute sayings, but nothing came to mind. Life was bittersweet. Didn't she know it?

CHAPTER THREE

TIFFANY

Tiffany Wright drove right home after work, glad the week was over. She loved her job, the ladies in the Fat Fridays group, even her boss, but it had been five days of hellish tension both at work and at home. She needed a couple of days to relax, to hang out with Beau and get back on track. She decided they'd barbecue chicken on the grill, have a few beers, and keep it nice and easy. It had been a while since they'd had a weekend like that. Maybe, then, things between them would seem better.

Pulling up to the front of the house, Tiffany let out a groan. Her father-in-law's fancy Mercedes sat in the driveway like a big black cloud of doom. Tiffany parked alongside it. She prayed Regard had left her mother-in-law, Muffy, at home, that he'd just stopped by on his way to or from Charleston and would soon be on his way.

Seeing Muffy's blond head in the window, Tiffany let out a sigh. Her mother-in-law was married to *the* Beauregard Wright Jr., a prominent lawyer in Charleston, and was a royal pain in the ass. Not that Tiffany could ever say that to her husband. Beau thought his parents, Muffy and Regard, were fine as far as 'rents went. But then, why wouldn't he think that? They spoiled him rotten.

The curse words Tiffany had grown up with flashed in her mind, but she'd learned not to say them aloud. Her mother-in-law's smooth, oversprayed hair would frizz in a minute if she knew what Tiffany really thought about her, the family's phoniness, and the stomach-clenching way they made her feel.

"Surprise!" Muffy burst from the house in one of her dressy St. John suits, wearing a bright smile that made Tiffany cringe.

Shit! Shit! Shit!

Tiffany forced herself to leave the safety of the car.

"Regard and I are taking you to the club for dinner," Muffy announced. "Regard had a speech to give in Atlanta and we've come for the weekend. We haven't seen you and Beau for a couple of weeks now."

Tiffany pasted a fake smile on her face, and told herself to chill, that it wasn't the worst thing that could happen. But really, she couldn't think of anything worse. She could never be herself with Muffy. Oh, yes, she put on a good show for her mother-in-law, for both her in-laws, really, but it was hard for her to hide who she really was. She was no debutante from the South. She was several rungs below the Wrights on the social ladder and always would be.

"How's our little princess?" Regard boomed when she walked into the kitchen. There was little real warmth in his voice.

Beau grinned at her. "Dad and I are going to play golf tomorrow. You and Mom can go shopping or whatever y'all want. Buy as much as you want, as long as you spend *their* money, not *ours*." He beamed at his parents as if he'd made a wonderful joke.

Tiffany's heart sank. She hated it when he became their spoiled little boy. They'd been married less than a year, and what with his parents constantly barging in, Tiffany sometimes felt as if she and Beau hardly knew each other. Regard and Muffy had bought them the house as a wedding gift, but that didn't mean his parents could drop in any frickin' time they felt like it, did it? Tiffany clenched her fists, so frustrated she wanted to cry.

Muffy eyed her with disapproval. "Maybe we'll go to a spa, get a nice massage. Our little princess looks like she could use it."

Beau and his father gave Tiffany looks of satisfaction, but she'd heard the not-so-subtle criticism behind Muffy's words. His parents hadn't wanted Beau to marry her. But their darling son had convinced them, and her, that it would work out, that he had no intention of marrying anyone else. He'd said they were meant to be together.

At first, Tiffany had thought so too.

Shopping with Muffy, having lunch together, Tiffany forced herself to be polite, but she wanted to let loose a rebel yell that would scare off Beau's family. She and Beau really needed some quality time together.

Getting ready for bed that night, Tiffany felt almost numb from hiding her frustration.

Beau frowned at her. "What's the matter? You've been acting weird all day."

Tiffany was about to spill her feelings and stopped. He didn't get it. He never had.

She slipped on her pajamas, climbed into bed, and lay down, careful to keep to her side of it. Beau slid over to her and gave her a hopeful look. Their sex life had always been good, and normally she might have responded. *Not tonight*, she thought, emotionally drained. Not once during the day had he defended her against his mother's subtle and not-so-subtle criticisms. And if she heard the words *little princess* again, she'd scream.

Hugging her pillow, Tiffany lay awake. When they first met, she'd thought Beau's parents were really nice and very sweet for wanting Beau to have the best of everything. Now, she knew his parents for the pseudopeople they were—as cold as a winter storm on the Kansas prairie where she'd grown up.

Muffy thought Tiffany was after their family name, their money. Nothing could be further from the truth. She wanted Beau to be the young man she'd thought she knew, the handsome guy in a T-shirt and torn jeans who helped her ward off a creep at a concert where they'd first met. There'd been no indication then that he was anything other than a regular college student having fun. He'd even had to borrow money from her to get a beer after the show.

Unhappiness gripped Tiffany like an iron fist. She let out a sigh and rolled over. *Maybe over time things will change,* she thought, blinking away the threat of tears.

Tiffany awoke to lemony sunshine curving through the slats of their window blinds like a welcoming smile. She got up and walked over to the window. The sky was the bright deep shade of blue that promised good things. Putting aside past worries, she pulled on a pair of jeans and a cozy sweatshirt and went downstairs.

Beau and his mother sat in the kitchen. Muffy was dressed for church, and judging by the resigned look on Beau's face, he'd already received a lecture from her.

She shot Tiffany a look of disapproval. "You two better hurry up and get ready. We're going to the ten-o'clock service at the Methodist church."

Beau shook his head. "But, Mom, I told you, we don't go there anymore."

Muffy's nostrils flared. She shot an accusing glance at Tiffany and turned to Beau. "I raised you to be a God-fearin' man, Beauregard Wright the Third. Now you and Tiffany go upstairs and get ready. You've got to make the right impression in this small town."

Beau gave Tiffany a helpless look and got to his feet.

Tiffany followed him up the stairs, glad there wasn't a gun in the house. She might've used it. She'd been raised a Catholic and was still trying to decide which church she wanted to attend, if any at all.

At church, Muffy and Regard headed directly to a front pew where they could be seen. The four of them settled on the pew's green cushions and sat, tensely ignoring one another. Beau put an arm around Tiffany's shoulder, as if they were as close as they'd once been. It felt good, though Tiffany wondered if this was for show, too.

It was quiet in the car on the way home from church. The minister's sermon had been about truth. Sitting in the back seat of the Mercedes, Tiffany felt like a fraud. She carried Beau's last name but she'd give it up in a minute if she could.

After a light lunch, Regard announced it was time for them to leave. The tension in Tiffany's shoulders eased. Seeing them off, Tiffany stood with Beau in the driveway and waved as their car disappeared down the street. She smiled and turned to Beau.

"Alone at last! I could hardly wait!"

Beau glowered at her. "Now don't go starting in on that. With my lousy salary at the firm, we could never afford to go out to nice restaurants, play golf at the club, and all that stuff. Stuff I'm used to."

"But, Beau . . ." she began.

He turned away from her and headed into the house.

Tears misted Tiffany's vision. Miserable, she went inside. The sound of a basketball game filled the downstairs. Beau had plopped down in front of the large-screen television they'd bought with the money from her last few paychecks. He never even looked up at her.

Sighing, Tiffany cleaned up the lunch dishes. Her thoughts wandered to her friends in the Fat Fridays group. As she thought of the way Sukie Skidmore's face had lit up at the mention of her daughter and hearing how close they were, an idea came to her. Maybe Sukie was someone who would listen, really listen, to her. And then she'd know how to make things better.

Tiffany went upstairs to the master bedroom, where Beau couldn't hear her, and picked up the phone. Her palms turned sweaty as she punched in the numbers on her cell and paced the thick green carpeting.

Sukie answered after two rings. "Hello?"

Too nervous to speak, Tiffany almost hung up.

"Hello?" Sukie said again.

Tiffany cleared her throat. "Hi, it's me. Tiffany Wright." Her dry tongue had trouble working. "I know we just met but I need to talk to you. Do you think . . . what I mean is . . . do you want to have lunch? Just the two of us?" Tiffany's stomach scrunched as she waited for Sukie's response.

"Tiffany? Lunch? How . . . how nice!" Sukie's voice was full of surprise.

Tiffany pressed on. "Could we meet for lunch sometime this week?"

Sukie paused. "I don't see why not."

Tiffany let out the breath she'd been holding. "I really need to talk to someone like you about a private matter. I'm taking a personal day off from work on Wednesday. How about meeting me then? Could you?"

There was another scary moment of silence.

"That'll be fine," Sukie said smoothly. "Why don't I pick you up at, say, eleven o'clock?"

Tiffany's knees weakened with relief. She gave Sukie directions to her house and hung up. Maybe talking to someone like Sukie would help her straighten out her life. She hoped so. Without it, she didn't know what she'd do.

CHAPTER FOUR
LYNN

Lynn Hodges unlocked the door to her small top-floor apartment and walked inside, happy that tomorrow was Saturday and she'd be able to sleep in. Glancing around, she sighed happily. She loved being in her own safe place. She'd moved around a lot over the years, but thoughts of permanently settling down in Williston had begun to fill her mind. Until now, she hadn't found a town good enough to think of staying put.

Williston was a friendly small town north of Atlanta, not so small, though, that you had to travel for miles and miles for your basic needs. She'd even allowed herself to make friends here, friends who had no idea what she was hiding.

Lynn tucked her purse in a kitchen cupboard, thinking of the ladies in the Fat Fridays group. They were real, nice women who didn't realize how much it meant to her that they'd welcomed her, a loner.

Her hand brushed the back of her favorite overstuffed chair as she passed by. Walking through the home she'd made for herself, Lynn felt like a kid at Christmas. At that whimsical idea, she shook her head.

Truth be told, that fat old man hadn't shown up very often in her life. That's just the way it'd always been for her.

She tiptoed over to the sliding glass door leading to the small balcony off the living room and drew the drapes as tight as she could. It would be dark soon and she didn't like knowing anyone could look inside.

Kicking off her shoes, Lynn turned on the television and went into her bedroom to change clothes. In her blue terrycloth robe, she prepared to settle down for a cozy evening in front of a movie. Something sweet. No murder mysteries for her. Sitting on her secondhand couch, glancing around the space that had become home to her, she could imagine living there for many years to come.

If only.

CHAPTER FIVE

CAROL ANN

Carol Ann Mobley remained in her bedroom for as long as she could. Most people couldn't wait for the weekends. She couldn't wait for the workweek to begin again. Striking a pose in front of the mirror over her dresser, Carol Ann spread her lips into a smile and arched her eyebrows to make her eyes look bigger, hoping to look . . . different.

Frustrated, she threw her hairbrush down on top of her dresser with a loud smack. No matter how much she tried to look like Tiffany Wright and some of the other hot girls at work, it didn't happen. She couldn't put herself together with their style. It wasn't just the way she seemed so plain next to them; it was everything. They were so full of confidence, so sophisticated. She was still stuck at home, living with her parents, saving money for a place of her own. She hated her pitiful life.

Her parents were like stones around her neck, weighing her down with their constant fighting, their low lifestyle, their clinging to her. With her sister gone and married, Carol Ann was the one left at home to put up with it. She gritted her teeth. She wanted a lot more from life and she was going to get it. She just didn't have a cotton-pickin' idea how.

Giving herself a last look in the mirror, Carol Ann practiced her Cameron Diaz smile.

"Carol Ann?"

Mama's shrill voice, calling from the kitchen, shattered her dreams as sure as if her mother had thrown a rock at the glass in front of her.

"Git the paper 'fore you do anythin' else," her mother said. "What time y'all be back from errands? Seein' it's Saturday, we'll git our usual supper."

Carol Ann clenched her jaw. Pizza. And every morning, without fail, she brought the paper inside for her parents. Just once, she wished Mama would let her do that without reminding her. At work, she handled some very important things for her boss. Why couldn't her mother understand she could damn well remember to get the paper on her own? And couldn't they, just once, have something other than crappy pizza on Saturdays?

"Carol Ann? You hear me?"

"Yes, Mama."

Carol Ann thought she'd have a better life by now. Thank God for MacTel. She loved the women, sweet as pie, in the Fat Fridays group. Regardless of their age differences, they were friends. They were the people who gave her hope that life could be different for her once she'd saved for the house on the other side of town she was determined to have.

"I'm waitin' on ya, Carol Ann."

She sighed and glanced around her bedroom, praying for that day. After her sister left home, Carol Ann had done her best to fix up the room that was now hers alone. She'd painted the walls a pale, pale pink and sent away for a country quilt and bed skirt at a price Mama never would have allowed her to pay. She was slowly paying off the loan on the bedroom suite she'd bought at a terrific sale. She'd also started a hope chest of sorts, filling it with household items on sale, praying for the day when she'd be gone, living on her own.

"Carol Ann? You payin' attention?"

"Okay, Mama," she answered, feeling about twelve years old. God! If she couldn't somehow change her life, she'd die.

CHAPTER SIX
SUKIE

It was one of those gray Sunday mornings when Sukie wanted to snuggle inside a warm sweatshirt and stay in jeans and fuzzy slippers all day. Alone, and with no plans, that's exactly what she intended to do.

She stepped over to the mirror above her bureau and gave her image an unflinching stare. Classic features coated with sadness—not too bad, considering the past several months. As usual, her stubborn hair sprang out in rebellious brown curls. She smoothed back the skin on her face. It had begun to show signs of giving in to gravity's relentless tug. Still, people never guessed her age. Elizabeth told her that if she'd let herself go, dress a little younger, kick up her heels a bit, they'd think she was Elizabeth's sister, not her mother. Funny, Sukie thought, it was always Ted who insisted she dress the part of conservative spouse to his bank presidency. *What a crock!*

The phone rang. *Elizabeth*. Sukie settled in an easy chair in her bedroom to talk to her daughter.

"I've signed up for the computer courses at the library," Sukie announced. "So I'm thinking it's time to spruce up my wardrobe."

"Great! Go for it! And get some cool clothes. You've got a good figure, Mom. Better than you think."

Sukie caught her lower lip with her teeth and nibbled nervously. No way could she deny her forty-three years. Not when her ex-husband was living with someone barely older than her daughter.

"I mean it, Mom. Show off your figure. Have fun! And while you're at it, put a little color in your hair. Highlights would look good on you. Who's going to stop you?"

"Absolutely no one." Sukie fought off the wave of depression that threatened to drown her good humor. Years of being part of a twosome were hard to ignore. She felt so adrift. There were still times she automatically set the table for two.

"Mom? I'm really proud of you. Those courses are bound to lead to something else."

At Elizabeth's encouraging words, Sukie didn't know whether to laugh or cry. It seemed as if their roles had reversed and Elizabeth was now supporting *her* emotionally. She wasn't even sure she wanted to be an admin, or whatever it was called, but she knew she had to protect herself. Ted's promises were as empty as gaily wrapped birthday gifts with nothing but tissue inside.

"I'm so mad at Dad for putting you through all this," said Elizabeth. "I won't even take some of his calls. He's being such a jerk!"

Sukie kept quiet. Her counselor had told her not to interfere with her children's relationships with their father.

"You know that cute guy I told you about?" Elizabeth said, quickly switching topics. "He's already got someone else. I found out after he put the squeeze on me. I was so bummed."

"Oh, honey, I'm sorry." *Are all men jerks?*

They chatted about school, and Sukie gave Elizabeth the latest news on the baby front. Elizabeth was as excited as Sukie about Rob and Madeleine's expected baby.

After Sukie hung up, she took a closer look at the items hanging in her closet. Safe. That's what they were. Neutral colors, and classic, almost rigid styles. Most of them were too big for her now. She pulled a navy dress out of the closet. Safe? Who was she kidding? It was just plain dowdy. Feeling as if she were discarding the past along with the clothes, she threw it down on the floor. A pile of other items soon joined it. Excitement coursed through Sukie.

She went to her desk to make a list of the new items she'd need. She'd choose basics and fill in with other things when she had the money. Wishing Elizabeth was there to help her, she tapped a pencil against her chin wondering where to begin.

After bagging her old clothes for charity, Sukie went down to the kitchen. Humming softly, she sorted through her ideas while she prepared a cup of hot, lemony tea.

Lowering herself onto a wooden kitchen chair, she gazed out the French doors at the wispy dark clouds racing across the gray sky. The last few days had been so interesting—meeting new friends and reaching out for new opportunities. Thinking of the women in the Fat Fridays group, she picked up her phone.

At Tiffany's hello, Sukie smiled and explained what she had in mind.

"Really? You want me to help you with your new wardrobe?" Tiffany's voice trilled with happiness. "Great! We'll do lunch at the mall. I can't wait!"

Touched by Tiffany's eagerness to help, Sukie went back to work on her closet. With every grunt of disgust, the pile of clothes grew larger.

Looking at them tossed on the floor, Sukie did a silly little dance. It felt so good to feel so free.

Waiting for Tiffany to appear for their shopping trip, Sukie sat in her car and studied the large, brick-faced colonial house—a house any couple would be proud to own.

Tiffany bounded down the sidewalk. With her ponytailed hair, designer jeans, and black high-heeled boots that matched her leather jacket, she looked like a teenager. A red Prada purse swung casually at her shoulder.

Sukie waved, and Tiffany opened the car door and slid into the passenger seat.

"I'm so glad . . ." they said together and burst out laughing.

Smiling at each other, they headed for the mall.

"Thanks for coming to lunch with me," Tiffany said. "It's no good talking to my mother and I have no one else."

"You and your mother . . ."

"Don't get along. Never did. Never will." Resentment crept into Tiffany's voice. "You'd think a grown woman would stop being cruel to her daughter, but it hasn't happened. Out-and-out jealousy is what my therapist called it." Tiffany took deep breaths before continuing. "See, my mother won a small beauty contest in the tiny town of Lovell, in western Kansas, back when she was in high school. It was the highlight of her life." A sad sigh escaped her. "According to my mother, I ruined her life by being born and making her stay in Kansas."

Sukie's heart constricted. "Oh, hon, that sounds so sad."

Tiffany gave Sukie a wobbly smile. "Yeah, well it's just the way things are between us. Now you understand why I would never go to her. I'd rather die first."

Sukie couldn't hide her dismay. "Are you in trouble?"

"Sorta."

Sukie's gaze rested momentarily on Tiffany. "Do you want to postpone the shopping?"

Tiffany shook her head. "No way. I figure we can talk about my problem at lunch. After that, I'll need to do something fun."

"All right. You're married to someone named Beau. How long have you kids been married?"

"Almost a year." Tiffany's chin quivered. "Our anniversary is next week." She let out a sigh and stared out the window for a moment before turning back to Sukie.

"So, how'd you get the name Sukie?"

Sukie smiled at the memory of the family story. "My maiden name was Susannah Keane. When I was little, I pronounced it 'sue-kee' and it stuck."

Tiffany grinned. "Cute."

Sukie found a parking place at the mall and they headed inside.

"What do you feel like for lunch? Another Fat Friday?" Sukie asked gaily.

Tiffany gave her a weak smile. "I shouldn't even do our regular Fat Fridays. I have to watch my weight. From the time I was little, my mother weighed me every day. She said she couldn't go around with a fat daughter; it would ruin her image even further."

Sukie felt her eyes widen. "But . . ."

Tiffany raised her hand. "I know, I know. Pretty screwed-up scene."

Sukie took a deep breath, wondering what she'd gotten herself into. Tiffany was a very insecure young woman from a background layered in rejection.

Inside the Salad Bowl restaurant, lettuce-green walls were offset by orange-topped tables and chairs whose cushions were covered in an orange, green, and yellow print.

After they were seated and their waitress left with their orders, Sukie turned to Tiffany. "Are you ready to talk now? You have me concerned."

Tiffany took a deep breath. "Before Beau and I were married, I had to sign a prenup. I was so in love with Beau I never questioned it. Now Beau says he's given me a whole year to myself, but we have to start a family; it's part of the agreement. He wants a baby now, and he's refused to discuss postponing it. See, it's a big deal in his family. They're waiting for a Beauregard Wright the Fourth." Her eyes filled. "You'd think they were fuckin' royalty or something."

Sukie frowned. "Didn't you and Beau discuss all this before you signed any agreements? That's a pretty major thing."

Tiffany let out a sigh. "We talked about having children, just not so soon. That's not all. He wants me to look perfect all the time. What is being pregnant going to do to me? To us?"

Sukie looked her straight in the eye, well aware of the physical results of her pregnancies. "I'm not going to lie to you, Tiffany. Having babies can change your body. But is that the only problem?" Sukie knew there had to be more to the story. Tiffany's hands were shaking.

"Beau has become somebody I don't know anymore. He's gone from being willing to defy his parents to doing everything they say. It's all about money. He told me I have an image to uphold, that his father is about to be appointed a federal judge like his grandfather was. The whole family is scheduled to have a photograph taken for a national magazine." Her eyes welled with tears. "I'm supposed to be perfect all the time. I just don't think I can keep it up. Beau grabbed me the other day and dragged me inside when I went out to get the newspaper in my robe. It really hurt, him grabbing me like that."

Sukie felt the blood drain from her face. "My God! Does Beau hit you?"

Wide-eyed, Tiffany shook her head. "No, he never has. It's just this image thing that seems to make him so mad. It's all so stupid."

Trying to understand, Sukie's mind raced. "Carol Ann mentioned he's handsome. Is he?"

Tiffany's features became hard-edged. "All Carol Ann thinks about is what Beau looks like and that he has money. No one seems to understand what living with him is really like."

"Have you talked to the other women in the Fat Fridays group about it?"

Tiffany shook her head. "I didn't dare bring it into the office. It would be bad for the Wright image and all that." Her laugh was sour. "Get it? Wright and right?"

Sukie nodded, letting Tiffany's words sink in. It sounded like something out of a soap opera.

"Image has always been important to his family," Tiffany continued. "Funny, I hadn't thought of it before, but Beau and I are both from backgrounds where appearance is more important than anything else."

"That's too bad," said Sukie. Appearance had been important to her parents, too, but only as it applied to their image in the church. They'd been furious when they'd learned she was already pregnant with Rob when she and Ted had rushed into marriage.

"You should have seen his mother at the wedding," said Tiffany, blinking back tears. "She planned it, you know."

"She did?"

"Oh, yes." Tiffany wrinkled her nose. "Even though Beau and I wanted something small, our wedding became a highlight of the season in Charleston. Nothing was too good for Muffy's only child. I was so stressed out I was sick to my stomach for weeks beforehand. And after, when we went to Hawaii for our honeymoon, it took me a few days to begin to enjoy myself."

"It sounds dreadful." Sukie thought about how much she would have hated a wedding like that.

"Like I said, it was a big social thing. You know how they handled me? They told everyone I was their little Cinderella and they'd rescued me, which was why I had no family at the wedding." Tiffany let out a snort of disgust and then wiped her eyes. "It's true. I'm a frickin' nobody."

Sukie straightened in her seat and took hold of Tiffany's hand. "Oh, honey, no. We're all somebody. You can't let anyone else take that away from you."

Tiffany blinked back tears. "What do you think I should do? What would you tell your daughter?"

Sukie thought of Elizabeth going through something like this and her heart ached for Tiffany. "I'd tell her to go to marriage counseling, that no one should have to put up with that kind of harassment."

Tiffany's sigh spoke volumes. "The way I see it, I can't win. I can't tell anyone what's going on because of the image thing, but, Sukie, I don't want to quit work to have a baby. Not now. Maybe not ever with Beau."

Sukie set down her fork and gave Tiffany a steady look. "Are you talking about divorce?"

Tiffany shrugged, looking confused. "I don't know. I don't like the person Beau becomes when his family is around. And that's more often than not. His parents gave us our house for a wedding present. Now, they feel they can come visit us anytime they want. I hate that I never know who's going to be there when I get home from work."

"Take it from me, divorce is an ugly thing," Sukie said. "On the other hand, you don't have children yet, so it would be easier at this stage in your life to do it now, if that's what you're determined to do. But, Tiffany, that's a huge, huge decision. No one can make it for you, and I certainly won't try."

Tiffany bit her lip. "Our anniversary is next week. After that, we're going to try for a baby." Her eyes welled with tears.

"Whoa! You just told me you didn't want a baby." Sukie frowned. "Why are you saying this?"

"Beau is going to throw me out of the house if I don't cooperate."

Sukie had gone through enough maneuvering with Ted to be enraged. She slapped the table with the palm of her hand. "That's blackmail!"

"But what can I do?" Tiffany sniffed and dabbed at her eyes with a tissue. "I have a big home and a nice car—in his name, of course, but mine to use. And, Sukie, if I were forced to leave, I couldn't make it on my own. I have huge debts from college, I don't make all that much at my job, and there's nobody else to fall back on."

Sukie fought for the right words. "Tiffany, there's a lot going on that I'm not sure I understand. I want you to think things through before you make any decisions. And if you can, find a therapist. That's something I'd tell my own kids."

Tiffany nodded and blew her nose.

"Do you want to cancel our shopping plans?" Sukie asked.

"No!" Lines of distress spread across Tiffany's forehead. Her eyes filled once more. "I need this time with you, Sukie. Please."

Sukie nodded. "Okay." She understood all too well the importance of filling time in difficult situations.

"I knew I could trust you to listen, really listen, to me." Tiffany's voice flooded with gratitude. "For once, my instincts were right."

Sukie gave Tiffany's hand a squeeze of encouragement and wondered if there was anything that could help Tiffany's marriage.

Tiffany led the way in and out of stores. Sukie soon discovered that Tiffany not only had wonderful taste, but she also had the innate artistic ability to tie together any outfit of Sukie's with the proper accessory to make it seem especially designed for her.

"Not bad," Tiffany said, as Sukie twirled in front of her in black silky slacks and a pink cashmere sweater, both on sale.

"Does it make me look hot?" Sukie teased.

"Oh, yeah." Tiffany fanned herself with her hands, and they both laughed.

By the time Sukie had stretched every dollar she could, it was four o'clock in the afternoon and she had several heavy bags full of bargains. She shot Tiffany a grateful smile.

"How about a cup of coffee? My treat."

Tiffany checked her watch and grimaced. "I can't. I need to be ready when Beau gets home from work. I promised I'd fix a special meal for him."

"Okay, we'll do it another day."

"You mean it?" Tiffany's smile brightened her features.

"Of course. It's been fun. I hadn't realized how much I needed this. You young women today are really something. Know that?"

Sukie's own young life had seemed so regulated, so full of expectations compared to the freedom of younger women. But then she realized Tiffany wasn't free, like Elizabeth was; she was caught in a golden trap.

Driving into Tiffany's neighborhood, Sukie took a closer look around and understood how intimidated Tiffany might feel. Her house, so large for such a young couple, seemed menacing now that Sukie realized why Beau's parents had given it to them. No wonder Tiffany felt threatened by Beau and his family.

Sukie pulled into the driveway and patted Tiffany's back. "Be sure to call me if you need me."

Tiffany nodded. "Wish me luck."

Sukie drove away, weighed down by the thoughts she'd pushed away all afternoon. From a wealthy background, Ted had introduced her to his friends and a lifestyle she'd never experienced. He'd led her to believe anything in life was possible. She'd loved him with all her heart.

It had been difficult telling Ted about her pregnancy. His look of dismay had turned to sharp disappointment, striking at the heart of her. She'd burst out crying, saying "I'm sorry, I'm sorry," over and over again, as if it were totally her fault. Ted had put his arms around her. "I suppose we were heading there, anyway. Don't worry, I'll marry you." She shook her head at the memory. It wasn't a very romantic way to begin a lifetime together. She wondered at her willingness to accept it.

Seeing things in a different light, she thought maybe Lynn Hodges was right. This whole divorce thing might turn out to be something good. If only she could get through all the humiliation, anger, and self-doubt.

CHAPTER SEVEN
SUKIE

Foil covered a good portion of her curls as Sukie sat in Henri's Hair Designs, deeply embroiled in a gossipy magazine she wouldn't be caught dead buying. She looked up as Katy Hartmann waltzed into the beauty shop, dressed in workout clothes. Wiggling her fingers to everyone, Katy made her way to the back.

She stopped and studied Sukie. "Why, Sukie, bless your heart, I didn't expect to see you here. Have you lost weight? You look fabulous." Katy poked her in the arm and gave her a teasing grin. "Maybe I should get rid of Jim, tell him it's okay to play around, if that's what divorce does for a woman."

Telling herself that it wouldn't do to choke a customer in Henri's place of business, Sukie forced herself to remain seated. If she made a scene, Henri might never let her come back. And in the future, she was going to need him a lot.

Unaware of Sukie's self-control, Katy continued. "By the way, I just came from the gym. Emmy Lou is looking a little ragged around the edges. Guess morning sickness must be getting to her."

"Whaaat!" Sukie's pulse pumped icy water through her body. Pregnancy had never been part of the equation—or so Ted had led her to believe. Betrayal burned brightly. The ice in Sukie's veins disappeared in a rush of heat.

"Oh, sorry, thought you knew." Wide-eyed, Katy covered her mouth with her hand.

Sukie looked away. She'd desperately wanted more babies after Elizabeth but it hadn't happened. Her doctor finally took her aside and suggested she enjoy the two children she had and stop trying for others. It was ruining her health.

"I really am sorry, Sukie." Katy gave her a pitying look before moving away.

Sukie told herself it didn't matter, that Ted's doings weren't her business anymore, but the news stabbed her heart. She pinched her lips. Why couldn't Ted and his bimbo have moved out of town, where she wouldn't have to see or hear about them?

As Henri washed, cut, and styled her hair, Sukie tried to concentrate her thoughts on her new friends and finding a job. After blowing her hair dry, Henri fluffed the streaked curls into a soft halo around the drawn features of her face. He leaned over and gave her a quick kiss on the cheek. "You're lovely, Sukie. Keep that in mind."

Grateful for his sensitivity, Sukie smiled at him. Inside, she was weeping.

Leaving the hair salon, Sukie decided to go to the library to check on reading materials for her upcoming computer course.

Julie Garrison, the head librarian, greeted her with a friendly wave. "Aren't you a ray of sunshine on this cold, wintry day! I love what you've done to your hair."

"Thanks. I'm here to pick up any material you have for the computer courses. I have to find a job. In college, I wanted to get a library science degree, but I got married instead. So, I guess administrative work is for me."

Julie's eyes rounded. "But didn't you attend some library science classes? I seem to remember that."

"I snuck into some courses, just to listen while my husband finished college. That's all. Why?"

A smile spread across Julie's face. "We've been looking for a children's librarian for some time, but the right person hasn't come along. The teacher we were going to hire decided not to take the job. You've been such a good volunteer, would you consider applying as a temporary fill-in?"

"Me?" Sukie's heart pounded. She'd always dreamed of working with children, introducing them to the joys of reading. Her own children were avid readers because she'd started them reading books at a young age.

"You'd be considered a temporary employee until someone with the proper degree comes along. It could be a matter of weeks or months. No guarantees on timing, but I'm sure, with my urging, the board would approve your temporary appointment," Julie's face lit up with enthusiasm. "Are you willing to take a chance on something like this?"

No guarantees? Weeks? Months? Nothing permanent? Sukie hesitated, then mentally waved away her concern. "Sure. Give me an application." She'd learned the hard way there were no guarantees in life.

On Friday, Sukie drove to the Fat Friday luncheon eager to see everyone. The new clothes Tiffany had helped her purchase, the bright streaks in her hair, and the fact that she'd applied for the job at the library combined to erode some of the despair that had undermined her these past few months. Even the news of Emmy Lou's pregnancy had been put in proper perspective, though there was a part of her that secretly hoped the baby would turn out to be colicky and on the ugly side.

She pulled into the parking lot of Bea's Kitchen. The low-slung, white clapboard building, a landmark in the area for years, was known for its down-home Southern cooking. Their collard greens, butter beans, and fried chicken were perfect for a Fat Friday meal.

Sukie entered the restaurant and joined Lynn and Carol Ann at a table covered with red gingham vinyl. "Where are Betsy and Tiffany?"

"They're coming along," Lynn responded. "Betsy's boss needed her to oversee lunch brought in for a meeting. No big deal. She was right behind us."

Carol Ann's eyes widened as she studied Sukie. "What did you do to your hair? I love it! And that sweater! Yummy! Tiffany told me y'all shopped together. You look great!"

Sukie playfully twirled around for them.

Tiffany and Betsy arrived in time to see her do it.

"Teeerific! Betsy exclaimed, giving Sukie a quick hug.

"Your hair looks really wonderful," said Tiffany. She pulled up a chair alongside Sukie's and edged in her designer-jeans-clad rear.

Lynn glanced at the menu. "What's everyone gonna have?"

The aroma of fried chicken wafted around Sukie in tantalizing whiffs. "I'm having the fried chicken-breast special. I haven't had it in ages."

"Sounds good to me." Lynn closed the menu with a snap. "Don't it smell delicious in here? I may even go for the peach pie."

"I guess I'll have the Caesar salad," said Tiffany, looking unhappy.

After their orders were placed, Sukie cleared her throat. "I've applied for a job at the library, running the children's department."

"Sukie, you'd be perfect for it!" gushed Betsy, clapping her hands with delight. "You were always so good with the kids when they were little."

"It's only a temporary position," Sukie explained, "but Julie Garrison thinks the board will agree to my taking it. It could be for just a few weeks, until they're able to hire someone with a degree. There's an outside chance it could last through the summer."

"How do you do it, Sukie?" A slight edge appeared in Carol Ann's voice. "New hairdo, new clothes, new job—I wish things like that would happen to me. And if I don't find a man soon, I don't know what I will do."

Betsy elbowed Carol Ann in the ribs. "You know what you need to do, Carol Ann? You need to register on a dating website. Everyone is into online dating now. They say it's easy."

Carol Ann made a face. "You have to post a picture of yourself and tell them all about you. What could I say? I work at MacTel and belong to a woman's group called Fat Fridays? I can see it now. Delete, delete, delete."

"Don't be such a pessimist!" said Tiffany.

Betsy began to sing softly. "You've got to ac-cen-tu-ate the positive, e-lim-i-nate the negative . . ."

Carol Ann rolled her eyes. "I'm serious about wantin' to meet a man. What am I going to do?"

"What harm could it do to try online dating?" said Betsy. "You talk about finding the right man, but how's he going to find you if you're at home hiding with your parents?"

Carol Ann's face turned shades of pink and then slid into reds. "Gawd! That's what I'm doing, isn't it? Okay, y'all want me to do this? Then I'm going to need help."

"Count me out." Lynn crossed her arms in front of her. "You don't need a man to make you happy. Any fool knows that."

Carol Ann glared at Lynn. "I want somebody to hold me, to love me, to make me feel good about myself. Somebody who will rescue me from the life I have."

Lynn shook her head stubbornly. "You've seen too many Cinderella movies."

Carol Ann's eyes filled. "You don't understand . . ."

"It's not so bad to want that, Carol Ann," Sukie said, stepping into the verbal fray. "I think what Lynn is trying to say is that finding a man won't be the answer to all your prayers. But it can be a wonderful thing."

"Not always," said Tiffany.

Sukie and the others stared at Tiffany. She sat at the end of the table, a woeful expression on her face. "I think I'm pregnant. I didn't get my period last week. It must have happened last month when my prescription ran out and the doctor's office was closed for the long weekend. Stupid me, I thought it would still be safe because it wasn't a fertile time of the month for me."

"Oh, honey, I'm so sorry," Sukie said.

Betsy frowned at Sukie. "What do you mean, you're sorry?"

Sukie held up her hands. "I know it sounds awful and I don't mean it that way, it's just . . ."

"Just that she knows I don't want a baby," finished Tiffany. "Don't scold Sukie. It's true. I don't want this baby."

"Oh, my!" said Betsy, not attempting humor, for once.

The color faded from Tiffany's cheeks. "Oh, no! I'm going to be sick!" She jumped up from the table and raced to the ladies' room.

Betsy turned to Sukie. "What's going on? I'd think she'd be delighted."

Sukie shrugged her shoulders. "Just like Tiffany said, she isn't ready for a baby." Whether it happened like this or not, Sukie had the feeling Tiffany would have ended up pregnant anyway.

"You'd think she'd know better," groused Lynn.

"Things aren't always what they seem," said Betsy, casting a look of concern at the ladies room.

"I caught her crying in the bathroom this morning. I thought it was her boss. Now I know why," said Carol Ann, looking worried.

"Poor kid," Lynn said, much more sympathetic now.

Sukie's gaze rested on Lynn. She was the one person in the group who remained a puzzle to her. She seemed so self-contained, so rigid.

Sukie had the troubling impression Lynn was hiding something but she couldn't figure out what or why.

Wearing a miserable expression, Tiffany returned to the table. "Sorry."

"It's all right, hon." Betsy patted Tiffany's hand. "I remember exactly what it was like, and my baby is older than you are!"

Tiffany let out a sigh. "It's that bad?"

Sukie put an arm around Tiffany's shoulders. "It shouldn't last too long. Usually, just for the first trimester. Have you seen a doctor yet?"

Tiffany shook her head. "I'm going to hold off as long as I can."

After eating their meal in relative quiet, each seemingly lost in her own thoughts, Lynn pointed to her watch and rose.

"Hey, we'd better get goin'." As everyone prepared to depart, Sukie took Tiffany aside. "Are you all right? Really?"

Looking as if she was trying not to cry, Tiffany shrugged.

Sukie gave her a steady look. "Remember, if you need anything, anything at all, call me."

Tiffany gave her a weak smile and nodded.

Carol Ann tapped Sukie on the shoulder. "Sukie? Can I have the phone number of your hairdresser? If I'm going to do this Internet dating thing, I want to look my best. I'll do anything to change my life."

Surprised by the tears that misted Carol Ann's eyes, Sukie wrote down Henri's number and gave it to her.

Carol Ann's lips quivered. "I'm not sure I even know how to begin to set up my profile."

Sukie didn't know Carol Ann's situation, but it was obvious she needed some support. "Do you want me to help you?"

Carol Ann's hazel eyes brightened. "Really? Do you mean it? That would be great!"

"Sure. Why not? Let's say ten o'clock tomorrow at my house." Sukie jotted down directions and handed them to Carol Ann.

Carol Ann all but skipped out the door of the restaurant.

Sukie couldn't help smiling. She understood all too well someone's desire for a different future.

Carol Ann arrived at Sukie's house promptly at ten, looking as hopeful as a Girl Scout with a big box of cookies to sell.

"C'mon in," Sukie said. "I have coffee brewing."

Carol Ann stepped inside and turned in a slow circle. "Your house is beautiful, Sukie. Like something I'd see in a home decorating magazine. I do that, you know—study the magazines so I'll know what to do when my time comes."

Sukie's heart constricted at the wistful note in Carol Ann's voice. She hoped Carol Ann would find the happiness she sought, but she knew things didn't always turn out the way one thought they would.

Sukie poured each of them a cup of coffee, and they settled at the kitchen table.

Carol Ann took a sip of coffee and nibbled on an English tea biscuit.

Sukie studied her. She seemed so young, so immature. "Tell me about yourself, Carol Ann. We haven't had much of a chance to get to know each other."

Carol Ann gave Sukie a shy smile. "It's pretty boring. People think I'm crazy for living at home, but my mother insists that after all she's done for me I need to help her with my father. He's got all sorts of health problems. And staying with them allows me to save money for a place of my own."

Sukie nodded. "It seems pretty practical, since it takes a lot of money for someone to purchase their first home."

Carol Ann shrugged. "I guess. When I finally get to leave, I want my new place to be nice. My sister Becky is four years older than me and eloped with her boyfriend right after high school. He's a teacher and doesn't make much money. It's been an awful struggle for them.

They have a small house, a big mortgage, and three wild boys. She says she's happy, but I don't see how she could be." She gave Sukie a sly look. "You and Tiffany were the smart ones, marrying someone who could give you nice things."

Sukie frowned. "There's so much more to it than that, Carol Ann."

Carol Ann dismissed Sukie's concern with a wave of her hand. "All y'all tell me the same thing, but I know what I'm looking for. That's why I'm going to do this online dating thing. There's not a man in Williston I'd be interested in dating."

"Nobody at work?"

Carol Ann shook her head. "The execs on our floor are mostly married. My boss, Ed Pritchard, isn't. But then, he's on the short side, balding, and a little pudgy. Not exactly a studmuffin."

"But, is he nice?" Annoyed by Carol Ann's attitude, Sukie sat back in her chair.

Carol Ann nodded. "He's great compared to Lynn's boss. Tiffany's boss, Glenn Mitchum, is the best—tall, dark, handsome." She sighed. "Too bad he's married with four young kids."

"How long have you women at MacTel known each other?" Sukie asked, curious how such diverse people got along so well.

"I've been with the company for two years, Lynn and Tiffany about eighteen months, and Betsy a little over a year. But it seems like we've known each other forever." Carol Ann smiled. "Working together, we bonded real quickly."

Sukie rose to pour more coffee and refilled Carol Ann's cup. "Why is Lynn so against men? What's her story?"

Carol Ann shrugged. "I don't know. She doesn't talk about her past, except to say she had a real bad marriage. She never mentions any kids." She wrinkled her nose. "I don't care what she thinks. I'm looking for someone exactly like Tiffany's Beau. I want out of my situation. You'll help me fill out the forms, won't you?"

Sukie hesitated, wondering how blunt she should be, and decided to be truthful. "It's not going to work well if you tell people you're looking for a handsome, rich man. Male egos aside, nobody likes to be judged that way."

"I just want to get away from home, have a much better life." Carol Ann's eyes grew moist. "My parents have never been able to take real vacations, have nice things, or just plain enjoy themselves. My father is dying of emphysema and my mother still yells at him for every little thing. God! I don't want anything like it."

Sukie nodded. "Okay. Let's begin. We'll come up with something that's both truthful and tactful."

Carol Ann grinned. "Thanks. And, Sukie, it'll be good practice for you."

Sukie shook her head. She couldn't imagine herself going through meet-and-greet sessions with strangers. Her mouth grew even drier at the idea of exposing her body to another man. *Unless . . .* Her thoughts flew to her new neighbor. She scolded herself for even thinking such a thing. He was taken, and there was no way she'd ever get involved with a married man.

By the time they finished working on the application for the dating site, Sukie decided Carol Ann wasn't as shallow as she'd first believed. She had a good heart.

The phone rang as Sukie was saying good-bye to Carol Ann. She hurried back to the kitchen to answer it.

"Sukie?"

All good humor vanished. "What do you want, Ted?"

"Guess you've heard Emmy Lou is going to have a baby," he began. "This is going to mean some changes in our agreement."

Stung by the note of pride in his voice, Sukie remained quiet.

"Well, I was wondering . . . you know that cradle that we used for the kids? Is it still up in the attic?"

"It's going to Madeleine and Rob," Sukie said with a firmness she felt to her toes. "Emmy Lou is not, repeat *not*, going to use it."

"Jeez, I just thought I'd ask," Ted grumbled. "So, how are you doing?"

"Good-bye, Ted." Sukie slammed the receiver down so hard it bounced in the cradle.

So much for thinking she was over the divorce.

CHAPTER EIGHT
BETSY

Betsy finished her coffee and put the cup in the sink, hoping the caffeine would help get her going. It was a listless day, one Saturday in which she didn't have Caitlin and Garrett staying with her. She was glad. They were great kids and she loved 'em like crazy, but crazy tired is what she got when she spent so much time with them. When she babysat them, it didn't help her mood to know that while she was running after the children, stopping fights, and keeping them entertained, Sarah was off shopping or lounging in some expensive spa. Then again, she and the kids were exceptionally close and she wouldn't trade that for anything.

Betsy picked up the phone. She and Sukie hadn't had a chance to talk privately after the Fat Fridays lunch, and she knew how lonely weekends could be for someone newly single.

When the call went into voice mail, Betsy hung up despondent. Between work and the time she spent babysitting her grandchildren, she hadn't had the energy to get back to some of her old activities or find new ones to keep her busy during down times. And she was someone who liked to stay busy.

The phone rang. She checked caller ID. Karen McEvoy. Betsy grinned. She and Karen had served on the Forsyth County jury together. It was she who gave Betsy the idea to take computer courses. After "we the jury" had found the shoplifter guilty, Betsy had signed up for the training. Over time she'd lost contact with Karen but she'd always liked her.

"Karen!" Betsy said. "I owe you big time. Guess what! I'm working at MacTel now."

"That's wonderful, Betsy," said Karen. "I was thinking about you the other day and decided to give you a call. I'm going to the movies. Want to join me?"

"Would I ever!" said Betsy, finding the day a whole lot brighter.

CHAPTER NINE
SUKIE

Monday morning, cold rain slanted against the bedroom windows, tapping against the glass like Jack Frost knocking for attention. But the gray, wet day failed to dampen Sukie's excitement. The computer course was to begin that evening.

Julie called from the library as Sukie was sipping her morning coffee. "Good news, Sukie! The library board has agreed to let you fill the children's librarian opening on a temporary basis. You can fill out the paperwork and start anytime."

Sukie hung up the phone and danced around the kitchen. She was living on court-ordered alimony Ted had guiltily agreed to, but she knew his cooperation wouldn't last. He'd find ways to delay payments, offering one excuse after another, making her life unsettled. Despite his wealth, Ted was far from generous. Sukie was sure that at some point in her life, she'd be forced to move out of the house, find something smaller, make her own way with little, if any, real help from him.

She eagerly changed her clothes and hurried to the library to check the layout of the children's section. She had a few ideas she wanted to try.

The library was a two-story, red-brick building next to the town hall, Williston's center of activity. White shutters accented the many-paned windows. A double black door served as its main entrance.

On this rainy March morning, the parking lot was mostly empty. Sukie pulled in, parked the car next to a white SUV, and hurried inside, avoiding as much of the lingering shower as she could.

Inside, Julie greeted her with a warm smile. "I'm so happy you're going to be part of my team. I hope you understand the job involves working on some Saturday mornings and a few Sunday afternoons. I forgot to clarify that when I called."

Sukie smiled. "No problem. I'll welcome it." Her once-busy weekends, now empty of social activity, seemed endless.

Julie motioned for Sukie to follow her. "I have the paperwork all set for you to fill out."

The office sat behind the circulation desk. A stack of books lay on the floor. Others lined both sides of a rolling cart.

Julie indicated the books on the cart. "These have already been cataloged. Volunteers will shelve them. As you know, we're a small operation here."

Sukie nodded. She'd been an active volunteer at the circulation desk when the kids were growing up and had continued to help ever since.

She filled out the paperwork and walked over to the children's section. Feeling like a chef surveying a well-stocked kitchen, she stood a moment, savoring the idea that it was hers to oversee.

A long table surrounded by several small wooden chairs sat in the middle of an open space edged by bookcases. A desk stood off in a corner.

"What do you think?" Julie asked, coming to Sukie's side.

"I'd like to make some changes to the layout," Sukie said, hoping she wasn't overstepping her new role.

Julie's eyebrows shot up.

"I remember the joy I had reading books as a kid. I'd put pillows all around me in the corner of my room near the window and sit and read for hours. That's what I'd like to see here—nooks and crannies where kids can escape into reading."

A smile spread across Julie's face. "I like it. Let me find the custodian and see if he can help us move things around."

Julie returned, accompanied by a short and stocky gray-haired man. "This is Bill Walters. Another man is on his way to help us."

Sukie smiled at Bill, then blinked with surprise as the tall man she'd seen in her neighborhood approached. He smiled a warm hello, reminding her of his innate kindness. "You're the welcome lady in my neighborhood."

"You know each other?" Julie said.

"We've met briefly." Sukie's heart pumped a flushed greeting she tried to control. Feeling foolish at her reaction, she held out her hand. "Sukie Skidmore."

"Cameron Taylor." The touch of his hand on hers snaked heat through Sukie's body. She quickly withdrew her fingers and steadied herself. "How's your little girl?"

"Chloe?" A tender look softened his features. "She's fine. At three, she's always running so she's pretty used to taking a tumble now and then."

Sukie smiled. Men today were so into helping to raise children. She remembered the many evenings Ted didn't arrive home until after Rob and Elizabeth were in bed.

The men moved her desk away from the corner, leaving a space for scattered floor pillows, and shifted the long table to an area off to one side, near the magazine shelf. *A better place for projects,* she thought.

"How's that?" asked Cameron.

Sukie hesitated. "Can you help me move a couple of bookcases?"

Cameron looked at Bill and shrugged. "Why not?"

Sukie hurried to unload some of the books from the shelves. The men wrestled with the bookcases, angling them at her direction, making it easier for children to browse for books on both sides.

"There, that's perfect." Sukie clasped her hands together, delighted with the effect.

"Much better," said Julie. "We've needed someone like you for some time."

Sukie turned to the men. "Thanks for your help."

Bill dipped his head and moved away.

Cameron stood a moment, frowning. "Sukie Skidmore. Didn't you sign up for the computer course?"

She nodded.

He smiled. "I thought so. I'm your instructor. See you tonight at seven." He waved and went on his way.

Sukie turned to Julie. "He's the teacher?"

"Yes. We're so lucky to get him. He's an independent consultant, working on a huge, long-term project for MacTel. I met him when he was looking for property. He came in to check out the library and get some recommendations for a preschool for his little girl."

"Very nice," Sukie murmured.

Julie grinned. "Very nice-looking, too. All the volunteers are drooling over him."

"Too bad he's married," Sukie said, and turned back to her new project. Her days of romance were over, but she understood how others might be disappointed to learn he wasn't available.

Later, Sukie lugged large pillows from her car into the library. She could hardly wait to see children gathered there for her first story hour. Even if the job might not last long, she wanted to make the best possible impression. Then maybe the board would decide to keep her on through the summer and even beyond.

"Excellent," said Julie, when she came to inspect what Sukie was doing. She helped Sukie arrange the bright-colored pillows in the corner.

At her desk, Sukie leafed through a selection of picture books. It had been some time since she'd read to children, and she needed to catch up on the latest books and reacquaint herself with old favorites.

The bright colorful illustrations brought back memories of many happy hours with her own children, hours she hoped to share with her new grandchild.

Funny, she thought, that she'd been excited about the news of a grandchild, but Ted had gone into a funk when he'd heard he was about to become a grandfather. He'd ended up acting like a spoiled baby himself. Looking back, she realized how many times he'd ruined happy moments for her.

That evening, as Sukie walked into the learning room at the library, Cameron acknowledged her with a nod. Five other people sat in front of computers on desks scattered throughout the small learning center. She took a seat at the remaining empty space.

"Thought you weren't going to show up," said Cameron, coming to Sukie's side to make sure she was logged on properly.

"I thought about it, especially after my first day at work," she said. "But after you helped me today, I couldn't let you down."

He grinned and turned to the others. "Okay, class, let's get started."

The time flew by. At the end of the hour, her mind spinning, Sukie turned off her machine. She'd learned more about computer programs than she'd thought possible. It now seemed silly she'd never taken a course like this before.

"How did you like it?" Cameron asked, packing up his teaching materials.

Sukie smiled. "It was great. You made it seem so easy. Julie told me you're going to be working at MacTel for a while."

He nodded. "It's a good opportunity for me."

"I know some administrative people who work on the executive floor. I'm sure they'd be happy to help you if you ever need it."

"Thanks." His deep blue gaze settled on her. "Are you always so helpful to strangers?"

Her cheeks burned. "I try to be."

"Nice," he said. "You don't find that so much anymore."

A warm glow accompanied Sukie all the way to her car. Something about the way Cameron Taylor had looked at her made her feel special. It'd been a long time since she felt that way.

Friday at noon, Sukie pulled into Bea's parking lot for the Fat Fridays lunch. She couldn't wait to tell the others about her job. She was also eager to see Tiffany and Carol Ann. She hadn't spoken to them all week.

Betsy hurried over to her as soon as Sukie climbed out of her car. "Sukie! You started the job. Good for you! I met Julie in the grocery store and she told me she's ecstatic about all you're doing."

"Thanks," said Sukie, pleased that nice, not hurtful, news was being spread about her. "I think it's going to be great."

Carol Ann drove into the parking lot with Tiffany. They waved hello and Sukie waved back.

"How are they?" Sukie asked, as Lynn joined them.

"Tiffany's been real quiet and Carol Ann has talked our ears off all week about the different men on the dating website she joined." Censure iced Lynn's words.

Sukie and Betsy exchanged knowing glances and turned as Carol Ann ran toward them.

"Sukie! Wait until I tell you about the responses to my profile! I'm so excited!" She hugged Sukie so hard, she almost knocked her over.

"Tell her all about it inside," said Lynn impatiently. "It's getting late."

Inside, the chatter of the noon crowd rose and fell as people laughed and called to one another. Sukie followed the others to a round table. The enticing aromas of home-cooked food swirled around her. Her mouth watered at the sight of Brunswick stew, pulled pork, and barbecued chicken breasts on the mounded plates waitresses carried by. In good spirits, she waved to a neighbor.

During the meal, Carol Ann kept everybody entertained, telling them about some of the men who'd responded to her singles profile.

"So which man are you going to date on Saturday?" Sukie asked, after taking a last bite of fried okra.

Carol Ann knotted her hands together. "Well, Rodney suggested we meet for coffee tomorrow at the Mall of Georgia. I'm gonna check him out and then meet John—the one who works for the insurance company—for a drink later that day." Her face lit up. "I never knew this could be so much fun!"

"Be careful," warned Lynn. "Some women have dated real losers."

"Oh, but Carol Ann can have her choice of dates," Tiffany said, defending her. "Her picture on the Internet is really cool. It's that new hairdo."

Carol Ann trailed her fingers over the sleek chin-length haircut Henri had given her and shot Sukie a grateful look. The new style did all kinds of wonderful things to her eyes, giving her a whole new appearance.

"Enjoy yourself, but Lynn is right," said Sukie. "Some of these guys aren't trustworthy. I've heard all kinds of stories about men stealing money away from women they've met online. That, and a lot of other crazy tales."

Carol Ann stuck her chin out, like a stubborn two-year-old. "Y'all, I'm going on as many dates as I can. You don't know what it's like sitting home night after night with my parents. Boring with a capital *B*! That's over, thank God."

Betsy piped up. "Like Mae West said, 'Too much of a good thing can be wonderful.' I say go for it, Carol Ann."

Sukie joined the rest in laughter.

Lynn checked her watch. "We'd better head back to work, ladies."

Tiffany held Sukie back. "I need to talk to you."

"You go ahead," Sukie called to the others. "I'll drop Tiffany off on my way back to the library."

Sukie sat back down and signaled the waitress. She came right over. "Whatcha want, hon? More coffee? Decaf, right?"

Sukie nodded.

In seconds, the waitress was back with an orange-handled pot. She filled Sukie's mug and left.

A whitish wisp of hot steam rose from Sukie's cup and caressed her face. Sukie inhaled, took a cautious sip, and waited anxiously for Tiffany to speak.

Tiffany leaned forward, her eyes shimmering with unshed tears. "I'm thinking about having an abortion," she said softly.

The coffee turned sour in Sukie's stomach. She set her cup down. "Is . . . is that what you want?"

Tiffany shook her head. "I don't know what else to do. If I go ahead with the baby, I'll never be able to leave Beau. He still doesn't know I'm pregnant. Do you know what he gave me for my anniversary present? One diamond earring. A huge one. I get the second one after the birth of our first child."

"That's awful!"

"Probably his mother's idea." Tiffany took a deep breath. "I hate her, Sukie. And I think she hates me. No matter what I do, it isn't right. And if I hear her talk about poor little Tiffany being a diamond in the rough one more time, I swear I'm going to frickin' kill her."

Stunned by the venom in Tiffany's voice, Sukie sat back in her chair. "Look, I know hormones go crazy when you're pregnant but, Tiffany, I hate to hear you talk that way. Do you really mean it?"

"About the abortion?" Tears filled Tiffany's eyes. "Probably not. I can't even step on ants. How could I hurt my baby? It's just that I have to get out all my anger before I burst. I've never felt this way before."

"Have you been to a doctor yet?" Sukie studied the dark smudges under Tiffany's eyes.

"No, because the minute I make an appointment, Beau will know. I've taken three pregnancy tests, wishing they were wrong." Her eyes welled again. "I never dreamed I'd be feeling this way. I've always wanted a family, in my own good time and with a man I was sure I wanted to be with for the rest of my life. How could I have been so stupid as to marry Beau? I guess I was blinded by everything—the way he looked at me, his background, everything." Tiffany's sigh wavered in the air, a sad note from a song gone sour.

"Perhaps you can talk to your minister," Sukie said, searching for ideas.

Tiffany warded off her words with a raised palm. "You don't understand. I can't talk to anyone else about it. Once Beau's mother finds out, any sense I have of freedom is gone."

"Tiffany, you can't hide this forever. Chances are she and Beau will find out you're having his baby. Think about it. Then decide where you want to go from there. Maybe Beau will be so excited about fulfilling his parents' wishes that things will be better between you." Even as Sukie said the words, she doubted it would happen.

"What should I do, Sukie?" Tiffany's eyes loomed large in her fine-featured face.

Sukie took a deep breath. "Well, I don't think you should do anything rash. How would you feel if you did end the pregnancy?"

"Awful, just awful." Tiffany's cheeks drained of color. "Oh, God! I think I'm going to be sick."

Tiffany dashed into the bathroom, leaving Sukie shivering at the table. She felt as if a frigid winter wind had blown through her.

Pale and silent, Tiffany emerged from the bathroom. Her hand cupped her stomach. Watching Tiffany's hand move in gentle circles over the slight bulge, Sukie felt the tension inside her ease. Whether Tiffany was aware of it or not, she'd already begun to comfort the baby.

Sukie dropped Tiffany off at work and headed back to the library. Her thoughts strayed to Ted and the life he'd recently started with Emmy Lou. It seemed so wrong that he should be able to have a whole new family after ditching the one he had with her. Now that he was about to have a baby with a younger woman, he strutted around town like a glowing ad for Viagra.

Darkening skies brought the afternoon to an end. Sukie headed home, grateful for her job. Weekends had become an agonizingly long period of time, but now she'd be busy.

She pulled into her garage, parked the car, and walked down to the mailbox. As she stood there, a white Lexus SUV pulled up beside her.

Cameron Taylor opened the front passenger's window of his car and leaned toward her. "I heard about the Nighty Night bedtime-story program you've started at the library. Is it too late to sign up Chloe?"

"No, it's fine. The more the merrier." Sukie leaned in the car window to talk to Chloe in her car seat. "It should be fun, honey. Come dressed in your jammies, all ready for bed."

Cameron gave Sukie a dazzling smile. "Thanks. It's a great idea. Gives parents the chance to have time to themselves."

Sukie nodded. "It's nice for the kids, too."

Cameron gave her a little salute and slowly pulled away.

Sukie watched the car travel down the road. The man did everything for his daughter. And he was hot. The way his leather jacket fit across his broad shoulders, the honey-colored hair, the slight cleft in his chin . . .

She let out a sigh. "Get real, Sukie."

At the mailbox, she lifted out a bunch of envelopes. Bills, bills, and more bills. A white sheet of paper floated to the ground. She leaned over and picked it up. Scrawled across it in bold, black letters was the single word HELLO.

A shiver did a spidery dance across Sukie's shoulders. The friendly word didn't seem friendly at all.

She looked around, but the street was empty and no one was in sight.

CHAPTER TEN
LYNN

Lynn wandered around her apartment admiring all the nice things she'd been able to gather together, items she'd bought at garage sales or at thrift shops. She picked up the small blue statue of the Virgin Mother from the end table by the couch and put it back down, uncertain what she believed anymore. The empty picture frame sitting nearby was a token of all she'd had and lost. She kept it out on display to remind her of the need to be careful.

Of all the places Lynn had lived in the past, this one had become most like a real home to her. She hoped to be able to stay in Williston for a long time, but she wasn't sure if she could. It was always that way. She'd just start to feel settled then something would come up and she'd worry about staying too long in one place and being found.

Lynn's heart shriveled at the idea of leaving. The ladies in the Fat Fridays group had become so dear to her. Their friendship was a real breakthrough for her. In the past, she'd never let anybody get so close to her. But each woman in the group was willing to accept her as she was—a woman all alone, restless and unsure of the future. Here, with them, she'd found something near contentment.

Sinking onto the couch, Lynn hugged a pillow to her, thinking of the little girl she'd once held close. She felt tired, so tired, from constantly running and living a nightmare few would imagine.

She wanted to stay in Williston. She really did.

Only time would tell if she could.

CHAPTER ELEVEN
SUKIE

Sukie awoke with fresh purpose. She'd always loved books—delighted in tracing the words across a sentence, inhaling the smell of the ink on the pages, holding the weight of the pages in her hand. As a child growing up in a small town, reading had played a big part in her life. She'd found it a joy to share that love of the written word with her children, to let them witness the unraveling of a story. Now she'd get to share that same joy with lots of other children.

She hurried through her daily routine and then went to the library, where she took up a morning post behind the circulation desk, helping to check out books, sorting returned books, and answering questions as simple as the location of the restroom. It felt good to be working . . . until Katy Hartmann walked in.

Sukie cringed and looked for a way to escape. Too late.

Katy waved and came right over to the desk. She'd casually thrown a pink sweater over a white tennis dress, which showed her long legs to good advantage, nicely honed from Emmy Lou's Pilates class, no doubt. Her eyes gleamed like those of a lizard that'd just spotted a juicy, fat fly.

The memory of Katy's smugness as she'd spread the news through town about Ted's affair sabotaged any good intentions on Sukie's part to be friendly.

Katy fluttered her eyelashes, and Sukie thought of bees, not butterflies. "Sukie, it's true. You *are* working here. I heard the news at the last meeting of the women's club."

Sukie nodded and remained silent, desperate to avoid a conversation with her.

"Say, I hear there's a new guy in town. All the women are talking about him. And, Sukie, he's right down the street from you. His name is Cameron Taylor. Does it ring a bell?"

"I've met him." Sukie fought to control the heat that shot defiantly to her cheeks. "He seems real nice. He's got an adorable little girl. I haven't met his wife yet."

Katy blinked, and her lips spread in a sly smile. "Sukie, he has no wife. He's single. That's why all the women, single or not, are going gaga over him."

Single? Sukie's mouth went dry. *Why hadn't he ever corrected her talk of a wife?* She felt like a fool.

"Well, I've got to go." Katy wiggled her fingers at her. "Just thought I'd stop by and say hello on my way to pick up fresh flowers. We're having a dinner party tonight. Catered, but still, I've got a lot to do."

Sukie feigned a smile. Once, she and Ted would have been included in Katy's dinners.

"Have fun!" Sukie forced herself to say, but the words got stuck in her throat.

After a quick supper, Sukie hurried to the library to greet the dozen or so children who'd signed up for the bedtime story hour. There, she arranged a number of pillows on the floor around the small stool she'd chosen for herself and paced the floor, awaiting the first arrival.

By seven o'clock, most of the children had appeared. Two overly excited boys began to hit each other with their pillows. Sukie pulled one of them aside, talked quietly to him, and placed the other boy close to her feet where she could watch him.

"Shall we begin?" Sukie said to the restless children, and looked up to see Cameron approach, Chloe in hand.

"Hi, Chloe! Come join us." Sukie smiled at her, trying her best not to stare at the jeans that perfectly outlined Cameron's trim, masculine, unmarried body.

Chloe ran over to Sukie and sat next to her, fitting into the curve of Sukie's side. Her light pink granny gown set off her pale curls.

As she read a Dr. Seuss book, Sukie loved the sound of the words on her tongue. By the time Sukie ended the session with *Goodnight, Moon*, a number of children were all but asleep, their tousled hair a rainbow of colors and styles.

Chloe climbed into Sukie's lap and nestled against her chest. Sukie held her close, inhaling the clean smell of her shampoo. She continued to hold Chloe even as parents came to pick up their children and departed. Cameron was the last to appear.

"Chloe? Ready to go?" He sounded out of breath, as if he'd been running.

Chloe clung to Sukie and shook her head. "I want to stay here with Miss Sukie."

Sukie smiled at Cameron and rubbed Chloe's back. "I think we both needed a hug tonight. I understand you two are alone." Chloe's eyelids fluttered sleepily, and closed.

He nodded. "It's always been that way." He trailed a finger down Chloe's cheek. "Her mother took off right after she was born," he explained quietly.

Sukie gently patted Chloe's back. "That's too bad. She's such a beautiful child, and so sweet."

"Yeah, she is." Tenderness softened the angles and planes of his face. He held out his arms.

Sukie placed Chloe in them and felt a stab of emptiness.

Chloe whimpered and settled in his embrace.

Cameron's blue gaze rested on Sukie. The yearning in his eyes sent a shiver of awareness dancing through her. Sukie looked away and back again, lost once more in his gaze. Damn! He was the sexiest man she'd ever met.

Cameron cleared his throat and stepped back, breaking the sexual tension between them. "Why don't I wait for you to lock up so you don't have to leave alone in the dark?"

"Yes, that would be nice." Sukie turned to get her purse, mortified by the fantasies that had crept into her normally practical thoughts. It was as if divorce had brought out a different side of her, or maybe it was realizing how shallow her marriage to Ted had become.

Cameron followed her to her car and waited until she was safely inside it before walking toward his SUV.

Sukie opened her window. "Thanks, Cameron!"

He turned back to her. "It's Cam, and you're welcome." He paused and walked back to her. "I see how you are with Chloe. Is there a chance you could help me out occasionally? With babysitting?"

Sukie swallowed hard. While she'd been fantasizing about his body and what he could do with it, making dreams of nothing, he'd been assessing her as a babysitter!

"Sure," she said, her voice hollow. "Give me a call sometime."

Sukie drove home, thinking she'd better pick up a romance novel. It was the only such excitement she was likely to experience in the coming months.

CHAPTER TWELVE
SUKIE

Waiting for the other women of Fat Fridays to arrive, Sukie set glasses, soft drinks, bottled water, and white wine on the kitchen counter and slid a chicken casserole in the oven. They'd all been excited to get her invitation for a casual get-together, and she was eager for the opportunity to get to know them better. They were such an unusual group.

The women's chatter outside her door signaled their arrival.

Sukie ushered them inside. "Drinks are set up in the kitchen and the casserole is in the oven."

Everyone fixed themselves something to drink, and they congregated in the living room.

Tiffany leaned back against the couch and let out a sigh. "I can't stay long. Beau thinks I'm working late on a special project. Even though he's out with his buddies, I shouldn't push my luck."

"Why are you letting a man control you like that?" Lynn growled.

Carol Ann shook her head. "Honestly, Lynn. Why are y'all so against men? Beau's a doll!"

"You've got your head in the sand, Carol Ann. No man is good enough to call *all* the shots," Lynn sputtered.

Tiffany said nothing, though her cheeks grew pink.

"I don't understand. Why do you feel so strongly?" Sukie asked. There was more than normal frustration in Lynn's voice.

Betsy winked. "It must be that mysterious past of hers."

"C'mon, spill," said Tiffany, giving Lynn a smile of encouragement. "You've never told us about yourself, yet all of you know more about me than my own in-laws."

Lynn twitched uncomfortably in her seat. After a moment, she straightened with a look of resolve. "Okay. You want the truth?" She drew a quivering breath. Her eyes became pools of sadness. "I'm not Lynn Hodges. My real name is Grace Jamison."

"Whaaaat?" Betsy's shrill cry pierced the shocked silence.

Sukie's jaw fell. "What are you saying? Why would you change your name unless . . ."

"You're not wanted by the cops or anything like that, are you?" Carol Ann fell back against the couch, looking as if she'd been punched in the stomach.

Tiffany's eyes narrowed with suspicion. "What are you running from?"

Sukie thought back to all the times Lynn had remained reticent about her past while the rest of them chatted away about anything and everything. It could mean so many things.

"Shh. You can't tell anyone what I've just told you." Lynn spoke in a tremulous whisper. "Nobody knows about my aliases. I couldn't talk about it, you see. It might mean my death." She twisted her hands in her lap.

Sukie stared at Lynn with shock. Lynn had always remained aloof, unreachable, but now all her vulnerability showed.

Betsy put an arm around Lynn. "You'd better tell us the whole story, hon."

Lynn had clutched her fingers together so tightly her knuckles had turned white. Now, tears flowed down her cheeks. "Six years ago, my ex-husband almost killed me and my daughter, Misty. She was only ten, but we survived."

Looks of horror distorted the faces of the other women in the room, mirroring Sukie's repulsion.

"Misty got away with some bruises and a few stitches, but he broke my arm as I was protecting her. He had a knife but I fought him for it." She held up her hand. A scar ran along the side of it. "The other scars you can't see."

Imagining the frightening scene, feeling the terror of it, Sukie struggled to breathe.

Tears ran down Lynn's cheeks, but no sound came out of her open mouth.

Observing her, Sukie had the odd feeling this way of crying was something Lynn had done for a long time, the pain so deep inside her it could not emerge.

"Oh, Lynn, what an awful, awful thing," murmured Betsy.

The pain on the faces of the other women told Sukie they were as upset as she. Sukie went to Lynn, handed her a napkin to dry her eyes, and gave her a hug. "It's okay, Lynn. We're here for you."

Betsy, Carol Ann, and Tiffany rose and hugged Lynn in turn, their faces ghostlike in their whiteness.

"What happened to your ex? Did he go to jail?" Betsy asked, clearly distressed.

Lynn nodded. "Yes, but they let him go after eighteen months. His lawyer claimed he'd been rehabilitated from his drug addiction and was no longer a threat to me or society. Fat fuckin' chance. After he got out, he threatened to kill me and Misty, no matter how long it took or where we went."

"Why?" Sukie's own eyes filled.

Lynn stemmed a fresh flow of tears with the napkin and took a deep breath. "He was convinced Misty wasn't his child. He thought I'd screwed around with a friend of ours while he was on the road, driving the truck. No matter how much I told him it wasn't true, he wouldn't believe me. He wouldn't even believe a DNA test! The man he accused me of screwing happened to drown in a nearby pond. I know damn well my ex had something to do with it, but I could never prove it. That's when I took off with Misty. No matter what anybody else said, I knew the sick bastard wouldn't give up until he'd killed us too."

"What happened to Misty?" Tiffany placed a protective hand over her stomach.

It took Lynn a moment before she could speak. "I sent Misty to a distant cousin he didn't know anything about and took off on my own. I had to do something to keep her safe, you know?" Lynn blew her nose. "I just couldn't let him get to her."

Sukie felt sick to her stomach. She thought about Elizabeth and all the happiness they'd shared through the years and couldn't imagine Lynn's pain. "I'm so sorry, Lynn. I truly am."

Studying her, Sukie realized Lynn wasn't nearly as old as she'd once thought. Years of running and hiding must have aged her. Worry lines etched her face and her hair had gone gray in places, but Sukie now guessed Lynn to be in her late thirties or early forties.

"What other names have you used, Lynn . . . I mean Grace?" Carol Ann asked awkwardly.

"Six or seven—Susan, Linda, Mary Ann, anything but Grace. Go ahead and call me Lynn. I'm used to it now." Her voice became bitter. "I have a sense of when I should move, change my name, and begin a different life. He's one of those guys who's a real smooth talker, able to convince a judge he's changed. But when he's alone with me, he can't control his temper. He has a violent streak to him that will never go away. He's been in and out of jail, but I know enough about the way he operates to believe he's gonna follow me here. He always finds me." She gave each of them a look of such misery Sukie felt her heart stop, then start again.

"I'm tellin' ya, he's a sick, evil man," Lynn said. "I should've left here a few weeks ago, but you've become such good friends and I'm so tired of running and hiding, I couldn't make myself do it."

Sukie felt cold, so cold. "We'll help you. We'll go to the sheriff and tell him your story. You can give him a description of your ex-husband, get help."

Lynn let out a derisive laugh. "What can the sheriff do? Get a restraining order for someone I can't see? Someone I haven't faced in years? Every time I thought I'd seen him or heard his voice, I'd take off. The thing is, unless he actually attacks or threatens me personally, there's nothing they can do."

The women sat together in the living room, silent, bonded together by all Lynn had told them.

Sukie's own problems now seemed small. Filled with determination, she stood.

"The rest of you begin to take notes while I get our dinner ready. We need a basic description of Lynn's ex. I'm sure he's changed since Lynn has seen him, but it's a start. Write down any other data that would be helpful to the sheriff."

"Lynn shouldn't be alone. She can move in with me," Betsy said.

Lynn shook her head emphatically. "Thanks, but no thanks. That's exactly why I can't stay here. If you help me, you're in danger too. He thinks anyone who is a friend of mine is in on the betrayal. I'm tellin' ya, he's really screwed up."

Sukie left them talking in the living room and rummaged through the refrigerator for the ingredients for a salad.

Betsy joined her. "I can't believe it. No wonder Lynn has always been so quiet. Bless her heart, she's had it tough."

"We've got to help her." It sickened Sukie to think how Lynn's ex had ruined her life and that of their daughter.

They sat and ate dinner, bouncing ideas around as to how they could help Lynn. By the time they finished their meal and reviewed the notes they'd made, it was dark.

"Tomorrow, I'll go see the sheriff," Sukie said. "We're not going to give in to this maniac, Lynn."

Tears filled Lynn's eyes. She rose from the dining room table, and they all gathered around her in a protective circle.

"Okay, I'll stay a while longer. I want to fight the bastard once and for all and then I'm going to get my daughter."

They hugged each other, no longer simply women meeting for lunch; they were each other's staunchest allies, willing to fight to protect one of their own.

Sukie stopped by the sheriff's office. Bill Michaels listened to the whole story and accepted the notes she handed him.

"I'll see what I can do, but without direct threats, as Lynn told you, nothing much can be done. I'll have my men drive through her neighborhood from time to time and check up on her apartment. Let me know immediately if you have anything else for me to go on. Otherwise, it's a waiting game."

The days moved forward. Sukie followed her normal routines but she knew things would never feel the same to her or the other women.

A somber group met for lunch on Friday.

Sukie decided to bring the issue into the open. "Lynn, I don't know how you do it, watching out for yourself, wondering if and when your ex might appear."

"Yeah, y'all, it's really spooky," said Carol Ann. "After hearing Lynn's story, I'm always looking over my shoulder, wondering if he's near."

"Me too." Tiffany's shoulders shook. "It's weird. I'm afraid to go outside alone in the dark."

"Yeah, well you can't let him control you that way," said Lynn. "That way, he wins. You gotta be careful, but you gotta go about your normal stuff. Remember, it's not you he's after. Like I told you, I get a sense of when he might be near. When that happens, I'll let you know."

"Lynn's right," said Betsy. "As FDR once said, 'We have nothing to fear but fear itself.' We have to keep living our lives."

They all nodded, but until he was caught Sukie knew she'd never feel safe.

CHAPTER THIRTEEN
CAROL ANN

Carol Ann climbed out of bed, aching all over. She didn't dare wake her parents. They slept in on Sunday mornings. No way did she want them to catch her like this.

She slipped on a T-shirt and jeans, tiptoed into the kitchen, and snatched up her car keys, grabbing hold of them tightly to keep them from rattling and giving her away. She started for the front door and hurried back for her cell phone. Slowly, she opened the front door and snuck outside, closing the door quietly behind her.

Climbing into the car, Carol Ann scolded herself. She'd been dumber than a box of rocks and needed to talk to someone. She punched in Sukie's number, praying she was at home.

Sukie answered right away. "H-h-hello?"

"Sukie? It's Carol Ann. Can I come over?" She couldn't stop her voice from shaking.

"Are you all right?" Sukie asked. "You sound upset."

"Yes . . . no . . ." Carol Ann's eyes flooded at Sukie's concern. Sukie had quickly become the center of their group, which had grown even closer now that they were helping Lynn.

"Hurry along, hon. I'll be here waiting for you."

Tears blinded Carol Ann as she hung up. Sukie wasn't like her parents. She wouldn't scold or nag or tell her she was stupid as all get out.

Carol Ann drove to Sukie's, cut off the engine, and sat outside in the car, taking deep breaths. After a few minutes, she got out, walked up to the front door and rang the doorbell, swallowing hard at the idea of having to confess what had happened.

Sukie opened the door with a smile that disappeared in a hurry. "Good heavens!" she gasped. "What happened? Your black eye . . ."

The fresh tears Carol Ann had been holding back ran down her cheeks. "It was John, the insurance guy I met for drinks last night."

Sukie put an arm around her. "Come inside. I've got coffee made. Extra strong. I think we're going to need it."

Carol Ann collapsed at the kitchen table. Sukie poured each of them a cup of coffee and took a seat in a chair opposite her.

"Tell me everything." Sukie studied her with a worried look.

Taking a sip of hot coffee, Carol Ann tried to pull herself together. She drew a deep breath. "It started out really nice. He's good-looking and not afraid to throw money around. He said we should start out the evening with a glass of champagne."

"Champagne? I don't know of any place in town who serves champagne."

Carol Ann swallowed hard. "He drove me to Buckhead. That was another thing. He seemed so polished, like he knew all the hot spots."

"You drove with him? Alone?" Sukie's cheeks flushed an angry pink that Carol Ann recognized.

Seeing how upset Sukie was, Carol Ann felt about five inches high. Words stuck in her throat.

"Oh, hon," Sukie said, shaking her head. "The dating services warn you to meet new dates in a safe place and to avoid riding in a car alone with them until you get to know them."

Carol Ann held up a hand. "I told him no, but he said with gas prices high and all the cool places bein' located in Buckhead, it'd be stupid for us to take two cars. When he said it that way, it made sense."

Sukie nodded. "I can see how it might seem logical, but . . ."

"I know I shouldn't have done it." Carol Ann fingered the puffy area around her eye. "But he's really hot and he's a good talker. We had a good time."

"So, what happened?"

Carol Ann gulped. She didn't want Sukie to think she was totally stupid, though in truth, she knew she'd acted dumb as an ox.

"Go ahead. Tell me," Sukie said softly.

"I had a lot to drink. More than I'm used to. When we got back from Buckhead, he dropped me off at the bar outside of town, where we'd met. He walked me to my car like a real gentleman. Then he said he wanted to come back to my house, maybe have a nightcap. I knew what he meant. I told him I couldn't; I lived with my parents. Dumb, huh? But what else could I say? It's the pitiful truth." Carol Ann sighed again. Her whole life was stupid.

"I told him that having a date didn't mean we had to end up in bed together. He got mad and called me a bitch. I tried to push him away. We struggled a bit and he shoved me up against my car. That's when he . . . he hit me."

"My God," gasped Sukie, studying Carol Ann, gazing into her green eyes.

Carol Ann sighed. Sukie didn't have any idea how some people, like her own parents, sometimes fought with a mean hand. "A couple of guys came out of the bar, ran over, and dragged him off me."

"Did you call the police?" Sukie clasped Carol Ann's hand with a look that told her Sukie really cared. "Did he hurt you anywhere else?"

"Uh-uh. Mostly my feelings got hurt, though I'm stiff and sore today." Carol Ann's eyes filled. "I thought we were perfect together."

Sukie frowned. "Seriously, Carol Ann, you should report this to the police."

Carol Ann shook her head. No way was she gonna do that. "Like I told the guys last night, it was just a silly fight between two people who'd had one drink too many."

"Any word from him?" Sukie's lips were pressed together in disapproval.

Of all the women in the Fat Fridays club, Sukie's opinion meant the most to her. Carol Ann wanted to magically disappear rather than keep admitting she'd been a fool. "There was a message on my cell this morning. He told me he was sorry, that he'd had more to drink than he should have. He said something like that had never happened to him before. He even asked me out for dinner, to make up for the horrible time he gave me."

"And?" Sukie's eyes drilled into her.

"I'm not going." Carol Ann wanted to collapse in tears.

She'd liked him a lot. He fit the image of the kind of man she wanted in her life—handsome, rich, savvy. Everyone had acted as if he was absolutely terrific. The waitresses in the restaurant had fluttered their long eyelashes at him like claps of applause, as if he'd won first place in a Mr. America contest or something. She'd been so proud to be seen with him. She felt like she thought Tiffany must feel with Beau.

"Good choice not to meet him again," said Sukie. "I'm glad of that." Sukie studied her, looking deep inside, as if she knew how much Carol Ann had counted on that date to help her out of her sorry situation. "I understand why men are attracted to you, Carol Ann. But I don't get why any of them would feel entitled to more than you want to give just because you agreed to a date."

Glum, Carol Ann nodded. "Like Lynn says, men are jerks."

Sukie shook her head. "Not all men, Carol Ann. You just had a bad experience."

"Yeah? Well, I can hear Lynn now when she sees me." Carol Ann took another sip of coffee, sorting through her feelings. "Maybe Lynn's right. Look at what she's gone through. I'm not so sure I want to do the online dating scene anymore."

Sukie's look of surprise threw her off. "But, Carol Ann, you're just getting started. Remember, not all men are like that."

Carol Ann shrugged. "Maybe I was meant to be an old maid." The thought sent a flood of acid to her stomach. She'd be stuck with her parents forever.

Sukie's voice softened. "I don't believe that for a minute."

"Well . . . maybe not." Optimism took hold inside Carol Ann. Bless Sukie! She'd made her feel so much better. Her situation wasn't the same as Lynn's. Not at all.

CHAPTER FOURTEEN
SUKIE

Sukie saw Carol Ann off and returned to the kitchen, filled with a restlessness that clung to her like a humid summer day. Carol Ann's episode with violence made her think of Lynn and all she'd gone through. Ted might be an ass but he'd never hit her. Thank God.

Thinking of Lynn, Sukie picked up the phone and called her, needing to know she was all right. All the women in the Fat Fridays group were making it a habit to check on her throughout the week—morning and night.

Lynn answered the phone. "Hey, Sukie, what's up?"

"Nothing much, just seeing what you're doing."

"I'm in the middle of a good movie. Just relaxin'."

"Okay, then. Go back to it and I'll talk to you later."

"Thanks, Sukie, it's real nice, you checkin' up on me."

Sukie said a quick good-bye and wandered around the house aimlessly. Rob and Madeleine were away for the weekend, and when she called Elizabeth, she was put through to voice mail. So much for a girly chat.

She tossed clothes in the washing machine and ironed a couple of shirts for the workweek ahead. When she could no longer stand the quiet, she put on her sneakers for a bracing walk through the neighborhood.

Outside, Sukie drew in a deep breath of cool air. Walking briskly, she headed east toward Betsy's house to begin her circle of the neighborhood. It felt good to march along, her arms in rhythm to her steps, working up a light sweat. By the time she reached the far end of the development, Sukie was humming under her breath. All seemed right with the world.

She approached Cam's house and absently noted how quiet it seemed. She'd taken just a few short steps beyond it, when she heard her name being called. Sukie stopped and turned around. Cam strode down the driveway toward her.

"Sukie, I need a favor," he said without preamble. "Chloe is getting a cold and I can't get her to take her medicine." His brow was creased with worry. "I don't know why she's being so stubborn about it. She's been cranky all day and I couldn't get her to take a nap. I've tried everything. Any ideas?"

Sukie smiled when she realized he'd manufactured an excuse to see her. "My daughter, Elizabeth, had a difficult time taking medicine. Maybe some of my old tricks can help."

She followed him inside, curious to see the interior. All the houses in the neighborhood had in common large kitchens, extra wooden trim throughout, and various upgraded features. How individuals decorated them was another matter, sometimes cause for gossip.

"Miss Sukie!" Chloe cried happily, jumping up from a large black leather couch that dominated the family room off the kitchen. She ran over to Sukie. "I gots a cold!"

Sukie leaned over and felt Chloe's forehead. It was warm.

"Come sit with me for a moment." Sukie took Chloe's hand and led her back to the couch. A large pink blanket lay bundled up in a corner.

A rubber doll with smudged eyes and hair pulled in all directions sat on a pillow at the edge of the blanket.

"Here, snuggle down," Sukie said, helping Chloe to slide under the soft covering. She turned to Cameron. "Have you taken her temperature recently?"

"Not for a couple of hours. It was ninety-nine point eight." He handed Sukie a thermometer.

"No." Chloe shook her head from side to side. "Don't want it."

"Well, maybe your dolly better have her temperature taken. How about it?" Sukie gave Cam a surreptitious smile.

Chloe's eyes lit up. "Can I do it?"

Sukie nodded. "I'll show you how to place it in her ear very carefully and then you can do it."

In a few moments, Chloe handed her the thermometer. "Sally has a tempsure. Like me."

Sukie pretended to read the numbers and shook her head. "I know what *her* temperature is, but I don't know the numbers for *you*. Let's check."

Chloe giggled, and within seconds Sukie had her temperature. "Ninety-nine. Daddy says it's time for more medicine. You give some to Sally and I'll give some to you."

Chloe pretended to pour some medicine into Sally's mouth with the special dispenser tube, and Sukie filled the container with red liquid for Chloe. She took it without a fuss.

"You're a good girl and a good mommy to Sally." Sukie wiped a blond curl from Chloe's pink cheek. "Now when Daddy says it's time for medicine, you'll know he's being a good daddy."

Chloe grabbed Sukie's hand and brought it to her smooth cheek. "Will you be my mommy?"

Heat rushed to Sukie's face. "Oh, honey. I don't think . . ."

"Miss Sukie is our special friend," Cam interjected, saving her from stumbling for an answer.

"I want her to be my mommy," Chloe whined. "I want her to stay here." She began to cry.

Sukie patted Chloe's back, aware of the sleepy side effect of the medicine. Chloe's eyelids were already fluttering. "How about me staying here until you fall asleep? Close your eyes and I'll rub your back. Soon you'll sleep."

Cam stood by Sukie's side, watching as Chloe's eyes closed and remained that way. Sukie waited until she was certain Chloe's breathing had slowed to a steady, slow rhythm, then she rose.

Taking her elbow, Cam lifted a finger to his lips. Sukie followed him onto the screened porch off the kitchen. Prince, the golden retriever, lumbered to his feet and walked over to her, wagging his tail.

"How about a glass of wine? Or maybe a beer? Sort of a thank you for your good deed?" Cam's warm smile invited her to stay.

"Thanks. A glass of wine sounds delightful." Prince looked up at her with large, brown eyes. Sukie rubbed the dog's silky ears, glad for something to do to cover up her nervousness at being alone with the man of her most recent dreams.

Cam left her to go inside. Sukie wished she was wearing something other than jeans with a trace of dirt at the knees and an old blue cotton pullover sweater that pulled a bit too tight across the bust.

Cam returned with two glasses and a bottle of red wine. "I found this pinot noir at Glenn's Gourmet, over in Millville. They have great prepared meals. It's an indulgence of mine when I can't face cooking another meal. I think you'll like it."

Sukie's eyebrows lifted. *He cooked, and he liked good food and good wine? How much more perfect could this man be?*

Cam indicated one of the cushioned wicker chairs for her. He sat down in its twin on the other side of the round table, sending her an approving look that sped up Sukie's pulse. He poured a small amount of red wine into a glass, swirled it, and raised it to his nose, making it seem a natural ritual. Swallowing a taste, his eyes shone with satisfaction. "It's as good as the guy said it'd be."

After he poured her a glass of wine, Sukie waited for him to fill his own. At a nod from him, she lifted hers and took a sip.

"Mmmm, delicious." It was rich and full, with a smooth finish.

Cam leaned back in his chair and studied her. "I appreciate you giving me a hand, Sukie. Sometimes everything turns into a royal battle between Chloe and me. It's at its worst when we're both overtired."

"Glad to help," Sukie said, meaning it. From what she'd observed so far, Chloe was an adorable little girl—affectionate and easygoing.

As they enjoyed their wine, their talk drifted to other things— the computer course, her work at the library, his work at MacTel. Conversation between them was easy. The glow of Cam's smile warmed her. His vitality permeated the air. Sukie cast secret glances at his full lips, wondering what they would taste like. She'd already noticed his attraction to her, the way his gaze took in all of her.

"You mentioned you had a daughter named Elizabeth. How old is she?"

"Twenty-two. My son, Rob, is almost twenty-four. He's going to make me a grandmother in June."

His look of surprise was sweet satisfaction. "Sukie, there's no way you're old enough to be a grandmother. What were you? A child bride?"

She laughed. "I got married very young."

"The marriage didn't last, I hear." He held up the bottle of wine. "More?"

Sukie held out her glass, and the damning words in her mind spilled out of her mouth in a rush. "Ted left me for another woman, a much younger one. He said he wasn't ready to be a grandfather."

Cam's blue gaze settled on her, and Sukie read a lot of things in it—compassion, understanding, and surprisingly, a hint of anger.

"Chloe's mother chose not to be a mother, other than to deliver her to me as soon as she'd recovered from the birth. We never married. I'm still a bachelor with one major difference . . ."

"Chloe," they said together, and laughed. Its musical sound rolled over them. They stared at each other silently, their interest in each other obvious.

Sukie's body grew liquid at his unspoken admiration. His gaze traced the outline of her body. It felt like the palm of his hand caressing her. He reached over and took her hand.

Sukie's heart stuttered a happy beat.

"How about staying for dinner? I'm going to pick up some pizza. I promised Chloe. It's her most favoritest thing in the whole wide world, as she says."

Sukie hesitated and nodded. Why not? There was no one waiting for her at home and she was having a wonderful time. "It sounds lovely. If you want, I'll stay with Chloe while you get the pizza, so you don't have to disturb her."

"Great," he said, rising. "Extra cheese okay?"

"My favoritest." They smiled at each other, and Cam headed for the kitchen to order the pizza. Sukie's breath caught as she watched the sexy rhythm of his jeans-clad rear as he walked away.

While he placed the order, Sukie wandered around the first floor of the house, attempting to order her lusty thoughts to go away. She was acting like a starstruck teen. It was silly, really, this attraction of hers.

Standing at the entrance to the small living room, Sukie stared at its white and beige emptiness. She felt, rather than heard, Cam come up behind her.

"A little bare, huh?"

His warm breath near her ear shot a prickling jolt down her spine. She turned around to face him. They stood and gazed at one another, nose to nose. The sexual tension that had been building all afternoon hovered above them like a hot-air balloon about to take them on a flight of fancy. Sukie's heart soared at the desire she saw in his eyes.

"Sukie?" His voice was gentle, full of questions.

She opened her mouth to answer and let out a soft sigh as his lips lowered to hers. His kiss was gentle and searching, but quickly became one of urgency. His body, pressed against Sukie's, was rigid and hard against her softness. After Ted's indifference to her, Sukie thrilled to the feel of Cam's manly response. Her heart pounded, sending her pulse sprinting through her.

Cam pulled away. His cheeks had flushed a deep red. A crooked smile swept across his face and then he cupped her face in his broad hands.

"God, I've wanted to do that ever since I saw you that first day, right after we moved in."

Delight shot through Sukie. She clutched her arms, hugging in the feeling. Then reality hit like a blow to the head. She stepped back, wishing she wasn't so practical, so realistic. "Cam, how old are you?"

He frowned. "Going on thirty-six. What's that got to do with anything?"

"The difference in our ages . . ."

Cam's melodious laughter stopped her. "Honey, I don't care how old you think you are, you've got all the right moves, the bod, the heat, everything a guy could want. Don't let anyone tell you differently." As if to prove his point, he drew her to him again.

Chiding herself for being so weak, Sukie wrapped her arms around his muscular body. His kiss had made her feel whole in a way she hadn't felt in a long, long time, if ever. She suddenly understood why Ted had wanted more than what they'd had.

Cam's fingers stroked Sukie's cheek, her hair. She laid her head against his strong chest, listening to his heartbeat keep pace with hers in a sexy tango. If this was only a dream, just a figment of her imagination, she never wanted to wake up.

She pulled away and gazed up into his face. "How did this happen? I never would have dreamed . . ."

Cam placed fingers across her lips, stopping her words. "Don't, Sukie. Don't ruin it."

Chastened, Sukie stepped away from him, certain she'd made a fool of herself. The wine had made her act like a sex-starved woman, she told herself, but she knew it was so much more. The man facing her had made her feel like a gorgeous young woman, unafraid of wherever life led. He'd had her whole body bursting with a desperate need.

Cam lifted Sukie's chin, forcing her to look into his eyes. "It's obvious we're attracted to each other. Let's see where it takes us. Don't make it complicated."

Sukie remained silent, letting his words and their implications work their way through her thinking. She was a planner, someone who always wanted to do the right thing. How could she handle being with a man almost eight years younger, someone who didn't want to do anything more than see what it all meant? She'd grown up in a very conservative family and had tried to teach her children to move cautiously.

"Sukie?" Cam's brow creased at her silence. "I can't promise you anything . . . anything at all . . . but I hope we can get to know each other a whole lot better."

She nodded, so confused by her emotions she couldn't bring herself to comment.

"We don't want to do anything to hurt Chloe," he continued. "So we have to be careful."

"I agree. She's never really had a mommy, but she shouldn't think it's me. Not like this."

"You're beautiful when you're so earnest, you know." Cam leaned over and kissed her again, tugging a little on her lips with his teeth.

Sukie kissed him back, like a hungry kitten lapping up fresh cream. The feel of him, the taste of him, the smell of him lit her senses.

"Daddy?"

Chloe's childish voice, calling from the family room, sent them reeling away from each other. Sukie straightened her sweater, pulling it back down, overwhelmed by the unbridled passion between them. Images of Elizabeth and Rob flashed in her mind. They'd be mortified if they knew what their mother was doing in the front hallway with a man somewhere between their ages and hers.

Shaken, Sukie followed Cam into the family room.

Chloe's eyes brightened at the sight of her. "Miss Sukie! You're still here!"

She smiled. "For a little while. But I'll have to go home right after supper."

"She's going to stay with you while I go get your favorite food." Cam lifted Chloe from the couch and gave her a playful squeeze.

A grin crossed Chloe's face. "Pizza?"

Cam laughed. "Yep, favoritest food for my favoritest girl."

Sukie watched them together, knowing he spoke the truth. Chloe was his favorite girl and always would be. That realization helped tamp down the desire that had enthralled her. They each had commitments and a life that wouldn't be receptive to a wild, passionate affair.

Cam left to pick up the pizza, and Sukie allowed Chloe to tug her upstairs to her bedroom.

"See?" Chloe pointed to a white Jenny Lind double bed, covered with a pink frilly spread. "It's my new bed. I'm a big girl. Daddy said so."

Sukie studied the room, charmed by the painted pink walls and the little white rocker in the corner of the room. Cam had done a wonderful job. There was no doubt in her mind that he'd do anything for his little girl. Sukie sat on Chloe's bed and leafed through a picture book with her, enjoying her bright little mind.

Cam found them in Chloe's room. The tender look he gave Sukie filled her with joy. He held out his hand. "Dinner's ready. Let's go downstairs."

Sukie took his hand, loving the way his strong fingers clasped hers, as if it were an everyday occurrence. Chloe looked from Sukie to Cam and grinned.

Chloe's chatter during dinner was offset by silent, lingering looks between Sukie and Cam. There was so much Sukie wanted to say, to hear. After he finished the last piece of pizza, Cam rose and took her hand.

"Let me drive you home. It's dark and I don't want you to walk alone."

Sukie nodded. Her emotions were still spinning from the passionate kisses they'd shared, the special connection they seemed to have.

She helped Cam get Chloe settled in her car seat, and climbed into the SUV. Cam slid behind the wheel, giving her an opportunity to study his profile. Strong chin, straight nose, classic features.

"Is this your house, Miss Sukie?" Chloe asked when they came to a stop in Sukie's driveway. "Can I come inside?"

Sukie glanced at Cam and turned back to Chloe. "Maybe some other time, honey. We'll see."

"Say good night to Miss Sukie," said Cam.

Chloe dutifully complied with a high-pitched "'Night."

Sukie opened the car door and got out. "Thanks . . . for a nice afternoon and evening."

Cam's eyes bored into hers, his interest still evident. "I really enjoyed it, Sukie."

"Me too," she said softly.

Unspoken words hovered in the air between them. Sukie waited for Cam to say something, anything, to let her know she hadn't made a fool of herself.

Cam smiled. "See you at class tomorrow night."

CHAPTER FIFTEEN
BETSY

Betsy drove past Sukie's house on her way to work Monday morning. She hadn't called her over the weekend as intended. Friday afternoon, Karen McEvoy had phoned. After learning Karen's carpets had been cleaned and wouldn't be completely dry for a day or two, Betsy had invited her to spend the weekend at her house.

Betsy smiled at the memory of their wonderful weekend. They'd been like two old sorority sisters, teasing as they'd challenged each other on their long walks, crying together as they'd watched old movies on television. And cooking in the kitchen, they were a real team. Betsy couldn't remember when she'd had so much fun.

Betsy slowed behind a school bus and wrinkled her nose at the smell of exhaust. Seeing happy faces in the bus's windows, her thoughts turned to her grandchildren. It hadn't gone well when she'd told Sarah she was too busy to babysit them. When Sarah had realized she'd have to cancel her plans, she became nasty, claiming Betsy should have told her she wouldn't be available, that babysitters were impossible to find at the last minute.

Even now, the memory of Sarah's mean sniping made Betsy grip the steering wheel so tightly her hands hurt. In the past, she'd willingly given up what she preferred to do in order to make Richie's family happy. But things were about to change.

Betsy drove into MacTel's parking lot, turned off the engine, and took several deep breaths in an effort to push aside her frustration. Working at MacTel was one thing Betsy wouldn't change. She loved her job.

Inside the building, Betsy walked over to her desk, mentally gearing up for a busy day. Setting down her purse, she caught a glimpse of Carol Ann's face and hurried over to her. "My God! What happened, shug?" A huge purplish welt next to Carol Ann's right eye showed through the light makeup Carol Ann usually wore.

"Follow me," Carol Ann whispered. She led Betsy to the privacy of the ladies room.

After checking to make sure no one else was in the room, Carol Ann leaned against a sink. Facing Betsy with an embarrassed sigh, she said, "It was John." A blush painted Carol Ann's cheeks as she explained how he'd pushed her against the car and maybe, probably, accidentally hit her.

Maybe? Accidentally? Uh-uh. Betsy didn't think so.

"This is nothing like Lynn, but still . . ." Carol Ann said.

Betsy debated what to say. Carol Ann was so . . . so . . . naïve about some things. For a young woman her age, Carol Ann sure didn't know much about how other people operated. And it was no wonder. Carol Ann was stuck inside that house with parents who treated her as if she were twelve.

Carol Ann dabbed at her eyes with a tissue. "I thought he might be the one to save me."

Seeing the heartbroken look on Carol Ann's face, Betsy filled with sympathy. "I'm sorry it didn't work out, Carol Ann. I really am."

Carol Ann blew her nose. "Do you think I should stop dating? I don't want to. Not really."

"Then don't." Betsy took a deep breath. She wanted to tell Carol Ann that no one else could save her from making such silly mistakes, that she should go ahead and have fun. Betsy tried to think of a saying that would fit the occasion, but she couldn't remember any. So she made one up.

"You can't catch the brass ring if you're not on the merry-go-round." Betsy winked at Carol Ann. "Somewhere there's a perfect match for you."

Carol Ann sniffled. "You really think so?"

Though she knew it didn't always work out that way, Betsy nodded.

Carol Ann threw her arms around her. "Thanks, Betsy. I needed to hear that. I hope you're right."

Aware of how badly Carol Ann wanted to find love, Betsy hoped she would find her match too. Who could blame her? Everyone needed love in their life.

CHAPTER SIXTEEN
SUKIE

Sukie pushed aside thoughts of her sexy weekend encounter with Cam and hurried inside the library. She had just enough time to review a report on the children's activities program she was proposing to the library board. As she glanced over the pages, her stomach fluttered nervously. It was an ambitious program, and she needed their support.

Moments later she walked into the conference room, papers in hand. A group of people had gathered around a coffee pot on a side table and were chatting together. Julie emerged from the group to greet her. She took Sukie's hand and led her over to the others for introductions.

Simon Prescott, the chairman of the board, was semiretired from Citizens' Fidelity and Trust, the largest private bank in town.

"I pride myself on being one of the first people to get behind the public library," he told her.

Julie nodded. "Simon was instrumental in getting the library funded. He's the real reason behind our being able to construct this new building."

Simon launched into the county politics involved in that project. "Yessir," he ended, "our town may be small, our county still growing, but there's enough politicking going on here to keep one very busy, indeed." His blue eyes twinkled below a wreath of snow-white hair on his otherwise bald head, reminding Sukie of a modern day St. Nick.

A tall, thin woman breezed into the room, attracting everyone's attention.

"Sorry I'm late," she said, tossing a notebook onto the table with a loud *whomp*. "I've had one important meeting after another." She turned and frowned at Sukie.

A shiver skittered across Sukie's shoulders. The woman's narrow face and small dark eyes reminded her of watercolor drawings of a weasel she'd recently seen in a picture book. She shook off her imaginings and scolded herself for being so judgmental.

Julie took Sukie's arm. "Come meet Edythe Aynsley." Under her breath, Julie murmured, "Be careful."

Sukie allowed herself to be led over to where Edythe stood, surrounded by a number of board members. Edythe directed her gaze to Sukie and then away, devoting her attention to a young woman talking earnestly to her.

Waiting for Edythe to turn to them, Sukie shifted from one foot to the other. She wondered why the delay. It was obvious she and Julie wanted to speak to her. After what seemed an extraordinary amount of time, Edythe turned to them, and Julie made the introduction.

Edythe narrowed her eyes at Sukie. "I've been meaning to ask you something. You wrote on your application that you'd taken some library science courses, but when I checked your college records there was no note of that."

At the sharpness of her words, Sukie stepped back. "I believe I wrote that I'd audited some library courses, not taken them." Sukie knew that was exactly how she'd written it.

"No one's accused you of lying, but when there is a discrepancy, one wonders, doesn't one? After all, it's a privilege to work at this library." She turned to Julie. "Isn't that true?"

Julie nodded. "Yes, of course. I'm sure it was just a misunderstanding. We're very lucky to have Sukie working here, degree or not."

A young man walked up to them. Edythe turned to him, dismissing Sukie and Julie without a backward glance. Sukie had the awful feeling she'd made an enemy of Edythe and she didn't know why.

Like most board meetings, this one seemed endless. No one made a comment on any subject without Edythe adding to it. The longer Sukie waited to make her short presentation, the more nervous she became. When she was finally called upon, Sukie handed out copies of the plan for her spring programs to Julie and all twelve members of the board. Conscious of all eyes on her, she took a deep breath.

"The Nighty Night series began this past Saturday. It was attended by twelve excited toddlers, dressed in their pajamas and eager to hear several good story books. The feedback I received from the parents was extremely positive. I'm very excited about it."

"I was wondering . . ." Edythe began, and Sukie wasn't the only person who let out a sigh. "Do you think there are any health issues involved in encouraging children to come to the library dressed for bed?"

Before Sukie could respond, Julie spoke. "In my opinion, children dressed in pajamas for the nighttime program are usually cleaner than in their play clothes, if that's your point."

Edythe glared at Julie. "Another thing we need to consider carefully is this idea of turning the library into a . . . a . . . pillow place. It isn't seemly. Instead of sitting at tables, the children are sprawled everywhere!"

"Yes, but what are they doing?" Sukie said, unwilling to let this woman destroy what she'd worked so hard to establish. "They're reading. That's what's happening."

"True enough," interjected Simon, "and that's the important thing here. Doesn't everyone agree?"

A few members of the board nodded; some looked away, obviously uncomfortable at being forced to go against Edythe. A heavy silence hung in the room.

A knock at the door dispelled the quiet.

Julie rose to her feet. "This must be our last speaker." She opened the door, and Cam walked into the room.

Sukie's heartbeat pranced, then broke into a gallop when he looked at her and grinned. Heads turned her way, and Sukie read questions in their curious glances. Feeling hot all over, she took a sip from the bottle of water she'd brought into the room.

"Well," said Julie with a bright smile, "it seems that Cameron knows some of you. Let me introduce him to the rest. Cameron Taylor is the teacher of the computer courses we're offering this spring. He's working as an independent consultant for MacTel. We're very lucky to have him. Cam, why don't you tell the group just exactly what you're doing and how successful you've been."

Cam began his presentation.

Sukie studied him. He was dressed in khaki slacks, an open-necked, cream-colored golf shirt, and a navy blazer, all of which did nothing to hide his masculine outline. Reliving the feel of his body against hers, a shiver of delight swept through her. She looked up to find Edythe staring at her.

At the end of Cam's talk, Julie rose. "Cam's right. We need more computers. We can use them for the genealogy group that meets here on a regular basis as well as for our patrons looking up information."

A vote was taken to purchase three new computers and the meeting was dismissed.

As Sukie was gathering her papers, Cam appeared at her side.

"How are you doing?" His voice was low and melodious.

"Uh, just fine," she mumbled, aware Edythe was heading their way.

Edythe held out her hand to Cam. "Cameron, I'm pleased you've taken such an interest in the library. We need young men like you to help us old matrons out. Don't we, Sukie?" Her smile was venomous.

Speechless, Sukie stared at her.

Edythe straightened her shoulders and moved away, calling to another board member to wait for her.

"I think she froze you with that look of hers," Cam whispered.

Sukie nodded, alarmed by Edythe's hostility toward her.

Julie hurried over to them. "What happened with Edythe? She looked ready to strike out at someone. Edythe Aynsley is someone to watch, Sukie. She can be very destructive. I suspect she might be a little jealous of you. I just hope she doesn't ruin your chances here."

"Jealous of me? Why?"

"For a lot of reasons, Sukie," Cam said. The "you are so hot" look he gave her made her believe he might be right. Any woman alive would want a man to gaze at her like that.

After all the board members had left and things were quiet in the library, Julie came over to Sukie's desk. "Sukie? Can we talk?"

Sukie nodded and braced herself for bad news.

Julie pulled up one of the kid-sized chairs. Her body folded upon itself, knees on chest, as she took a seat, but there was nothing childish about her worried expression or her troubled sigh.

"I'm sorry to have to even bring this up, but I just got a call from Edythe. She noticed the attention Cam was giving you and wanted me to warn you that as the children's librarian you have a special obligation to behave in a seemly way. Those were her words, not mine."

Sukie felt her body sag. "Why is she doing this to me?"

Julie looked off into space and began to play with the thin silver bracelets on her left wrist. Their tinkling sounds broke the ominous silence between them.

"Edythe hasn't been happy for a long time. She married a man much older than her, thinking, I suspect, that her days would be happy because Arthur Aynsley was a very wealthy man. It didn't turn out that way. He left her for another woman. An older one. All of Atlanta was aghast at the news. Edythe moved to what they called their country home up here in the northern suburbs and has become our voice of society, if you can call it that. She's a bitter, angry woman."

"And obviously hates me," Sukie added, wishing she'd never met the woman.

Julie gave her a thoughtful look. "So, do you and Cam have something going?"

Sukie stared at Julie with confusion, wondering what to say.

Julie waved her hand in dismissal. "Don't answer that. It's none of my business. But you know what a small town this is. Even though we're growing by leaps and bounds, it stays a small town in many ways. It pays to be careful."

After Julie left her, Sukie's mind raced. She and Cam hadn't even gone out yet and it was already causing all sorts of trouble for her because of the age difference. She'd thought that kind of thinking had long since disappeared. It was the twenty-first century, for God's sake!

Drained of all energy, Sukie drove home from work, still upset by the day's events. She was a private person, used to successfully fulfilling every task, but she had the uneasy feeling that she'd have to fight for both her privacy and respect.

At home Sukie poured herself a glass of red wine and took a seat at the kitchen table, trying for perspective as she reflected on the day. For a moment she wondered if she should cancel computer classes with Cam, then reminded herself of the bigger picture. She needed training. And the way things were going at the library, she'd better prepare for a different job. Edythe Aynsley was a formidable woman. Her maliciousness was already at work.

Sukie checked her voice mail and listened to a message from Mr. Prescott's bank. Ted, it seemed, had not paid the mortgage as promised. Furious, Sukie called him at the office. He answered with a crisp hello.

"Ted? It's Sukie. I received a phone call from the bank regarding the mortgage payment. Haven't you paid it yet?"

"Sukie, we're going to have to rethink our agreement," Ted said in an irritating tone he'd used on their children when they were especially rambunctious. "With a baby coming, I've got new family responsibilities." His tone was smug.

Sukie gritted her teeth. "But you and I agreed . . ."

"That was before I knew about the baby. Emmy Lou says we can't stay in the condo, that it isn't big enough. I was thinking maybe we could make a trade . . . you know, even though we'd agreed to something different . . ."

"A trade? This house for your condo? You've got to be kidding!" Sukie realized he wasn't kidding at all; he was that dense. "Pay the mortgage, Ted, or I'll see you back in court."

Rocked to the core, Sukie slammed down the phone. It had taken a much shorter time for Ted to back out of what he'd promised her than she'd thought. She'd fight him on it, of course. She had to. This house was hers in every sense of the word. She was the one who had cared for it, nurtured her family inside it, and now needed the familiarity of it to make the other transitions in her life more tolerable as she worked to become an independent woman able to survive on her own.

Though she was no longer hungry, Sukie made herself eat a cup of soup before class. Taking computer courses was just one way she'd prepare herself for the uncertain future.

Cam looked up from his paperwork and smiled at her when she hurried into class. Sukie's spirits lifted. Throughout the class, she listened carefully to him as he went over some of the finer points of various programs.

"Next week, we'll go over some extra things you can do on the computer to make your life a whole lot simpler," he announced at the end of the session.

Sukie gathered her materials together, grabbed her purse, and headed for the door.

"Sukie? Wait!" Cam called. "I need to ask you something."

Puzzled, she stopped. The two other women remaining in class glanced his way and hurried out of the room.

Cam grinned at her. "I have to entertain a businessman and his wife from out of town on Friday. I was wondering if you'd join us for dinner."

A date? Sukie wanted to say yes, she really did, but she knew it would be better for her, for him, for them, if she didn't.

His smile faded. "What's the matter?"

"Edythe Aynsley called Julie after the board meeting and asked her to warn me about unseemly behavior, as she called it. Ted is trying to back out of our spousal agreement, and I can't do anything to jeopardize my job." She hated the way tears stung her eyes.

Cam's look of sympathy soothed her. "A bad day, huh? That Aynsley woman needs to be shaken. I told you, Sukie, she's jealous of you."

"Yes, but . . ."

"You're not serious about letting her dictate how you spend your time, are you?" His voice held a hint of disapproval.

An inner debate began in her head. Even in those few moments they'd had together, he'd made her feel whole in a way she'd never known. The idea of their being together was crazy and yet so wonderful. Confused, she covered her cheeks with her hands.

Cam tilted her chin and stared into her eyes, silently seeking permission. Then his lips covered hers with a sureness that made it seem undeniably right. Desire swept through Sukie.

When they pulled apart, Cam's lips spread. "Like I said last night, let's see where this takes us. We'll take it one step at a time, beginning now. What do you say? Will you go with me on Friday?"

Sukie drew a deep breath. This wasn't really a true date. She'd be with other people. It was just dinner. A business dinner. Right?

CHAPTER SEVENTEEN
TIFFANY

Tiffany lay in bed, miserable. She'd thrown up until there was nothing left inside her. She pulled the silky gold covers of their king-sized bed up to her neck. No way could she consider going to work, even if it meant she'd miss the Fat Fridays lunch.

She'd been reading that raging hormones could make you think crazy thoughts, but Tiffany swore every time she raced to the bathroom to barf that Beau looked proud and happy. It made her want to scream at him. She rubbed her belly in slow circles and asked herself how any teeny, tiny baby could make her feel so sick.

Beau poked his head through the bedroom doorway. "You take care of our son while I'm at work."

Tiffany groaned. His parents had gone nuts when he'd told them about the baby a few weeks ago. They'd immediately declared it had to be a boy, to carry on the family name. It made her feel woozy to even think of it. If the baby was a girl, she'd have to face their disappointment.

Again.

Beau went off to his job at the law firm of McDonough and Stiles—a job his Dad had landed for him, and a job he hated.

Tiffany rolled over and closed her eyes, relieved to be left alone in the bed her in-laws had given them. Her thoughts drifted as she lay there. She rubbed her belly from time to time, telling herself she felt fine, that things would work out.

At the clicking sound of the front door being unlocked, Tiffany froze. Her heart pounding so hard she grew light-headed, she sat up. The cleaning lady wasn't due until Monday. Was it Lynn's ex? Would he attack her like he'd done to Lynn and their daughter?

Tiffany rose on shaking legs, tiptoed to the top of the stairs, and peered over the railing. Ready to call 911, she gripped her cell phone.

Shit! Her mother-in-law was heading up the winding staircase, carrying two large plastic bags.

"What are *you* doing here?" Tiffany asked, furious at the intrusion.

Muffy jumped guiltily.

Seeing the look of fright on the face of Beau's mother, Tiffany couldn't help the sense of satisfaction that filled her. It served Muffy right for coming in unannounced.

"What am I doing here? I might ask the same of you," said Muffy, all composed once more. She stared at the old T-shirt of Beau's that Tiffany had worn to bed and sniffed. "Aren't you supposed to be at work? Is everything all right with *our* baby?"

Trying to control her irritation, Tiffany shrugged. She hated it when Muffy said "*our* baby," as if she'd been the one throwing up. "I didn't get much sleep last night so I decided to take the day off. I still feel sick."

"Oh, pooh, Tiffany, it's just part of the process." Muffy moved past her and set the bags down on the hallway carpet. "When you hold that little boy in your arms, it will all seem worth it."

"It might be a girl . . ." Tiffany began.

"Nonsense." Muffy waved a hand in dismissal. "Not in this family. I don't even want such a thought mentioned aloud. Regard needs to know there'll be Wright men following in his footsteps. When you come from a prominent family like his, it's very important to know the family name will go forward."

At Muffy's words, Tiffany's stomach churned. But she'd be damned if she'd throw up in front of her. "What's in the bags?"

Muffy gave her a sly smile. "I ordered a whole set of towels with the Wright monogram on them. Black lettering on white terry. I detest colored towels, don't you?"

"But . . . but I just bought towels to match the bedspread I picked out. Dark green won't show dirt, and besides . . ."

Muffy picked up the bags and marched into the master bath.

Tiffany watched helplessly from the bathroom doorway as Muffy took the green towels from their racks and threw them down on the floor. "Let's see how these new ones look. Beau knows he can't get away with wiping unclean hands on a white towel. That's how I trained him to wash up correctly."

Tiffany turned on her heels and climbed back into bed, too tired to fight her mother-in-law. It was always like this. She punched her pillow. *Why did it always have to be this way between them?*

Muffy came into the room and stood over her. "This morning sickness of yours should be over soon. I suggest you get up and get going before long. Be ready for Beau when he comes home tonight. A man needs to come home to a clean house and an attractive wife or he'll end up not coming home at all."

Tiffany blinked in surprise. Did Muffy really believe all that 1950s bullshit? In today's world, her ideas were so old-fashioned, they were laughable. And whose fault was it that she was in this wretched condition? Didn't Muffy get that?

Muffy waved. "Okay, dear. I've done my good deed for the day. I'm off to a luncheon with a friend and then Regard and I are going to meet our favorite senator for dinner in Atlanta. Give Beau all my love. And don't dawdle in bed too long."

She left, and Tiffany curled up in a ball, wondering how her life had gotten so out of control. She didn't even know who she was anymore.

CHAPTER EIGHTEEN
SUKIE

Sukie arrived at Anthony's restaurant shortly after noon and wove her way through the noisy lunchtime crowd to the back booth where Betsy, Carol Ann, and Lynn sat chatting.

"Hi," she said, sliding into the booth next to Betsy. "Where's Tiffany?"

"She called in sick." Betsy gave her a worried look. "That poor girl has gone through hell with this baby."

Sukie clucked her tongue. She wished there was more they could do for Tiffany.

"Here's the waitress," said Lynn. "We'd better order. We're running late."

As soon as they'd all ordered the special—chicken and goat-cheese ravioli and side orders of garden salad—Carol Ann launched into the latest responses to her online dating profile. She made everyone laugh when she told them about her date with a guy who'd posted a picture of his handsome roommate instead of himself.

Carol Ann turned to Sukie with shining eyes. "Guess what! There's a new guy at work, a consultant named Cameron Taylor. He's a total looker. I keep trying to come up with excuses to deliver mail to his office, anything to get his attention, but he mostly ignores me. All the women are crazy for him. There's a rumor racing through the office that he's got some hot date this weekend."

"Yeah. His date must be gorgeous, because like Carol Ann says, this guy is something else," Betsy said.

Sukie felt the blood leave her face. *Hot date? Is that how Cam thought of it?*

The conversation turned to other matters, but Sukie's thoughts remained stuck on Cam. Maybe he expected some kind of wild romp after dinner, something a hot date would supply. Her pulse pounded with dismay at the thought. She wasn't that kind of woman. It just proved to her how out of sync they were and how foolish she was acting.

While waiting for Cam to pick her up, Sukie paced her bedroom floor, moving from the full-length mirror beside her closet to the smaller mirror in the bathroom, needlessly primping. She felt like an innocent young teen going to her first big school dance, wondering whether her young date expected a French kiss at the end of the night. If she were smart, she'd call and tell him she was sick.

The doorbell rang.

Pulse racing, Sukie went downstairs and opened the door.

Cam's eyes rounded when he saw her. "Wow! You look great." He leaned over to kiss her. "Mmmm, you're so beautiful. You taste good, too. Like peppermint candy."

Sukie's nervousness evaporated in a rush of pleasure. She grabbed her shawl and headed out the door with him.

On the way to the nearby Village Inn Motel, Cam explained they were picking up Mary and Bob Anderson. Bob, he further explained, was a semiretired computer consultant who sometimes worked with him on projects. "They're folksy, down-home people from the Spartanburg, South Carolina area. I especially enjoy their company."

Mary and Bob were waiting outside when Cam and Sukie pulled up to the front of the motel. Cam introduced her to them. Bob was a jovial man who smiled easily. His wife Mary was equally pleasant.

During the drive to Atlanta, Bob kept them entertained with stories of projects he'd worked on, making them laugh with all the missed deadlines and crazy programming he'd done in the past.

"Which restaurant are we going to?" Sukie asked.

"Jasper's," Bob said. "I picked it. It's one of the hottest new restaurants in Midtown. They're known for their classic French cuisine."

Mary smiled at her. "Beneath that computer geek of mine is a very good chef."

Sukie laughed.

Bob grinned. "One of the specialties of the house is sautéed sole with a light beurre blanc sauce topped with fried capers. How's that sound?"

"I can taste it now." Sukie's mouth watered at the thought of the fish in a tart buttery sauce. It had been a long time since she'd had a fancy meal like that. Looking back, she wondered just when she and Ted had stopped planning evenings out.

Cam reached over and took hold of Sukie's hand.

Sukie smiled, pleased to be with him.

Fighting the Atlanta traffic, they made their way to a tall building on Peachtree Street and pulled into a circle at the side of the building, where a valet met them. He helped them out of the car and whisked Cam's Lexus away.

Cam led them inside, and Sukie followed the maître d' to a table in the corner of the dining room. After being seated, she and Mary exchanged approving glances. Dark wainscoting met green-painted walls. The color of the walls was duplicated in the Oriental rugs that covered most of the wooden floor and brought out the burgundy hues of the brocade-covered chairs. Crisp white table linens and gold-rimmed china added to the classic elegance of the room. Crystal lighting fixtures hung from wooden beams like bright-colored stars.

"How lovely," commented Mary. "And the piano music is perfect—nice and soft."

Cam ordered a bottle of French champagne.

Sukie sat back, truly content for the first time in many months. She sighed with pleasure, but then sat up with a start.

"What's wrong?" Mary whispered, grabbing hold of her hand. "Are you okay?"

Sukie shook her head.

Katy Hartmann approached their table with a dangerous smile. "Sukie! Sukie Skidmore! What a surprise! I had no idea I'd see *you* here." Her gaze swept over Cam and Bob and Mary and came to rest on Cam.

"And you are?" Katy said to Cam before Sukie could find her voice.

Cam rose to his feet and held out a hand. "Cameron Taylor."

The glint in Katy's eyes as she looked from Cam to her made Sukie's stomach feel like she'd swallowed a huge rock.

"Pleased to meet you, Cameron. I'm Katy Hartmann." She beamed at Cam as if he were a double-fudge brownie and she was the biggest chocoholic in the world.

Cam introduced Mary and Bob Anderson.

Sukie clutched her hands, wishing she could evaporate. She'd taken a chance that no one from town would see her on a date with Cam. Now she knew it wouldn't be long before everyone in Williston would know they'd been out together.

After Katy left their table, Sukie explained to Mary that Katy was head of the neighborhood women's group and the biggest gossip she knew.

"Well, let's just enjoy the evening." Mary gave Sukie's hand a comforting squeeze.

Sukie forced a smile and told herself to relax, though she had the sinking feeling that the waves Katy would cause would drown her carefully laid plans for financial and emotional independence. Neither Ted nor her children would be prepared for a surprise like this.

Cam smiled at her. "It'll be all right. You'll see."

Sukie hoped he was right. Putting aside her worries, Sukie concentrated on enjoying the evening. The conversation was pleasant. Mary clearly adored her husband, and they treated Cam like one of their own. When Mary found out Sukie was about to become a grandmother, she couldn't hide her surprise. "All grandmothers should look like you," Mary joked. A grandmother herself, she launched into the joys of being able to spoil and play with her own grandchildren and then walk away at the end of the day.

They ended the meal by sharing crème brûlée and chocolate pots de crème, teasing each other over the calorie count in each delicious bite.

The ride home was quiet. Like the others, Sukie was sated with excellent food and wine. She leaned back against the front passenger seat of the car, floating in good humor as the radio played softly.

Cam reached over and took hold of Sukie's hand. "I'm glad Chloe is staying overnight at her teacher's house," he murmured. He gave her a sexy smile that turned Sukie's body hot, then cold. The promise of intimacy was something she wanted, and something she dreaded.

After dropping Mary and Bob off at the motel, Cam turned to Sukie with an adorable crooked smile. "I've waited all evening to get you alone."

Sukie bit her lip. "You're okay with Katy blabbing all over town that we were together? And everyone at MacTel is talking about a hot date you have this weekend . . ."

"What?" Cam frowned. "Where'd you hear that?"

"Friends of mine work in the executive area," Sukie said. "Carol Ann Mobley is one of them."

"Carol Ann? Oh, yeah. She's the one who keeps trying to deliver stuff to my office."

"Wait'll she hears about tonight," Sukie said, unable to let the subject drop. "She's not going to believe I'm your so-called hot date."

Cam pulled into Sukie's driveway and brought the car to a stop. Reaching over, he stroked Sukie's cheek with his thumb. "You don't have any idea how sexy or how beautiful you are, do you?"

She let out a soft sigh as his lips found hers. His tongue entered her mouth. The taste of after-dinner mints lingered in his kiss. When it became apparent they both wanted more, he pulled away from her.

"Let's go inside."

Taking Cam's hand, Sukie drew him inside the house.

Cam led her to the sectional couch in the dimly lit living room. "Let's just settle here."

Sukie tossed her shawl on a chair and sank back onto the couch's plush cushions and into his strong arms. It felt so right to snuggle up against him.

Cam kissed her. Caressing Sukie's body, his hands moved to her breasts.

Her nipples tightened under his touch.

"Mmmm, you're so responsive," Cam murmured. He gently tugged Sukie down so they were lying, facing each other.

Sukie snuggled up to him. The feel of his hard arousal against her abdomen sent anticipation through her.

They spent precious moments together, kissing and discovering the shape of each other. After some time, Cam slid his hands under her dress and stroked the intimate parts of her. A sigh escaped her. She hoped he'd never stop.

"I want to see you. All of you," he murmured.

Sukie rolled to one side, and he unzipped the back of her dress. She stood and let it fall to the floor. Then swallowing nervously, she stepped aside, clad only in her lacy black bra and matching panties.

He tossed his shirt to one side, and struggled to get his zipper undone. The deliciously large bulge in his pants didn't help. Sukie admired his sleek, muscular body, his trim waist, his firm erection. A stab of insecurity made her pause. She had stretch marks from her pregnancies and her body was not as young as his.

Naked, Cam came up beside her, as virile as any Greek god. Smiling, he undid Sukie's bra. His fingers trailed over her breasts and then he cupped them. "Beautiful, Sukie."

He bent and took one nipple in his mouth. Sukie leaned her head back and let the pleasing sensations roll over her.

Cam helped Sukie onto the couch and slid her panties down. Lying next to her, Cam traced the scars on her belly with his fingertips. Sukie sucked in her breath, waiting for a response.

"Amazing, isn't it?" he said. "What women go through for babies."

Sukie let out a sigh. Cam was mature beyond his years, and though he was extremely handsome, it was so much more than his looks that had attracted her to him. It was his innate kindness. She'd never loved another man more.

Cam stroked Sukie until her body quivered with the need for more of him. She pulled him to her and, arching joyously, took him inside. They moved together, exploring, testing, urging each other, until their rhythm became hard and fast, driving them toward their goal.

Later, Sukie traced the strong line of Cam's jaw. "Did you feel it?" she asked softly.

"Feel what?"

"That special connection between us."

He chuckled. "Weird, isn't it?"

"Wonderful," Sukie answered, knowing what they had together was very rare.

Later, they moved upstairs, carrying their clothes with them.

"I'm not through with you yet," teased Cam, drawing her up against him.

Her pulse dancing, Sukie indicated the door to her bedroom. Ted's ghost had been chased away. For good.

Sukie awoke the next morning with a vague sense of wonder. She rolled to her side and gasped softly. Cameron Taylor lay next to her, enticingly naked beneath the sheets. She gently touched his chest, almost afraid to believe he was there.

Cam blinked sleepily. A grin spread across his face, which showed the beginnings of a beard. "Hi, beautiful," he said, reaching out and cupping her breast.

Sukie filled with happiness as he pulled her into his arms. It hadn't been a dream after all.

Sometime later, Sukie gazed at the clock, wondering how she could ever move her body out of bed. It had been a marathon of lovemaking and she was feeling the effects of it. "What time were you to pick up Chloe?"

"Around ten. Why?" Cam mumbled, nestled against her.

"It's nine forty-five."

Cam came wide awake with a start. "Whoa! I'd better get going. How about fixing me a cup of coffee while I take a quick shower?"

"Fair enough." Sukie rose and covered her nakedness with a robe.

Downstairs in the kitchen, she listened to the water running in the shower and realized how much she'd missed the sounds of sharing a house with someone.

Cam appeared, his hair still wet.

Sukie gave him a quick kiss and handed him a cup of steaming coffee.

"Thanks." He took a long sip, keeping his gaze on her. "Think we can get together later this weekend? Sunday, maybe?" He wiggled his eyebrows playfully.

Sukie laughed. "Call me."

He took another sip of coffee and set the cup down on the counter. "Have to go."

They kissed good-bye in a way that proved to Sukie how much he wanted to stay. She dreamily wondered how it would be to have him kiss her that way every morning.

After Cam left, Sukie sat at the kitchen table, sipping coffee, reliving every wonderful moment of the past several hours. The whole thing was crazy—cautious, careful her, lost in a passionate affair as if she were sixteen with no cares in the world. But Sukie loved the way she'd come alive. She'd been given a second chance at romance, and she wasn't about to throw it away. The connection between Cam and her was so strong, so compatible, so right.

She knew their relationship would face challenges. Many in their conservative small town would not like the idea of her and Cam together. Her children were still reeling from their father's defection. She didn't think they'd be happy with the idea of her dating so soon, especially someone as young as Cam. It was too close to what their father had done.

The phone rang. Ignoring the protests from her body, Sukie got up to answer it.

"Hi, Mom," came Elizabeth's cheerful voice. "I tried to get you last night but there was no answer. Out on a hot date?"

Words stuck in Sukie's throat.

"Don't worry, Mom, I was just kidding," Elizabeth said before Sukie could answer. "I've decided to take some summer courses. A professor of mine suggested it and it would help me tremendously. I've already talked to Dad. He didn't sound too happy about it, but he finally agreed to spring for the tuition when I told him it would mean graduating earlier."

Sukie instantly became alert. "Tuition shouldn't be a problem. A college fund has already been set aside for you. We started it when you were just a baby."

They talked of other things—a new restaurant Elizabeth had discovered, a cute guy in one of her classes, an upcoming interview with a marketing firm for a part-time intern position, and other exciting details of Elizabeth's daily life.

"You're awfully quiet," Elizabeth complained. "Are you doing all right? It's got to be hard for you in the face of Dad's behavior. Can you believe how proud he is of that baby? What was he thinking, fooling around with someone so young? For God's sake, she's not much older than I am."

At the anger in Elizabeth's voice, Sukie's body went cold.

"It's downright disgusting to even think of it!" Elizabeth continued, letting her feelings out in a blast of resentment. "I'm glad I can count on you to be different, Mom. Dad's embarrassed me. All my friends back home know about his . . . his affair. Why did he have to go and get mixed up with her?"

"I'm not sure what he was thinking," Sukie said as steadily as she could. Just hours earlier she and Cam had made love on the couch like two hormonal teenagers.

"Well, listen, I've got to go. Love you, Mom. Be good! Don't do anything wild. Promise?"

"Love you, too, honey." Sukie hung up the phone, shaken. No doubt about it. Elizabeth would not like her dating Cam.

It was noon by the time Sukie was able to pull herself together enough to shower and begin a load of laundry. She made a grocery list, checked to see if Lynn needed anything, and was about to walk out the door when the phone rang.

"Sukie? Can I come over?" Tiffany sounded as if she'd been crying. "Beau is golfing with his father, and his mother is away for the weekend at some spa in western Georgia. So, I finally have a chance to get out of here."

"Sure. I was going to call you later. We missed you at our Fat Fridays lunch yesterday."

"Yeah, well, I couldn't make myself get out of bed. I felt sick and I'm so damn depressed I don't know what to do. I'll be right over."

Amazed by how much her life had changed since she'd joined the Fat Fridays group, Sukie waited for Tiffany to arrive. Belonging to the group meant so much more than meeting for lunch. And Lynn's predicament had bound them to each other in a way nothing else could. Not a day went by that Sukie didn't think of Lynn and wonder if and when her ex would appear, calling them to action.

When Tiffany arrived, she looked terrible. Dark smudges colored sleep-deprived pouches under her eyes. She'd obviously lost weight.

Dismayed, Sukie gave her an encouraging hug. "Come on in."

Tiffany stepped through the doorway. "I know, I know. I look just awful, and the sicker I become, the more ecstatic Beau acts. Like my throwing up is proof of his manhood or something."

"You surely have spoken to a doctor about it, haven't you?" Sukie said, leading Tiffany into the kitchen.

Tiffany nodded. "I've got medicine for the sickness but it isn't all that reliable. I should be getting over the worst of it very soon, he told me. After the first trimester, things usually get better."

"Would you like to try some hot tea? Or some saltines and ginger ale?"

"Maybe ginger ale. Thanks." Tiffany sank down on a chair at the table with a long sigh.

"I guess Beau must be pretty excited about the baby," Sukie said, gently probing as she poured Tiffany a drink.

"Oh, yeah." Tiffany made a face. "It has all worked out according to his plan. His whole family is going crazy. Thank God his mother was already scheduled to go to the spa or else she'd be camped out at the house, telling me what to do. She's impossible!"

"You're definitely having the baby?" Sukie slid in a chair opposite her. Studying her, Sukie was reminded of the difference in Tiffany's appearance between their first meeting and now. Tiffany was still beautiful, but she seemed so defeated. Her shoulders slumped. Her mouth drooped with sadness.

"It's too late to do anything about the baby. Besides, little stinker that it is, I want this baby. I already feel as if it's mine, you know?" Tiffany's expression softened.

At the show of Tiffany's maternalism, Sukie relaxed. "Good for you."

Tiffany's eyes filled with sadness. "The thing is, I'm more certain than ever that I don't want to stay with Beau. He and his family are making me so miserable." Her cell phone rang. She glanced at the display and a look of despair crossed her face. "It's him."

Sukie rose and walked over to the sink to give her some privacy, but Tiffany made no effort to lower her voice.

"I'm at Sukie Skidmore's house. No, I didn't fix lunch for you. I thought you and your father were going to eat at the club. Tomorrow? Okay, I'll ask her. Bye, Beau." Tiffany sighed noisily, pushed the off button on her phone and laid it down on the table.

"Beau wants to meet you, Sukie. He told me to ask you to come to dinner tomorrow. His father is taking us out to the club."

"Can you do that, go out to dinner, what with being sick and all?" Sukie knew how difficult that could be.

Tiffany let out a snort. "I make myself do whatever my in-laws want. Believe me, it's much easier that way."

"Well . . ."

"Please, Sukie. I really am feeling better. Will you come to dinner with us? It would mean so much to me, and it might help Beau understand that my friendship with the women of the Fat Fridays group is all right."

Sukie hesitated.

"Please, please, please!"

At the desperation in Tiffany's voice, Sukie caved in. "Okay."

"Great! I'll call you later with the time." Relief put a glow on Tiffany's face.

Sukie was pleased to see her smile. They chatted about babies' names, how Lynn was doing, and then Sukie told Tiffany about Carol Ann's latest online conquests.

"Maybe Carol Ann will have better luck than me," said Tiffany. "But if all she wants is handsome and rich, it's not going to be easy. She makes me so mad with all that kind of talk." Tiffany checked her watch. Her expression turned grim. "I'd better go."

Sukie showed Tiffany to the door and returned to the kitchen. Lowering herself onto a seat at the kitchen table, she stared out at the garden, lost in thought. Life was complicated for everyone.

Too restless to sit still for long, Sukie paced the room. Earlier, she'd thought that she and Cam were soul mates because their connection was so deep. But maybe, she thought unhappily, she was simply trying to justify her uncharacteristic behavior. Cam hadn't made any promises to her, had even said he couldn't. Maybe their tryst was just a one-night thing. A hot date, like everyone thought.

CHAPTER NINETEEN
LYNN

Fear stalked Lynn like it was her ex himself. Not so much fear for herself, but for the brave women of the Fat Fridays group. *Bless 'em,* Lynn thought as she hung up the phone. Not a day went by that she didn't get phone calls from at least two of them to check up on her. The whole idea of a showdown with her ex was scary, but also exhilarating. The other women were right. It was time for her to stop running. And maybe, just maybe, she could have a normal life, use her real name, even keep her drapes open for as long as she liked.

Lynn drew a deep breath. She'd told the women in the Fat Fridays group that she'd stay in town. She was determined not to let them down. But at the same time, she couldn't let anything bad happen to them. So she watched out for them as carefully as they watched over her. And unbeknownst to them, Lynn called people who'd helped her in the past to see if they had any information on her ex's activities. She'd even gone to see the sheriff herself, because she knew damn well her ex was a psycho.

As she traveled back and forth to work and did necessary errands, she was determined to put on a brave front. But in many respects she still thought of herself as a captive to her ex's threats. She was constantly looking over her shoulder, twisting in circles at the hint of a shadow, checking out parking lots, scouting for any sign of the son of a bitch who wanted to hurt her.

So far, she hadn't caught sight of anyone who looked even close to Buck. While he might not be easy to find, he had those big hands that had slapped so hard. And one of his shoulders slumped to one side from an old fight.

Taking a stack of rental movies into the living room, she went over to the window and pulled the blinds away from it, just enough to peek out.

Nothing suspicious.

Maybe, Lynn thought happily, he'd messed up again and was sitting in a jail cell in some faraway place, cooling his heels for doing something damn stupid.

She let the blinds fall against the window and pulled the drapes closed, shutting out the growing dark.

CHAPTER TWENTY
SUKIE

Sukie hung around the house, pacing restlessly from room to room, picking up and putting down magazines, wondering when Cam would call and what she'd say to him when he did.

Determined to stop the spinning thoughts in her head, she picked up a romance novel and curled up on the couch. After reading a few pages about a woman falling in love, her mind drifted. Making love with Cam, she'd felt a real meeting of their souls, something she'd never experienced with Ted. Her dreamy thoughts ended abruptly when she thought of her children. Elizabeth wouldn't like the idea of her dating Cam. And Rob? He probably wouldn't like it either. Conflicted feelings tore her emotions into painful shreds. She leaned back against the cushions and closed her eyes.

The ringing of the phone startled her awake. Disoriented, Sukie stumbled into the kitchen and checked the digital clock on the microwave. Midnight. The caller ID screen read "Private Caller." Sukie's thoughts flew to her children. Rob and Madeleine were away, visiting her parents. Elizabeth had told her she was going to bed early.

"H-h-hello?"

The sound of partying blared in the background. A man's breathing came through the phone—steady, stealthy breaths.

Sukie's hand froze on the phone. "Who's there?"

No answer.

"Who's there?" she said in a trembling voice, frightened now.

The phone clicked and went dead.

Unable to shake the creepy feeling that swept over her, Sukie thought of Lynn. She quickly dialed her number.

"Yeah?" Lynn answered sleepily.

"It's Sukie. I'm so sorry to wake you, but I needed to make sure you're all right. I just got a hang-up call and it scared me. Do you think it was your husband?"

"Oh, hon, that's not his style. Get some sleep. Hear?"

"'Night," Sukie said sheepishly and hung up. She'd overreacted, she knew, but ever since she'd heard Lynn's story, she and the other women in Fat Fridays had been on edge. Her thoughts turned to Ted. Would he do something stupid like that? She shook her head. That wasn't his style, either.

She climbed the stairs, put on her nightgown, and slid into bed. Under the covers, she inhaled Cam's scent on the pillow next to her. Wishing he was there beside her, she hugged it to her.

After a restless night of tossing and turning, Sukie told herself to face facts. Cam's silence had sent a strong message. She decided that casual sex was probably all it meant to him. She could well imagine everyone in town laughing at her foolishness for thinking that one evening was the beginning of something that might last.

Feeling the need to settle her feelings, Sukie decided to go to church. It had been a while since she'd gone. She dressed and drove to the white clapboard building in the center of town and took a moment, as she always did, to admire the tall steeple that seemed to reach for heaven. Williston Congregational was one of the oldest churches in town and stood as a symbol to Sukie of all that was noble.

She parked and entered the church, trying her best to ignore the curious stares cast her way. In the past, sitting beside Ted in their pew, Sukie had always enjoyed the light coming through the rainbow-hued glass windows. Alone, she closed her eyes and concentrated on finding peace. She told herself that somehow her life would straighten out, but niggling worries snaked through her thoughts.

When Sukie got up to leave, she found Katy Hartmann on the other side of the aisle, right in her path. The gleam in Katy's smile made Sukie's stomach clench. She gave Katy a reluctant nod, hurried down the aisle, and came to a frustrating stop in the midst of the crowd waiting at the doorway to shake the minister's hand.

Katy came up behind her. "It was such a surprise to see you the other night, and with Cameron Taylor, no less. No wonder you looked like your hand was caught in the cookie jar. Some cookie!"

Sukie gave Katy a cold stare. She shook the minister's hand and moved away before he or Katy could engage her in further conversation. She was halfway down the marble steps when Katy's voice brought her to a halt.

"Sukie, hon, wait for me!"

Several people turned and stared at Sukie. She pressed her lips together and turned to face the biggest gossip in town.

Katy hurried over to her. "I want to hear more about that gorgeous hunk you were with. The women's club has been abuzz about him ever since he moved into the area. I had no idea you really knew him." She elbowed Sukie in the ribs. "You know, it's got to be great being with a younger man. It makes spouses seem pretty unappealing. Lucky you, you don't have to contend with a spouse anymore, do you?"

Refusing to take the bait, Sukie clamped her teeth together.

Katy's husband, Jim, came over to them. "Hello, Sukie. Long time no see." His gaze swept over her and came to rest on Sukie's breasts.

Frowning at her husband, Katy tugged on his arm. "C'mon. Time to go." As they walked away together, Katy turned back and shot Sukie a warning look.

Sukie shook her head at the implied threat. If she wanted to fool around—and she didn't—Jim Hartmann wasn't even in the running.

Tired of the emotional ups and downs of the past months, and now with Cam, Sukie exchanged her skirt and sweater for jeans and a sweatshirt. She headed downstairs. There was nothing like working in the garden to ease her stress.

Outside, Sukie loosened the dirt in the small vegetable garden and sat back on her heels, inhaling the distinct scent of sun-warmed soil. New life.

"Miss Sukie! I want to see your flowers!"

She turned to see Chloe running toward her. Smiling, Sukie held out her arms. Chloe ran into them and gave her a joyful hug. Sukie hugged her back, feeling an empty part of her fill with warmth.

Cam crossed the lawn, smiling. "Chloe insisted upon stopping to see you. Hope this isn't bad timing."

"No, it's fine," Sukie said, wondering if he would've come on his own.

Cam's eyes captured her in their blueness. "I've been thinking about you . . ."

Chloe tapped Sukie's arm, interrupting her father. "What are those flowers? Over there, those yellow ones. What are they?" She pointed to the clay pots sitting at the edge of the patio.

Sukie and Cam exchanged resigned looks, and then Sukie led Chloe over to the multicolored pansies and told her a little bit about taking care of plants. Moments later, Chloe became distracted by a red cardinal and went racing off in its direction, frightening the bird away with her loud, excited cries.

Cam approached Sukie. "Can I see you tonight? Maybe you could come for supper."

"Afraid not," Sukie said with real regret. "I'm going to dinner with the Wrights tonight. Tiffany insisted I join her and Beau and her father-in-law, the judge. Poor girl, she's going through a hard time."

"I see," Cam answered, clearly disappointed. "I thought . . ."

"I thought you'd call me after our wonderful evening together," Sukie blurted out, unable to hold back the insecurities that gripped her like a tightening fist.

Cam's features hardened.

Sukie observed the changes in him but pressed on. "Friday was very special for me. I believed it was for you, too."

Cam's eyes narrowed. "Are you judging my feelings for you on the basis of whether I called you or not?"

At the irritation in his voice, Sukie's heart pounded with dismay. With her mouth dry, she searched for the right words. "Maybe I should explain that sex is not something I do casually."

Cam's lips thinned. He shook his head as if he couldn't or wouldn't answer.

As they stared at each other, Sukie's heart fell. It seemed hopeless. She hadn't even mentioned how Elizabeth felt about things.

"Look, I'd better go before I regret what I say." Cam turned away from her and called to his daughter. "C'mon, Chloe! We've got to go to the grocery store! You can help me pick out some things."

Chloe came running over to them, her face alight. "Sugar bears?"

"I guess." Cam ruffled Chloe's curls.

"Bye, Miss Sukie!" Chloe waved at her cheerfully and dashed away to catch up to her father who was marching away like a man on the run.

Crestfallen, Sukie watched them leave. Tears blurred her vision. She pulled a tissue out of her pocket and dabbed at them. Why, she wondered, couldn't he have understood how vulnerable she was, how much she needed reassurance from him? One phone call was all she'd wanted. She realized then that she and Cam were on very different emotional levels. And there was the Mars and Venus thing, too. Bottom line, she'd been a damn fool.

Grieving for what might have been, Sukie went back to her gardening. She worked steadily through the rest of the afternoon, weeding and putting down mulch, trying to tell herself that ending it with Cam was for the best. But the memory of their lovemaking made her wish it could go on and on.

Shortly before five, Sukie showered and dressed carefully for her meeting with the Wrights. She selected black slacks and a silky green blouse she and Tiffany had chosen together. Though Ted continued his membership there, she hadn't been back to the Green Valley Country Club since the divorce, and she was nervous about going there.

Sukie pulled up in front of Tiffany's house. Once again she admired the colonial design of it. Most young people Sukie knew, including Madeleine and Rob, would be thrilled to own such a large, luxurious home. But Sukie knew what a high price Tiffany was paying for such fine surroundings.

She made her way up the brick walkway, climbed the porch steps, and rang the front doorbell, wishing she hadn't agreed to come. Too fragile emotionally from her conflict with Cam, she wasn't in the mood to be social.

The large black door swung open and a tall, young man with light brown hair stared at Sukie. A frown creased the space between his dark brown eyes.

"Beau?"

A brilliant smile transformed his features. "You must be Sukie. Come on in. Tiffany's still getting ready. You know how women are."

"Of course she does, son," drawled an older version of Beau, coming forward to clasp her hand. "A beautiful woman like you knows all about it." He raised Sukie's fingers to his lips in an old-time Southern gesture.

He was equally as handsome as Beau, though his hair had turned a distinguished gray and his body had taken on a substance that was lacking in his son. She'd read about Judge Wright but was bowled over by his dramatic presence.

Tiffany descended the stairs and smiled at Sukie. "You've met my father-in-law, Regard?" The look of amusement in Tiffany's eyes told Sukie that Tiffany understood why she might be ill at ease.

"I was just about to introduce him," Beau snapped at Tiffany.

Hurt flashed across Tiffany's face, making Sukie even more uncomfortable.

"Ah, yes," the judge said. "Let me do the honor. Regard Wright, at your service."

"And I'm Sukie Skidmore." She gamely shook his hand before moving to Tiffany's side and giving her a quick hug. "You look lovely." The brown dress barely showed a baby bump.

Tiffany smiled. "Thanks. I'm feeling better."

"We've got to take care of this little lady," the judge boomed. "She's having my grandson."

"It might be a girl . . ." Tiffany began.

"Not in the Wright family," Regard said, cutting Tiffany off, chuckling heartily at his own double entendre.

"I have each—a boy and a girl. They're both very special," said Sukie, coming to Tiffany's defense. "We just wanted a healthy baby."

Beau clapped his father on the back. "Don't worry, Dad. If it's a girl, we'll keep trying until we get our boy. More fun for me."

Beau turned to her. "Come on into the family room, Sukie. Dad and I are having some bourbon. Would you like one? Or a glass of wine?"

"Wine would be nice, thank you." Sukie followed them into the sizable family room off the kitchen. The large-screen television that filled most of one wall was displaying the score of the Falcons football game.

"We're looking at a taped replay of a Falcons game. You a football fan?" Regard asked Sukie.

She shook her head. "Not really."

"Best game around. Teaches you a lot about life. Right, Beau?"

Beau didn't answer, and Regard continued. "Yessir, my boy played quarterback for his high school. Too bad a knee injury prevented him from playing in college. He could've been real good."

Sukie wondered how Beau felt about the sport his father loved. With his thin build, he looked more like a tennis player.

"Here's some chardonnay. It should be good. Dad bought it." Beau handed Sukie a tall-stemmed glass of pale gold liquid.

Sitting beside Sukie on one of the beige-tweed love seats in front of the fireplace, Tiffany wrinkled her nose at the glass Beau handed her. "Orange juice."

Beau shook a finger at her. "No alcohol for you."

Regard frowned. "Sukie Skidmore . . . You're not by chance related to Ted Skidmore, are you?"

Sukie choked on the sip of wine she'd just taken. "Ted is my ex. Why?"

"I put a boat up for sale. A man named Ted Skidmore from Williston phoned me about it. Said his wife wanted a boat to use at their lake house. Only trouble is, he refused to pay a fair price for it. Thought you might know something about it."

Boat? Lake house? What next? "We've gone our separate ways." Sukie's lips were stiff as she responded. Inside, she was seething. Ted had given Elizabeth a rough time about tuition money. He'd better not have undermined her college fund so he could spend money on Emmy Lou and himself, she thought. If so, she'd personally kill him.

The sounds of televised football competed with their conversation, making it difficult to discuss anything of substance. Occasionally, shouts of encouragement from Beau and his father reverberated in the room. Tiffany and Sukie talked a little about the Fat Fridays group, but Sukie noticed how stressed out Tiffany was with her father-in-law, and they both grew quiet.

The game ended with a field goal by the Falcons, and the four of them headed outside to go to the country club.

"Why don't we all go in my car?" Regard indicated the large black Mercedes in the driveway.

Beau and Tiffany climbed into the backseat, leaving Sukie standing alongside Regard.

"Sit up front with me." Regard took Sukie's elbow and ushered her around to the passenger's side and helped her into the car. Sukie felt awkward sitting in his wife's seat, but Regard didn't seem to notice. He slid behind the wheel, and they took off. Regard drove with confidence, as if the road under his wheels were his alone. Sukie had the feeling it was pretty much the way he ran his life and that of his son.

The country club sprawled atop the hilltop like a white beacon overlooking the rolling sea of golf course green. It was, by far, the most sophisticated gathering spot for members of their small suburban town.

The moment Regard pulled up in front of it, a valet rushed to help them out of the car. Regard took Sukie's arm and led her inside. Tiffany and Beau followed. Sukie noticed that though Beau helped Tiffany over the curb, he didn't continue to hold her hand.

People in the noisy wood-paneled bar off the front entrance hall turned to watch them make their way to the dining room. Some tipped their heads in acknowledgment or waved to Regard.

Outside the entrance to the dining room, Sukie felt a tap on her shoulder and swiveled around.

"What are *you* doing here?" Ted growled. He glanced from Regard to her with glassy eyes.

Realizing Ted must have been at the bar for some time, Sukie's heart fell. He reeked of liquor and cigarette smoke. She scowled at him, silently warning him to back off.

"You okay, honey? Ready to go inside?" Regard asked, aware of her distress.

The flush on Ted's cheeks deepened as he glared at Regard.

"Yes, please." She knew from past experience that when Ted was in this state, any conversation would quickly escalate into an argument.

The judge took her elbow, and they moved forward. At each step, Sukie felt Ted's stare stabbing her in the back.

They were quickly seated at a table. Regard orchestrated the selections for dinner, cajoling the waitresses and acting generally as host. Beau was surprisingly silent, but later the two men began talking about their golf game.

Tiffany leaned over to Sukie. "I wonder how Carol Ann's latest date went." She clucked her tongue. "I've been to her house just once, to deliver something she'd left at the office. I can understand why she's so anxious to leave it. Her parents bicker all the time. I could hear them going at it from the front door."

Sukie let the matter drop and turned the discussion to the latest sale at one of their favorite stores at the mall.

Later, between the main course and dessert, Sukie excused herself from the table. She'd eaten more than she'd really wanted and it felt good to get up and move around. Glancing at the various tables in the room, she checked to see if Ted was anywhere nearby and slipped into the ladies' room unnoticed. She'd just stepped inside a booth when she heard the door to the ladies' room open. The sound of laughter followed.

A woman spoke. "Can you imagine? Ted Skidmore told me I was sexy as hell. I all but laughed in his face. The guy is impossible."

"He's become a first-class lech and a drunk," Sukie heard another woman say, and she stifled a gasp.

"If you ask me, Emmy Lou is taking him for a ride for his money," said the first woman. "Who's to say that baby is his? She's been known to put out for others."

"Yeah, and they're not even married! What's with that?"

"Who knows? Let's hurry and get back to the table. Katy Hartmann has some juicy news for us."

Sukie's stomach churned. She hid in the booth until the women left. Had she and Ted been the laughingstock of the club? And, God help her, was Katy about to spill the beans about her date with Cam? Sukie took a deep breath. She wanted to run out of the club and never come back.

She stepped out of the booth and patted her face with cold water. Humiliation fought anger. She drew herself up straight. Quaking inside, but determined, she left the ladies' room and walked back to the table, ignoring the hushed comments along the way.

Regard and Beau got to their feet as Sukie approached. Their polite gesture made her grateful, though she knew it would set off more speculative talk.

Tiffany gave her a worried look. "You okay, Sukie? You were gone for such a long time."

"I'm fine," Sukie answered, though she wasn't fine at all. It'd been an awful day and it wasn't over yet.

Sukie took a few nibbles of the moist chocolate cake Regard had ordered for the table. It was the specialty of the club. But with the events of the weekend playing over and over in her mind, the rich dessert tasted like mud.

"Ready to go?" Tiffany asked when the meal was over. "I'm exhausted and I can't miss work tomorrow. My boss has a big meeting this week. I've got to get ready for it."

"I thought you were going to give up your job." Regard gave Tiffany a disapproving stare. "You know you don't need to work as long as Beau, here, keeps his job."

Beau shuffled his feet uncomfortably. Tiffany's lips tightened.

Standing, Regard motioned for Sukie to walk in front of him as they left the dining room. Katy Hartmann noticed them and beckoned them over to her table. Regard, always one to enjoy an audience it seemed, went right over to the table of eight. Sukie held back.

"Where's Muffy?" Katy asked Regard, eying Sukie.

"At the Golden Door," Regard said. "You ladies seem to enjoy those spas."

"Oh, yes," said one of Katy's dinner companions, giving him a coquettish smile. "But y'all love it when we come back feeling like new women."

Regard laughed heartily.

Sukie exchanged glances with Tiffany, silently urging her to move on.

"Sorry to rush away but I've got to work tomorrow," Tiffany called to them sweetly.

Sukie nodded. "Me too."

She and Tiffany moved toward the front door while Regard shook hands with the gentlemen and gave each lady a kiss on the cheek. Beau stood to one side looking as if he were caught in the midst of a bad play.

"Beau hates all the bullshit," Tiffany whispered, "but that's part of the role he has to play with the family legacy and all."

"It's too bad," Sukie said softly, wondering how he'd ever be able to grow up on his own.

"Well, we'd better get these little ladies home," boomed Regard, drawing everyone's attention to them.

Sukie cringed as every person at the table turned to look at them.

Ted lurched out of the bar and faced her, weaving unsteadily. "You're going home with Regard? A married man, Sukie?"

Tired of all the crap he'd put her through, she clenched her fists. "It's none of your business what I do anymore, Ted."

Giving her a look of concern, Tiffany took Sukie's elbow. "Let's go."

Regard and Beau came up behind them, like knights on white horses.

Ted glared at the judge, but Sukie kept on moving. More emotional upheaval would undo all the confidence she'd worked so hard to build. As it was, she wanted to break down and cry.

CHAPTER TWENTY-ONE
SUKIE

Sukie hurried to get ready for work, thankful she had a reason to keep busy. It had been an upsetting weekend to say the least.

When she arrived at the library, the parking lot was surprisingly full. It was then that Sukie remembered that the Friends of the Library was holding its monthly meeting.

Julie grabbed her arm as she entered the library. "Sukie, can you give a quick, impromptu report to the Friends about the Nighty Night program? I was talking to the president and I believe they'll give us funds for refreshments. They might even fund the awards program you wanted to initiate for preschoolers."

Sukie flushed with pride. "Sure. Give me time to pull together my notes and I'll be ready."

Excitement building inside her, she hurried over to her desk. There was so much she wanted to do to encourage families to read together. Her own childhood had been filled with reading books from the bookmobile that appeared on a regular basis throughout her rural Pennsylvania neighborhood.

By the time Julie came to check on Sukie, she had enough copies of her report in hand.

"Good girl," said Julie, giving her a pat on the back. "Go for it! We need their help!"

Sukie followed Julie into the conference room, which was awash in loud chatter. Conversation stopped. Debbi Warren, Katy Hartmann's best friend, gave Sukie a sly smile.

Doing her best to ignore the chill that slithered across her shoulders, Sukie glanced away and handed out her report.

Julie introduced her, and Sukie gave a quick summary of both children's programs and told the committee how they could help fund them. The Friends' president put it to a confirming vote, and with a sense of triumph, Sukie left the room.

Her phone was ringing when she returned to her desk. Still savoring her victory, she picked it up and said a cheery, "Hello?"

"Sukie? My God, why didn't you tell us you were Cameron Taylor's date?" Carol Ann's voice quivered with indignation. "The whole office is talking about it!"

Sukie's breath left her in a whoosh. She collapsed in her chair. "What do you mean?"

"One of the girls in the accounting department was visiting another couple in the city. They saw you together at Jasper's in Atlanta. She asked Cam about it and he told her it was true."

Sukie stirred uncomfortably in her chair. "Is Cam there?"

"No. He's out at a client's. Oh, Sukie, I can't believe it. You and Cameron? Wow! Is he as hot as he looks? He's gotta be. You'll have to tell us *all* about it on Friday," Carol Ann babbled, oblivious to Sukie's silence.

Sukie's head began to pound. She felt as if her whole body were caught in a vise. What she'd intended as a very private evening had turned into another public nightmare.

"I've got to go," she said, feeling sick to her stomach.

"Yeah, well, don't forget. Fat Fridays women stick together. I'm so excited!"

Sukie hung up the phone and held her head in her hands. She'd thought she and Cam would have privacy away from town. She'd misjudged, yet again. Now she'd be forced to confront her children.

Somehow Sukie made it through the day, though every triumph at work was counterbalanced by the thought that she'd have to speak to Cam that night about ending their relationship.

Still fragile from the divorce, her underlying insecurity began to play games with her mind. Cameron was in his thirties and could attract any woman he wanted—a much younger, much hipper one than her. Sukie couldn't understand why he'd wanted to be with her. Images of their lustful time together flashed in her mind. She swallowed hard. There *had* been something wonderful between them. But still . . .

Exhausted from all of her inner turmoil, she left the library.

At home, she sipped a glass of white wine and waited for a frozen diet meal to heat. It was the best cooking she could do on her Monday work schedule.

The phone rang.

Sukie checked caller ID and turned away. She was not about to talk to Ted; she could well imagine the tone of his conversation if news of her dating had reached him.

Just as the microwave beeped, the phone rang again. Madeleine. Sacrificing a hot dinner for details regarding her forthcoming grandchild, she picked up.

"Hi, Sukie. Just wanted to let you know we're back in town. How are things going?" Madeleine's cheery voice washed over Sukie in soothing waves.

"I'm going through a difficult time," Sukie told Madeleine honestly. "But I'll be all right. How's the baby?"

Madeleine laughed. "Kicking and turning. I think there's a real football player down there. Rob says he doesn't care if it's a boy or a girl, but I think deep down he wants a boy. We'll see. I'm glad we decided to wait to find out."

They chatted a few more minutes and Sukie hung up. In a couple of months, she would have her first grandchild to hold. She could hardly wait.

Sukie reheated her dinner and gulped it down so she wouldn't be late for her computer class. The hint of teriyaki on the chicken tasted wonderful and reminded her of the appetizers she'd had at Jasper's in Atlanta a while ago. It had been, Sukie reflected, a magical evening. Too bad it had turned into a public spectacle.

She arrived at the library to find the classroom empty. Disappointment roared through her.

"Has the computer class been canceled?" Sukie asked the woman behind the circulation desk.

The volunteer nodded. "Mr. Taylor called to say his daughter was sick and he couldn't find a babysitter. Class will be the same time next week."

All the energy Sukie had built up to face Cam whooshed out of her, leaving her weak-kneed. She had to get this situation under control or she'd feel like hiding in her house again.

She went back to her car and sat a moment, stewing. She wouldn't— she couldn't—rest until she'd faced Cam.

She drove into the neighborhood. The lights were on in Cam's house. She hesitated and pulled into his driveway, determined to resolve the issue of whether they were dating once and for all.

"Hey, there!" Cam's pleasure at seeing her when he answered the door shot warmth through Sukie. Her emotions whirled in confusion. Caught off guard, she stumbled for something to say.

"Is Chloe all right? I went to class and was told she was sick."

Cam nodded. "Poor kid has the flu. It's going around her preschool. She's sleeping now, but she was really sick." He waved Sukie inside with a sweep of his arm.

Her hands icy cold, Sukie stepped through the doorway. She hated confrontation, had always veered away from it.

"You look like you've got something on your mind," Cam said, studying her a moment.

Sukie let out the breath she'd held. "It's everything—our relationship, the talk around town about us, everything. You're young. You can have anyone you want. I'm about to become a grandmother. My children won't like us being together. I don't know what got into us—me—the other night."

"You don't?" His mesmerizing blue eyes stayed on Sukie as he covered her cold hands with his warm ones and drew her toward him. "Sukie, what are you really worried about?"

They stood, holding hands, gazing at one another. *It's more than lust,* Sukie thought, as she observed his concern. "I don't know where we're going, why I'm even here . . ."

His lips came down on hers. Soft, gentle, probing. Sukie couldn't prevent herself from responding. In his arms she was a different woman—not the organized soon-to-be grandmother everyone knew and counted on, but the young, adventuresome, lusty woman she hid inside.

Cam's eyes were shiny when they pulled apart. "Why are you so concerned about your age? I'm not that much younger than you. I'm what my mother calls a late bloomer, and you obviously are not. You had your children young."

"Everyone is talking about us, you know." Sukie waited for his reaction.

Lifting Sukie's chin, Cam forced her to look into his eyes. "Does that bother you, Sukie?"

She nodded. "My whole life has been on display lately. And, I don't know . . ."

"Aha. It really upsets you that I can't give you any promises, doesn't it? Well, let me ask you the same thing. Any guarantees from you that this is what you want?"

Sukie's teeth caught the corner of her lip, seeing the situation in a whole new light.

Cam cocked an eyebrow. "Maybe it's time to take a chance on us, Sukie. For you, as much as for me. No guarantees."

"It's more than just the sex for you, isn't it?" Sukie's voice quivered with the need to know.

He gave her a reassuring grin. "The sex was great but, yeah, it's more than that. You know that thing, that connection, you mentioned? It's there. Damned if I know what it is about you, but I want to keep it going."

"Have you ever felt like this before?"

Cam swept a lock of hair away from Sukie's face, his fingers gentle. "No."

Joy and wonder filled her. She learned enough in that single gravelly word to know that she also wanted to give him, her, them, a try.

Cam reached for her and Sukie gladly went into his arms. His lips met hers with a deep-seated need she recognized. Tears of happiness misted her vision. Maybe some chances were worth taking.

CHAPTER TWENTY-TWO
BETSY

Betsy had planned to talk privately to Sukie after the next Fat Fridays luncheon, but she decided she couldn't wait that long. As soon as she got settled at her desk at MacTel, she punched in Sukie's number. Waiting for her to answer, Betsy's stomach did a series of somersaults.

"Hello?" Sukie finally answered, sounding a little out of breath.

Betsy drew in fresh air. "Sukie, may I stop by your house after work today? There's something I need to discuss with you. Something personal."

"Sure," Sukie said. "Are you okay?"

Tears came to Betsy's eyes. Her life was such a mess. "I just need to talk to you."

"All right, Betsy. I'll be waiting for you."

"Thanks." Betsy hung up more grateful for her dearest friend than she could say. She trusted Sukie to be honest with her and fervently hoped they could still be friends.

Throughout the day, Betsy carried out her duties at work with a worried heart. She imagined different scenarios with Sukie. Would Sukie understand what she was about to do? Would anybody?

As Betsy was getting ready to leave the office, Lynn came over to her. "Hey, are you okay? You've been real quiet today. I didn't know if you were sick or what."

Touched by Lynn's concern, Betsy pasted a smile on her face. Of all the people in the Fat Fridays group besides Sukie, Lynn would be the one who might accept what Betsy had done.

"Thanks. I'm fine," Betsy told her, amazed how easily she could fib when the situation called for it.

She waved good-bye to Carol Ann and Tiffany and hurried into the elevator, anxious to get out of the office before anyone else asked how she was doing. The truth was, she was scared to death.

Betsy pulled into Sukie's driveway and took a moment to gather her thoughts. It wouldn't be easy to tell Sukie what was on her mind. She'd hidden the truth for years. The therapist she'd talked to recently had helped Betsy understand it would be better if she faced reality head-on.

Sukie greeted Betsy at the door with a hug, stepped away, and studied her. "What's wrong, Betsy? You look so worried. Come on in. I've fixed some appetizers and chilled a bottle of white wine."

Betsy followed Sukie into the kitchen and stood by while Sukie poured wine into two long-stemmed crystal glasses, then handed one to her.

"I really need to talk to you." Unable to hide the sting of tears, Betsy took a sip of wine to steady her frayed nerves.

"Is everything all right? Is Richie okay?" Sukie gave her a worried look.

Betsy nodded. "He's fine. It's me. Oh, Sukie, I'm so confused."

Sukie took her by the elbow. "Come. We'll sit outside, have our wine on the patio, and you can tell me whatever is troubling you."

On the patio, they settled at the glass-topped table and eyed each other curiously.

Heart pounding, Betsy cleared her throat. "I need to talk to somebody about what's going on with me. Sure you don't mind listening?"

Sukie gave her an encouraging smile. "That's what friends are for, isn't it?"

Toasting each other, they clinked their wine glasses together. Betsy hoped that by the end of her visit Sukie would still feel the same way about being friends. She swallowed hard, wondering where to begin, and blurted, "I'm falling in love."

Sukie beamed at her. "Betsy! That's wonderful! The black car I've seen in your driveway so often . . . does that belong to him?"

"Yes . . . I mean, no," Betsy answered, bursting into tears.

Sukie reached over and clasped her hand. "My God, Betsy! What is it?"

"The car belongs to Karen McEvoy." Betsy gave Sukie's hand a squeeze. "What am I going to do? I love her. I really do. It's what I've waited for my whole life, to feel like this. Poor Rich, poor Richie." Betsy pulled a tissue out of her pants pocket and blew her nose. "It wasn't Rich's fault, but I could never love him to this extent. Richie is going to be upset. He adored his father. What am I going to do?"

"You're gay?" Sukie's eyes widened with surprise.

"I know it's a shock . . ." Betsy gripped her hands together, waiting to hear what Sukie would say next. Her stomach knotted. After years of making herself do and say the right things, she was allowing her secret feelings, the ones she'd hidden for years, to emerge.

Sukie frowned. "Are you sure about this? I know how hard it is to live alone after so many years."

Betsy laughed—a sad, bitter sound she knew so well. "I've been alone all my life, it seems. And, yes, I'm very sure about wanting to be with Karen. She makes me feel alive, fulfilled. We share so many common traits and interests. Sukie, I'm terrified by my intense feelings for her."

"Does she know?"

Betsy sniffed and nodded. "Yes, she knows how I feel about her." Betsy could feel her lips spread into a quivering smile. "Karen says she feels the same way about me. I've decided to follow my heart. I've asked her to move in with me."

Sukie sat back in her chair, silent.

Betsy watched her with dismay. She could almost see Sukie's mind working, trying to absorb the news she'd sprung on her.

"I've talked to a therapist about this," Betsy said, trying to make Sukie understand. "She says I need to be straightforward, unashamed. But, Sukie, I'm worried about the neighbors. Do you think they'll put up a stink about it?"

Sukie shook her head. "I don't know. I suppose those that would are the same people who might be upset by me seeing a much younger man."

Betsy drew herself up. "You know what I say, Sukie? I say, to hell with 'em. We have a right to live our lives the way we want. Right?"

"Right." Sukie raised her glass and saluted her, but Betsy could tell Sukie was troubled. Her heart sank.

Betsy waited for Sukie to say something, do something. Their friendship meant so much to her. She knew there would be others who would turn away from her—a lot of them from her church—but she couldn't bear for Sukie to be one of them.

"You remember Karen, don't you?"

Sukie nodded. "I met her a month ago, when I ran into you and Karen at the mall in March. She seemed nice."

Betsy gripped her hands together so tightly the blood left her fingers. "What do you think the girls in the Fat Fridays group will say when they hear about this?"

Sukie drew a breath. "They'll be surprised."

"Will they let me stay in the group?" Betsy's voice shook. She'd grown to love them all, even with their differences.

Sukie rose and gave her a hug. "If they don't, I'll leave too."

Fresh tears rolled down Betsy's cheeks. "We've all become good friends and since you've joined Fat Fridays, we've become even closer. And now we have to stick together for Lynn."

Sukie gave her a pat on the back. "I'm pretty sure they're not going to abandon you, Betsy. You're the one who's brought everyone together. We all love you."

Betsy choked back tears. "Oh, Sukie, I'm so scared. It's such a big step for me to take. Yet I know how unhappy I'd be if I didn't acknowledge my true self, the one who's tried so hard to fit in, to be proper, to do the right thing." She blotted her wet eyes. "I deserve to be happy, don't I?"

Sukie nodded. "Why don't you make it easy on yourself? Why don't you simply continue the relationship without having Karen move in with you?"

"She has a chance to sell her condo—the owner of the one next door to her wants to buy it to expand his space. In this slow market, if she doesn't sell now while she's got a good offer, she might not get another chance for a long time."

"I see . . ."

Betsy gripped Sukie's hands. "I've told no one else about how I feel. My therapist suggested one person, one step at a time. I came to you first because I knew you'd be honest. Honest and fair. I don't know when I'll tell the others. I haven't even told Richie. I'm not ready for that."

Sukie gave her a worried look. "I understand how hard the whole process will be for you."

Betsy swallowed hard, glad the awkward situation was out in the open. "I'm going to take baby steps, like the therapist said. One thing at a time. Eventually everyone will know, but for now I'm just getting used to the idea myself."

"That sounds reasonable. Good luck, Betsy. I'm happy for you. I really am," Sukie gave her another encouraging smile.

Betsy took a calming breath, relieved she'd started the process of telling people with Sukie.

"Karen is going to be with me this weekend. Any chance you'd come for brunch on Sunday? You and Cam?"

"I'll ask him," Sukie said, "but that means he'll know too. Is that what you want?"

Betsy nodded, rose, and gave Sukie a hug. "You're a dear, dear friend, Sukie. Thanks for hearing me out and supporting me. I'd better go now. I'm meeting Karen for dinner."

Sukie walked her to the door. "Everything will be fine, Betsy. You'll see."

Betsy nodded, but she knew things were never that simple. Like it or not, in a small town like theirs, there would be ugly consequences for her. But she'd already decided she couldn't be her real self if she was too afraid to tell people the truth.

Her heart skipped a beat. Telling her beloved son would be the hardest thing of all.

CHAPTER TWENTY-THREE
SUKIE

Betsy is gay?

Sukie's body felt numb with shock as she watched Betsy walk down the sidewalk, get into her car, and drive away. She knew Betsy well enough to know this wasn't something she'd decided abruptly. Betsy had told her before that she hadn't been happy with Rich, that her life with him wasn't satisfying. Sukie had no idea then what it all really meant. Maybe Betsy didn't either.

Sukie wandered into the kitchen to fix herself a light supper. Betsy's situation forced her to look at her own in a new light. She wondered how Rob and Elizabeth would handle it if her relationship with Cam grew into something permanent.

A new feeling of self-worth filled Sukie. She'd fight their disapproval, if forced. Like Betsy, she deserved to be happy. It had been years since she'd known real happiness. With Cam, she was fulfilled in a way she hadn't believed possible. He made her feel beautiful—heart and soul. She and Betsy had each done their duty, raising their families with love and commitment. Now it was time to discover who they were and who they might become.

Sukie's feelings were reinforced when Cam called that night and she told him about her conversation with Betsy. "What do you think will happen when the news gets out?"

"Some people will be upset," he admitted, "but she can't deny what has happened and how she feels. I won't say a word to anyone else, of course, but eventually she'll have to deal with everyone in this small town."

Sukie's heart swelled with affection. Cam was a good man, a kind man. Under the same circumstances, Ted would have been disgusted and warned her not to have anything to do with Betsy. She liked—no, loved—Cam for so many reasons.

At noon on Friday, Sukie hurried into Anthony's restaurant, gingerly elbowing her way through the line of customers waiting to be seated. Betsy called to her. Sukie went over to a round table in the back room and took a seat between Betsy and Tiffany. "Sorry I'm late. I was talking to a local author of children's stories. She's agreed to come and read one of her picture books at the Nighty Night program next week."

"Sounds good," said Betsy.

"Sukie, you look wonderful." Tiffany's eyes twinkled. "But then, Cameron Taylor could make anyone look wonderful. Right, girls?"

"Yeah." Carol Ann leaned forward with a grin. "C'mon, Sukie, we've been waiting for you. Spill!"

Sukie held up her hands. "All I can tell you is that we've had only one real date. I got to know him through being neighbors and by being in the library computer course. We're just taking it one day at a time."

"Is it better with a young man?" Carol Ann asked, fluttering her hands.

They all gaped at her.

Carol Ann's cheeks flushed bright red. "I meant overall, not the way all y'all are thinking. Good heavens!"

Sukie grinned. "Actually we're not that different in age and, yes, I like being with him."

At their smug smiles, Sukie's cheeks flamed.

"What are we going to order?" Lynn's impatient tone interrupted the moment.

Betsy waved her hand for attention. "You know what the filmmaker Fellini said? 'Life is a combination of magic and pasta.' I think this is the perfect day for their pasta specials." She beamed at everyone around the table, and they all chuckled.

Sukie chose lobster-filled ravioli with a light, lemony cream sauce. Everyone else but Tiffany ordered pasta of some kind. Tiffany stayed with a salad.

"I don't want to gain too much weight," Tiffany explained after the waitress left with their order. "Now that the word is out that I'm pregnant, Beau's family is unbearable. I'm getting endless lists of instructions from my mother-in-law. Beau's mother even sent a special maternity diet for me to follow, as if I don't already watch what I eat. She doesn't trust me to do the right thing on my own."

"Poor Tiffany," Betsy said. "Your mother-in-law would be difficult for anybody."

Tiffany grimaced. "My father-in-law can be worse. He doesn't want me to work. You heard him, Sukie, at dinner on Sunday. After you left that night, he sat me down and told me that I would hurt the baby if I worked. Is that weird or what?"

"Wait a minute!" said Carol Ann, turning to Sukie. "You had dinner with Tiffany's father-in-law?"

"I had dinner with Tiffany and Beau and her father-in-law. A family dinner. That's all it was," Sukie said firmly, mortified by the idea of another wild rumor about her racing through town.

"Wow! Two dates in one weekend. You've got to give me lessons." Carol Ann studied her.

Sukie stiffened, determined to put an end to that kind of talk. "Whoa! Dinner with Tiffany's father-in-law was no date, Carol Ann. Remember that."

"Still . . . After all the dates I've had in the past few weeks, I haven't found someone I'm wild about." Carol Ann's lips jutted out in a childish pout. "That insurance guy still sends me emails. I've ignored them, but maybe I'll give him another chance. He was kinda interesting, even if he did get out of line just that once."

Sukie and Betsy exchanged silent glances of disbelief.

"Has anyone received crazy phone calls?" Betsy said. "I had one the other night."

"I had a strange one, just before midnight last Saturday." Sukie glanced around the table. "I heard sounds of partying and then just heavy breathing. No one spoke. I asked who it was, but the caller wouldn't answer me."

"Sukie called me right after that, but that was the only phone call I got, except for one from Tiffany earlier that evening," said Lynn.

Sukie turned to Carol Ann. "At first, I thought it might be you, at a party or something."

Carol Ann's eyes widened. "Me? No. Michael, my new date, and I were getting along just fine at the movies. But I don't think he'll call again."

"Why not?" Betsy asked.

Carol Ann grimaced. "It was stupid, really. Nothing important. Just a little argument."

Sukie exchanged another meaningful glance with Betsy. Carol Ann was doing okay getting first dates, but she hadn't been asked out for a second date yet, unless you counted the insurance guy who kept emailing.

They finished their meal and paid the bill.

The MacTel women, late for a meeting, left in a flurry of hugs and good wishes.

Sukie climbed into her car, feeling pleased to be part of the group. As quickly as the Friday lunches went, they brought the women together, building the friendships between them and providing a support system for Lynn.

The next morning was warm, humid, and gray, the kind of Saturday morning meant for staying inside and completing household chores. Sukie pulled on a pair of jeans and an old T-shirt and padded around the house in bare feet, trying to decide which task to tackle first. She opened the refrigerator to get milk for her cereal and knew she had no choice. Plastic containers holding old leftovers and half-eaten sandwiches had taken over every available space. It was sad to live like this, she thought, stacking most of the containers in the sink. Living alone had taken all the fun out of cooking. Eating had become a necessity, not a shared moment of enjoyment. She missed that.

On an impulse she called Cam. "Instead of you taking me out to dinner and the movies like we talked about, why don't you come here? I've got a sudden urge to do some cooking."

"Sounds great! I've got a sudden appetite."

Sukie laughed. They chatted for a couple of minutes before she hung up to prepare a grocery list. Cooking had always been a way for her to show affection. Though his waistline suggested otherwise, her cooking efforts had obviously been wasted on Ted.

Later, when she was almost out the door, the phone rang. She raced to answer it.

"Hi, Mom! What's up?" Elizabeth's cheerful voice chirped in Sukie's ear, sending waves of panic through her. She didn't want to mention Cam until she was more certain about the relationship.

"Nothing much. I'm having a friend over for dinner tonight."

"Hmmm. Betsy?"

"Uh, no . . ." Sukie evaded. "Someone I met recently. What's going on with you?"

Elizabeth launched into describing her activities, leaving Sukie responsible for one- or two-word comments, nothing more.

"Gotta go. Amy's here," Elizabeth abruptly announced. At the click of Elizabeth's phone, Sukie heaved a sigh of relief. She knew she was a coward for not telling Elizabeth about Cam, but she didn't want anything to destroy the evening she'd planned with him. In time, if she and Cam continued to date, her savvy daughter would surely understand. Wouldn't she?

Saturday at World Foods was always a mob scene. Sukie darted inside the store, intent upon quickly getting in and out. She hurried to the back of the store. Katy Hartmann was standing at the meat counter. Sukie ducked into the aisle of seasonings, praying Katy hadn't seen her.

The next time Sukie peeked around the corner, Katy was gone. Letting out a breath of relief, she hurried over to the meat counter and took a ticket.

"Hello, Sukie!"

She tensed.

Betsy grinned at her. "It's only me. Don't worry, I've already encountered the Mouth of the South, and I'm not talking about Ted Turner."

Sukie laughed. It had been foolish to try to hide. Cam was an attractive man—okay, a studmuffin—and he'd chosen to spend time with her. There was nothing wrong with that. Everyone said she didn't look or act her age. Besides, it was nobody else's damn business.

Sukie completed her shopping and, humming softly, headed home.

A couple of hours later, she reviewed the outcome of her labor with satisfaction. Tangy barbecue sauce rested in a jar next to the garlic-and-herb salad dressing that had become a family favorite. Cleaned leaves of romaine were stored in the refrigerator near the mushrooms she'd marinated for an appetizer. The pièce de résistance was the lemon meringue pie, a recipe that she'd become noted for at PTA fundraisers.

When her chores were done, she took a long soak in the tub, reveling in the fact this was one Saturday night she wouldn't spend alone. While getting dressed, she put a dab of perfume behind each ear. When she was satisfied she was ready, she drifted downstairs to wait for Cam.

He arrived with a bottle of wine. He wrapped his arms around her and gave her a kiss that sent her pulse racing. Wearing a sexy grin, he said, "Should we forget dinner?"

Sukie laughed. "What time do you have to be home?"

"I told the babysitter I'd be back by midnight."

"Good." She smiled. "We've got time to do both."

Cam chuckled and followed her out to the patio.

A bottle of chilled pinot grigio sat on the table, along with the mushrooms and an assortment of cheeses garnished with frosty green grapes.

Sukie took a seat and breathed in the air, fragrant with the scent of flowers. The evening still held a bit of the day's warmth. The flowers she'd recently planted along the edges of the patio bobbed their colorful heads in the soft breeze that danced with them, adding bright color to the green spread of lawn beyond.

"Very nice." Cam took a seat and stretched his long legs out in front of him. Sukie admired the muscular shape of them beneath his khaki pants. Her gaze traveled up his buff body to his rugged face.

Cam looked at her, his blue eyes full of questions. "Everything all right?"

"Oh, yeah." The chemistry between them was on high alert. "What do you suppose it is between us that makes our connection so unusual? It's almost too good to be true." Sukie took a deep breath, wishing she could see into the future. "Are you . . . are you going to end up breaking my heart?"

Cam leaned over and gently caressed Sukie's cheek. "I'll try not to, Sukie. I know what it's like to have your life turned upside down by someone else."

"Do you hate her? Your ex-girlfriend?"

He shook his head. "No. Remember, she gave me Chloe. But I don't give a damn anymore what she does or who she's with. She simply doesn't matter to me." His mouth formed an unpleasant twist. "She wants no part of Chloe. She'd rather have her drugs and other men who will give them to her. End of story."

"But you'd like to find someone else . . ."

"Sure." He gave Sukie an endearing smile that made her heart turn over with joy. "But, Sukie, many of the women I've dated are so spoiled they can't see beyond themselves. I already have one child to raise. I don't want more."

Sukie leaned back in her chair, letting his words settle inside her.

"It isn't just about the sex, which is great with us, Sukie. It's about how I want to spend my time, and with whom. I have so little time to myself, taking care of Chloe and all. It's got to feel right. Know what I mean?"

Sukie nodded. She knew exactly what he meant. Her divorce had changed her views about a lot of people. She was no longer willing to waste her time with those people who'd be only too glad to stab her in the back. Sukie's counselor had mentioned the need to be around positive, active people, who supported one another. She understood. That's why the Fat Fridays group had come to mean so much to her. That's why she and the other women in the group were willing to fight to keep Lynn with them, safe and sound.

Cam poured the wine into the stemmed glasses she'd set out and moved a glass across the table toward her. A few drops of wine spilled on the glass tabletop. Sukie wiped them up with her finger.

Reaching for her hand, eyes steady on her, Cam sucked the liquid from her finger. His tongue and lips absorbed the chill from the wine and sent fiery heat racing through her. Sukie almost swooned from the effect. God, this man knew how to get to her. And it felt so good.

Cam leaned over and kissed her on the lips. She knew from the way his tongue caressed hers that he was aroused, too. When they finally broke apart, he said, "Let's enjoy what we have. Time will take care of the rest."

After they'd sat for a while, talking, Sukie got up and handed Cam an apron with "Kiss the Cook" scrawled across the front of it.

He looked at the saying and grinned. "Better do it before the chicken goes on the grill."

She knew enough to do exactly what she'd been told.

They ate in the dining room. The formal setting of the room, with its crystal chandelier and white wainscoting etched below hunter-green walls, did nothing to stem the tide of sexual tension that rippled invisibly between them.

Sukie served a salad and garlic oven-fried potatoes and watched with satisfaction as Cam dug into the meal. To her delight, he asked for seconds of everything.

Coffee accompanied the pie.

"Delicious," Cam said, scraping the last remnant of lemon filling off his plate.

Leaving Cam to finish his cup of coffee, Sukie went into the kitchen to straighten up. She was standing at the sink when she felt Cam's arms fold around her. She leaned back against him, loving the feel of his strong body pressed to hers.

Cam nuzzled her neck. "Forget the dishes. We've got better things to do." He held out his hand. Pulse racing with anticipation, she took it.

CHAPTER TWENTY-FOUR

CAROL ANN

Carol Ann had been so excited about dating that, at first, she didn't care who she went out with. Now, after a number of dates with guys she had no interest in, she found herself thinking more and more about what she wanted.

The only man she'd really liked—in every way but one—was John, the insurance guy. He was cute, he had a nice car, and he didn't mind spending money. She shook her head. So, things got out of hand one night because they'd both had too much to drink. That didn't make him a monster like the women in the Fat Fridays group seemed to think, did it? It was a pretty puny excuse for giving up on him.

They didn't have to live with her parents.

She did.

They didn't have to go out on one lousy date after another.

She did.

Carol Ann paced her room, thinking of all of the reasons why she should be in touch with John. Sukie had Cam; Tiffany had Beau. And Betsy? Carol Ann wasn't sure, but she thought Betsy might have some guy on the side. Something was going on with her. Lynn, Carol Ann knew, would never be interested in a man.

John continued to send emails, asking her for another chance, and Carol Ann decided she was going to give it to him.

CHAPTER TWENTY-FIVE
SUKIE

Sunday morning, Sukie stretched like a cat sated with cream, languishing in satisfaction. Months ago, she would never have dreamed how her life would change. It still stung that Ted had been so cruel, but she was more than happy to discover this new side to life. Though she was about to become a grandmother, she felt younger and more alive than she had in years. She was free to be herself, the real Sukie, not the mother, the wife, the community volunteer defined by others, but the person defined by her own new sense of self.

She got out of bed and tossed her nightgown aside. Catching a glimpse of herself in the mirror, she stopped and peered at the image staring back at her. Not bad. Her body wasn't perfect, of course. It never would be. But it attracted the man with whom she'd already fallen in love, and that's what most mattered to her.

The jarring ring of the phone startled her. Sukie checked the digital bedside clock. Ten after seven on a Sunday morning. *Oh my God! Is it Lynn?*

"H-h-h-h-hello?"

"Mom?"

Sukie lowered herself to her bed, her heart racing. "Rob? What is it? Is everything all right with Madeleine and the baby?"

"Yes, they're fine. It's Dad. He came over here last night ranting and raving about you seeing some younger man. What's going on?"

The smell of Cam's spicy aftershave wafted up from the sheets. Sukie's pulse pounded. She wasn't ready to divulge her deepest feelings to her son. Not yet.

"Is it true?"

"I've met someone very special," Sukie answered as calmly as she could. "He and I are seeing each other. I'd like you to meet him in time. You and Madeleine."

"So, it's true. I heard he has a three-year-old daughter. Geez, Mom, you're about to become a grandmother. Don't you think it's a little weird?"

"A difference in our ages shouldn't matter to anyone else. Look at your father. He left me for someone Madeleine's age, for God's sake. Why should it be an issue with me?" Sukie hated her defensive tone but the injustice of it filled her with resentment. "His age isn't all that different from mine; I had you young, remember?"

"So, who is he?"

"Cameron Taylor, an IT consultant who's working at MacTel on a special project. He's a remarkable man, someone I'm sure you'll like." As if Rob could see her, Sukie clutched the blankets to her, covering her nakedness.

"Uh, Mom? Madeleine wants to talk to you. Here she is."

"Sukie?"

She tensed, wondering what her daughter-in-law had to say. It couldn't be good if Rob was so upset.

"I just want you to know that Rob and I disagree on this being weird," Madeleine said. "If you've moved on and found someone you're interested in, I'm all for it. This idea that a difference in ages is wrong for a woman but right for a man is ridiculous."

Sukie's breath escaped in a rush of relief. Bless Madeleine. Sukie had always loved her.

"Don't worry. Rob will come around. But Sukie, I've never seen Ted so angry. He's absolutely furious that you've embarrassed him."

Sukie's blood pressure rose in pounding pulses. Through teeth clamped together she ground out, "He has no reason to be upset with me. I'm the one who's been embarrassed by him parading his pregnant girlfriend all over town."

"Just a warning. Talk to you later."

Sukie hung up the phone trembling with fury. She was still fuming over the unfairness of Ted's behavior, when she received a call from Betsy. "Just checking. You and Cam are still coming for brunch, aren't you?"

"Yes, but we have to bring Chloe. All right?"

"That's fine. I've got plenty of toys here for her to play with. See you soon."

Thinking of Ted, Sukie shook her head. If he knew of her support of Betsy's relationship with Karen, it would send him into another tizzy. He'd become so full of self-importance in his role as bank president that somewhere along the line he'd lost the ability to be kind. Earlier, she'd accepted it as part of who he was, but now she couldn't and wouldn't condone it.

Betsy was all smiles when she greeted Sukie, Cam, and Chloe at the door. Karen stood behind her wearing a look of uncertainty.

"Come in, come in," Betsy said. "I've set up brunch in the sunroom. It's my favorite room in the house!" Her cheeks colored prettily as she ushered them inside. "Sukie Skidmore and Cam Taylor, I want you to meet Karen McEvoy, my . . . partner."

Cam smiled and shook Karen's hand, and Sukie followed suit.

"Hi there, Chloe." Betsy knelt on the floor and opened her arms. Chloe ran into them. "I've got some toys for you to play with. My granddaughter Caitlin keeps a whole basketful of them here."

Chloe's eyes danced. "For me?"

"For a while," said Betsy cheerfully, rising and leading the way.

Sukie turned to Karen. "I understand you're going to move in with Betsy. When?"

Karen's eyes rounded. "Betsy hasn't told you?"

Sukie shook her head.

Karen sighed. "Probably never. Richie called her yesterday. He and Sarah are having some problems, and he asked Betsy if he could move in with her for a while. I've gone ahead and rented an apartment nearby. There's no way either one of us feels ready to spring our relationship on him. Not when he's so vulnerable."

"I'm sorry." Sukie didn't know what else to say. Betsy had a family to consider.

While Chloe played with the Barbie dolls she'd pulled out of a wicker basket, Sukie sat with the other adults at the round rattan and glass table. Betsy had loaded it with brunch items—an egg and cheese casserole, sausage patties, fresh fruit, sweet rolls, and an assortment of pastries. As they ate, Karen talked about her work as an IT analyst. While Cam and Karen discussed a new program she was working on, Sukie turned to Betsy.

"Karen told me about Richie coming to stay with you."

Betsy nodded. "I have mixed feelings about it. Naturally I'm disappointed Karen decided to rent an apartment nearby rather than move in with me, but I'm pleased Richie is taking a stand with Sarah. They need to work several things out. It's about time he faced that."

Sukie told Betsy about the phone call with Rob and Madeleine and how angry she was with Ted.

Betsy shook her head. "As Gloria Steinem once said, 'A woman without a man is like a fish without a bicycle.' Who needs 'em when they pull stuff like that?" She nudged Sukie with her elbow. "So, how's it going with Cam?"

Sukie glanced over at him, deep in conversation with Karen, and felt a flutter of excitement as she recalled him naked in bed with her.

"You don't have to say a word," Betsy whispered, beaming at Sukie. "It's written all over your face."

Sukie could feel herself blushing.

Betsy clasped her hand. "It's okay, Sukie. You guys seem to be doing fine."

"I hope so," Sukie whispered.

Sometime later, the sound of the doorbell brought Betsy to her feet. "I wonder who that is?"

Chloe darted out of the room, carrying the doll she'd been playing with. Sukie hurried after her.

"Hey! She's got my doll!" came a shriek Sukie recognized as Caitlin's voice.

By the time Sukie reached the front hall, Caitlin was holding the doll and Chloe's face was already streaked with tears. Sukie put her arm around Chloe as she began to cry in earnest.

Cam came up behind them.

Richie stood to one side, a hand on Garrett's shoulder. He shot Sukie a look of surprise.

"Hi, Mrs. Skidmore. Whose little girl is this?"

"Mine." Cam picked up Chloe and patted her back.

Betsy took the doll from Caitlin and handed it back to Chloe. "Next time, ask for it politely," she admonished Caitlin.

"But it's mine!" Caitlin wailed.

"How about a trade?" Sukie suggested. "Let's go see the other toys."

They all crowded into the sunroom. Sukie was able to persuade Chloe to let go of the doll in favor of a musical game.

"Well, now that that's settled, how about more food for everyone?" Betsy announced. "Richie?"

He nodded. "Sounds good. I took the kids to their favorite place for lunch but couldn't force another burger down my throat. Meals have been on our own all week." He slumped in a chair.

Betsy served him a heaping plate of food.

Watching Richie dig into his mother's cooking with gusto, Sukie was amused. Sons were all alike. She looked around the room and saw that Karen had moved as far away from Richie as possible.

Between bites, Richie said to his mother, "I know Mrs. Skidmore. Who are the others?"

Betsy's hands fluttered in the air nervously. "Oh, my! In all the confusion, I forgot to make the introductions. Cameron Taylor is a new neighbor. Chloe is his daughter. And this is Karen McEvoy, a special friend of mine."

The tinkling notes of the musical game echoed in the silence of the room that followed. Richie stared from Betsy's bright cheeks to Karen's look of discomfort.

Sukie shifted uneasily in her chair.

Chloe whined and threw the game down on the floor.

Cam caught Sukie's eye. "Time for us to get Chloe home for nap time."

Richie's eyebrows formed arcs of surprise. "You two are together?"

Cam gave him a thin smile. "Not really. We're just friends."

Sukie froze in her seat. *Just friends?* Elizabeth had told her all about friends with benefits. Is that what Cam meant?

"Are you sure you have to go?" Betsy asked.

Sukie realized Betsy was nervous to have Richie and Karen in the same room, but she needed some time to herself. She was so confused.

Outside, Cam gave Sukie a seductive grin. "We'll walk you home— unless you want to help me put Chloe down for a nap and stay for a while."

She swallowed hard. "Better not. I've got a lot of things to take care of before the busy workweek ahead."

Cam gave her a puzzled look and lifted her chin. "You okay?"

Sukie nodded, hoping he wouldn't notice how mixed up she felt.

They came to a stop in front of Sukie's house.

"I'll call you this week." Cam gave her a quick kiss on the cheek.

Chloe lifted her arms up for a hug. Sukie bent down and picked her up.

Wrapping her little arms around Sukie's neck, Chloe gave her a hard squeeze. "Gimme a bear hug."

"Grrr. Love you," Sukie responded, as she had to her own children years ago.

"My mommy." Chloe gave Sukie another hug.

Aware of Cam's steady, troubled gaze, Sukie said, "No, honey. We're special, special friends, you and I. Okay?"

Chloe's blue eyes seemed to fill her face as she stared at Sukie for a moment. "I want to get down."

Sukie set Chloe on her feet.

Cam shook his head. "Sorry about that mommy business. She really likes you and doesn't understand why she can't have one too."

"I understand," Sukie enjoyed the feeling of Chloe's small arms squeezing her into a hug.

"Well, gotta go. She's too far ahead of me." Cam took off in a loping run.

Sukie watched him, her mind whirling. Her life had gone from a quiet, almost boring existence to one filled with so many ups and downs she couldn't keep track of them.

Still upset over Cam's statement about being just friends, Sukie changed her clothes and went out to the garden. The warm dirt in her hands, the colorful flowers, even the weeds she'd plucked from the ground—all gave her a better sense of self. Chiding herself, Sukie decided her angst was because of her existence between two different social worlds. She'd never give her body, her heart, her soul to someone without it meaning more than being just friends.

A car pulled into the driveway. Sukie tensed. She might have sorted out a few things but she was in no mood for company. Grumbling to herself, Sukie headed toward the front of the house.

Carol Ann greeted her halfway. "I'm sorry I didn't call first, but I had to get out of the house. My parents are at each other again and I was going crazy. I knew I could find peace and quiet here with you."

Sukie smiled. "C'mon! You can help me."

Carol Ann laughed. "I thought we might end up in your garden so I wore my ratty old jeans."

Suddenly, it felt good to Sukie to share her space with someone who had no expectations beyond conversation. She handed Carol Ann a trowel and set her to work loosening the soil around the plants she'd just weeded.

They worked in companionable silence for a while, with the sweet trilling notes of birds as background music. Sensing something was on Carol Ann's mind, Sukie waited for her to speak.

Carol Ann finally broke into the quiet. "I've decided to date John again. You know, the guy from the insurance company. He called me last night."

Alarm shot through Sukie. "Isn't he the one who got rough with you in the parking lot?"

"Yes, but that was a onetime thing. He promised me it won't happen again. He said he'd had way too much to drink and it made him crazy when he knew we didn't have anywhere to go."

Sukie shook her head in disbelief. "What's going to be different now? You still live with your parents."

Carol Ann flashed Sukie a triumphant smile. "He's got a new apartment. One of the condos by the lake was up for rent."

"That's pretty expensive." Ted and Emmy Lou lived there, and Sukie knew exactly how much they sold for. "When did all this come about?"

"He got a raise two weeks ago and decided to get out of his old place and into something more suitable for a manager." Carol Ann spread her arms out. "Sukie, he's good-looking, and he has a nice car and a great apartment. What's not to like?"

Sukie studied her, uncertain what to say. They'd all told Carol Ann those weren't the most important things to look for in a man.

Carol Ann clucked her tongue. "Oh, I know he's not as handsome as Tiffany's husband, or as rich, but living with him would be a whole lot better than living with my parents."

"Whaaat! You're already talking about living together?" Sukie couldn't hide her dismay.

A blush crept up Carol Ann's cheeks. "No, no. He doesn't know I've been thinking about it, but it might be an answer to my prayers. Finding someone to share an apartment with, getting out of my parents' house . . ." Her voice trailed off.

Sukie placed a hand on Carol Ann's shoulder and gazed into her eyes, trying to understand. She didn't know whether Carol Ann was just plain naïve or so desperate for a change she wasn't thinking clearly. "I want you to promise me you'll go slowly."

Carol Ann nodded. "I will, though he seems pretty anxious to get together." She clasped her hands together. "I'm so glad everyone got me started on Internet dating. I can pretty much pick and choose who I want to go out with. And John wants me, just me, he says."

"More reason to go slowly." With encouragement from the Fat Fridays group, Carol Ann had emerged from her shell, had begun dressing differently, and was well aware of the different ways men were reacting to her. Observing her low-cut halter top that barely contained her breasts, Sukie wondered if they'd created a monster.

"Thanks for listening to me, Sukie." Carol Ann gave her a weak smile.

Sukie's heart went out to her. "Just be careful." Time would help Carol Ann regain her equilibrium. Until then, Sukie would worry about her.

They finished working, and Sukie brought out sweet tea and cookies to the patio. Carol Ann stretched out on one of the lounge chairs and accepted her drink with a lazy smile. "Your house is so beautiful, Sukie. I can't wait to have one like it."

Sukie let out a sigh of frustration. "Carol Ann, it takes a whole lot more than material things to make someone happy."

Carol Ann waved away her words. "I know, I know. But it doesn't hurt to have nice things. Take a look at Tiffany. She doesn't appreciate all that handsome husband does for her. She's got it all and still she complains."

It took all Sukie's will power to keep from blurting out the truth about Tiffany's marriage. She'd promised to keep the information to herself, but it was hard not to tell Carol Ann how it really was for Tiffany. "Sometimes things aren't what they seem."

"I guess I shouldn't criticize her. I know she's been real sick with this baby. Still . . ."

"Still, we're not going to judge her. Right?"

At the stern look Sukie gave her, color flooded Carol Ann's face. "I'm sorry, Sukie. I really am."

Sukie gave her a quick hug. "Let's just relax and enjoy the last of the sunny afternoon. We're due for some rainy days this week."

Carol Ann left a short time later. Sukie sat outside, finding pleasure in the warm April weather, knowing it wouldn't last. Her thoughts turned to Cam. A deep sense of loss knotted her stomach. If all he wanted was a "friend with benefits," their relationship wouldn't last.

CHAPTER TWENTY-SIX
TIFFANY

Tiffany stood in front of her long bedroom mirror, rubbed her round tummy, and turned from side to side. With morning sickness pretty much gone, she was in awe of what was happening to her body. "Who are you?" she whispered, sending the baby silent "boy" messages. Beau kept saying having a son was the one thing he would've finally done right to please his parents. She tried to tell him their baby might be a girl, but he didn't want to listen.

She turned away from her image and sighed. The whole thing about the baby being a boy and Beau having to please his parents was pretty weird. She sometimes felt it was better to have been raised by a mother who didn't really want her than to be raised by Beau's parents, who insisted Beau follow their rules.

"See you later." Beau waved to her from the bedroom door. "Remember, I have a meeting at the club tonight so I need an early dinner. Have it set for me. Okay?"

Tiffany nodded and went back to searching her closet for a jacket. If only she and Beau could live far away from his parents, take on a different name, live a totally new life, she thought wistfully, things would be better. But then she wasn't sure she even wanted to stay with Beau. If the baby was a boy, maybe Beau's parents would be content to leave them alone until the little one was born.

Several days later Tiffany lay in bed, worrying. She'd find out the sex of the baby that afternoon and her life would take a turn for better—or worse. Rising, she flung off her nightshirt and went into the shower, wishing she could wash her anxiety away.

Tiffany was brushing her hair when Beau came up behind her and nuzzled her neck. "I'm going to try to get home early. My father has bought a bottle of champagne to celebrate, so come right here after your appointment."

"Beau . . ."

He held up his hand. "I don't want to talk about it. I'll see you this afternoon."

Tiffany finished getting ready for work and went downstairs to the kitchen. She managed to swallow her vitamins but could hardly taste the dry piece of wheat toast she nibbled on between sips of orange juice.

Her morning at work passed quickly. The execs were caught up in preparation for an upcoming companywide meeting, and she was given a ton of work to do. It wasn't until she was driving to the Fat Fridays luncheon at Bea's that her heart kept skipping beats at the thought of having to face Beau's parents with bad news.

Sitting at a table with the other women, she hid her anxiety and ordered a fruit salad as if nothing were wrong. But when she lifted her fork to eat her lunch, her stomach turned. She shifted in her chair, wondering if she should get up and leave the table.

"What's going on with you?" Carol Ann asked. "Are you gonna be sick again?"

Tiffany took a deep breath. "No, but I find out the sex of my baby this afternoon. I don't know what I'll do if it's a girl."

Sukie frowned at her. "The important thing is the health of the baby." She gave Tiffany a pat of encouragement. "This should be an exciting time. I hate to see you worry so, Tiffany. It will be what it will be."

"Yeah. Too late for changes, hon," Lynn said.

Tiffany nodded, attempting to calm her pulsing nerves. She was glad Betsy wasn't there to give her one of her crazy sayings.

"Say," said Lynn. "Have any of you noticed anything different? See someone strange? Had any creepy calls?"

"No, why?" said Carol Ann, clasping her hands together.

"Are you sensing something, Lynn?" Sukie's eyes rounded. "Should we be more aware?"

Lynn shook her head. "No, don't worry. It's just that this is the longest I've ever stayed in one place. I guess we're in a holding pattern. But if any of you feel like anything weird is going on, you let me know. Hear?"

Tiffany nodded with the others and listened as Carol Ann, then Sukie, took over the conversation.

When it was time to leave, Lynn unexpectedly hugged her. "Good luck, Tiff!"

Sukie gathered her purse and turned to Tiffany with a smile. "Let me know how you do this afternoon. I'll be thinking of you."

"Yeah, me too," said Carol Ann, giving her a sympathetic look.

Tiffany's eyes filled. The women of Fat Fridays had become so dear to her. She didn't know what she'd do without them.

Tiffany lay on the examination table at the doctor's office. Watching the ultrasound screen, her heartbeat thumped uneasily in her chest. "Please, God . . ." she whispered and stopped. She wouldn't go there. Sukie was right. She just wanted a healthy baby.

"Looks like a beautiful little girl." The doctor's voice faded in and out over the humming that broke out in Tiffany's ears.

"Are you sure it's not a boy?" said Tiffany, feeling as if she was about to faint.

"Yes, we have a clear shot of her. See? There's one leg here and another and, there, you can see the shape of her back as she turns over."

Tiffany tried to take in what the doctor was saying, but the beat of the baby's heart combined with hers sounded like warning thumps of a drum.

"Come into my office. We'll talk," said the doctor, oblivious to her emotional pain.

Tiffany nodded numbly. How was she going to break the news to Beau? She could feel his anger already.

After her talk with the doctor, Tiffany left his office and sat in her car, afraid to go home. Beau hadn't been able to get off from work to accompany her, but he'd be waiting for her now. Muffy and Regard would be there, too. The thought of facing them was too much to handle. She needed to talk to someone. Someone like Sukie.

Tiffany found Sukie at her desk, leafing through picture books. "Sukie! Sukie! Thank God you're here. I just came from the doctor's office. It's a girl. What am I going to do?" Tiffany felt the sting of tears.

Sukie blinked in surprise at her, then drew her eyebrows together. "What are you going to do? You're going to have a baby girl. That's what you're going to do. You do know about X and Y chromosomes, don't you? It's the male who determines the sex of the baby, not the female."

Tiffany clutched her hands together. "Yes, but Beau and his family won't see it that way. They'll find some way to blame me. I just know it. It seems so silly, but it's a big deal to his family."

"You better sit down and tell me about it, hon." Sukie's soft soothing voice caught Tiffany's attention. She sank into a chair and dabbed at her eyes.

"The doctor said the baby seems healthy but she's on the small side. He wants me to gain a few more pounds."

Sukie's eyes bored into her. "Has Beau been watching your weight?"

Misery washed over Tiffany. He'd scolded her the other day when she ate a couple of cookies. "He doesn't want me to get too fat."

Sukie slammed her hand down on the desk. "Dammit, Tiffany. He can't have everything his way. Don't you see?"

Feeling like a total failure, Tiffany hung her head.

Sukie grabbed hold of Tiffany's hand. "Oh, hon, I'm sorry. It's not you I'm angry with. Now, what can I do to help you?"

Tiffany lifted her head and looked at the woman who just might be her best friend. "Will you come with me to my house? I can't face all of them alone."

Sukie's eyebrows rose. "Shouldn't this be a private moment between you and Beau?"

"It's not private at all. It never is. Regard and Muffy will be there, too, waiting for the news." Tiffany held back a sob of frustration. She felt like she was married to three ornery people. Not one.

Sukie shook her head. "I can't intrude on family matters. It wouldn't be right." She stood and wrapped her arms around Tiffany. "You can do it, Tiffany. I know you can."

Wishing her life was different, Tiffany clung to Sukie.

Resigned to face the family alone, Tiffany gave Sukie a pseudo thumbs-up and left the library. She struggled to build her courage as she headed home. A block from her house, she pulled over to the curb and vomited. Preparing herself for the ordeal ahead, she rinsed her mouth with water and continued down the street.

Pulling into the driveway, she eyed Regard's black Mercedes and Muffy's powder-blue Porsche and let out a groan from deep inside her. There was no way she could avoid them.

Tiffany entered the house through the back door and found the three of them—Beau, Regard, and Muffy—lined up in the kitchen, their expressions eager.

"Well?" A smile spread across Muffy's face.

Tiffany swallowed hard. "It's a girl. A healthy girl."

"Dammit!" Beau's face flushed an angry red. His eyes shot daggers at Tiffany.

She could feel her knees grow weak. "You're the one with the chromosomes . . ." Tiffany began, but Beau had left the room.

Muffy hurried after him.

Regard looked at Tiffany, disappointment stamped on his face.

Bile rose in Tiffany's throat. "I'm sorry . . ."

"Don't you worry, little gal," said Regard. "We'll try as soon as we can for our little boy. No stopping til it's done."

Muffy returned to the kitchen and faced Tiffany, her hands on her hips. "Why are you so late getting home? Your appointment was for two. It's after four."

"I stopped at the library to see Sukie," Tiffany said defiantly, rebelling against the demanding tone of Muffy's voice.

"Sukie who?"

"Sukie Skidmore. She's my best friend. We both belong to the Fat Fridays group and meet for lunch every Friday."

"Oh, well, that will soon come to an end." Muffy turned on her heels, leaving Tiffany blinking in shock.

"Now, don't y'all mind Muffy," Regard said in his exaggerated drawl. "We've had a bit of a shock and she's upset. We're tryin' to get used to the idea of a granddaughter." He gave Tiffany a meaningful stare that made her skin prickle.

There was no shouting, no screaming—just painful words and pointed looks that pierced Tiffany's heart. She straightened as maternal juices flooded her body. She covered her rounded stomach with her hands, hugging the baby. *We're going to be just fine, baby girl. You and me.*

No one, she silently vowed, would be allowed to hurt her precious daughter. Unlike her own mother, Tiffany would make sure this child never knew she wasn't wanted.

CHAPTER TWENTY-SEVEN

SUKIE

After Tiffany left her, Sukie sat at her desk, sickened by all she'd been told. Cruelty was just part of the game played by Beau's illustrious family. Sukie wondered if they knew how much damage they'd done to Tiffany and to their son's marriage.

On her way home, Sukie pulled into Betsy's driveway. She'd never been known to miss a Fat Fridays luncheon and she wanted to make sure Betsy was all right.

Richie answered the front door. "Hi, Mrs. Skidmore. My mom's not home. She's gone to New York."

Sukie blinked in surprise. "New York? I thought maybe she was sick."

He shook his head. "Her friend Karen won a free trip to the city and they decided to go up there for the weekend." He gave Sukie a troubled look, one that reminded her of him as a young boy. "What's going on with Mom?"

Sukie gulped. No way would she say anything to jeopardize Betsy's relationship with her son. "I'm just pleased to see your mother so happy. Aren't you?"

He shrugged. "I have so many problems of my own, I haven't given it too much thought."

"Please tell your mother I said hello." Sukie returned to her car and let out a sigh. Talk about complications! How could a group of five women have so many problems?

At home, Sukie could hardly wait to get out of her business clothes and into something more comfortable. She pulled on a pair of cutoff jeans and a knit shirt and slid her feet into a pair of sandals, glad it was Friday. The rain the weatherman had promised had fallen most of the week, encouraging growth in the garden. She went out to the backyard and examined the burgeoning blooms and new batch of weeds. Too tired to deal with yard work, she went inside, fighting feelings of depression.

Cam hadn't called her all week. Disappointment ate away at her good memories of the two of them together. Sukie told herself that in today's world, Cam didn't owe her a thing and that so-called friends with benefits didn't have to keep in touch on a regular basis. But it stung.

She plunked down on a bar stool, wondering what she'd gotten herself into. It was driving her crazy that she hadn't heard from him. She smiled at the imaginary headline she conjured up in her mind:

WOMAN ADDICTED TO LOVE SHOOTS OUT CELL TOWER WAITING FOR CALL

She'd just poured herself a glass of wine when the phone rang. Cam.

"Oh, thank God you're there," he said without preamble. "Sukie, I need your help. We're deploying three new computer applications at work and it's been a mess, with all sorts of failures. I'm going to have to work all night. Is there any way you could take Chloe for me? Her preschool teacher is going away this weekend and I don't trust Emily Warren to babysit her all night."

Sukie heard the worry in his voice. Still . . .

"Will you do it?"

She thought of sweet little Chloe alone and frightened, left with a veritable stranger. "Okay, bring her down. She can stay here. We'll make it a fun sleepover."

"Ah, Sukie, you're a doll."

She grimaced. Right. A babysitter with benefits.

"Sorry I didn't call earlier, but like I said, it's been a helluva week. I'm on my way to pick up Chloe from school now."

"I'll be right here," Sukie said, already trying to come up with ideas to occupy an active three-year-old.

Chloe's look of joy when Sukie answered her soft knock on the door warmed Sukie's insides. With her bright smile and wide blue eyes, Chloe was as pretty as any of the dolls Elizabeth used to play with. Sukie gave her a big hug.

"Thanks again." Cam handed her a pink-canvas, princess-adorned suitcase, Chloe's special blanket, and her favorite doll, Sally.

Cam's face was drawn into tired lines. Dark smudges rested below his eyes.

Sukie gasped. "You look awful! Are you sick?"

"No. Like I said, it's been a bad week. My work is sometimes like this. You think you have everything programmed just right and nasty little surprises pop up. It's all part of the process."

"Have you eaten?" she asked him.

Cam shot her the crooked smile she found so disarming. "We've ordered pizza for the entire crew." He reached for her, and she fell into his arms.

He let out a long sigh that told Sukie how much he'd missed her. She settled against his broad chest.

Feeling a tug on her shirttail, Sukie looked down. Chloe held her arms out to Sukie.

Sukie pulled Chloe up into the circle she and Cam had formed, feeling as if all was right with the world once more.

"Gotta go," said Cam, reluctantly pulling away.

"Don't worry about us girls," Sukie said, still holding Chloe. "We're going to have a fun sleepover." They made a show of waving good-bye to Cam, and then Sukie and Chloe went into the kitchen.

Chloe's lips, which had quivered at seeing Cam off, quickly turned into a beaming smile when Sukie suggested a picnic. While Chloe showed her doll Sally around the kitchen, Sukie peeled and cut up carrots and apples and sliced some cold chicken.

Outside, Chloe helped Sukie spread a blanket on the ground and they sat down to their impromptu meal. Chloe pretended to feed Sally while Sukie encouraged her to eat something herself. Sukie liked Chloe. She was a sweet child—imaginative and even-tempered—unlike many of the children she'd observed at the library. Chloe ran around the backyard shrieking with delight as she chased colorful butterflies that fluttered and swooped toward the flowers. Listening to her, Sukie wondered how Chloe's mother could have given her to Cam and walked away.

The sound of a car pulling into the driveway disturbed the peaceful moment.

Sukie rose and called to Chloe, and led her around the side of the house. Her heart stopped at the sight of Ted's BMW.

He emerged from the car, his expression dour.

"Ted? What are you doing here?" My God, he'd gone and dyed his hair. He looked foolish.

"We need to talk, Sukie. I've just come from the country club and I've had it with your behavior. I've become the laughing stock of all my buddies!"

Sukie crossed her arms and stood her ground. Chloe hid behind her and clutched her legs. "And just why do you think it has anything to do with me?"

He shook a fist at her. His face turned a deep, angry red. "Because you've been fucking some young stud! That's why!"

At his angry tone, Chloe began to cry. Sukie drew Chloe out from behind her and picked her up. Holding back a venomous reply, Sukie narrowed her eyes at Ted.

"Who's that?" Ted's lips thinned. "I get it. It's his daughter, isn't it? So where is he, this big stud of yours? Why isn't he out here facing me?"

"Stop talking like that." Sukie fought to keep her voice controlled so Chloe wouldn't become even more frightened. "He's not here and I'm not discussing this with you. Leave. This isn't your home any more, and there'll be no fighting in front of this child. I mean it, Ted." It occurred to her that in the past, she'd often caved in to Ted's wishes rather than fight in front of the children.

His face twisted into an ugly expression she found repulsive. He shook his fist at her. "I'll go, but this isn't over, Sukie. Not by a long shot. I will not, repeat *not*, be made a fool of by you."

"You don't need me to help you with that." Her body shaking, Sukie turned on her heels and walked away from him. Didn't he see how hypocritical the whole scene was? And what was with the dyed hair? She wondered why she'd ever been attracted to him.

"I don't like that man," Chloe whispered to Sukie as Ted climbed into his car and roared off.

Sukie hugged Chloe closer. "Neither do I."

They cleaned up the picnic items and headed back inside. Chloe proudly carried the blanket while Sukie held Sally and their dishes.

Upstairs, Sukie ran a warm bubble bath for Chloe. Giggling, they made a game of forming bubble crowns on Chloe's head. Most women at some time in their lives had had wishful thoughts about being a real princess. Sukie was no different. Now, this much later in her life, Cam made her feel that way. Maybe that's why she'd fallen so hard for him.

Sukie dried Chloe with a fluffy towel and dressed her in a soft pink cotton nightgown. Some of Sukie's friends would call her crazy, but she liked going back to mothering duties. Lynn would probably tell her to get a dog, but Sukie was happy doing this type of thing.

Tucking Chloe in Elizabeth's old bed, Sukie wrapped Chloe's blanket around her and placed Sally in her arms. They picked out a storybook together and Sukie read to her until Chloe's eyes stopped fluttering and remained closed. Then she tiptoed out of the room.

As she was dressing for bed, Sukie wondered, as she did so often, just where her relationship with Cam was headed. It was all so confusing— falling in love with a younger man, a single father, someone who could have his choice of many others. From every aspect, it was so new and unsettling.

Sukie was deep in sleep when she felt a tug on her arm. Startled, her eyes flew open. Chloe stood next to Sukie's bed, peering up at her in the semidark room. "Can I get in bed with you?"

Sukie glanced at the bedside clock. Six o'clock. She held back a groan. This was one aspect of caring for a three-year-old she hadn't missed. "Sure, honey. Come on up."

Chloe tossed Sally up on the bed and Sukie helped Chloe climb in beside her. Her little feet were chilly against Sukie's warm body. Sukie put her arm around Chloe and drew her close, inhaling the sweet smell of the bubble-bath soap on Chloe's skin. They lay side by side for a few minutes, quietly talking about preschool.

Chloe turned to Sukie. "Sally's hungry."

Sukie yawned and stretched. No more lounging in bed. "Okay, we'll get up and have breakfast." Chloe jumped off the bed, and Sukie grabbed her robe.

After breakfast and getting Chloe dressed, Sukie pulled on a pair of jeans, a white tank top, and a crisp white shirt. Chloe lay on the bed, watching her.

"Wait!" Chloe ran over to the closet and pulled out a pair of strappy red heels. "Here."

Sukie laughed, amused Chloe seemed to be into fashion already. "Thanks, but these brown sandals will do."

They left the house and headed to World Foods.

Sukie walked through the entrance of the market, pushing Chloe in a cart. Debbi Warren looked up from the fresh fruit and wiggled her fingers in greeting. Giving Chloe a meaningful look, Debbi's eyebrows lifted. She came right over to Sukie. "Emily's been trying to reach Chloe's father for some time. She's hoping for more babysitting jobs for him. I didn't know you'd gone into the babysitting business, too. I must say, Sukie, you're very ambitious—working at the library and now this."

Words tumbled in her brain and got stuck in her throat.

"Wanna go faster!" Chloe swayed in her seat, rocking the cart.

Sukie pasted a bright smile on her face for Debbi's benefit and patted Chloe on the head. "I guess I'd better keep moving."

At home, Sukie settled Chloe at the kitchen table with new crayons and a coloring book and put away the groceries. She'd planned a special dinner for Cam—filets of beef, grilled asparagus marinated in a soy-garlic dressing, fresh sliced tomatoes, and a gooey chocolate dessert she thought he'd like.

The phone rang. Sukie eagerly picked it up, hoping it was Cam.

"Hi, Mom!" Elizabeth said.

"Elizabeth! What a nice surprise! How are you?"

"Not too good. I need to know what's going on. Dad called me this morning and I just got off the phone with Rob. Is it true? Are you seeing some guy a whole lot younger, someone who has a three-year-old? Dad was furious. Rob didn't sound too happy about it, either. He says the whole town is talking about you and who Dad called your young stud."

Sukie's entire body felt like it had been flash frozen. Her own children were becoming sucked into the idea that what she was doing was somehow wrong. This, after what Ted had done to her. Tears stung Sukie's eyes.

"Mom?"

"What?"

"It's just that Dad is really upset. He's afraid all this talk is part of the reason he's being reassigned to the branch bank in the new development north of town. It's a demotion of sorts."

"Whaaat?! He didn't mention anything about his job to me."

"It seems he's known about it for a while. He told me it might affect my tuition payments, that you might have to sell the house and move to something smaller."

The headache Sukie had tried to fight off earlier pounded behind her eyes with renewed force. Ted wanted her to sell the house, yet he was looking into a new lake house for himself. Resolve stiffened Sukie. She'd spent years sacrificing her own comfort, sometimes her own happiness, to keep her family content. No more.

She spoke in as calm a voice as she could muster. "Money for your tuition was set aside a long time ago, Elizabeth. You remind him of that, will you? And remind yourself and your brother that I wouldn't do anything to make you ashamed of me. Got it?"

"Geez, Mom . . ."

Her body trembling with outrage, Sukie hung up the phone. She and Elizabeth never fought. What next?

Chloe patted her legs. "Is Sukie sad?"

Sukie tried to smile and decided the hell with it. Tears streamed down her cheeks. "Yes, Sukie is sad."

Chloe held up her arms. Sukie picked her up and hugged her, grateful for the comforting arms the sweet little girl placed around her neck. She'd been raised to care what others thought and said about her and to behave in such a way that nobody could find fault with her. Now, apparently, except to the women in Fat Fridays, she was a big loser.

Sukie set Chloe down and led her outside. The fresh air might do them both good. Sukie pulled a big rubber ball out of the storage bench beside the patio and tossed it on the lawn. Chloe squealed gleefully and ran after it.

Sukie was playing a running game of ball in the backyard with Chloe when Cam appeared. Chloe shrieked with delight and raced over to him. He smiled at Sukie as he picked up Chloe, then walked over and gave Sukie a kiss. His damp hair hung in a curl over his forehead, exuding the essence of his spice-scented shampoo.

Sukie inhaled the scent of him and smiled. "You look much more rested."

He grinned. "Thanks for babysitting Chloe. You should do this more often."

Her nerves on edge from all she'd been through that morning, Sukie tensed. "You're asking me to be your babysitter?"

He shrugged. "A babysitter with benefits. Right?"

Sukie's jaw dropped. My God! It was all too real.

"What's the matter?" Cam shot her a puzzled look.

"I can't do this anymore. Whatever I thought we had together has . . ." Nausea made her stop. "Sorry, Cam. I'll get Chloe's things and you can go."

"What in the hell are you talking about? Did I say something wrong?"

Heartbroken, Sukie turned back to him. "This whole thing with us is wrong. Everyone thinks I'm a fool, and they're right. I can't pop in and out of your bed and have it mean nothing more than being your babysitter with benefits. I'm not made that way."

"What? You know how I feel about you . . ."

Sukie cut him off, seeing the situation in a whole different light. "I'm afraid I do." Her voice broke. Everything she thought was true was turning out to be a lie. Ted was trying to go back on his word and Cam couldn't give her any promises, and at this point, Sukie didn't trust herself to make decent decisions regarding him or anybody else.

"I'll get Chloe's things and meet you at your car." Sukie fled into the house, gathered Chloe's belongings together, and marched out to Cam's SUV. "Here."

"What in the hell is the matter with you?" Cam asked, strapping Chloe into her car seat. He straightened and faced her. "If you're telling me it's over, fine. It's over. I don't come begging, Sukie."

Sukie shook her head. "I can't do it. My children, my ex, the women in the neighborhood, they all think I'm a fool. You, yourself, called me a babysitter with benefits. How stupid of me not to see it that way before."

Cam's eyes widened. "Is that what you think, Sukie?"

"I don't know what to think anymore," she said, miserable.

Cam got into the car without saying another word. He backed the car out of the driveway and took off down the road. The roar of his engine let Sukie know just how angry he was.

She went inside, packaged up the steaks, and put them in the freezer. Her head aching, she lay down on the couch in the den, wondering how she could have been so foolish. The phone rang, but she refused to answer it.

Much later, Sukie awoke to the sound of her neighbor mowing his lawn. The heat of the day was gone. Sleepy-eyed, she got to her feet and wandered into the kitchen. The message light on her phone was blinking. She studied it for several moments before retrieving them. Julie had called from the library to say that Monday's last two computer classes had been canceled, Elizabeth had called to say she was sorry, and Carol Ann had left a message about the gorgeous condo John was renting and invited her to stop by to see it.

Sukie grabbed the chocolate candy bar she'd hidden behind the vinegar in the cupboard and went back to the den. She wanted nothing to do with anybody else until her feelings were squared away. As if they ever would be.

CHAPTER TWENTY-EIGHT
SUKIE

When Sukie arrived at the library, a Friends of the Library regular Monday meeting was already in progress. Julie waved her over and asked her to give them an impromptu report on her activities. Sukie was kept busy from then on, until she dragged herself out of the library at five-thirty. The pace continued that way for the entire week, one activity after another. She even skipped a Fat Fridays luncheon to cover for Julie at a Friends awards luncheon while Julie made a speech at the Rotary Club. Sukie carried out all her duties in a state of numbness over what she'd lost with Cam.

Betsy called her that night. "Sukie? Are you all right? We missed you at Fat Fridays."

"Yes . . . no . . . I will be," Sukie answered, forcing an upbeat note to her voice.

"Wanna join Karen and me for dinner? We're going to Peppino's, the new Italian restaurant over in Meridon. I hear it's good."

"Thanks, but I'm going to stay right here." The house was once more becoming her safe haven.

"Sukie Skidmore, you're not going to go back to square one, are you?" Betsy's voice became stern. "I've heard rumors that Cam is taking someone else out for dinner tonight. Is that what this is all about?"

Sukie's knees buckled. She found a chair and sank into it. "He's dating someone? Who is it?"

Betsy let out a sigh. "I wasn't supposed to tell you, but here goes. I'd rather you hear it from me. It's one of the IT consultants on his team. Her name is Marilyn Embers. She's not nearly as pretty as you are and, between you and me, aside from IT stuff, she doesn't appear to be too bright. None of us knows what he sees in her."

The thought of Cam dating someone else was like a stab to Sukie's heart. She took a deep, painful breath.

"I'm sorry, Sukie. I really am. It could be just a business thing . . ."

"I don't think so, but thanks for trying to make me feel better. Have fun with Karen."

"Sukie, I'm not going to let you hide inside your house for long."

"I know. I just need a little more time."

Tears stung Sukie's eyes as she hung up. How could she have been so wrong about Cam?

Sukie woke up Saturday morning determined to make peace with Elizabeth. She'd tried to phone her earlier in the week, but Elizabeth hadn't returned the call. Sukie hated conflict, and fighting with her children had made her stomach a burning fire.

Needing some sort of settlement, she dialed Elizabeth's number. "Elizabeth?"

"Mom? I'm sorry, I can't talk. I'm on my way out. I'll be late for my special Saturday class."

Disappointed, Sukie hung up, and reached for an antacid pill. Still in her pajamas, she poured herself a cup of coffee and stood staring out at the garden through the French doors of her kitchen. Gray clouds scudded across the May sky, playing hide and seek with the sun. Rain was sure to follow. She decided to go to a matinee to see a thriller movie to vent her frustration. Or maybe she'd choose a sappy romantic story where she could cry as much as she wanted. She searched the paper. *Love Always* was a highly rated romantic tearjerker—exactly what she needed to get the last of Cam out of her system.

That afternoon, Sukie sat in the dark interior of the theater caught up in the love triangle being played out on the screen, letting her emotions play along, sobbing long after others had stopped. When the lights came on in the theater, Sukie wiped away the last of her tears and headed out the door.

Outside, she'd almost reached her car when a voice called out to her. "Sukie! Sukie Skidmore!"

Mary Anderson hurried toward her, smiling. "Hi! I thought that was you."

Sukie worked to put a smile on her face. She hadn't seen Mary since that fabulous dinner in Atlanta, on her first date with Cam. "What are you doing in town?"

Mary gave Sukie an affectionate peck on the cheek. "Bob is here working on another special project for MacTel with Cam and his team. I came along for the ride and needed to kill some time on my own. I'd love it if you and Cam could join us for dinner tonight."

Sukie bowed her head and struggled to maintain an air of calm. Taking a deep breath, she faced Mary boldly. "Cam and I aren't seeing each other anymore."

Mary's eyebrows rose with surprise. "Really? You two seemed so happy together. I'm so sorry. Take care, Sukie." She gave Sukie a quick hug and left.

Sukie returned home emotionally drained. Crying about someone else hadn't cured the tears she still felt inside over Cam. She slid a frozen dinner in the microwave, ignored a phone message from Ted, and resigned herself to another lonely evening.

The sound of the doorbell brought Sukie to her feet. She tensed. If Ted wanted to do battle with her, he'd chosen a bad moment. Sukie was ready to scrape every dyed hair off his head for everything he'd put her through.

She cautiously walked to the door and peered through the peephole. Betsy, Karen, and Lynn stood outside. Pink balloons bobbed in Betsy's hand.

Sukie grinned and threw open the door, so relieved to see her friends, she wanted to sob.

Betsy beamed at her. "The others will be here soon, but we wanted to give you fair warning. We're going to party!"

Sukie threw her arm around Betsy. "Come on in! I sure could use one."

Betsy handed Sukie the balloons. "Great! I didn't think you'd mind all of us barging in on you."

"Mind it? I love it!" The Fat Fridays group was exactly what she needed.

Tiffany drove up in her SUV. Carol Ann's Probe pulled into Sukie's driveway. They gathered on Sukie's front porch, chatting among themselves, and then went inside. Holding the festive balloons, Sukie led them into the kitchen. Karen, Tiffany, and Lynn set paper bags down on the kitchen counter.

"We've ordered pizza for later." Betsy pulled a bottle of red wine out of Karen's bag and held up a container of juice. "The lemonade is for Tiffany."

"Good thing Beau is away at a golf tournament with his father or I never would have been able to make it," Tiffany said. "What's going on, Sukie? You'll have to tell us everything."

"Let's see what we've got to eat." Lynn lifted a large bowl of salad out of one of the bags. "This is the only healthy thing we brought."

"Mmmm, chocolate-chip cookies," Tiffany said, looking into another bag. "Maybe I'll allow myself to have one."

Betsy frowned. "One? How about two? Here, hand two to me. I'll break them in half. There. Remember, a broken cookie is half the calories."

They all laughed.

Sukie's spirits lifted as she set out plates and bowls for the cheese and crackers, pretzels, cookies, and chips and salsa they'd brought with them.

"Looks good," said Lynn, eying the food. "It's what I call going on a junket."

Sukie smiled at Lynn's play on words, amazed by Lynn's resilience in the face of the constant fear under which she lived. Seeing her friends gathered in the kitchen to cheer her up, Sukie went to each one and hugged her close.

The evening was still warm. Twilight had yet to fill the sky. They carried food and drinks out to the patio, pulled chairs into a circle around the table and sat like chattering teens at a hen party.

Carol Ann waved her hand in the air to catch everyone's attention. "Sukie, you weren't at lunch to hear about my date with John last weekend." She gave Sukie a triumphant look. "I think he's *the one*. His condo is beautiful and he says he wants me to think about moving in with him. He knows I'm saving money for a house but says we could get a good deal on this condo. A doctor bought it for an investment but wants out."

Betsy and Sukie exchanged worried glances.

"Isn't he moving awfully fast?" Sukie said.

Carol Ann's cheeks turned a pretty shade of pink. She clasped her hands together, joyfully. "He says he loves me. Really loves me."

At the suddenness of Carol Ann's plans with someone who'd once hit her, Sukie wasn't sure what to say. But then she'd already proved to herself and everyone else that she had no ability to judge men.

At the silence in the group, Carol Ann's brows formed a V. "Why can't y'all be happy for me? This is what I've wanted all my life."

"Things aren't always what they seem," said Lynn. "There are a lot of bastards out there. Believe me, I know all about them. If it weren't for all of you looking out for me, I would have moved. I've never been able to stay in one place too long."

"No word, no inkling of trouble?" Betsy said.

Lynn shook her head. "Not yet. The minute I hear or feel like he's near, y'all be the first to know. You and the sheriff."

Sukie hid a shiver. The fear of Lynn's ex showing up haunted them all. Just yesterday, a man, a stranger to her, had stared at Sukie as she got out of her car at the grocery store. Her heart froze to a stop. It wasn't until another woman got into a truck with him and drove away that Sukie was able to take a calming breath.

She turned to Betsy. "Did you and Karen have a good time in New York?"

Betsy grinned. "It was great. Karen won the trip as part of a radio promotion by the local smooth jazz station. It included everything—our hotel room, meals, a tour through Radio City Music Hall, and tickets to a show." She glanced at Karen, her expression soft with fondness. "We had such a special time together."

Sukie observed the affection between Betsy and Karen and smiled.

Carol Ann wagged a teasing finger at Betsy. "I saw the way you smiled at Karen, Betsy. Better be careful! People might start to talk."

Betsy's cheeks turned white, then bright red.

Karen looked down.

Sukie sucked in her breath and waited for Betsy to say something. As far as she knew, Betsy hadn't mentioned a word to the others about her relationship with Karen.

"Omigod!" Carol Ann's eyes rounded. "You two?"

"Don't look so worried," Tiffany said to Betsy. She smiled at the two of them. "If you two are happy together, it's more than most couples have." She turned to Carol Ann. "Stop acting so shocked. Who are you to judge?"

"Who are you to act so high and mighty?" Carol Ann shot back. "You've got it all—a rich husband, his famous family, fancy cars, a big diamond, everything."

"It might not be everything," Sukie interjected, hoping to stop a fight before it got nasty.

"What do you mean by that?" Carol Ann glared at Sukie.

All eyes turned to Sukie. She glanced at Tiffany.

"What she means," Tiffany said, "is that I live with a man I've grown to despise. He and his family dictate how I'm going to live, what I should look like, everything. They even want me to continue to dye my hair blond so I'll fit into their all-American image. The one thing they haven't made me do yet is quit my job. That'll happen when the baby is born, so they're not pushing it. Then I'm to be given enough time to recover from this baby girl so I can make a boy for them." Tiffany's lips trembled.

Total quiet descended.

"That's called abuse." Lynn's lips twisted into a grimace. "It don't have to be physical, ya know. If he controls your movements, calls you stupid and other names, and tells you what you can and cannot do, it's abuse. Sound familiar, Tiffany?"

Tiffany's eyes filled. She nodded. "That's exactly what it's like. His mother and father are part of it, too. I'd never even be here with y'all if Beau wasn't away."

As if on cue, Tiffany's cell phone rang. She glanced at it. "It's him."

"Better get it." Lynn's voice held urgency. "Keep his suspicions at bay. We'll all be quiet."

Tiffany rose and walked away from the group, phone to her ear.

"I had no idea," Carol Ann whispered. "Did you, Sukie?"

Sukie nodded. "Some. It's not good, especially when it's all said and done in a smooth, sophisticated way. Strangers wouldn't suspect it's so bad. Image is everything to the family and Tiffany has been told she's not to let anyone else know anything about the family situation."

"We have to be there for her, help her in any way we can." Betsy studied each one of them in turn. "Right?"

"I'm there," Sukie said.

"Me too." Carol Ann looked sheepish.

"You bet your ass." Lynn flexed her fingers as if she wanted to punch someone out. Studying the ferocious look on her face, Sukie suspected Lynn could do just that. It gave Sukie some comfort to know Lynn was so strong.

"I had a friend in the same kind of situation," said Karen. "We have to be very careful not to make circumstances worse for her than they already are."

Tiffany returned to the circle. "Beau doesn't know I'm here. I told him I was sitting outside on the patio at home which is why I didn't hear the home phone ring. But I can't stay too late."

Betsy checked her watch. "Well, let's make the time count. Our pizza should be here soon."

"So, Sukie, are you going to tell us about you and Cam?" Carol Ann asked.

It seemed like a good time to get it all out in the open. Sukie held nothing back. She told them how her children had reacted to the relationship, Ted's objections, the gossip she'd overheard from women in the neighborhood, her encounter with Debbi, and Edythe Aynsley's threats to her job.

"The final blow was when Cam referred to me as a babysitter with benefits. That really hurt. So I've ended it. It just seemed like the sensible thing to do." Sukie's stomach knotted at the memory of his car roaring down the street, away from her.

"Whoa," said Tiffany. "Don't you think you might have made a mistake? Cam was teasing about the babysitter bit, wasn't he?"

"I don't think so. He's eight years younger than I am . . ."

"Pooh!" said Karen. "Age means nothing when you reach a certain point. You started having children early and he's a little late. So what?"

"There's got to be more than that going on with you," said Betsy.

Sukie reached inside for some deeper answers. "I guess the real issue is that I can't believe he'd want me when he could have his pick of anyone. And my children are upset by the idea, more so than I would've guessed. I can't do anything to destroy my relationship with them."

"I know what you mean," Betsy commiserated. "Richie moved in with me for a few days while he and Sarah were fighting, but he couldn't wait to leave when I finally told him about Karen and me."

Karen shook her head. "I tried to tell her not to discuss it with him, not while he had so many problems of his own to work out."

"Richie took it all wrong, told me I'd destroyed the memory of his father and that he wasn't sure he could ever forgive me." Betsy took a tissue from her pocket and wiped her eyes. "I'm sorry, Sukie. Here we are, come together to cheer you up, and we've all ended up crying or coming close to it."

Sukie took hold of Betsy's hand. "Isn't that what friends are for? Sharing laughter and tears?" She turned to the others. "We have to stay together and be strong. For each one of us. Right?"

The other women nodded.

Betsy put away her tissue and gave them a devilish grin. "Strong? It reminds me of a quote from Judith Viorst. 'Strength is the capacity to break a chocolate bar into four pieces with your bare hands—and then eat just one of the pieces.'"

Laughter spilled out over the patio. Sukie passed the chocolate-chip cookies.

The doorbell rang and Sukie left to get the pizza. Tiffany joined her.

"I'm glad I have you alone for a minute," Tiffany said. "Beau wondered if you could come to dinner tomorrow. His father is going to take us out and he wanted you to join us. Muffy is away again."

Sukie's lips parted in surprise. "You're kidding. Why would he want me to come? To fill in for Her Highness while she's away? I don't think so. Besides, I've already promised Rob and Madeleine I'd have dinner with them."

Tiffany looked miserable. "I told him I didn't think you could do it, but Beau made me promise to ask you. I think his father likes you."

Sukie took a deep breath. She wanted to help Tiffany, but there was no way she wanted to be more involved with Beau's family. Sukie placed a hand on Tiffany's shoulder. "Call me or come here anytime you want. Any of us would be glad to help you."

Tiffany nodded. "I know. I don't know what I'd do without you and our Fat Fridays group."

Sukie's mind lingered on that thought as she and Tiffany worked in the kitchen and prepared to call the others inside. Fat Fridays, which had begun as a way to celebrate the end of the workweek, had become so much more than that. The women had formed a real support group for each other. Though they were of different ages and backgrounds, each of them would do whatever was necessary to help the others.

It was good their relationships had deepened to this extent, thought Sukie. She had the uneasy feeling more heartache lay ahead.

CHAPTER TWENTY-NINE
CAROL ANN

Carol Ann left the party at Sukie's and made her way home. Pulling up to her parent's small, run-down house, she parked in the driveway and studied it with dismay. If everything worked out the way she hoped, she'd soon be out of there.

Fisting her hands, Carol Ann vowed not to give up on her dreams. She'd prove to the women in Fat Fridays she was no moron, that she could move forward with her life with a man who loved her. Frustration gnawed at her. The other women sometimes treated her as if she were a baby. But she wasn't one. Not anymore.

She hadn't told the other women about the way John talked dirty to her or the way he liked to make love—fast and furious. Even now, just thinking of it, her pulse raced. He was the first guy who'd ever told her that he loved her. She'd been even more flattered when he told her that he wanted to live together.

A sense of pride filled her. John was ambitious and wanted nice things. Like her. He'd told Carol Ann that he had everything planned out. They'd use her money for a down payment on the condo. In a few years, they'd sell the condo and move up to a house like Sukie's. Maybe someday they'd even join the country club and play tennis and golf. Carol Ann could hardly wait. It would be a far cry from the life of her parents.

Longing for the day when she could leave, Carol Ann went inside the house and tiptoed past the living room, hoping to get to her room without anyone hearing her. She'd just reached her bedroom door when her mother appeared in the hallway.

"That you, Carol Ann? You be quiet now, hear?"

Carol Ann clenched her jaw and bit back a nasty remark. Her Daddy had taken a stick to her when she'd sassed her mother as a child. Carol Ann had never forgotten the sting of it. She sighed. She was still that child to them. Nothing in their house ever changed. She couldn't even make it safely to her room without having her mother spy on her.

Though she wanted to slam the door in her mother's face, Carol Ann said softly, "Good night, Mama."

CHAPTER THIRTY
LYNN

"Good-bye. Thanks for the ride."

Hoping to appear nonchalant, Lynn climbed out of Betsy's car and glanced around, searching for the figure that haunted her dreams. It seemed so unfair to be forced to live life this way. Her ex should have been jailed for years and years for all he'd tried to do to her child, her body, her soul.

"Go ahead inside, Lynn. We'll wait for your signal before we leave." Betsy waved Lynn toward the door.

Lynn lifted her hand in farewell, stole another quick glance around her, and hurried inside the apartment building. She'd purposely chosen an apartment on the third floor, thinking it would give her more options to escape should she spy the bastard she'd like to see dead.

She stood inside her small apartment, keeping the door behind her unlocked until she had a sense that she was alone. Then locking the door, she crossed the living room and turned on the light next to the couch. She flicked it on and off several times to let the other women know she was safe inside.

Taking off her clothes, she wondered at the size of them, remembering when she'd been young and thin and happy, thinking she could build a better life than she'd known growing up in her small hometown in Iowa. Vain, her mother had called her. Glancing at herself in the mirror and turning away, Lynn knew she had no real reason to be vain any longer. She looked older than her years. Heartache had changed her face into a duplicate of her mother's—lined and hollowed out by the life she seemed unable to escape.

"Men," she uttered with disgust. Her father hadn't threatened to kill the family but he'd destroyed it anyway, with his drinking.

Sighing for what she couldn't change, Lynn put on her nightgown and slid into bed. From the bedside table, she picked up the photograph of a young girl with dark curls and sparkling brown eyes.

Lynn's eyes filled as she stared at the picture. She pressed her lips to the glass.

"Someday, baby girl, Momma is going to see you again."

CHAPTER THIRTY-ONE
BETSY

Betsy pulled into her driveway, pushed the button on the garage-door opener, and drove the car inside the garage. She sometimes felt as if she and Karen were playing parts in a mystery television series. To keep her affair with Karen quiet, they'd ended up sneaking around like international spies, entering and exiting her home, cloaked in secrecy, hoping no one would see them.

The garage door closed behind them. Karen opened the car door and climbed out. Betsy followed suit, and they went inside.

Lingering in the kitchen, Karen turned to her. "So how do you think it went, Betsy? The women in the Fat Fridays group seemed to accept us."

A sense of pride filled Betsy. "Sukie thought everyone would be fine with it. I'm so glad they were."

"Me too." Karen threw her arm around Betsy's shoulder. "It's a good group."

Betsy nodded. "I wish Sarah and Richie would feel the same way about us. What am I going to do if Richie doesn't come around?" Her eyes filled.

Karen gave her a steady look, then drew her close. "I don't know about Sarah, but Betsy, Richie is your son. I think he'll come around."

"I hope so." Betsy gazed at the woman she loved, wondering how her life could be so mixed up. "Come on. Let's get settled for the night. It's been another long day."

CHAPTER THIRTY-TWO
SUKIE

On Sunday morning, the sound of the phone jarred Sukie awake. She checked caller ID. Elizabeth. Sukie sat up and grabbed the phone. "Hello."

"Mom? I'm so sorry about what I said the other day," Elizabeth exclaimed in a rush. "You're right. You can live your life the way you want. I just don't want you to get hurt. You know?"

Relief trailed through Sukie, leaving a warm path behind. Elizabeth hated confrontation as much as she did. "It's all right, honey. It's over. I've decided not to see Cam anymore." Her voice caught on the last sentence.

"Damn. He hurt you, didn't he?"

Sukie worked hard to downplay the pain she still felt. "I guess I was just a diversion for him. He's fairly new in town . . ."

"Oh, Mom, I'm so sorry. Is there something I can do? I wish I could come home for a few days, be there for you."

At the concern she heard in her daughter's voice, her whole body softened. "That's sweet, Elizabeth, but I'll be all right."

"Mom? I spoke to Dad and told him I knew the money for my tuition had already been set aside. He got really mad, but I wanted him to know he couldn't hide that from me. He said it didn't change things between you and him and he was going to talk to you about selling the house. Maybe I can help by getting a full scholarship for next year. I'm going to look into it."

Working hard to keep from drawing Elizabeth into the battle between her and Ted, Sukie ground her teeth together. It was their fight—not Elizabeth's. And Sukie intended to fight tough.

"Mom? I've gotta go. I love you."

"I love you, too, Elizabeth." Sukie hung up, proud of the strong young woman she'd raised.

Later in the day Sukie headed over to Rob and Madeleine's house. It was a small, attractive brick ranch, much nicer than the first place she and Ted had owned when they'd started out. Madeleine had a flair for taking something simple, like a set of pillows, and dressing up a hand-me-down leather couch. Because of her, their first house was a real home.

Sukie loved her son. Almost twenty-five, Rob hoped to rise to partner in the large accounting firm where he worked. Though he looked a lot like his father, with the same hazel eyes, Rob's curly brown hair came from her. Sukie liked to think Rob's personality came from her, too—he'd turned out to be a nice, generous, thoughtful man.

Sukie greeted Rob and Madeleine with heartfelt hugs and eagerly followed Madeleine upstairs to the baby's room. Charming hand-painted nursery-rhyme characters populated a yellow banner bordering the pale blue walls. A white wicker chest and white spindle crib sat waiting for the tiny baby Sukie and everyone else couldn't wait to meet.

"It's adorable." Gazing at the rocking chair, Sukie anticipated the day when she could finally hold her grandchild in her arms. "How many weeks left?"

Madeleine rubbed her bulging stomach. "The doctor thinks about six. I'm ready now, but he won't induce labor unless it's necessary."

Sukie smiled affectionately at her. She turned to go, but Madeleine pulled her back.

"I'm sorry about you and Cameron Taylor. You sounded so happy when you began dating him. Ted is the one who got Rob riled up. It was really rotten of him to try to blame his job change on that sort of gossip."

"What are you two talking about?" Rob said, joining them.

"Ted's new position," Madeleine answered.

Rob frowned. "When Citizens' Fidelity and Trust bought out Williston Savings and Loan, Dad thought he'd naturally be made president of the new bank. Then Simon Prescott from Citizens' interviewed him and mentioned he'd met you through the library. Soon after, it was announced that Dad was to be transferred to the boonies to 'help them achieve their growth objectives.' He's convinced he would've gotten the job of president if word wasn't going around town about you dating a much younger man."

Sukie's nostrils flared with frustration. "Doesn't your father understand that it was his own behavior that tipped the scales against him?"

"Ted's drinking could also have contributed to the decision," added Madeleine.

Rob studied Sukie. "What happened to the two of you? Dad went crazy and so did you. I don't know what to think about any of it."

"If it will make you feel any better, I'm not dating Cam anymore." Still hurting, Sukie swallowed hard.

"Sukie, you should be able to date anyone you want," Madeleine said with conviction. "You can't let narrow-minded people make that decision for you."

"Right now, I'm worried about finances. Ted is trying to weasel his way out of paying Elizabeth's tuition. He's been telling her I'm going to have to sell the house."

Madeleine snorted. "It's Emmy Lou. She wants a new house on the lake, a new car, and everything in the world for that baby. She's furious you wouldn't give her the cradle and we got it instead."

Sukie's pulse bubbled at the news. Emmy Lou was such a greedy witch.

"I don't think Dad is all that happy with her," Rob said. "He sure doesn't act that way."

Sukie didn't really care if Ted Skidmore was happy or not. He'd ruined any chance of sympathy from her. Downstairs, she helped Madeleine put the meal together—pot roast and vegetables done the old-fashioned way in a Dutch oven.

Watching her son attack his food at dinner, Sukie said, "I'm going to make casseroles for you to freeze for when the baby comes."

Rob's eyes lit up. "How about some of your lemon chicken casserole?"

Pleased, Sukie grinned. By the time she left that evening, Sukie felt in sync with Rob once more. Madeleine, bless her heart, would always stand by her.

Driving by the mailbox at the end of her driveway, Sukie remembered she hadn't picked up the mail from Saturday. She parked the car in the garage and walked down to the mailbox, pausing to study the stars sparkling in the ebony sky. Somehow she'd work things out with Ted, but selling the house at this stage of the game was not going to be part of it.

Sukie gathered the assortment of magazines, letters, and ads from the mailbox. A folded piece of paper fell to the ground. She picked it up and tucked it in the stack of mail, her thoughts still on Ted and the house.

Sorting through the mail in the kitchen, Sukie came upon the folded paper. Thinking it was an ad for lawn services or perhaps a note from Betsy, she opened it and staggered back.

"BITCH!" in shocking, bold letters marched across the page.

Sukie's stomach knotted like a tightened fist. Was it some kind of sick joke? Her jaw tightened. Had Ted gone completely off his rocker? Was he now resorting to this juvenile kind of retaliation? Her heart pumping overtime, Sukie held on to the edge of the kitchen counter. She punched in Ted's cell number and tapped her foot impatiently, waiting for him to pick up.

"Yeah?"

All the fury Sukie felt over his shenanigans came pouring out of her. "What are you trying to prove, Ted? How could you leave me a slimy note like that?"

"What in the hell are you talking about?"

"The note in the mailbox, the one with the word *bitch* scrawled on it. Are you that mad? That childish?"

"Whoa! You've got the wrong guy," he snapped. "Stop blaming me for things I haven't done. You know what, Sukie? That note says it all."

Sukie was too stunned to form words. If not Ted, then who else could hate her enough to leave a note like that?

"Good night," she managed to say and hung up.

Thinking of Lynn, she quickly phoned her. "Are you all right?"

"Yeah, what's happening? Did you see someone lurking around, someone suspicious?"

"No, nothing like that, just an ugly note in my mailbox. I thought it was Ted, but he said it wasn't."

"Do you think you should call the sheriff?"

"No, it's probably the kids in the neighborhood. They've been acting up lately. Glad you're fine. Talk to you tomorrow."

Still upset, Sukie checked the locks on all the doors and sank into a kitchen chair, racking her brain for clues as to who might have left the note for her. Cam wasn't that kind of person. Certainly Edythe Aynsley wouldn't do anything so common. But someone had. Who?

Sukie left a kitchen light on and made her way upstairs, trying to convince herself that it was nothing more than a prank. A nasty one at that.

Julie greeted Sukie with a smile when she arrived at the library. "Some of the books you ordered arrived early this morning."

"Great." In addition to some of the old classics, she'd ordered some popular contemporary picture books. She sat at her desk and pulled out the preliminary report she'd written on Friday to present to the board of directors today.

The phone rang as Sukie finished editing the report. "Sukie? It's Tiffany. I have to talk to you. I got into a big fight with my mother-in-law last night and I'm scared."

"Scared? Why? Did she threaten you?"

"Not exactly. I told her to stop trying to control me. I said I was going to work as long as I could and I was going to continue to see my friends. She doesn't like you, Sukie, or any of my friends. She said the Fat Fridays group was full of misfits. And, Sukie, she had all of you investigated by someone on Regard's staff."

"Whaaaat? What right does she have to do that?" Sukie could well imagine the dirty kind of details any investigation like that could dig up. And would it jeopardize Lynn?

"I'm sorry." Tiffany's voice ended in a sob. "They're hateful people. I won't drag you into my life any longer. I'll resign from Fat Fridays."

"Resign? No. You. Won't." No one, not even Muffy Wright, was going to destroy the group Sukie had come to love. "You've got to make a stand, Tiffany. We'll all help in any way we can."

Tiffany sniffled. "Thanks. I was hoping you'd say that. Uh-oh! My boss just walked in the door. Gotta go."

Sukie sat at her desk, outraged.

Julie dropped off a load of the new books on Sukie's desk. "Anything wrong?"

Sukie shook her head. She needed time to digest what Tiffany had told her. She had nothing to hide, but the others might not feel so comfortable. Especially Lynn. And Betsy hadn't come out to the community yet.

Still stewing about the situation, Sukie gathered her papers and headed into the conference room for the board meeting. If good fortune were with her, Edythe Aynsley wouldn't be there. No such luck. Edythe's strident voice could be heard all the way down the hallway.

Sukie took a seat at the conference table next to Julie, acknowledging smiles from everyone but Edythe, who managed to avoid meeting Sukie's eye. At the proper time, Sukie gave the board members a brief summary of the activities she'd overseen in the previous month, along with a financial summary of the money spent on new books. "Any questions?"

Edythe waved her fingers annoyingly. "As you are someone just temporarily filling in and without a degree in library science, I would certainly hope Julie oversaw the purchase of the books, and that you didn't encourage her to buy any books about burping dogs and the like."

Sukie's temper reared its ugly head. "I believe you mean the book about *farting* dogs."

Edythe's bright red cheeks brought Sukie some satisfaction.

"As a matter of fact," Sukie continued, amid chuckling from others in the room, "that was one of the books we considered purchasing. Although it has been requested many times, Julie and I decided to postpone buying it because so many other books are also in demand. Any more questions?"

Edythe's eyes bored into her the entire time Sukie responded to questions from members of the board. Sukie tried her best to ignore Edythe's glares but antagonism rose from her like a poisonous green mist.

After the meeting ended, and Sukie and Julie were alone in the conference room, Julie spoke quietly to her. "You've made a real enemy of Edythe. Be careful, Sukie. She wields a lot of influence in different circles."

"Edythe's never given me a chance to prove myself," Sukie said, frustrated. "After seeing me with Cam, she made up her mind to get rid of me."

"You may be right, but you need the job and I need you."

Sukie realized she'd been foolish to lose her temper, but she'd felt so bombarded by so many people's expectations lately that she'd been unable to hold back.

"Speaking of Cam," Julie said, "he's offering to give money back to the people who took his computer class and lost out on the last two classes. He says he taught everyone the basics but he'd wanted to do more. It seems he's been very busy, working weekends and traveling a lot."

Sukie wondered who was taking care of Chloe but said nothing. Chloe was no longer her concern. Come this Saturday's Nighty Night gathering, it would be a relief to know Chloe would, most likely, be absent and Sukie wouldn't have to face Cam. Still, Sukie would miss her. And though she didn't want to admit it, even to herself, Sukie would miss seeing Cam stride into the room, holding Chloe's hand.

She finished picking up discarded meeting agendas from the conference table and went to her desk, vowing to do better with Edythe. She had to keep the job. Her computer skills were shaky and she had no other training. If Ted and she were forced to go back to court, Sukie wanted to be able to prove to the judge she'd done more than sit around, doing nothing.

When she got home from work Sukie called Ted, determined to resolve the issue of housing. Ted gave her a churlish hello.

Sukie ignored his tone. "Ted, we need to talk about this house. You've been telling the kids that I'm going to have to sell it. I'm well aware of the fact you're looking into building a lake house. Judge Wright told me you talked to him about buying his boat. I don't think any judge is going to look kindly upon those facts. So, back off."

"What's happened to you, Sukie?" Ted snarled. "I didn't write that note you called me about, but I'm not surprised you got it. I have a new family to think about. Don't you get that?"

Sukie steeled herself. "What I get is that you're trying to bully me into something I don't want at this stage, all because of . . ." She stopped. This conversation was going nowhere. "I meant what I said, Ted. Any more threats of taking this house away from me and we'll go see the judge."

"You *are* a bitch!" He slammed down the phone before she could say anything else.

Sukie's body thrummed with an unspoken, angry response. *Stay strong,* she reminded herself. *Stay strong.*

CHAPTER THIRTY-THREE
SUKIE

The days and weeks flew by in a blur of projects. Now that people knew there was a children's librarian, Sukie was called upon to give talks to community groups, hold story hours for two different age groups, and perform research to broaden the inventory. Of all her duties, the Nighty Night program was her favorite. The response to the series had been outstanding and the board was enthusiastic about keeping its success going.

Sukie drove into the parking lot of Bea's Kitchen, eager to see everyone in the Fat Friday's group and receive her weekly serving of acceptance.

Betsy was already seated at a table when Sukie walked in.

Concern filled Sukie as she noted the dark circles under Betsy's eyes, the downward turn of her mouth. "How are you?"

"Richie and Sarah are back together." Betsy's lips quivered. "She made him promise not to see me until I regain common decency, as she put it. She said I'm an embarrassment to her. She's telling everyone else I've had a nervous breakdown. Richie called to say he'll pick up the last of his things from the house on Saturday while Sarah's on a shopping trip to Atlanta."

Sukie reached over and clasped Betsy's hand. "I'm sorry. That hurts."

Betsy's eyes filled. "I was afraid this might happen. I'm not saying much to anyone else, but I'm heartbroken."

Carol Ann and Lynn arrived, followed by Tiffany. They all exchanged quick embraces and settled at the table in front of their menus.

"Think I'll have the pork chop today." Lynn slapped her menu down on the tabletop with an air of finality.

Studying Tiffany surreptitiously, Sukie selected the baked chicken and waited for the other women to place their orders. Tiffany looked healthier than Sukie had ever seen her. Perhaps it was the glow of pregnancy that some women seemed to wear like a crown.

Tiffany glanced over at Sukie and smiled.

"Did anyone else get strange phone calls this week?" asked Lynn. "I got one, asking if I'd been working at MacTel for long and if I'd be interested in purchasing life insurance. I hung up right away, but something about it has been bothering me ever since. I don't think it has anything to do with Buck, but it didn't sound right."

"Oh, no!" Tiffany clapped her cheeks with her hands.

They all turned to her.

Tiffany looked as if she was about to cry. "I bet it's this whole thing with my mother-in-law." She proceeded to tell them about the investigations her mother-in-law had ordered. "I'm so sorry. I had no idea she'd gone ahead and done this."

Carol Ann looked annoyed, and Betsy, angry. Lynn wore a frightened expression that made Sukie's stomach clench.

Tiffany's eyes filled. "I told Sukie I'd be glad to leave the group, if that's what y'all want."

"No," Lynn said, commanding attention. "You mustn't let them control you like that."

Betsy took hold of Tiffany's hand. "Sweetie, you're part of us."

"It wouldn't be the same without you," added Carol Ann. "You gotta stay."

Tiffany gave them a tremulous smile. "Thank you. It means so much to me."

"I told Tiffany we'd all help her in any way we can," Sukie said, and the others nodded their agreement.

Their meals were placed before them, and the table grew quiet as they dug into the Southern home-cooked food.

"I've got a bit of good news." Happiness brightened Carol Ann's features. "John has agreed to let me have an open house at the condo on Saturday. You're all invited to come. He wants to thank everyone in the group for convincing me to try online dating."

Carol Ann gave the details of the party. "All y'all will come, won't you?"

Sukie glanced at the other women. They all nodded.

"We're agreed, then?" said Betsy. "We'll meet at the condo at eight, and if any of you want to join Karen and me for dinner ahead of time, just give me a call."

"I might just do that. I like these Saturday-night get-togethers," said Lynn with uncharacteristic enthusiasm.

As people were rising to leave, Tiffany pulled Sukie aside. "I found out why Muffy doesn't like you. The ladies at the country club told her about your date with Regard."

Annoyed, Sukie burst out, "It wasn't a date!"

"I know, but Muffy thinks it was. I'm sorry if I've made it uncomfortable for you."

Sukie sighed. "Don't worry about it. We all need to stick together."

As Sukie left the restaurant, she wondered how her life had become so complicated. The thing with Muffy Wright was silly. She had no interest in breaking up Muffy's marriage or anyone else's.

At the library, Sukie glanced through the new books she'd ordered and selected four for the upcoming Nighty Night program. The stories had to be fast-moving and allow plenty of acting out, or else she couldn't hold the attention of restless toddlers. It was a challenge, but she loved drawing the little ones into the stories, sharing the action and pictures with them.

"Hello, Sukie."

Sukie looked up from her desk to see Mary Anderson approaching. "Hello, Mary! What are you doing here?"

Mary smiled. "You told me you were the children's librarian. Bob is back in town helping Cam, so I thought I'd drop by to see you. Have a minute?"

"Sure." Sukie was happy to see her. She'd been so welcoming when they'd first met.

Mary pulled up a chair. "Bob told me not to interfere but, Sukie, I feel I have to say something. Cam needs your help."

Sukie felt the blood leave her face. "What's wrong? Omigod! Is something wrong with Chloe?"

Mary shook her head and stared at Sukie in silence.

Suspicion grew. An entirely different thought entered her mind. "I suppose he needs me to babysit, right? The same old babysitter-with-benefits routine?" The look of satisfaction on Mary's face made Sukie stop.

She clasped Sukie's hand. "Good. You still care."

"What are you talking about?"

"Cam has been miserable these past weeks and I think I know why. He won't come out and tell me everything, but I know enough to realize it's because of you. He's a stubborn man, and I doubt he'll come to talk to you on his own, but you've hurt him. For what it's worth, he told me you didn't want to see him anymore. He said you just didn't get it."

"Get it?" Sukie's nostrils flared. "A babysitter with benefits? Certainly not."

Mary had the audacity to laugh at her. "He told me that part, too. Sukie, have you no idea how difficult a time this man has had? He'd never do that to you."

"I'm too old to do this . . . this benefits thing. What I felt for him was so real, so deep." Tears came to Sukie's eyes, but she quickly brushed them away.

"He cares about you, too. That's why I'm here, though both Cam and Bob would be furious if they ever found out. Do you have it in you to call him, Sukie?"

Sukie shook her head. "It's become so much more than that. My job is in jeopardy. I can't lose it. And my children and others weren't happy about my seeing Cam. He's just starting a family and I'm about to become a grandmother. In so many respects, we're worlds apart."

Mary sat silently, continuing to study her. "I thought I knew you better than that, Sukie. I never should have come here. Enjoy that grandchild of yours. I must go."

Mary left, and Sukie put her head down on her desk, trying to hold in her tears. No matter how much she might wish things were different, they never would be.

Time alternately dragged and flew by as Sukie awaited the children's arrival for Saturday night's story time. Their excitement when they saw her dressed in a granny nightgown over her clothes was contagious. Gathering the children around her, getting them settled on comfy pillows, Sukie relaxed. She was well into a story about a pet pig saving a tightrope walker at a circus when she heard someone call her name.

"Miss Sukie!" Chloe ran toward Sukie, her arms held out. Just before Chloe reached her, she tripped on her blue nightgown and fell into Sukie's arms.

Sukie glanced up to find Cam staring at her. Without saying a word, he turned and walked away. Watching him leave, Sukie's heart pounded with dismay. Cam hadn't even cracked a smile at her or waved good-bye to Chloe.

Chloe climbed up on Sukie's lap. The other children moved restlessly, waiting for Sukie to continue. She picked up where she'd left off, trying to concentrate on the words and pictures in front of her.

As Sukie read one book, then another, she couldn't stop thinking of Cam's stern expression. Even if she might have wanted to talk to him, Sukie knew "keep away" signs when she saw them.

Every time an adult appeared to pick up a child, Sukie tensed. When only Chloe remained, she began to wonder if Cam had planned it that way. Thinking of being alone with him, her body grew cold, then hot.

"Where's Daddy?" Chloe's little voice echoed in the empty room.

"Here," came a deep voice.

Cam walked toward them, his expression grim. Without looking at Sukie, he took Chloe by the hand. "Say thank you to Miss Sukie."

Chloe stamped her foot. "I want to stay with her!"

His face darkened. "Come on, Chloe. It's time to go."

"No! Sally wants to live with Sukie. Me too!" Chloe let out a woeful wail that made Sukie want to gather her in her arms.

Sukie knelt beside her. "We'll always be special friends, Chloe. Remember that. I've got to go, too. I'll be late for my party."

"Will you come visit me?" Chloe wiped her eyes with the sleeve of her nightgown.

Sukie rose and gave Cam a helpless look.

"Maybe, someday, I can drop you off at Miss Sukie's house for a visit." Reluctance slowed his every word.

Chloe's lips curved. "Promise?"

His jaw working, Cam looked away. After a few awkward seconds, he nodded.

Chloe danced out of the room, circled back, and left again, playing in the hallway.

Moving restlessly from one foot to the other, Cam stared at Sukie.

She started to say something, then stopped, unable to trust her voice.

"I'm sorry," Cam said, and turned away.

"Cam?"

He faced Sukie and waited for her to continue.

"I . . . I wish things could have been different between us. I really do." She fought tears.

"Me too." He walked away.

Sukie wanted to run after him, beg his forgiveness, tell him what a fool she'd been. But she stayed resolutely in place, knowing it was not what he wanted. The memory of their lovemaking, their laughter, their ease with one another was like a sharp-edged knife ripping at her. Grateful no one else was there to witness her misery, Sukie took out a tissue, wiped her eyes, and blew her nose. She told herself it was for the best. Her family and coworkers would be happy it had ended. Talk about her in this small town would finally die down.

Sukie locked up the building, wishing she hadn't promised to go to Carol Ann's open house. The pieces of her broken heart were rubbing her insides raw.

CHAPTER THIRTY-FOUR

CAROL ANN

Carol Ann and John drove into the upscale complex to the condo they were about to share. The three-story condos lined the shore of the lake, providing water views from ground level decks and middle-floor balconies. Studying the brick and clapboard buildings, Carol Ann could hardly believe she might live here permanently. With its style and sense of exclusivity, it was everything she'd always wanted.

John pulled Carol Ann's car into the garage, and Carol Ann unloaded the groceries she'd bought at World Foods. Desperate for the Fat Friday ladies' approval, she wanted to make a good impression.

Inside the kitchen, Carol Ann unloaded her CD player and turned on music, so it played it softly in the background. She placed cheese on a platter, arranged crackers next to the cheese, and added green grapes for color. She stood back and gazed at them, proud of the effect. Checking her watch, she opened a can of peanuts, poured them into a plastic bowl, and slid frozen appetizers into the oven. Doing these simple preparations, she was filled with excitement. It was the first time she'd entertained friends like this.

The doorbell rang. Anxiety curled through her in nervous twists and turns as she hurried to the door. Betsy, Karen, and Lynn stood together on the doorstep.

Carol Ann ushered them inside eagerly. "Look around, y'all. I'll be right there. I'm going to open a bottle of wine."

A few moments later, the sound of the doorbell rang out again. Carol Ann excused herself from the others and answered it. "Sukie! You're just in time. I'm about to give a tour of the condo."

Once everyone had a glass of wine, Carol Ann led them downstairs to the large family room in the basement. "This level has a nice fireplace and there's a half bath down the hall." She slid open the glass sliding door and walked out onto the large wooden deck. "We have a great water view."

"Very nice," commented Betsy.

"Much larger than the apartment I'm renting," said Karen. A touch of envy coated her voice.

Carol Ann filled with pride. "Come see the upstairs. Two bedrooms, two baths, and a study are up there."

They climbed to the main floor and on up to the third level. John joined them at the top of the stairs. Carol Ann was pleased he was wearing the new shirt and pants she'd bought him. She made introductions, and he followed the group into the master bedroom. An air mattress sat on the floor opposite a TV. John had stored a couple of boxes and his clothing in the closet.

"Where's all the furniture?" Lynn asked.

Carol Ann didn't know how much to say. She and John had had an argument about it. "We haven't picked it out yet."

John turned to Sukie. "What do you think of the condo?"

Carol Ann held her breath, waiting for Sukie's answer. Of all the women in Fat Fridays, Sukie's opinion meant the most to her.

"It's attractive," Sukie said. "My ex lives here in the complex."

"John wants me to move in with him. I've saved enough money to furnish the whole place," Carol Ann said in a rush of excitement.

John gave Carol Ann a wink and she wanted to throw her arms around him. He loved her. He really did.

Sukie frowned. "I thought you were saving for a house, Carol Ann." An uneasy silence fell over the group.

John's eyebrows formed a *V* of irritation. "This is a way for Carol Ann to get out of the trap she's in. She moves in with me, gets us some furniture, we fix the place up, and then we try to buy it."

Silent disapproval radiated from every woman in the Fat Fridays group. Carol Ann shrunk inside. John had made it seem as if it was her responsibility to do everything. She was sure he didn't mean it that way and tried to think of something positive to say.

"Hello? Am I too late?" Tiffany's voice sailed up the stairs. Carol Ann breathed a sigh of relief, thankful to end the awkward moment.

Tiffany appeared at the top of the stairs, her eyes swollen and red.

"Are you okay?" Carol Ann asked.

Tiffany nodded. "I wasn't sure I'd make it, but Beau finally agreed to drop me off. He'll pick me up at ten."

"Well, now that everyone is here, let's go downstairs," Carol Ann said. "I've fixed some appetizers." She couldn't help her note of delight. For years, she'd dreamed of entertaining friends in a nice place like this.

She handed Betsy the tray of cheese and crackers, Karen, the peanuts, and she fixed a plate of mushroom appetizers for Sukie to carry in. "Let's eat in the living room," Carol Ann suggested. "We'll do it picnic style on the carpet."

"Who wants something to drink?" John asked. "We have more wine, Diet Coke, and Sprite."

Betsy held up her plastic glass. "More wine sounds good to me!"

Karen laughed. "I'll have more too."

Sukie and Lynn quickly joined them.

Tiffany sighed. "Sprite for me. Thanks."

Carol Ann slid in some CDs, mellow stuff from the saxophone player David Mandeville and others, and they sat in a circle on the rug.

John came into the room and gave them a little salute. "Well, ladies, I'll leave you to your fun and go upstairs. Baseball's more my style."

Carol Ann smiled at him. He'd turned out to be a nice host.

Tiffany took a sip of her soda and sang a few bars of the music softly. Her musical notes floated in the air.

Surprised, Carol Ann turned to her. "Wow! You've got a beautiful voice, Tiffany. Good enough for professional singing."

Tiffany smiled. "Thanks. I used to be in a glee club in high school and did some singing in college."

"You did?" said Betsy. "Will you sing for us now?"

Tiffany drew in a breath. Could she? "I don't know. I haven't sung in a while. I was asked to sing at one of the country club dances but you-know-who said '*we* do not perform in public.' I tried to make her change her mind, but I finally gave in."

They all groaned.

"You've got to be shitting me," said Lynn. "That's all the more reason to sing for us now. Right, ladies?"

A broad grin spread across Tiffany's face. She rose to her feet, grabbed an imaginary microphone, and began to sing along with the new Kristy Keene CD *For Now and Forever Mine*.

Carol Ann could see by the expressions on the other women's faces that they were as stunned as she was by Tiffany's pure, sweet voice. Even pregnant, she had a star's dramatic appearance with her long, blond hair, beautiful features, and sense of style. Watching her perform, Carol Ann thought Tiffany seemed like a totally different person, completely at ease with herself. She felt a tiny prick of envy that someone so beautiful could be so talented. It didn't seem fair. Her own singing was terrible.

Tiffany finished singing, and they all clapped enthusiastically.

Thrilled the evening was turning out so well, Carol Ann poured more drinks. She turned to Sukie. "Don't you think I ought to move in here? It's so beautiful."

Sukie shook her head. "Not until you get to know John better."

Disappointment soured Carol Ann's stomach. "But I don't want to wait. I told John I'd have to think about it, but seeing you all here, as if it really were my house, it makes me want it more than ever."

"Just be patient," said Betsy. "It's hard to wait for things to work out, I know, but most times they do. That's what I keep telling myself."

"Did Richie come by?" Sukie asked Betsy, and they turned their attention to her.

"He called at the last minute and canceled. He was afraid one of the kids would tell Sarah about seeing me. How do you like that?" Betsy's voice quivered. "It's Richie I'm most worried about. I hope he'll at least tolerate Karen. Sarah's the problem. She's worried about her so-called social status and is still sticking to the idea that I'm having a breakdown. If she turns Richie away from me permanently, I don't think I could bear it."

"Give him a chance to become used to the idea and he'll be okay," Sukie said sympathetically. "He's a lot like his mother."

Betsy's eyes filled. "Karen is even more worried about it than I am. She knows how much I love my family."

Karen's lips thinned with anger. "I'd like to really, really hurt Sarah for treating Betsy like this."

Tiffany turned to Lynn. "So how are things going with you? No more freaky calls because of my mother-in-law?"

Lynn shook her head. "It's been real quiet. Thank God."

After some time, the sound of a car horn interrupted conversation and brought Tiffany to her feet. "It's Beau. I've got to go. I can't keep him waiting. Thanks, Carol Ann! 'Bye, everyone."

She left, and the conversation turned to ways in which the women could support Tiffany. She was another one in a tough situation.

"Like I said, it's abuse, pure and simple." Lynn's cheeks became a deep red. "We've got to keep our eyes on her."

Poor Tiff, thought Carol Ann. She, at least, had John. Later, when they were alone, she'd tell him she'd move in with him for sure.

CHAPTER THIRTY-FIVE
SUKIE

As Sukie drove away from Carol Ann's party, she noticed a new Mercedes SUV sitting in Ted's driveway. She gritted her teeth. No doubt Emmy Lou had finally gotten her way with a new car. Emmy Lou wouldn't be satisfied until she got everything she could out of Ted, Sukie thought sourly.

Sukie pulled up to her house and slammed on the brakes. Cam's SUV was blocking the driveway. Pulse pounding, she parked at the curb and walked over to his car. The driver's window of his car was wide open. She peered inside.

Cam was sound asleep, head thrown back, mouth open. Chloe lay curled up in the backseat, her blanket and her doll Sally snuggled up next to her. Her small back rose and fell in peaceful sleep.

"Cam?" Sukie shook his shoulder gently.

His eyes flew open. "Wha . . . Oh, damn, I must have fallen asleep."

"What are you doing here?"

Cam ran a hand through his hair and blinked rapidly, struggling to come awake. "Can we talk?"

Sukie's heart did flips inside her chest. "How long have you been here?"

He checked his watch. "It's eleven o'clock? We got here a little before nine."

"You woke up Chloe to come here?" Chloe usually went to bed at eight.

Cam nodded.

Tears sprang to Sukie's eyes. Cam had awakened his daughter and hung around for two hours, waiting to speak to her. "Come on inside. Chloe can sleep in Elizabeth's bed while we talk."

Cam got out of the car, reached into the backseat, and lifted Chloe into his arms. She murmured in her sleep and nestled against his chest.

Sukie led the two of them inside the house and up the stairway to the second floor.

Gingerly, Cam placed Chloe atop the pink sheets on Elizabeth's bed. Sukie stood with Cam, gazing down at her. With her rosy cheeks and curly blond hair, Chloe resembled a cherub. Her mouth was pursed in sleep as if she were kissing angels.

Sukie placed a hand on Cam's arm. "Come downstairs." At the bottom of the stairs, she turned to him. "Would you like some coffee?"

"How about a drink instead?" he said. "I could really use one."

"Sure. Is everything all right?" Sukie's mind raced with possibilities.

Cam held his head in his hands. "No. Everything is not all right."

Sukie knotted her fingers. "I'm standing here imagining all kinds of horrible things. Is Chloe all right?"

His lips curved into the crooked smile she loved. "Yeah, right as can be." His blue eyes fastened on hers, sending a message Sukie couldn't deny. Her pulse sprinted. *This really was about them?* She'd refused to let herself think about that possibility, coming up with every other excuse she could think of for his sudden appearance.

Cam reached for her, and his lips found hers. They were warm and sure and demanding, letting Sukie know how much he'd missed her. Sukie's body responded in warm ripples of pleasure that quickly escalated into waves of passion. In that moment she didn't give a damn about his age or hers. When they were like this, nothing else mattered.

They finally pulled apart. Sukie gazed up into Cam's face. The lines of stress she'd noticed earlier had smoothed out. She knew exactly how he felt—as if the world was a friendly place once more.

"We need to talk," Cam said.

Sukie nodded. It was much more complicated than simply realizing how much they craved each other. She knew that.

Her thoughts spinning, she opened a bottle of wine and pulled out a couple of glasses from the cupboard. Cam poured the wine, handed her a glass, and lifted his for a toast.

"Here's to straightening out our lives."

They clinked their glasses together. That musical note hovered in the air, sending a wave of optimism through Sukie.

His expression both tender and tough, Cam studied her. "Chloe and Sally aren't the only ones who might want to live with you." He paused. "I'm not promising anything, Sukie, but I want us to be together to see if that would work. What I'm trying to say is I want you to give it another try. Will you?"

Sukie took a deep breath. Could she trust her instincts? For once, could she do something for herself without worrying about other people?

"It scares the crap out of me, this idea of something permanent." Cam gave her a steady look that spoke volumes.

She understood. She was scared, too. But he'd come to her after saying he wouldn't come begging, and in his arms she'd felt as if she'd found the home she'd always wanted. Thinking of all the challenges ahead, Sukie's mouth became dry. According to Julie, Edythe Aynsley was working hard to find a replacement for her. Ted was a problem that wouldn't go away. Her children? They'd said the right words, but the idea of any relationship with Cam bothered them. They'd have to understand she was her own woman now. Madeleine, bless her heart, already supported her.

Sukie cradled Cam's face in her hands. She kissed him tenderly on the soft skin covering his eyes, each bristly cheek, and finally his smooth lips. Cam wrapped his arms around Sukie and drew her close enough for her to hear the soft sound of pleasure in his throat as he held her tight.

She smiled at him, as certain as she'd ever been. "I'd like to try, too."

They spent the next couple of hours filling each other in on what they'd been doing during the past few weeks and how they'd coped with being apart. Sukie talked about her childhood—parts of which she'd never even shared with Ted. Cam told her more about Chloe's mother. Sukie spoke about her marriage and its increasing disappointments, not dwelling too long on it because from this moment on she wanted to think only of Cam. Cam told her how his parents had turned away from him when he decided to leave the West Coast and raise Chloe on his own.

"Would you like to stay the night?" Sukie asked, wanting him so much her body trembled.

Cam gave her the teasing smile that always made her pulse quicken. "With benefits?"

Sukie laughed. They'd already discussed the subject ad nauseam and had reached the conclusion it was a term they both hated.

Upstairs, they looked in on Chloe and went into Sukie's bedroom. Her pulse fluttered in anticipation as they tossed their clothes aside and climbed into bed.

Cam lay facing her. "I've missed you." He ran his hands down the length of Sukie's naked body and smiled at her. "Just like I remembered." He fondled her breasts, exciting the nipples, sending heat to her center in pulses that matched her racing heart.

Her hands trailed down his body until they reached his manhood. He groaned and pulled her to him. A shiver of desire swelled in Sukie and grew to a fiery passion only Cam could satisfy.

Later, they lay curled in each other's arms. Watching him sleep, Sukie smiled. All was right with her world once more.

◆ ◆ ◆

After work on Monday, still full of joy from her decision to be with Cam, Sukie pulled into her driveway, got out of the car, and dashed through raindrops to snatch the mail. She laughed out loud. Life was so good.

Inside the kitchen, sorting through the mail, Sukie was happy to see fewer bills. A crumpled piece of paper among the envelopes caught her eye. She opened it warily.

"CUNT!" was hand printed in slashing dark strokes. The world spun crazily around Sukie. She gripped the counter. Who would do this to her? She'd received two such ugly notes. Why? Who was after her?

Her heart skipped in nervous beats. Desperate to hear his reassuring voice, she called Cam at the office. The receptionist informed her he was in a meeting and couldn't be disturbed.

Sukie hung up and sank onto a kitchen chair. It was all so confusing, so terrifying. She'd let one note go, but she couldn't do the same with this one. Someone wanted to hurt her.

Sukie checked her watch and called Betsy. "I need the help of everyone in Fat Fridays. Ask the others if they'd be willing to come with you to my house after work. I need to talk to all of you about something. Something important."

"What's going on?" Betsy asked, sounding alarmed.

"We'll talk later."

Sukie took out a digital voice recorder Ted had kept in the den and put in fresh batteries. As she and the other women discussed possibilities, she'd record them so they'd have as many facts as possible before going to the authorities.

Waiting for the others to arrive, she paced the living room floor, reviewing every possibility in her mind. But none seemed to make sense to her.

The women arrived in a group at five thirty, all talking at once.

Sukie ushered them into the living room.

Carol Ann gave her a puzzled look. "What's going on? You're so serious, Sukie."

"She wouldn't tell me a thing," Betsy pouted.

Tiffany took a seat on the couch, eying Sukie curiously.

"Someone is leaving ugly messages in my mailbox. A couple of months ago, I received a note that just said "Hello." Nothing harmful, just weird. In the past several weeks I've received two more. The first one just said "Bitch." The note today says "Cunt." Sukie clutched her hands together, feeling as if someone had rubbed dirty hands all over her body. "I need your help in figuring this out." She held up the notes and handed them over to Tiffany. "Ted was furious when I suggested he sent the first nasty one, and I can't think who else it might be."

Tiffany studied the papers and passed them on to Carol Ann. "Oh my God! Who would do this? It's so freaky."

Lynn cleared her throat. "I have something to say." Her face turned white. "Sukie, I don't think those notes are for you. I think they're for me, from my ex. Buck has probably seen us together. It's his way of letting me know he's here, just waiting for the moment when he can get to me. Like I told ya, he's a sick, evil man."

Sukie heard the quiver in Lynn's deep breath and a shudder went through her. She couldn't stop herself from looking outside. The idea of Lynn's ex being on her property made her queasy.

Lynn shook her head. "I knew I should've left here, but when you all offered to band together to keep an eye on me, I thought I could stay for a while longer. Now, I have no choice. I'll leave. It's become a sick mission of his to find me. I can't let anything bad happen to you."

Sukie's heart twisted. It was such an awful scenario. She put a hand on Lynn's shoulder, keeping her in the chair. "No, don't go, Lynn. If we don't face him down together, you'll never be able to stay anywhere. We'll go to the sheriff and tell him he's on your trail, have him help us."

Lynn let out a derisive snort. "The thing is, unless Buck actually attacks or threatens me personally, what can the sheriff do? Buck knows that, which is why the notes went to you, someone he knew I was in contact with. Women are threatened like this in little ways every day but can't do anything about it. Believe me, I know."

They sat in the living room, silent, bonded together by all they'd shared in the past several months.

Sukie stood, filled with resolve. The women of Fat Fridays would stick together, now and always. "The rest of you take notes. I'm going to put together a little dinner. Let's get a basic description of Lynn's ex. I'm sure he's changed a great deal since she's seen him, but it's a start. Write down any other data that would be helpful to the sheriff. I'm going to his office first thing tomorrow morning."

"Lynn can move in with me," Betsy said. "She shouldn't be alone."

Her eyes welling, Lynn shook her head. "Thanks, but no thanks. That's exactly why I can't stay here. If you help me, you're in danger too. He thinks anyone who is a friend of mine is in on my betrayal. Look what's happened to Sukie. I'm tellin' ya, he's really screwed up."

It frightened Sukie that Lynn's ex had pulled her into the dangerous battle for Lynn's safety. But unless this monster was stopped, none of the women in Fat Fridays would be safe.

It was growing dark by the time they reviewed the notes they'd made on Lynn's ex. As they stood to leave, the women formed a circle around Lynn for a group hug.

"We're not going to give in to this maniac, Lynn," said Sukie, doing her best to hide her fear.

Tears filled Lynn's eyes. She thrust her chin out. "You're right, Sukie. I'm not leaving. I'm going to fight the bastard once and for all and then I'm going to get my daughter."

The next morning, Sukie stopped by the sheriff's office. Bill Michaels listened to the whole story and accepted the papers she handed him, including the two latest notes.

"I'll see what I can do, but without direct threats, as Lynn told you, nothing much can be done. His anger seems to be focused on all you women and you in particular Sukie. He's a man used to being able to intimidate. Maybe that's all it is. But as a personal favor, I'll have my men drive through your neighborhood on a regular basis, check up on your house and the apartment where Lynn is staying. Let me know immediately if you have anything else for me to go on." The sheriff's expression was grim. "I'll put a few feelers out, but from what you tell me, he's well acquainted with the system and doesn't want to get caught, which is why his threats to her are coming through you. He's a real slime ball."

"Thanks, Bill. I appreciate it. We're all pretty scared." Sukie had been haunted by nightmares all night. Her new life with Cam was just starting to come together; she had no wish to have her life end.

Even after visiting the sheriff, Sukie had trouble feeling safe. Her small town seemed even smaller and she felt much more vulnerable in it, with danger stalking her and the other women. At the hint of any shadow behind her, she caught herself looking over her shoulder. Her heart pounded at the sight of any male stranger coming toward her. She and Cam made a practice of setting their home security systems on whether they were in the house or not. They made sure Chloe was with one of them at all times. Patrol cars glided through her neighborhood, cruising by at odd hours of the day and night, giving her some comfort. But Sukie knew she wouldn't rest until the man who'd penned those notes was in custody. Even then, they'd all have to make sure he wasn't dismissed as merely an unhappy ex or a disgruntled neighbor.

The days continued in a tense pattern. When Cam and Chloe weren't at Sukie's house for the evening, she was with them at Cam's house. The one good thing that came from their vigil was the amount of time Sukie and Cam had to discuss the day's happenings or life in general, adding substance to their relationship. Contentment with Cam wrapped itself around Sukie, silky and warm, even as she continued to worry about Lynn and the other women.

Sukie arrived early for lunch at Anthony's. Betsy waved at her listlessly from a corner booth.

"What's the matter?" Sukie asked her, sliding into the booth opposite her.

Betsy sat slumped in her seat, looking lost. Her eyes filled. "It's Sarah. I called to speak to her about summer plans. Caitlin answered the phone. When she heard it was me, Caitlin said, 'I'm not supposed to talk to you. Mommy says you're bad.' Then she slammed the phone in my ear." Betsy reached across the table and gripped Sukie's hands. "What am I going to do? Those children mean the world to me."

Sukie's heart ached for her. "Have you talked to Richie about it?"

Betsy shook her head. "I left a message at his office, but he hasn't returned my call. I know he's busy and he's trying to save his marriage, but it isn't fair!"

Sukie didn't know what to say. After meeting Sarah at some club events, Sukie had thought her quick to find fault, to gossip, to hurt others.

"You know what Karen says?" Betsy wrung her hands. "She says we ought to get even with the bitch."

"Karen said that?" Sukie's eyebrows rose with surprise. She couldn't imagine Karen using language like that. She'd always struck Sukie as being very ladylike.

"Karen feels guilty over what's happened between me and my family. I've told her it's not her fault, but now she's sure she's ruined my life. It's all such a mess!"

"Hey, everyone! Good news!" Carol Ann waved and slid into the booth next to Sukie, all smiles, oblivious to the anxiety that surged out of Betsy in waves of despair. "Lynn and Tiffany are in the parking lot. I'll wait to spill the news until they get here."

Carol Ann smiled at Sukie. "You look terrific, Sukie. Did you do something to your hair? Change your makeup?"

"Tell you later," Sukie said happily.

Tiffany and Lynn arrived and slid in on either side of the long booth.

"Where'd all these kids come from?" grumped Lynn. "I had to circle the parking lot twice to find a space."

"Like John says, Williston is growing by leaps and bounds," said Carol Ann. "I've heard they're putting up a new restaurant over on Columbia Street. A steak house, I think."

Betsy straightened in her seat, giving them a weak smile. "Yay! A new place for Fat Fridays."

They ordered quickly—pizza, salad, and diet sodas—and chatted about the unusually hot weather.

"Okay," said Sukie, finishing off a slice of vegetarian pizza. "Anyone have any calls or see anything strange that we can report to the sheriff?"

At the shake of heads, Sukie relaxed. Another Fat Friday had gone by without any sightings, calls, or notes from Lynn's ex.

Carol Ann beamed at the members of the group. "Now that we're all together, I am pleased to announce that John and I are dating exclusively. He asked me last night, and I accepted. No more online dating, just him." She twisted a lock of hair behind her ear and smiled. "We're going furniture shopping this weekend in North Carolina. He says we can get good buys there on furniture direct from the manufacturers. I can hardly wait! It's like we're engaged or something."

Sukie couldn't hide her alarm. Things were moving too rapidly, though Sukie had to admit she shouldn't be the one to find fault. Look what'd happened so quickly between her and Cam. Still, she couldn't hold back. "Hold on! Has there been any mention of a wedding?"

"Carol Ann, I'm not sure . . ." Betsy began.

"There's something about this whole setup . . ." Lynn said at the same time.

The sound of Carol Ann's wail stopped them. "Why can't you just be happy for me?" She lowered her voice. "It's the first time in my life I have a boyfriend who's really, really serious. God knows it's hard to meet anybody decent in this town. Want to know something weird? My boss posted information about himself online with the same dating service I used. What a joke!"

Tiffany frowned. "Ed Pritchard is very nice. I like him."

"For a man, he's not bad," Lynn added, surprising them.

"Well, he's losing his hair and he's boring. I want somebody younger and handsome. Not somebody like him." Carol Ann lifted her shoulders in an exaggerated shudder.

Sukie's fingers tightened. She wanted to shake Carol Ann for being so shallow. The expressions on the other women's faces told her she wasn't the only one who felt that way.

"You've got to be sensible, Carol Ann." Betsy's outrage spoke for them all. "Listen to us. Go slowly, and for heaven's sake, don't spend the money you've been saving for a house on furniture for this guy."

"Maybe I should ask my mother-in-law who she uses for private investigations," joked Tiffany. "We could have John investigated."

"Don't you dare!" Carol Ann's loud protest worried Sukie. No matter what they said, Carol Ann wasn't about to listen to any of them.

The waitress appeared with more food, and talk quieted as she passed around the plates. They were almost finished eating when Carol Ann broke through the small talk.

"So, Sukie, what's going on?"

Sukie hesitated. After warning Carol Ann about going too fast, she wasn't sure she wanted to get into her relationship with Cam.

"I bet I know what it is." A devilish grin spread across Betsy's face. "I've seen a certain white SUV at your house the last couple of weeks."

"You're back with Cam?" Tiffany's face lit up. "That's wonderful, Sukie!"

Sukie couldn't hide her delight. "We're taking it nice and slow, learning more about each other, testing to see how daily routines work for us. I haven't discussed it with my family. I've waited to tell you until I felt comfortable with how things are developing."

"And?" Betsy arched her eyebrows.

"And it's wonderful. Each day is so much better with Cam a part of it. For once, I don't care what anybody else thinks. As Rhett Butler would say, 'Frankly, my dear, I don't give a damn.'"

"And like Scarlett, you can worry about any of that tomorrow," added Betsy, and they all laughed.

"Seriously, though," Betsy continued. "Don't you think it's time you talked to your family?"

Sukie's stomach knotted at the thought, but she knew Betsy was right.

When she got home from work, Sukie phoned Madeleine.

After saying hello, Madeleine happily announced, "The baby has dropped. The doctor said it could be any time now. I'll continue to work until I absolutely have to stop, but believe me, I'm more than ready to have this baby."

Madeleine's enthusiasm was contagious. Sukie could already envision a sweet little face and imagine holding the baby in her arms. "That's wonderful! I can't wait!" She drew a deep breath. "I called to ask you and Rob to dinner tomorrow. There are a couple of people I want you to meet. One, in particular."

"Is it who I think it is?"

Sukie heard the smile in Madeleine's voice and the tension in her shoulders loosened. "Cam and Chloe are with me every day now. We're trying to see if we really have a compatible future together."

"Oh, I'm so excited! Has he . . ."

"I'm taking it one day at a time." Sukie couldn't think too far ahead or she might be disappointed all over again.

"Good luck, Sukie! I think it's wonderful. Of course we'll come for dinner. Wild horses couldn't keep me away."

Sukie could have hugged Madeleine for her support. They chatted for a few minutes longer and Sukie hung up the phone tingling with excitement. Her grandbaby was about to make an appearance!

As Sukie finished putting together a macaroni-and-cheese casserole for Rob and Madeleine, Cam walked through the door with Chloe.

"That for dinner?" Cam asked, before leaning over and giving her a kiss.

"Not this time. We're ordering in." Sukie told him about her conversation with Madeleine.

Cam put his arm around Sukie and drew her to him. "Will I have to start calling you Meemaw?" he teased.

Sukie laughed. "Not if you want to keep living!"

"Look what I got!" Chloe handed Sukie a small paper kite she'd colored at day care.

Sukie gave Chloe a hug. "Good job. Let's hang it up for everyone to see."

Chloe watched as Sukie taped it to the front of the refrigerator. Then she patted it proudly. "Mine."

Cam and Sukie smiled at each other. It seemed so right to have it hanging there. Sukie gave Chloe another little hug. The sweet little girl had become a part of her in so many ways. How would her children feel about that?

CHAPTER THIRTY-SIX
SUKIE

Sukie waited anxiously for Rob and Madeleine to arrive for dinner. Betsy's family had been torn apart by her decision to partner with Karen. Sukie didn't want that to happen to her family.

Chloe in tow, Cam arrived early. When Chloe saw Sukie standing on the front porch, she shouted Sukie's name and came running toward her, arms outstretched.

Cam looked on, smiling, as Sukie swept the little girl up in her arms. Observing Chloe in a new pink sundress, with a pretty matching bow in her hair, Sukie's eyes misted. She kissed Cam hello. "She looks darling. Thank you."

Cam caressed Sukie's cheek affectionately. "I know how important this dinner thing is for you. Don't worry. We'll all get along. If Rob is anything like his mother, he'll understand about us." He put his arms around Sukie and gave her a comforting squeeze. She hoped he was right.

They walked out to the patio. Chloe ran ahead, onto the grass, chasing a ball. Cam and Sukie took seats at the table. Though he acted nonchalant about the evening, Sukie sensed he was nervous too. He'd slicked his blond hair back in a style that made him appear older, though his healthy, trim physique indicated a young man in his prime.

At the sound of a car pulling into the driveway, Sukie rose and glanced at Cam. He gave her a thumbs-up sign, and she went out front to greet her guests.

Sukie's heart squeezed with affection when Madeleine got out of their Jeep looking as if she'd swallowed a watermelon. Madeleine waved and moved toward Sukie in a rolling gait. Rob rushed to her side and held onto her elbow.

"Looks like we have a baby on the way," he joked.

Madeleine gave him a jab in the side. "You try this, mister, and we'll see how *you* do."

They all laughed, and Sukie gave each of them a hug. "C'mon in. We're going to have appetizers on the patio. Cam and Chloe are waiting there."

They stopped at the sight of Chloe coming around the side of the house.

"Sukie! Wait for me!" Chloe sprinted toward Sukie, her blond curls bouncing, her pink dress puffed out like a balloon. Her eyes glowing, Chloe ran into Sukie's embrace, wrapped her arms around Sukie's neck, and stared wide-eyed at Rob and Madeleine.

"I guess she couldn't wait to meet you. This is Chloe." Sukie turned to her. "Can you say hi to Mister Rob and Miss Madeleine?"

Chloe buried her face in Sukie's shoulder and peeked at them coyly.

Sukie smiled. "Oh, here's Cam now."

Cam strode toward them. His long legs stretched easily to cover ground in a hurry. Sukie walked over to meet him and they approached Rob and Madeleine together.

Her face alight with pleasure, Madeleine smiled and shook Cam's hand. "I'm *very* glad to meet you."

Cam put a protective arm around Sukie and shook hands with Rob. Chatting about the weather, the four of them moved with Chloe into the house and headed out to the patio.

In the kitchen, Madeleine caught Sukie's arm and held her back. "He's gorgeous, Sukie!" she whispered. "No wonder Ted is in such a stew about it. Have they met yet?"

Sukie shook her head. That was one meeting she wanted to avoid.

She and Madeleine went outside, where the two men stood facing each other, looking as if they were prepared to choose swords for a duel.

"So, how long are you planning to stay in town?" Rob asked Cam, sounding like a sheriff talking to an outlaw in an old western movie. It was definitely not one of Rob's friendlier moments.

Madeleine led Sukie away from them. "I don't know if this parenthood thing is getting to him, but Rob is becoming so protective of you, it's silly."

Sukie smiled. "Let them duke it out with words. Get comfortable. What would you like to drink?"

"Ice water's fine." Madeleine eased into a lounge chair and stretched her slightly swollen legs out in front of her.

Sukie poured her a glass of sparkling water, filled a plastic cup halfway with juice for Chloe, and settled her at the table with a coloring book and large round crayons.

Turning her face up to the sky, Madeleine leaned back in her chair and closed her eyes.

"How are you doing?" Sukie asked her, taking a seat opposite her.

Madeleine sighed. "I don't know. The baby has dropped even more, but that might be from all the activity. I mopped the kitchen floor this morning and did a thousand little household chores I've put off. I think I'm ready now. Is it always this difficult near the end?"

Sukie nodded. "Pretty much. Just rest there. I'm going inside to get the appetizers."

Through the kitchen window Sukie observed Cam and Rob, chatting amicably now. Her nerves settled. They were the two most important men in her life and she wanted—no, needed—them to get along.

Sukie carried a tray of appetizers out to the patio.

Madeleine looked up from where she was resting, a quizzical expression on her face. "I feel so strange . . ."

Sukie studied Madeleine's flushed face. "Are you all right, honey? You've spilled your drink. I'll get you another." She set the tray down on the table and picked up the bottle of sparkling water before realizing Madeleine's glass was still full. She glanced at the puddle on the flagstones. "Madeleine! Your water has broken. The baby is on its way!"

Conversation between the men stopped. Rob ran over and took hold of Madeleine's hand. "Oh my God! Does it hurt?"

Madeline puffed out a breath. "I've got the worst backache in the world. It comes and goes every few minutes but I don't think . . ."

Sukie's heart raced as Madeleine stopped talking and grimaced. The signs were unmistakable. "Rob, you'd better get her to the hospital immediately. I'll meet you there."

The color drained from Rob's face. "Hang on, Mad. I'll get the car started." He took off at a full run.

Sukie took one of Madeleine's arms, and Cam the other. They helped Madeleine walk around the side of the house, letting her set the pace. She stopped once and panted until the pain went away.

Sukie gave Cam a worried look. Thank God, the hospital wasn't far—just one town over. Ten miles, max. When they reached the car, Madeleine grabbed Sukie's hand.

"You'll stay with me, won't you, Sukie?"

Sukie glanced at Cam.

"Go," he said. "I'll clean up, find a sitter for Chloe, and meet you at the hospital. I know where it is."

They helped Madeleine into the backseat of the car. Sukie got in beside her. As soon as the car doors slammed shut, Rob took off with a roar of the car's engine that matched the roar of excitement inside her.

In record time, they pulled up to Gilbert Regional Hospital. With the ease of much practice, the emergency room nurses had Madeleine in a wheelchair and on her way to the maternity ward before Rob could finish the administrative paperwork. Sukie sat on the edge of her seat in the waiting room, needing Cam's presence more than ever. Awaiting the birth of her first grandchild was one of the most important moments of her life.

Rob trotted over to her. "Keep your cell phone on. I'll be in touch. Will you call Dad?" He hesitated. "Never mind. I'll call him later, when I know more about what's happening."

Sukie was sitting in the waiting room, flipping through a time-worn magazine for the umpteenth time, when she looked up to see Ted walking toward her. She jumped to her feet.

Ted gave her a hesitant smile. "Rob called. Said the baby is on its way and that with the way things were going, it shouldn't be too long. Guess she's one of the lucky ones. Not like you with him or Elizabeth."

Sukie was touched by the tenderness that had entered his voice. Both deliveries had been difficult, along with two miscarriages that had been painful to her.

"I've been so excited about this," Sukie said. "I've heard grandchildren are gifts to make up for the relatives you'd rather not have."

Ted frowned. "Well, I'm not there yet. My new baby is due in a couple of months and I'll be glad when it's over. Unlike you, Emmy Lou's not too happy about the whole process."

"I can imagine," Sukie said, biting back any further comments. No doubt, Emmy Lou had him waiting on her hand and foot—anything for more attention. The helpless female act had worked before on a number of men. Why not, Ted?

Ted's gaze lingered on her. "You look great, Sukie. I mean it. You've lost weight, done something to your hair . . ."

He leaned over to kiss her.

Sukie quickly stepped back. *After all he'd done, her ex was hitting on her?*

"There you are, hon." Cam approached them. "Rob called to tell me it wouldn't be long. I got Emily Warren to sit for Chloe, so we're set."

Sukie waved him closer. "Cam, meet Ted Skidmore. Ted, this is Cameron Taylor."

Cam held out his hand.

Frowning, Ted hesitated, and finally shook it. Though he didn't reach Cam's height, he raised his chin. "I was just telling Sukie I have a baby coming soon."

"How about that," said Cam in a controlled voice. "My daughter is three. They grow very fast, don't they?"

"Cam hasn't met Elizabeth yet, but he will," Sukie said to Ted, wanting him to understand her relationship with Cam was serious.

"Yes, she'll be coming home to see her new little sister or brother," responded Ted in a game of one-upmanship.

Cam ended it by turning to her. "Elizabeth called home while I was cleaning up. She wants you to give her a call as soon as you know anything definite about the baby. Let's go outside." He took Sukie's elbow and led her away.

Sukie glanced back at Ted. The fury on his face was frightening. She turned away. Maybe, she thought, he was beginning to realize by tossing her and all their married years aside, he'd given her a chance to be happier than she'd ever been.

She took a seat next to Cam on a bench by the entrance to the emergency room. Cam took her hand. "Whew! If looks could kill, you'd be dead! What's his problem? He left you—not the other way around."

Sukie gave him a heartfelt smile. "I'm so glad he did."

Cam put his arm around Sukie and pulled her close. "Me too." He gave her a long look. "Be careful with him, Sukie. He's one pissed-off guy."

A shiver crossed Sukie's shoulders. The Ted Skidmore of the past was someone she knew. The man he'd become had made a lot of bad decisions. Now he was paying the price and might be blaming her for all his problems. Sukie's thoughts flew to the nasty notes she'd received. Had Ted sent them? Was that why no one had seen or heard from Lynn's ex?

The click of heels warned Sukie someone was approaching. She turned and held her breath. Emmy Lou walked toward them. With her enlarged breasts and bulging stomach, she barely resembled the sleek instructor who'd enjoyed making Sukie sweat in her Pilates class.

Emmy Lou's eyes widened when she saw Sukie. "H-h-hello . . . Sukie." Her gaze fled to Cam and lingered. "I heard you were seeing someone . . ." She turned and waited for Sukie to introduce her.

Cam stood. "You must be Ted's . . . er . . . friend. I'm Cam Taylor."

Emmy Lou turned a megawatt smile on him and fluttered her eyelashes at him, almost comically. "Emmy Lou Rogers."

After an awkward moment of silence, Emmy Lou waved to Sukie and disappeared inside.

"Ted left you for her?" Cam's expression was incredulous. "You've gotta be kidding."

"She's a lot younger than I am," Sukie reluctantly admitted.

Cam laughed and hugged her. "My God! He's a fool."

If Sukie didn't love him already, she would have fallen in love with him right then. She was one lucky woman, and she knew it.

Her cell phone rang. She snatched it out of her purse.

"Mom?" said Rob. "Madeleine says for you to come upstairs. She wants you in the delivery room as her second coach. Things are moving right along."

"Really? I'll be right there." Sukie jumped to her feet and turned to Cam. "I can go into the delivery room!"

"Good luck!" Cam said. "Call me with the news. I'll go home and rescue the babysitter. It's early yet and Chloe will still be up."

Sukie gave him a quick kiss and hurried inside.

Ted called to her as she rushed toward the elevator. She waved and kept going.

Upstairs, the nurses met Sukie and directed her to a scrub area where she could wash up. There, she slipped on a green gown over her clothes. The birthing rooms were at the end of the hall. Rob met her. Sukie entered a room to find Madeleine lying on a gurney, her feet in stirrups.

"How're you doing, hon?" Sukie took Madeleine's hand as another contraction hit her.

"Great," Madeleine growled, crushing Sukie's fingers. When she could get her breath, Madeleine gasped, "Wanted you to see this."

"Thank you." A look of affection passed between them.

Rob and Sukie worked in unison to help with Madeleine's breathing exercises.

After a short time, the doctor entered and checked her. "The baby's crowning. I see lots of dark hair. Let's find out what we have here."

Madeleine bore down and let out a cry as the baby emerged.

"It's a boy!" Rob's eyes lit with excitement and filled with tears. "It's our son, Jonathan." He put his arms around Madeleine and murmured softly to her.

Sukie observed her beautiful, perfect grandson. He was flailing his arms and bellowing now. She stepped into the hallway to give Rob and Madeleine privacy, and wiped tears of joy from her face.

CHAPTER THIRTY-SEVEN
BETSY

Betsy dialed her son's number and waited for Richie to pick up. He'd told her things were better between him and Sarah. She hoped they'd want some time to themselves so she could take the children. She'd missed Caitlin and Garrett like crazy. A new Disney movie was playing and Betsy was sure the kids would love it.

"Hello?"

At the sound of her daughter-in-law's voice, Betsy's heart sank. "Hello, Sarah."

"What do you want?" Sarah snapped.

Caught off guard, Betsy gulped. "I called to offer to take the kids for this weekend so you and Richie can have some time alone. Just like I've done so many times before."

"Not on your life," said Sarah. Her voice rose. "Do you have any idea what an embarrassment you are to me? My friends know all about your . . . your perversion, and if you think I'd let you contaminate my children, you're wrong!" Her shrillness hurt Betsy's ears and her heart.

Finding it hard to breathe, Betsy fought to get words out. "Karen won't be around this weekend and you know as well as I do, my being with Karen does not harm my grandchildren. I want to see my grandchildren. I want to spend time with them." Tears stung her eyes.

"Sorry. You've made some bad choices lately. My children are not going to be part of them. Good-bye." Sarah's words, coated with ice, froze Betsy's insides.

She collapsed in a kitchen chair, too stunned to do anything but sob as hot tears streamed down her face. She recalled all the times she'd tolerated Sarah's obnoxious behavior for the sake of peace in the family. No more.

Anger took over. Betsy's hands balled into fists. How dare Sarah do this to her!

Betsy awoke feeling as if she'd run a ten-mile race in quicksand. Her eyes were swollen and her body dragged as she forced herself out of bed, showered, and got ready for work. The loss of her grandchildren was like a drain on her soul, emptying her of life.

At the office, Betsy automatically followed her daily routines, but her mind whirled in endless circles, reliving the blow of Sarah's cruel words to her. Sarah knew damn well her children would be safe with her. Betsy had practically raised them herself so Sarah could go away on weekends and be needlessly pampered.

By early afternoon, Betsy had worked herself into such a state, she couldn't sit still. She got up and knocked on her boss's door.

He looked up from his desk. "What is it, Betsy?"

Betsy swallowed the tears that threatened. "I need to leave early. Personal reasons."

His concern apparent, he studied her a moment. "Sure. Leave any time you want. And, Betsy, let me know if there's anything I can do for you."

"Thanks." Betsy went back to her desk, gathered her purse, and hurried out the door.

Inside her car, she took a deep breath. Sarah was *not* going to destroy her relationship with her grandchildren. They were her flesh and blood!

Making her way to their school, Betsy pressed her foot down too hard on the accelerator and had to consciously slow the car. *Easy does it*, she reminded herself. She didn't want to get arrested for speeding. That would ruin everything.

Betsy parked her car on a side street next to the school and gazed around, scouting for the best way to proceed. The school buses were already lined up in the school yard, their engines churning. A school bell rang. Children burst out of the building in groups and formed lines in front of the buses. Betsy searched eagerly for Caitlin and Garrett, but neither one was among the students.

She hurried around to the front of the school, past cars lined up in the front circle. Garrett and Caitlin were standing together by the school's entrance. Waving, Betsy called to them.

They saw her and ran over to her.

Tears of joy blurred Betsy's vision as they flung themselves into her arms. She hugged them hard. A high-pitched noise echoed in the air around them. It took a moment for Betsy to realize it was someone shrieking.

Sarah came running toward Betsy, her teeth bared. "Get away from my children!" Sarah pushed the children away and threw herself at Betsy.

Betsy teetered back on her heels and landed on the sidewalk with a painful grunt. Staring at the satisfied expression on her daughter-in-law's face, Betsy's self-control snapped.

"You . . . You . . . !" Betsy lunged at Sarah with a strength she didn't know she had. They tumbled to the grass. Sarah screamed and kicked. A crowd of students and teachers gathered around them, but Betsy held on, all her anger and frustration spilling over.

"Stop! Stop it now!" A uniformed resource officer rushed forward and grabbed each of them by an arm and jerked them to their feet. Gasping for breath, Betsy stood facing Sarah.

Sarah glared at Betsy and turned to the officer. "Officer, call the FBI. This woman was about to kidnap my children. I told her to stay away from them."

"No, sir, I was not. This . . . this . . . witch . . . won't let me see my grandchildren."

"Children, go to the car!" shouted Sarah. "Now!"

Wide-eyed, they hurried away, glancing back at Betsy.

"Go on about your business and leave these women alone," the officer ordered the crowd. The circle of onlookers began to disperse.

While the officer was distracted, Sarah grabbed a lock of Betsy's hair and pulled. "Leave my children alone."

Betsy swung her fist back and hit Sarah as hard as she could. The blow caught Sarah on the side of the face.

"Owwww!" Sarah put a hand to her red cheek and narrowed her eyes at Betsy. "Officer, arrest this woman!"

"Now, now, both of you calm down. You're out of control. Let's go inside and talk this over."

"There's nothing to talk over," said Sarah. "I'm going to my children." She whipped around and marched away as a sheriff's car rolled into the driveway, its red light flashing.

Betsy turned to leave, but the resource officer grabbed her elbow. "Stay right here."

Bill Michaels left his car and walked over to them.

Betsy's cheeks flooded with shame. She knew the sheriff from her community volunteer work and hated to have him see her like this—her dress torn, her hair a mess.

"Sorry, Betsy," he said, "but I'm going to have to take you down to the office. We can sort things out there. The school called, said you were trespassing, and got into a fight."

"But, Bill . . ." Betsy began, sickened by all that had happened. "She won't let me see my grandchildren!"

He nodded. "Let's go and allow the school to resume their business. We can talk about it on the way."

"Please don't do this to me," Betsy said, panicking.

Giving her a sympathetic look, he shook his head. "I'm sorry, Betsy. Let's go."

He led Betsy to his patrol car. She slid into the backseat, as miserable and angry as she'd ever been. Caitlin and Garrett's eyes were round with shock as they stared at her from the window of their car. Betsy gazed at them and swore she'd never forget this mortifying moment, all because of their mother's narrow-mindedness. No, she wouldn't forget what Sarah had done to her, not in a hundred years.

The sheriff's office was in a one-story brick building a block off the town square. Bill parked the car, and helped Betsy out of it and into the building.

Inside his office, he listened to her story and quickly agreed it was little more than an ugly family feud.

"Would you like to call someone to come for you?" he gently asked, offering Betsy a tissue. He stood. "You can wait in one of the back offices for better privacy. I'm sorry about this, Betsy. I thought it best to get you away from the school to defuse the situation. I was told your daughter-in-law wanted to call in the FBI. Having the feds involved is the last thing we'd want. Trust me."

Bill led Betsy to an office behind double doors, at the end of a long hallway. She knew she'd overreacted to Sarah's obnoxious behavior. But even now, if she came face-to-face with Sarah, she knew she wouldn't be able to control her anger. Left alone, Betsy dialed Sukie's number and asked for a ride.

"My God, Betsy! Are you all right? What happened?"

The words came tumbling out of Betsy's mouth. "I had a terrible fight with Sarah. She told me I couldn't see Caitlin and Garrett again. I was so mad and hurt, I decided to go to their school to see them. Sarah accused me of trying to kidnap them. It was awful. We ended up in a physical fight. She left and Bill made me come here to cool off." Her voice quivered. "Can you imagine what my grandchildren think? They saw me put into a patrol car and driven off. Caitlin's eyes were round as could be. Garrett ducked down in the car as we drove past."

"I'll be right there," said Sukie. "Take a deep breath. Somehow we'll get all this straightened out."

Feeling like a truant sitting in the principal's office, Betsy waited for Sukie to arrive. She thought about calling Richie and decided against it.

Sukie arrived and gave Betsy a sympathetic look.

"I can't believe she did this to me," said Betsy. "I swear I hate her, Sukie."

Sukie shook her head. "Take it easy. Remember, you don't want to lose Richie. Be careful when you talk to him. He's caught between the two of you."

"Don't I know it?" Betsy wouldn't put it past Sarah to make him disown her.

"C'mon, let's go home." Sukie's voice was full of understanding.

Feeling twenty years older, Betsy stood and grabbed her purse. A glance at her reflection in the only window in the office showed her a defeated woman. For that reason alone, she'd willingly assault Sarah all over again.

"Why don't you come to my house for a while?" Sukie said gently.

"Thanks. I don't want to be alone right now. Karen's away."

Betsy's cell phone rang. Richie. She picked it up eagerly. He'd always been a good son. They shared many common traits. But before she could begin talking, he launched into a diatribe about her and Sarah fighting like seventh graders, humiliating him and his children. "This has got to stop, Mom. Enough is enough."

"But . . ." Betsy began, and realized he'd already hung up. She turned to Sukie, sick to her stomach. "He's furious at me. Oh, crap! I've ruined everything."

"Hold on!" said Sukie. "Give everybody time to settle down, including yourself. What you need right now is a hot cup of coffee or maybe some tea."

"What I need right now is a glass of wine. It's got to be five o'clock somewhere."

Sukie grinned. "As a matter of fact, it's quarter to five right now."

They got settled in the car and, exhausted, Betsy leaned back against the passenger seat and closed her eyes.

Sukie's cell phone rang. She picked it up. "Hi, Tiffany. Betsy? As a matter of fact, she's here with me now. We're on our way to my house." She paused. "Okay, great."

Sukie hung up and turned to her. "That was Tiffany. Everyone in the group is coming to my house. They're worried about you leaving the office so abruptly."

Gratitude filled Betsy. Sarah wasn't the only one who'd turned against her. Several women in the neighborhood club had looked the other way when she approached. And some people in her church refused to talk to her. She'd even been asked to resign from the Greeting Committee.

Rejection made Betsy more determined to be true to herself. All her life, she'd wondered what was wrong with her as she'd struggled to meet the expectations of others. When she and Karen had finally voiced their feelings for each other, Betsy felt as if she'd been given a gift—the gift of her true self, the one she'd hidden for so long. As painful as the situation was, Betsy couldn't change who she was, not even to be near her grandchildren.

CHAPTER THIRTY-EIGHT
SUKIE

Sukie went to work putting together snacks for the group. Betsy sat at the kitchen table, sipping a glass of pinot grigio, looking totally drained.

Sukie was chilled to the bone by Sarah's actions. The sheriff had told her he considered it nothing more than a nasty family feud and that no formal charges were pressed, but Sukie saw how destroyed Betsy looked. Her eyes were swollen and red-rimmed. More than that, her natural bubbly spirit was broken.

The doorbell chimed. Sukie went to answer it.

Standing on the front porch, Carol Ann peered over Lynn's shoulder. Tiffany stood behind her. Sukie's heart warmed at the sight of them. Their friendship worked because they each had issues to sort out, and sharing them made it easier and them stronger.

After greetings and hugs were exchanged, they poured themselves assorted drinks and gathered around the kitchen table. Sukie passed around cheese and crackers and carrot sticks with dip, set a bowl of nuts on the table, and listened as Betsy told them the whole story.

The antique ogee clock in the living room chimed six times. Tiffany jumped to her feet. "I've got to go. I told Beau I had to work late, but he'll still be wondering why it took me so long to get home."

"You didn't tell him you were coming here?" Sukie asked Tiffany, walking her to the front door.

Tiffany shook her head. "No way. He doesn't like me being part of this group or any other group."

Sukie pressed her lips together.

Tiffany sighed. "Regard called a family meeting Sunday night and it did not go well. I'm fighting back, Sukie, and they don't like it."

Observing the pain etched on Tiffany's face, Sukie studied her. "Are you all right?"

Tiffany's eyes welled. "I can't talk about it now. I have to get home."

Sukie stopped her. "If you ever need a place to stay, you can come here. Got it?"

Tiffany nodded and gave Sukie a shaky smile. "I might just do that. See you."

Sukie stayed by the door, watching Tiffany climb into her car. It was the first time Tiffany had admitted things were so bad she might have to leave Beau.

It was one of those humid summery days that clung to Sukie. The air was heavy with moisture, scarcely allowing her to catch her breath. It drained the energy from her as she hurried from the library to the car to meet the women for another Fat Fridays lunch. Sukie's mouth watered at the thought of Bea's famous chicken salad. The cold chicken and fruit concoction was one of her favorites.

Sukie was the last to arrive. She slid onto the empty chair at the table, catching the tail end of Carol Ann's conversation.

"Sorry I'm late. What's going on?"

Carol Ann sighed. "It's John. We had a fight. Last weekend, we picked out some furniture for his place. I told him I couldn't afford to buy all of it, and he got mad. He's just started a new job at an insurance agency and he doesn't have the money to buy it himself. I told him what y'all had said about not spending all my money on furniture and he blew up."

"He didn't rough you up, did he?" Sukie asked, recalling their first date.

Carol Ann shook her head. "No, he didn't touch me, but he was really, really angry. Today, he told me he'd have to rethink our exclusive relationship." Her mouth turned down. "He's the first man who's wanted to date me exclusively. Know what I mean?"

"He's asking you to give up all you've worked so hard for," Lynn said forcefully. "What is he giving up in return? You gotta be firm. He's not the only guy around."

Carol Ann nodded glumly. "Yeah, but then I'll end up with someone like my boss Ed Pritchard. Ugh!"

"There you go again. If you want my opinion, I'd take Ed over John any day. He's really nice." Tiffany shook her head. "Carol Ann, Ed's a far better catch."

Carol Ann's face became pinched with anger. "Just because you have someone handsome and rich like Beau doesn't give you the right to tell me who I should or should not date."

Tiffany bowed her head and took a deep breath. The rest of them remained quiet in the tense moments that followed.

Sukie turned to Betsy. "How are things going?"

Betsy let out a sigh that told its own story. "I've written letters to Caitlin and Garrett. Richie promised to see that they get them. At least they'll know that I still love them." Her voice cracked on the last two words.

The waitress appeared, and they placed their orders.

After the waitress left, Tiffany spoke up. "Beau's parents are paying for us to spend the weekend at Château Élan."

"See?" said Carol Ann bitterly. "You've got it all."

Tiffany glared at her. "At our family meeting last Sunday, his parents decided we needed to get away—just the two of us—so I wouldn't be so uppity. Pampering, they said, would calm my nerves. How do you like that?"

Sukie understood what a barbed gift they had offered. By accepting their invitation, Tiffany was forced to agree she'd been on edge; by refusing to go for the weekend, she would be considered nervous, as Beau's family put it. It was a no-win situation.

"Maybe it will help make things better between you and Beau," said Betsy tentatively. "I hope so."

Tiffany shrugged. "I said I'd go, but I don't think much is going to help us out. On top of everything else, Beau hates his job and he takes it out on me. He's afraid to leave it and try something new."

"How does he take it out on you? He hasn't hit you, has he?" Lynn's voice was low but it held a hardness that no one could miss.

Tiffany lifted her shoulders and let them fall. "After his parents left on Sunday, we got into it. He slapped me, but he didn't hurt the baby."

A collective gasp rose from their table.

Lynn's face turned an ugly red. Eyes narrowed, she leaned forward. "If that bastard ever touches you again, let me know." She looked around the table at each of them. "Are we together on this? Anything happens to Tiffany, we're there for her?"

They all nodded solemnly.

That night, Sukie told Cam about her concerns for Tiffany.

As he listened, his brow furrowed. "Tiffany had better be careful. Sounds like a volatile situation to me."

"I suppose a number of people from prominent families like Beau's feel undue pressure to succeed," Sukie said. "I can't imagine how it must be for him, with parents like Muffy and Regard Wright."

Cam nodded. "Like I said, it's a disaster waiting to happen."

A shiver crossed Sukie's shoulders. *Why do so many men turn violent?*

She got up to pour Cam another cup of coffee. "I talked to Elizabeth today. She's thrilled to be named Jonathan's godmother. She's planning on coming home in two to three weeks." Setting his coffee in front of him, Sukie tweaked Cam's cheek playfully. "She's anxious to meet you."

He grinned at her. "What do you think? Will I pass the test?"

Sukie chuckled and settled on his lap for a hug. "You've already passed all of mine."

Cam smiled. "Things are going well, aren't they?"

"Very well," Sukie murmured and immediately wished she hadn't said it. It was sure to bring bad luck.

At home alone later that week, Sukie pressed a shirt for work and then curled up on the couch to watch a movie with a bowl of buttery popcorn. The phone rang during a crucial love scene. She checked the number on caller ID. Nobody she knew. Probably a sales call, she told herself, turning back to the movie.

A short while later, the chiming of the doorbell brought Sukie to her feet. Fear stiffened her body. She wasn't expecting anyone. Cam was staying at home with Chloe. With her heart pounding and skipping beats, Sukie tiptoed to the front door, turned on the front-porch light, and peered through the peephole in the door.

Tiffany stood in the circle of light cast around her, a rolling suitcase at her feet.

Sukie swung the door open. "Tiffany! What are you doing here? Are you all right?"

"I tried to call you earlier," Tiffany said. "I'm leaving Beau. Can I stay here?"

"Sure. What happened?"

Tiffany took a deep breath, and Sukie knew the effort it cost her to keep from breaking down. "He hit me in the stomach. Not hard, but, still . . ."

Sukie pulled her inside and looked her over. "Are you sure you're all right? Any bleeding? Is the baby still moving?"

Tiffany nodded. "It really wasn't that hard . . ."

"He struck you, Tiffany. That's wrong."

Tiffany buried her face in her hands. "Sukie, he's become a monster since we married. First, I never measured up to his standards. Then, the baby turned out to be a girl. Next, his job fell apart. Now, he's gone from shouting at me to shoving me around."

She looked up at Sukie with eyes that were so sad, Sukie drew in a breath. "When he struck out at my belly, I knew I had to leave. I've had it. I can't do all this pretending anymore. No matter how well-off his people are, things at home suck. I hate him and his hoity-toity family." Her hands fell to her sides and her shoulders slumped in defeat. "I'm pretty sure he's taking drugs."

"Does Beau know you're here?" Sukie couldn't help glancing out at the night.

Tiffany shook her head. "He thinks I've gone to a motel. He told me he'd give me overnight to straighten up, then I was to get my fat ass back home before his mother found out I was gone." Tiffany's face crumbled. "They don't like me, but they won't let me leave. Weird, huh?"

Sukie's lips tightened. It was a power issue as well as an image problem.

"Come on, sweetheart." Sukie picked up the suitcase and led Tiffany up the stairs to the guest suite at the end of the hall. "Can I get you something? Water? Juice?"

Tiffany shook her head. "If you don't mind, I'd like to lie down for a few minutes."

Sukie gave her a gentle pat on the back. "Poor thing. You must be exhausted."

"I am." Tiffany slipped off her shoes and lay down on the bed. "Thanks, Sukie. I'll come downstairs in a bit."

Sukie checked on Tiffany several times, worried about any injuries, but each time she checked, Tiffany was sleeping peacefully. Sukie covered her with a light blanket and finally headed to bed herself.

The next morning, Sukie rose early and went into the guestroom to make sure Tiffany was all right. She was still asleep, so Sukie tapped gently on her shoulder.

Tiffany's eyes flew open. Uttering a soft cry, she hunched her shoulders and curled her body around her belly.

Sukie's heart contracted at the sight of such self-defense. "Tiffany? It's me, Sukie. Time to get up."

Tiffany came fully awake and sat up. "Wow . . . I slept the whole time, huh?"

Sukie sat down on the edge of the bed. "What's going to happen to you, Tiffany? Isn't there a minister, a marriage counselor, or someone else you can talk to? Someone to help you and Beau sort things out?"

Tiffany lowered her head. When she raised it, sparks seemed to fly from her eyes. "Like I said last night, I can't do it anymore. He's taken everything away from me—my self-esteem, my talent, everything, including my love for him. I'm just a freakin' shell. I'm afraid of him, and I know from listening to you and the other women in the group that things are not going to get better. He won't go for help. He said he'd kill me if I tried to see a counselor. I never should have let him talk me into marrying him."

Sukie put her arms around her and felt the shudder that rippled through Tiffany's body.

Tiffany's eyes pleaded with her. "You'll let me stay here, won't you?"

"Yes, but we're going to have to let Beau know where you are and lay down some ground rules. If he needs to talk to you, it can be done by phone or somewhere else. I don't want him showing up here unannounced."

"Once he realizes how serious I am, he'll drop all pretense of wanting to be with me. He's already told me over and over again that I'm just a worthless piece of shit."

Anger burned a path through Sukie.

Tiffany drew in a breath. "I'll probably have to go on welfare or something."

"I wouldn't be so sure about that," Sukie said. "I'll give you the name of my lawyer. Beau has responsibilities he can't shirk."

While Tiffany took a shower and got dressed, Sukie called her lawyer to let her know the situation. The lawyer advised Sukie to be firm about Beau not coming to the house, telling her it was too soon to have any kind of legal restraining order in place.

Sukie hung up and raced upstairs to get ready for work. Later, Tiffany joined Sukie in the kitchen. "There was no answer at the house when I tried to reach Beau."

"Maybe he went out for breakfast," Sukie said hopefully.

Tiffany shook her head. "I bet he headed right over to his parents' house." She let out a sigh. "This is no idle threat of mine, Sukie. I'm leaving him."

"Just be careful. Here's the number of my lawyer. You might want to meet Beau there and explain the situation to him. Whatever you do, don't agree to meet him alone."

"Okay, but sometime I'll need to go to the house and get more of my things."

While they were together in the kitchen, Tiffany tried to reach Beau several times again. She turned to Sukie. "That's it. I can't take the time to keep calling him. I'll be late for work. He can reach me there, if he even bothers to try."

After Tiffany left, Sukie checked all the doors of the house to make sure they were locked securely. As she did every morning since she'd learned about Lynn's situation, Sukie punched in the numbers for the security system. There had been a time she hadn't felt the need to do that. No more.

Still lost in thought about Tiffany's situation, Sukie pulled into the library parking lot and nearly hit Edythe Aynsley. Edythe glowered at her and made a point of taking her time to move out of the way.

"Sorry!" Sukie called out the window to her.

Edythe hunched her shoulders and hurried into the building. Sukie's heart sank. It was not going to be a good day. Like Julie said, Edythe was a bitter woman who'd had it in for her from day one.

Sukie was sitting at her desk when Edythe approached. Sukie stood, anxious to make things right. "I'm sorry about the parking lot incident. I didn't see you . . ."

Edythe cut her off. "I'm not here to talk to you about that. I just got a call from an old friend of mine. Muffy Wright. She's furious. It seems you're interfering with her son's marriage. I'm warning you to back off. You need to mind your own business."

Sukie's jaw dropped. "What I do is none of *your* business."

"We'll see." Edythe's smirk stung. "I've got a candidate lined up to take over for you. I've already talked to Julie about it. She agrees my candidate is much better suited for the job than you are."

Edythe walked away, leaving Sukie speechless. She clenched her fists. No one was going to tell her she couldn't help a friend. Tiffany needed all the friends she had in the battle ahead.

A short while later, Julie approached her.

Sukie stopped typing. "Is it true? Edythe has a candidate for my job? I'll be replaced?" Her stomach felt hollow.

Julie nodded. "I'm sorry, Sukie. I really am. The person she's found for the job has all the necessary qualifications. She'll still have to be approved by the board, but that's a mere formality. I'm sure Edythe will have the board members' support lined up before the meeting next month."

Sukie's whole body collapsed inward.

"I feel terrible about this," said Julie. "Why don't you take some online computer courses, programs that'll be helpful to you at other jobs? They're free here at the library."

Sukie swallowed hard. "I guess I will."

"If it's any comfort to you, you're the best children's librarian we've ever had. I'll fight to keep you on through the summer. We'll say you're training the new person and going through a slow transition so the children have a chance to get used to the idea."

Sukie let out a sigh. "That would be wonderful. It'll take a while for me to find something else."

Busy with details for the library, Sukie managed to make it through the day, but her stomach was churning. Even though Ted had initially agreed she could stay in the house and have enough alimony to pay for the expenses of running it, he'd started pushing to get out of the agreement. If any adjustments were made to it and without her job, there was no way Sukie could make it financially. What in the hell was she supposed to do? Move to a motel?

At the end of the day, Sukie hurried home, changed her clothes, and tried to reach Cam. He'd been in business meetings all day and she hadn't had a chance to tell him about Tiffany. She finally reached him on his cell on his way to pick up Chloe early from day care. The teacher had called to tell him Chloe wasn't feeling well.

"Hi, sweetheart," he said in the low musical voice she'd come to adore.

She held back a sob.

"What's wrong? Are you okay?"

"No," Sukie choked out. "It's everything. Edythe Aynsley found someone to replace me at the library and told me to stay out of the Wright family's business and Tiffany moved in and I don't know how I can stay in this house."

"Whoa! Calm down and tell me one little part at a time."

Sukie sniffed, took a deep breath, and started all over again.

"That's all?" he said, when she'd finished.

Sukie realized he was kidding and felt a laugh begin to bubble up in her. It felt so good to share her concerns with him.

"Just take it one step at a time, Sukie. I'm going to take Chloe home. Stop by when you get a chance."

"I will. I have a feeling Tiffany will need some time alone and I can't wait to see you."

"Me too. Later."

Sukie hung up the phone, thinking how much she loved him. During the weeks and months of late winter and spring that they'd been together, he'd shown her that he loved her too, but she was still waiting to hear him say those three important words.

She was in the kitchen putting together a chef's salad when Tiffany walked into the room. "How'd it go?"

Tiffany shrugged. "We met at the lawyer's office, like you suggested. Beau tried to tell me I couldn't take clothes or any of my things out of the house, but after his father found out, Beau agreed it was only fair. Beau's father told him to let me go; I'd come to my senses within a week. He also told Beau to tell anyone who asked that I'd gone on a minivacation to get ready for the baby."

Tiffany shook her head. "They won't listen to me when I tell them things have gotten out of hand. They say I've got to stop annoying Beau."

Sukie shook her head. "Classic enabling. When are you going to pick up your things? Do you want me to go with you?"

Tiffany's face lit up. "Will you?"

Sukie nodded. No way was she going to let Tiffany go back to that house alone.

CHAPTER THIRTY-NINE

TIFFANY

Tiffany gathered several large garbage bags together, grateful Sukie had offered to go to the house with her. She'd probably never get another chance to pick up her things after Beau's family realized how serious she was about leaving him. Tiffany checked her watch. Beau was going to stay with his parents, so it would be safe for them to go to the house now. She and Sukie put a few empty boxes into the SUV and took off.

Pulling up in front of the house, Tiffany remembered how proud she'd been of it when they'd first moved in—but then she'd realized it wasn't really hers and never would be.

Sukie grabbed some of the boxes and the plastic bags. Tiffany got the rest and they walked up to the front door. Tiffany unlocked it and stepped inside, feeling like an intruder in her own house. She stood a moment, eying all the furniture and decorative things Muffy had chosen. She was more than ready to leave it all behind. Now, she wanted to get in, snatch her personal things, and get out as fast as she could.

Crossing the marbled entry, Tiffany led Sukie up the stairs and into the master bedroom. The oversized room contained massive carved-walnut furniture, filling the room with a heavy look Tiffany never would have chosen for herself. Even the hangings at the window had been selected by Muffy, as if she and Beau couldn't have picked anything out for themselves. The only things she would miss about the room were the number of drawers in her dresser and the space in her closet. *Pretty sad,* she thought.

Tiffany opened the drawers and tossed most of their contents onto the king-sized bed—lingerie, nightgowns, silk scarves—anything she thought she might need in the future. It all ended up in a heap in the center of the bed, but she didn't care.

Sukie began to gather Tiffany's things together and place them into plastic bags.

Tiffany sat on the plush carpet in the closet and shoveled the shoes she wanted onto the floor behind her. Taking a garbage bag, she scooped them up and dragged the bag out of the room, down the stairs, and into the car. Sukie followed with two full bags of clothes.

They kept up a steady pace, taking things on hangers in bunches down to the car, dragging full plastic bags out of the house. Tiffany's heart clutched with sadness. Her life with Beau was being reduced to items on hangers or in bags to be carted away.

Tiffany took the last load from the closet to the car while Sukie began on the bathroom.

When she returned, she found Sukie staring at an ornate wooden box. "What's this?" she asked. "Should I pack it?"

Tiffany opened the lid of the jewelry box and stared at the pieces of silver, gold, and assorted precious stones that sparkled against the dark-blue velvet lining. "It's mostly stuff Muffy gave me, back when I thought we'd be able to get along."

Sukie lifted out a gold chain with a large topaz pendant and studied it. "You'd better take it with you. It's valuable. You might need some of this later."

Unsure, Tiffany shut the lid and placed the box on the bed. "Before we go, I want to check on one thing. The nursery was supposed to have been painted yesterday."

Holding back a sob, Tiffany ushered Sukie down the hallway to the room she and Beau had chosen for the nursery. Nothing had turned out the way she'd once imagined. Even so, she wanted to view the room she'd intended for her baby.

"I selected shell pink for the color of the room, a pale shade just perfect for a little girl," she explained to Sukie. She opened the door to the room and stumbled back. Struggling to keep on her feet, she clung to the door frame and stared in shock at the writing on the wall.

"FUCK YOU!" was scrawled across all four pink walls in bright blue paint.

Sukie grabbed hold of her as Tiffany sank to the floor. Seeing those foul words, Tiffany felt as if she'd been socked in the stomach.

"Oh my God! Who would have done this?" Horror was etched on Sukie's face. "It's just like one of the notes."

"Beau did it. I'm sure," Tiffany said, trying to catch her breath. It was so like Beau's sick behavior lately. It had to be the cocaine, though he'd promised to stop taking drugs.

Sukie grabbed hold of Tiffany's shoulders. Her eyes were wide with fear. "Tiffany, we've got to get out of here. Now!"

They hurried to the master bedroom for the box of jewelry. The sound of the front door being thrown open stopped them.

"Tiffany? Where the hell are you?"

Tiffany felt the blood leave her face. "It's him!" She could tell he'd been drinking or worse. His words were slow to come out but they were filled with fury.

"Stay behind me. I'll protect you." Sukie's voice quaked, but Tiffany knew from the ferocious scowl on her face that Sukie meant it. She wanted to weep with gratitude.

Beau met them at the top of the stairs. His glassy eyes peered from a face that had become the angry mask of a stranger. "What are *you* doing here?" he snarled at Sukie.

Though her knees were about to buckle, Tiffany stood firm. "I asked her to help me. We're leaving now."

"You're not going anywhere." Beau grabbed Tiffany's arm. The jewelry box went flying, spilling its contents over the carpet in shiny patches.

Sukie positioned herself between Tiffany and Beau. She glared at him. "Leave Tiffany alone or I'll call the police."

"Stay out of our business," snapped Beau. "She's not really going to leave me."

"Your father agreed that you should let her go. Right?" said Sukie.

Beau bowed his head and dropped his hand. "What the fuck does he know?"

Sukie tugged on Tiffany, and they moved down the stairs as fast as they could, leaving the jewelry behind.

With her pulse sprinting, Tiffany turned and looked back.

Weaving on unsteady feet, Beau stood at the top of the stairs and shook his fist at her. "You're going to be sorry."

She and Sukie scrambled into the car. Gasping for breath, Tiffany started the engine and pulled away from the house with a shriek of tires that matched the howl in her heart.

CHAPTER FORTY

LYNN

Lynn flipped off the six-o'clock news on the television, wondering if she was right to feel suspicious. A series of small robberies was taking place in the next town. The description of the man who'd tied up an older woman and taken all her money had sounded eerily like Buck. Not enough details had been given, though, to make Lynn certain it was her ex. There'd been no mention of huge hands, no talk of a heart tattoo with "Grace" written across it, but then the robber had been wearing dark clothes that had covered his arms.

She shook her head, telling herself her imagination was being overactive. Sighing at all the bad things that had happened in her life, Lynn went into the kitchen and took out the makings of a chicken Caesar salad. Since joining the Fat Fridays group, she'd taken to eating healthier meals, daring to believe she might live longer than she'd always thought possible. She wondered how her sweet daughter was. Had she grown into those long, skinny legs of hers? Did she understand about the mother who loved her so much she'd been forced to abandon her?

Tears stung Lynn's eyes. Someday this running would all come to an end. But when?

CHAPTER FORTY-ONE
SUKIE

Sukie suspected Tiffany was still in a state of shock, like her, as they headed back to her house. They hadn't spoken a word to each other. Finally Sukie said, "I had no idea things had gotten so bad."

Tiffany sighed. "Like I said, they've been getting worse and worse."

As much as Sukie wanted to protect Tiffany, she couldn't help but feel sorry for Beau. She'd bet it wasn't the first time he'd cried out for help and been ignored. "Beau needs help. I hope his parents come to understand that."

Tiffany shrugged. "They'd probably tell him it's too public a move to seek counseling or rehab, that Wrights keep their business private and don't need other people to tell them what do to." The bitterness in her tone told a story of its own.

Tiffany turned the car ignition off, and they sat a moment in silence. Shame colored Tiffany's face when she turned to Sukie. "I don't want to put you out, Sukie. I'll try to find another place as soon as possible."

Sukie squeezed Tiffany's hand affectionately. "Stay as long as it takes. It's important for you to get settled and remain as calm as possible—for the baby's sake, as well as your own. Things will work out. You'll see."

Tiffany lowered her head on the steering wheel. Her chest heaved in and out with heartbreaking sobs. Sukie gave her another loving pat and got out of the car. There were times when people needed to be alone. This was surely one of them.

A short time later, Tiffany entered the house, her eyes red and puffy.

Sukie put her arm around her. "It'll be all right, hon. Somehow things will work out."

Tiffany handed her a bag of cosmetics. "Here. I'll start to unload the car."

"Let's eat some dinner before we think about doing that." She'd already called Cam and told him she wouldn't be able to see him after all. Then she'd phoned Betsy to suggest she and Karen stop by on their nightly walk together.

Conversation was kept to small talk as they ate their simple meal. Sukie suspected Tiffany's stomach was as upset as hers. They were just starting to clean up after dinner when Betsy showed up with Karen, Lynn, and Carol Ann. Betsy carried a floating pink balloon that read "Happy Birthday."

"What's this?" Tiffany asked, smiling as she accepted it from her.

Betsy grinned. "Like they say, today is the first day of the rest of your life. So it's kind of like your birthday."

Sukie was happy to see Betsy acting more like her old quirky self.

"We're here for you," said Lynn, giving Tiffany a hug.

They all trooped out to Tiffany's car, grabbed the bags and boxes, and went upstairs to help Tiffany settle things in the guest suite. Sukie was now grateful that in the hopeless days following Ted's departure, she'd spent hours cleaning and straightening closets and drawers. There was plenty of room for Tiffany and her belongings.

As they unpacked Tiffany's things, talk and laughter echoed in the bedroom. To Sukie, it felt like an old college sorority gathering. Carol Ann oohed and aahed over each dress, skirt, pair of pants, or blouse that she and Sukie hung in the closet. Betsy unloaded all the shoes and arranged them neatly on the closet floor. Lynn took the bag of cosmetics into the bathroom and Karen stored sweaters, knit tops, and other items in bureau drawers. Tiffany went from one to another of them, supervising.

After things were settled, Tiffany gave each of them a hug. "Thanks. I don't know what I'd do without you."

Their earlier gaiety disappeared as the women looked at one another, aware their worries were far from over. Looking as if she were ready to collapse, Tiffany sank onto the bed.

Sukie waved the others out of the room and followed behind. Downstairs, she bid everyone good night, shut and locked the door, and leaned back against it. It had been one hell of a day.

In the morning, Sukie gave Tiffany a key to the house, showed her the alarm system, then prepared for work. She believed Regard Wright when he told Tiffany they'd give her a week to calm down and figured the situation would remain fairly quiet for the next few days.

After a busy day at the library, Sukie returned home, excited by the prospect of spending time with Cam and Chloe. It had been two days since she'd seen them. She stopped at the mailbox and pulled out the usual stack of mail, leafing anxiously through it for hand-folded, ugly notes—she breathed a sigh of relief when she found none. Still uneasy, Sukie glanced around, but saw nothing unusual. She slipped into her car, remembering the days when she'd felt safe in her own yard.

"Sukie! Sukie!" Chloe shrieked, running toward her with outstretched arms. Sukie hugged Chloe to her and laughed when Cam wrapped his arms around both of them. She'd missed them terribly.

Chicken fingers and carrots were two of Chloe's favorite things, which meant dinner was without the coaxing they sometimes needed to do to get her to eat.

After their meal, Sukie helped give Chloe a bath and then tucked her into bed. Sukie studied her sweet face ringed by damp curls. In just a few years, Chloe would be heading into the tween years and soon after would become a full-fledged teenager. The idea caught Sukie off guard. Elizabeth hadn't been as difficult as some girls her age, but no teen girl was easy. Helping Chloe through those years would require a huge commitment on her part. Sukie kissed her good night and left Chloe and Cam alone to go through their nightly rituals.

Sitting at the bottom of the stairway, Sukie's thoughts whirled. There were so many things to think about when considering her future.

Cam came down the stairs and sat on the bottom step next to her. "God! It's only been what? Two days? I've missed you." His eyes sparkled with humor. "And your cooking."

Sukie laughed. "Everyone loves my cooking. Even Ted."

The smile left Cam's face. "Sukie, I've heard rumors around town that things are not going well for Ted and Emmy Lou. He'd better not decide he's made a huge mistake and come trotting back to you, asking your forgiveness."

Sukie couldn't hide her surprise. "Why would you think that? Cam, I could never go back to Ted Skidmore, no matter how much he threatens to take the house away from me."

Cam frowned. "He's threatening you? Maybe he's the one sending those nasty notes. Don't count that out. I've seen the looks he's given you, seen his anger."

A niggling thought entered Sukie's mind. With her out of the picture, Ted would have the house free and clear and no alimony to pay. A shiver rippled across her shoulders. No new notes had shown up lately, but maybe they'd been wrong about it being Lynn's ex. The man she'd married was someone she didn't know anymore.

Cam tilted Sukie's chin and placed his warm, soft lips on hers. All worrisome thoughts evaporated as he told her how much he cared. Locked in his embrace, she thought of only him.

CHAPTER FORTY-TWO
LYNN

Lynn sat in her dark apartment in a complete funk. Seeing and hearing what Tiffany was going through had brought back many unhappy memories. Like Tiffany, she'd started out thinking she'd found the man she could happily live with for the rest of her life.

Caught up in the past, Lynn paced the living room. Maybe if Buck hadn't been a long-distance truck driver, things might have been different. But he'd come back after being away for several days and had quizzed her—asking her who she'd seen, what she'd done in his absence, and why she hadn't answered the phone every time he'd called. That was how it had started.

Then he became suspicious of anyone she knew, claiming she was out to hurt him. He even refused to believe that Misty—sweet, precious Misty—wasn't the child of their next door neighbor back in Scranton, Pennsylvania. She'd tried to tell him there was nothing going on between her and Jack Spofford. In fact, Lynn had always suspected Jack was gay, but Buck wouldn't listen to her or anyone else.

Lynn went into the kitchen and washed her hands, remembering how bloody they'd been when Buck had exploded one day and chased after her with a knife, threatening to kill her. She'd fought him with every bit of strength she'd had. Thank God neighbors called the police when they'd heard her screams.

She dried her hands and headed back to the living room. Even with the hope the women in Fat Fridays tried to give her, she'd lived with being hunted down for so long she couldn't believe she'd survive. Time was against her. She was sure he'd eventually find her. Those were the odds, pure and simple.

She peered through the curtains in her bedroom to the darkness outside and wondered where that sick, brutal man was.

CHAPTER FORTY-THREE
CAROL ANN

My life might as well be over.

Gasping for breath, Carol Ann hung up her office phone and gripped the edge of her desk, holding on as the room spun in sickening circles.

Staggering, she hurried to the ladies room and threw up. As she was washing up afterward, her stomach heaved in dry gulps at the thought of having to tell anyone what she'd just found out. She'd been such a stupid fool.

One of the girls in the office opened the door to the bathroom. "There you are, Carol Ann. Ed needs to see you in his office."

Carol Ann patted cold, wet paper towels against her face and braced herself for the meeting with her boss. She took another glance at herself in the mirror and tried to smile. She didn't want anyone else to know about the disaster called her life. She needed time to sort things out. Telling herself to be brave, she took a deep breath and made her way to Ed's office.

"Carol Ann! Come in!" Ed said, looking up from the papers on his desk. His smile became a frown. "Anything wrong?"

Carol Ann shook her head and burst into tears.

Ed rose from behind his desk and closed the door. "What's going on? Anything you want to tell me?"

"No . . . yes . . . maybe . . ." Carol Ann dabbed at her eyes, willing them to stop flooding. "It's . . . I've been robbed," she finally got out.

"What! Have you called security?" Ed sank down in his chair and gave her a worried look. "What happened? Can I do something for you?" Ed's offer of help brought fresh tears to her eyes.

He handed Carol Ann a bunch of tissues. "Why don't you tell me what happened." His tone was gentle, and more tears threatened.

Carol Ann drew a trembling breath. "I called the furniture company to verify delivery of my new furniture and found out my boyfriend had canceled the order. I told the woman on the phone there must be some mistake. John had told me the arrangements were all set. He'd said we'd get a big discount for paying with cash."

She took a shuddering breath. "The woman said, 'Honey, that's one of the oldest scams going. You'd better check out the story with your guy.' I tried to call John but . . . but his cell number has been disconnected." Carol Ann couldn't stop tears from rolling down her cheeks. "Yesterday I gave him a check for eight thousand dollars." Feeling sick all over again, she buried her face in her hands.

Ed's voice broke through the haze that surrounded her. "Well, now, let's see if we can stop payment on that check. Give me the name of the bank and the account number. Maybe we can catch the bastard."

Carol Ann looked up, surprised at the anger in Ed's voice, the way his nostrils flared. She gave him the information and sat back as he made the call, seeing him in a different light. She'd made fun of him with the ladies in the Fat Fridays group. Now, seeing him in action as he tried to help her, he seemed almost . . . well . . . nice looking. Nobody had ever fought for her like this.

Ed hung up the phone and shook his head. "Too late. The check has already been cashed. Anything else you need to worry about, Carol Ann?"

She let out a trembling sigh and the whole story came tumbling out. "I was so stupid. He didn't want to date me exclusively. He wanted my money. Me and my big mouth. I told him on our first date that I had a lot of money saved up for a house. Then he went and stole it." Her voice rose as it hit her all over again. "Do you know how long it took me to save up that much money?"

Ed's expression grew grim. "Think now. What else might he have done? Where was the furniture to be delivered? Do you have any liability anywhere else?"

Carol Ann's mind raced. "He wanted me to sign my name on the lease for the condo. Thank God I didn't. He has no other information of mine that I know of."

"You'd better call the bank to make sure you're protected on all your credit cards and accounts. Do you have anything left in the condo? You should probably get it out of there." He studied her a moment. "Give me a minute. I'll cancel my meeting and we'll go together."

"I'll meet you in the parking lot." Carol Ann felt weak with relief she wouldn't have to go to the condo alone. She left Ed, went to get her purse, and quickly headed out the door before anyone could ask any questions.

Ed arrived in the parking lot a few moments later. "I'll drive." He led Carol Ann to a silver BMW.

As they drove into the condo complex, Carol Ann's throat tightened. She'd had such high hopes of living there. Ed noticed her reaction and gave her an encouraging pat on the back.

They entered the condo, and Carol Ann steeled herself. Disappointment sank into her stomach heavy as a rock. She'd left a few items in the kitchen along with her CD player. Ed was right. She needed to remove any trace of her presence there. She suspected John had run off without paying the rent.

"Nice place," Ed commented, walking into the living room. "Mind if I look around?"

Carol Ann shook her head and hurried into the kitchen and grabbed a box. Glasses, a few plates, dish towels, silverware, and some other items were still where she'd left them. She quickly gathered them up and looked for her CD player.

She climbed the stairs, hating the emptiness of the condo. It matched the emptiness inside her.

The master bedroom was cleared of any signs that a man named John had lived there. No air mattress, no television, no clothes in the closet. No CD player of hers!

Carol Ann sank to the floor and let the tears flow. He'd taken it, along with her money, her pride, her dreams, her hopes.

CHAPTER FORTY-FOUR
SUKIE

Sukie was immersed in budget details for the summer children's program when she received a call from Tiffany. "I don't know what's going on," Tiffany said, "but Carol Ann is in Ed Pritchard's office, crying. But the real reason I called was to tell you I won't be home for dinner. I'm going to get my hair cut. This long hair is too hot and hard to deal with now that I'm getting big with the baby. I don't have to please Beau anymore, so I can do what I want with it."

Sukie hung up, amused. She'd always thought at this stage of her life she'd be slowing down and living a simpler life, but she seemed to be going backward—dating a younger man, mothering his three-year-old daughter, and sharing a house with a woman her daughter's age.

After work, Sukie went to see baby Jonathan. She tried to stop by every day or so to see him. Holding him in her arms, she reveled at how much he looked like his father. A deep love stirred inside her as she caressed his soft cheeks. Babies always reminded her of possibility.

In her arms, the baby stared at her, his dark eyes studying her seriously. She smiled, certain he knew who she was. She kissed his soft, precious cheek.

After leaving Rob's house, Sukie drove home. As she entered her driveway, Betsy pulled up behind her, got out of the car, and came right over to her. "Can we talk?"

Noting the concern on Betsy's face, Sukie said, "Sure. Come on in."

They sat outside on the patio in the shade, sipping cold sweet tea. A light breeze danced playfully around them and cooled their bodies, but its playfulness couldn't erase Sukie's worry.

"What's going on, Betsy?"

Betsy cleared her throat. "I wanted to tell you myself. Karen is going to move in with me as soon as she can get out of her lease. There's no point in trying to deal with Sarah. She's still refusing to let me come to their house. Richie has finally agreed to bring the children to the park on Sunday afternoon. That's the only way I'm going to see them." Her voice grew shaky with emotion. "It's like having visitation rights, for God's sake. To think of all the weekends Sarah and Richie dumped the kids off so they could go away for a couple of days!"

Sukie studied her friend. Dark shadows colored the skin under Betsy's eyes. Lines of worry etched her face.

"Will it make things worse to have Karen move in with you?" Sukie asked, wishing life wasn't so difficult.

Betsy shrugged. "Richie has inherited some of his father's basic fairness, but I can't predict what Sarah will do. I figure there's no reason to wait until everyone is used to the idea. That might never happen."

Knowing Sarah as she did, Sukie doubted the two of them would ever come to an agreement.

"Something else," said Betsy. "Carol Ann was crying in Ed Pritchard's office this morning and I haven't seen her all day."

"Tiffany mentioned it, too. Maybe we'd better call her to make sure she's all right." Sukie punched in Carol Ann's cell number.

Carol Ann answered on the first ring. "Oh, Sukie!" she wailed. "It's awful! John took the money I gave him for furniture and skipped town."

"What? How did that happen?" Sukie couldn't believe that after all the warnings the women in Fat Fridays had given her, Carol Ann would just hand John money.

"I know what you're thinking, but John told me a friend of his was picking up the furniture to save shipping costs. He said we'd get a deep discount for paying with cash. It seemed like a good deal, so I gave him a check." Carol Ann's words grew shaky.

A sick feeling crawled through Sukie. "Is all your money gone?"

"Most of it." Carol Ann sniffled loudly.

"Oh, no! Can you stop payment on the check?"

"Ed Pritchard made a call to the bank, but it was too late. The jerk already cashed it."

Sukie's heart sank. She knew what that money represented to Carol Ann. "How much did you lose?"

"Eight thousand dollars!"

"Oh, honey, that's awful! Just awful!" Sukie shook her head, giving Betsy a thumbs-down sign.

"Sukie, he didn't want to date me exclusively," Carol Ann whispered, as if she couldn't bear to say the words aloud. "He just wanted my money."

Sukie ached for her. "I'm so sorry. Is there anything I can do for you?"

"Ed is going to help me sort things out. We may be able to press charges, if we can find out where the . . . the . . . bastard went." Carol Ann lowered her voice. "Sukie, you wouldn't believe how wonderful Ed has been to me."

"That's really nice," Sukie said, and realized Carol Ann had just grown up a lot.

Betsy's eyes were riveted on Sukie as she and Carol Ann murmured good-byes. "Let me guess. John took the money for the furniture and ran off."

Sukie nodded. "Bingo. Carol Ann has learned a hard lesson, but some good has come of it. She's seeing Ed Pritchard in a whole new way."

"Good for her!" Betsy checked her watch. "I know how disappointed she must be. I'll call her later. Now, I'd better be going."

Sukie walked Betsy to the door. "Cam's picking me up soon. We're going to have dinner at Bea's tonight. Midweek break."

"Karen and I haven't gone there yet, but someday we will," said Betsy with a determination Sukie admired.

Sukie held Chloe's hand as they entered Bea's. When Chloe saw the lollipop basket by the cash register, she pulled away from Sukie and ran over to it.

"No, Chloe. Not now. After dinner, maybe," Sukie said quietly, taking Chloe's hand and leading her away.

"Noooooo! Now!" Chloe let out a rebellious cry and continued crying as the hostess showed them to a table by the window and seated them. Sukie buckled Chloe in her booster seat and turned to see Ted striding toward them.

Ted glared at Sukie. "What are *you* doing here? With him? And her?"

Sukie's temper rose. "This isn't your private club, Ted. If you need to talk to me, you can call me at home."

Ted's mouth worked as if he wanted to say something nasty, but he turned and walked away.

Sukie breathed a sigh of relief. Tension between her and Ted was at a breaking point. Unless he backed off, it wouldn't be long before she'd have to take him to court.

"Be careful, Sukie," Cam said quietly, after she was seated. "He's really, really frustrated. No doubt he realizes what he's lost." Cam gave her a "but look what I've found" smile that warmed her insides.

As they sat looking at menus, whispers circled around them. Sukie ignored the sound of them, along with the cold stares Ted assailed them with like missiles of hate. Her back straightened. She and Cam had every right to be together, in that restaurant, eating a nice Southern meal. The hell with what others might think of their relationship.

Ted left as Cam was paying the bill. Sukie watched him get into his car alone and was unable to prevent herself from comparing Ted to Cam—a comparison that wasn't in Ted's favor.

As Cam dropped Sukie off at her house, a sheriff's car slowly drove by. Sukie's thoughts turned to the anonymous notes. Maybe Ted had been the one behind them all along, no matter what he claimed. The looks he'd given her at the restaurant were murderous.

Cam leaned over and gave her a kiss.

"Me too, Sukie. I want a kiss," said Chloe from her car seat in the back.

Cam and Sukie broke apart, laughing. Sukie blew noisy kisses to Chloe and got out of the car, waving good-bye until they'd driven too far for her to see.

Tiffany greeted Sukie at the front door. Her newly cut hair swung at her shoulders, giving her a carefree look. "Good news!" Tiffany's eyes sparkled with excitement. "Karen's moving in with Betsy and she said I could sublet her apartment. And it's at a price I can afford."

"Wonderful!" said Sukie. "When is this going to happen?"

"Sometime in the next couple of weeks. I have to take care of some legal issues with Beau first, but he's not fighting me on this." She clasped her hands together. "I'm so relieved."

"Great." Sukie gave Tiffany a quick hug, surprised by how fast everything was moving. It all sounded simple. Too simple.

Cam called as Sukie was getting ready to leave work Friday afternoon. "I'm at Glenn's Gourmet. How does beef Wellington sound? That, a salad, and a bottle of good red wine?"

"Wonderful." Sukie smiled happily. Cam liked good food and wasn't shy about working in the kitchen. It was just one more thing to love about him.

Sukie drove directly to Cam's house. As she pulled into the driveway, Cam was carrying a couple bags of groceries inside. His eyes lit up at the sight of her. "Chloe's preschool teacher's daughter wanted to have a sleepover with Chloe, so we have the whole night to ourselves." He gave her that sexy look she loved.

She grinned, grabbed the last two bags from the SUV, and followed him inside. Cam took the bags from her, set them down on the counter, and took her in his arms. His blue eyes danced with pleasure. "I have something very special planned."

"Oh? A special dessert?" Cam had a sweet tooth and Glenn's Gourmet was known for its excellent pastries.

Cam grinned. "Not exactly." He took Sukie's hand and led her upstairs.

Her pulse raced with anticipation. It was so nice to be alone with him.

Cam opened the door to his bedroom with a flourish. "For you."

Sukie's breath caught. The bedcovers on his king-sized bed were turned down. Red rose petals formed a trail from the door to the bed and lay scattered atop the sheets. Unlit candles were placed on the bureau and tabletops. A bucket of ice containing a bottle of champagne sat on the floor near the bed. Two tulip-stemmed glasses rested nearby.

Clasping her hands together, Sukie fought tears. It was the sweetest, most romantic thing anyone had ever done for her.

"This was supposed to be for later," Cam said, smiling at her. "But let's not wait." He swept Sukie up in his arms and carried her over to the bed. "They say champagne tastes best before dinner and I know what I want for dessert."

"Yes," Sukie happily agreed. "Let's skip the rest."

Sukie later woke up and stretched lazily in Cam's bed, wondering if every morning with Cam would be as wonderful. Cam reached for her and she rolled toward him. She loved the feel of his naked, strong, virile body wrapped around her. It still amazed her that he found so much pleasure in hers.

"Sukie? What do you say you move in with Chloe and me?"

Sukie sat up in bed and stared at him. "Here?"

"Yeah. Ted is giving you a hard time about the house. Maybe it would be smart to sell it and move in here." He grinned. "I want to wake up like this every morning."

Cam put his arms around her and Sukie nestled against him, her mind trying to get comfortable with the concept of living together without a wedding. It was so against her nature to leave things open-ended.

After another bout of lovemaking and a quick breakfast, Sukie returned home. An unfamiliar car was parked behind Tiffany's SUV. She immediately became wary.

At the front door, Sukie quietly slid the key in the lock and slowly opened it. Sticking her head inside, she listened. At the sound of a familiar voice coming from the back of the house, she grinned. Elizabeth.

"Mom!" Elizabeth, in a T-shirt and pajama bottoms, hung up the phone, jumped up from the kitchen table, and came running over to her.

Sukie threw her arms around Elizabeth. They rocked back and forth in a heartwarming embrace. "I tried to call you yesterday but had to leave a message."

Elizabeth laughed. "I was on my way here. It's pretty obvious you didn't expect me." She nudged Sukie with her elbow. "I came home to find you were having a sleepover with your . . . friend."

"Friend? I'll have you know he's asked me to move in with him," Sukie retorted, not wanting Elizabeth to get the wrong idea about their relationship. This was no friends-with-benefits situation, no matter what others might think of their age difference.

"Ohhhhh. So, it's moving right along," Elizabeth said. Her expression grew pensive. "Sit down, Mom. We've got a lot to talk about. Jeez, I leave for a few months and everything changes." She tucked a strand of honey-blond hair behind her ear. "Okay, fess up. What's he like? Madeleine says he's hotter than hell."

Sukie chuckled. "He is."

"Yeah? Well, you're looking pretty hot yourself. I love what you've done to your hair. Tiffany said she helped you with your wardrobe."

"Yes. All the women in Fat Fridays have been a great support to me."

"That's nice, Mom, but let's talk about Cam. Am I going to have to call him Dad if this goes any further?"

At her teasing tone, a nervous laugh rolled out of Sukie. *God!* It felt so awkward to be talking to her daughter like this—all topsy-turvy, as if Elizabeth were the mother and she, the child.

Elizabeth's laughter ended. "Speaking of Dad, I promised to spend the night with him and Emmy Lou. It's a short visit; I have to leave tomorrow afternoon. But I had to come home to see everybody. I've been feeling left out."

Sukie hid her disappointment. "Will you come to Sunday brunch tomorrow? I'd like you to meet Cam. And, of course, Chloe."

Elizabeth sighed. "Okay, but I'm not sure I like having all these little ones around the family. First, Dad. Now, you."

Hating to be compared to Ted, Sukie forced a smile. "Wait until you meet Chloe. She'll steal your heart. And she's going to be thrilled to meet you. She wants a sister. I'll just have to explain to her that you're not a baby like she wants."

Elizabeth returned Sukie's smile. "I went to see Jonathan last night. He's so perfect. I can't believe Rob and Madeleine are parents. They're a real family now. Nice, huh?"

Sukie nodded. "So far, they seem to be doing well with him. He looks just like Rob at that age. It's brought back a lot of memories."

Elizabeth twirled a ring on her finger and looked up at her with a worried frown. "Mom? Do you think it's a good idea for you to do this thing with Cam? He's so much younger and it's kinda like you're starting a family all over again."

Sukie clasped Elizabeth's hand. "Nothing will ever take the place of the children I have, Elizabeth. And it will take a while for me to move in with Cam. I've got to sell this house first."

Elizabeth's eyes filled. "I know. It's just that it's going to take me time to get used to the idea of you being with him and all."

Sukie leaned back in her chair, seeing things from her daughter's point of view. She *was* starting all over again. And it was scary. In time, Sukie was sure she and Cam would have a more traditional situation. For now, she was taking a giant leap of faith.

The next morning Sukie woke to unsettling weather. Gray clouds boiled in the sky but spilled no rain. Warm summer air swirled in affectionate bursts around the flowers edging the patio. Not taking a chance on showers, Sukie set the table in the dining room. Maybe, she thought, a little formality was in order. It would be the first time her family—new and old—would all be together.

Cam and Chloe arrived early as she'd asked. Sukie added a blue bow to Chloe's curls, while Cam grabbed a cup of coffee and stood ready to greet her children. Sukie sensed he was as nervous as she, but, as usual, his manner was calm.

Elizabeth arrived next. Sukie rushed forward to embrace her. "Glad you're here. Come meet Cam and Chloe."

"Are you my sister?" Chloe asked, looking up at Elizabeth with her big, blue eyes. "You're so big."

The guarded expression on Elizabeth's face softened. She knelt before Chloe. "You don't want a big sister?"

Chloe shook her head firmly. "No. I want a baby sister."

Cam gave Sukie a look that implied he was ready to try for one any time.

Sukie's cheeks flushed and then grew even hotter when she noticed Elizabeth gazing at the two of them with an amused expression.

The doorbell rang, shattering the awkward moment.

"I'll get it!" Chloe shouted and ran out of the room. Sukie followed closely behind.

Madeleine came through the front doorway carrying Jonathan in her arms. Rob trailed her, weighed down by a diaper bag, a baby seat, and an extra blanket.

"It's the baby!" Chloe exclaimed happily.

"And the baby's packhorse," said Rob, and they all laughed as they crowded around them.

Jonathan opened his eyes, let out a huge yawn, and then went right back to sleep.

Rob shook hands with Cam and leaned over and gave Sukie a kiss on the cheek.

While everyone chatted and fussed over the baby, Sukie finished coordinating things in the kitchen. When all the food was laid out, she called to everyone and took her place at one end of the dining room table. Cam waited until everyone else was seated and took a place at the far end of the table. Chloe sat beside Sukie, next to Elizabeth. Jonathan lay in his infant seat on the floor between his parents' chairs, still asleep. They all held hands while Rob said a short grace and then everyone dug into their food.

Sukie automatically began to cut up Chloe's egg and cheese casserole for her.

"No, Mommy!"

Chloe's unexpected words split the air like a jagged bolt of lightning.

"Where did that come from?" The look on Rob's face told Sukie that while she might think of it as one big happy family, he didn't. Not yet.

"Wishful thinking on Chloe's part," Cam said apologetically.

"It's so surprising to hear you called that, Sukie," said Madeleine, saying what they'd all been thinking.

Elizabeth nodded. "Yeah. Really weird."

Sukie exchanged silent looks with Cam and decided to let the matter drop. It was too much, too soon. For everyone.

After the meal and cleanup, Madeleine took the baby home. Cam and Sukie agreed Chloe needed a nap and he left with her. Rob and Elizabeth decided to visit their father together.

Sukie picked up a novel she was reading and went into the den, feeling very alone in the quiet house. Settling in her favorite comfortable chair, she let out a sigh that came from deep within her. Trying to blend families would take much more time and work than she'd thought. Rob's silence and Elizabeth's horrified expression at hearing Chloe call her Mommy were clear indicators how far they were from embracing the idea.

Later, Elizabeth returned to the house and joined Sukie in the den. Sitting on the arm of the chair, she gave Sukie a look of regret. "I've got to head for the airport soon."

Sukie squeezed Elizabeth's hand. "So? How did it go with your father? No more trouble with your tuition, I hope."

Elizabeth shook her head. "No, but Mom? I don't think this thing with Dad and Emmy Lou is going to work out. All she wants from him is his money. You should hear the way she talks to him."

Sukie pressed her lips together. "He'll have to work things out for himself, Elizabeth."

"I know, but at least he's not married to her. I could never think of her as my stepmother. Gawd!"

"And Cam?" Sukie held her breath.

Elizabeth paused. "There's no doubt he loves you, Mom. That's so important to me. I saw how Dad sometimes treated you. I'm going to try to get used to the idea of you being with him. And, like you said, Chloe is adorable."

Sukie let out a sigh of relief. "Thank you, Elizabeth. I needed to hear that."

"Sure," Elizabeth replied, looking pleased. "I hope one day some man looks at me the way Cam looks at you. I just don't want you to get hurt, Mom. You deserve something better than that." She checked her watch. "I'd better go."

Sukie rose. They walked arm in arm out to Elizabeth's rental car. "I haven't had a chance to ask, but how did your finals go?"

"I got an A and three Bs," Elizabeth said, proudly.

"That's my girl," Sukie said, giving her a squeeze.

They hugged good-bye, then Sukie stood in the driveway, watching her daughter leave. She loved her so much. Her thoughts turned to Tiffany. It was sad, really, that she'd never known such love.

CHAPTER FORTY-FIVE
CAROL ANN

Holding her bank savings book in her hands, Carol Ann stared at the dismal numbers, feeling wretched. *Why didn't I see what kind of man John really is?* she wondered. All he'd ever wanted to talk about was money—how much she had and what *he* wanted to do with it.

Carol Ann paced in her bedroom, too restless to sit still while her whole life had unraveled. Her thoughts flew to the women in Fat Fridays. They hadn't said much about her being such a fool, but they didn't have to. She knew how stupid she'd been, all because of a handsome man who'd talked big. They'd warned her about John, but no, she'd been too stubborn to listen. They'd also tried to tell her Ed Pritchard was a really nice guy.

Who knew when she went to him with her troubles, she'd end up sobbing in his arms? And when she'd broken down at the condo, he'd pulled her up into his arms and held her. At the memory, she let out a sigh. She couldn't forget how it felt when his strong arms came around her or how solid his chest was when she'd leaned against it or forget his sweet murmurs of encouragement. No one had ever made her feel so cared for, so protected.

Even now, remembering it, thinking how their lips had met, sending messages neither of them could say aloud, there was a tugging inside her body. It was the best kiss she'd ever had. How could she have been so stupid about men? She'd gone for a jerk when a really good guy was right before her.

Carol Ann grabbed the keys to her car off the top of her bureau and picked up her purse. She'd promised to meet Ed for Sunday brunch to discuss ideas about how she could strike out on her own. Thinking of him again, Carol Ann decided the wispy hair on top of his head was kind of cute. Or maybe it was the way Ed's bright blue eyes lit up at the sight of her that filled her with an unexpected joy. God! He made her feel positively beautiful.

In such a short time, Carol Ann thought, he'd become someone who could one day be everything she'd ever dreamed of in a man. Well, almost. Maybe . . . more.

CHAPTER FORTY-SIX
SUKIE

Sukie arrived at the library, grateful no presentations were required from her for the Friends of the Library meeting. Her replacement would be taking over that task in just a few weeks.

Julie waved at her from behind the circulation desk. Lifting her hand, Sukie waved back and headed for her desk, hoping to take some personal time for an online course on Excel.

"Wait, Sukie! I have something to tell you." Julie crossed the room toward her as Edythe Aynsley entered the building.

Edythe gave Sukie a disapproving look and turned to Julie. "You and I were to meet promptly at nine. Your conversation with Sukie will have to wait."

Julie's face turned an ugly red. "I need to talk to her. I'm hoping Sukie will be willing to overlook your interference and help train her replacement for as long as she can."

"Well?" Edythe said, turning to Sukie.

Tired of Edythe's interference and her narrow thinking, Sukie's nostrils flared. "I would be happy to do that for you, Julie, but I am not going to deal with Edythe during this transition period. I hope that's clear."

Gasping like a goldfish whose bowl has just been shattered, Edythe stared at Sukie wide-eyed.

Sukie turned and walked away. She didn't care what a spiteful woman like Edythe Aynsley thought of her. She may have lost her job because of the woman, but she hadn't lost her sense of self.

Sukie spent most of the day writing up instructions for the young woman who'd replace her. Regardless of how she felt about Edythe, she wanted to leave the responsibilities of the position well-documented. She'd just finished the last report when Tiffany called.

"Sukie? After work, meet me at Betsy's. We've got a lot to celebrate!"

At the enthusiasm in Tiffany's voice, Sukie grinned. "What's happening?"

"I've made an agreement with Beau to try living on my own. Carol Ann has some big news, too."

"Who's bringing the champagne?" Sukie joked.

Tiffany laughed. "I will, even though I can't have more than a taste."

"Deal. I'm on my way."

Sukie drove to Betsy's, full of excitement. The luck of the ladies in the Fat Fridays group appeared to be changing.

Betsy greeted her at the door with a smile. "Sukie! Come on in!" She led Sukie out to the porch where Carol Ann and Karen were deep in conversation.

When Carol Ann saw her, she jumped up. "Oh, Sukie! You're here!" Her eyes shining, she rushed over to her. "I think I've found the man of my dreams! And it wouldn't have happened without you."

"Somebody new?"

Carol Ann grinned at Betsy. "Should I tell her?"

Amused, Sukie waited, knowing full well Carol Ann wasn't about to keep it to herself for long.

"It's Ed! Ed Pritchard. He was so nice about helping me out with the stolen check that when he asked if I'd go out with him on Saturday, I said yes." A pink tinge crept to Carol Ann's ears. "He's a real good . . . um . . . kisser. And that's not all. We met for brunch on Sunday. He thinks he can find a small house for me through a government program for first-time homebuyers. Isn't he the best?"

"It sure sounds that way." Sukie gave Carol Ann a hug. "Congratulations!"

Tiffany and Lynn arrived together and joined them on the sunporch.

Tiffany held up a large green bottle. "I've got some chilled bubbly." She handed the bottle to Betsy and turned to the group with a smile. "I can't believe it! Everything is turning out so well for all of us!"

Betsy brought out six tulip glasses on a tray and set it down on the table. They gathered around the table and watched as Lynn helped Tiffany open the bottle. At the pop of the cork, they cheered.

Tiffany poured a little champagne into each glass but her own. Raising her empty glass, she said, "Beau has finally agreed to hold off on taking any legal action against me until I've had a chance to live on my own for three months. His parents were mad as hell at him for agreeing to this, but for once, he stood up to them. We've even begun talking about getting help for him."

"We'll drink a toast to that!" said Betsy.

"Here! Here!" Sukie cried. She clinked glasses with Tiffany, realizing what a major step this was for Beau. "Did you get the agreement in writing?"

Tiffany shook her head. "I know he'll follow through on this. He made it a point to tell me."

"You make sure he doesn't strike out at you again," warned Lynn. "Sometimes things happen when you least expect it."

Sukie nodded. Life delivered one surprise after another. A little less than a year ago, she'd thought she was happily married.

◆ ◆ ◆

Judith Keim

The next morning, Sukie dressed and ambled out to the front porch for the morning paper. Sleepily, she bent over to pick it up and froze. A neatly folded note lay on top of the paper. Heart pounding, she scooped it up and opened it. "IT'S OVER, BITCH!"

The bold typed letters wavered in front of Sukie's eyes. She clutched the sheet of paper so hard it crumpled in her hand. Shaking, she scanned the area but couldn't see anyone. Shivers, like an army of a thousand ants, marched up and down her back. Someone had been standing in her yard in the early morning light while she'd stirred sleepily in her bed, thinking happy thoughts about a future with Cam. Her stomach clenched. She hurried inside. It was time to bring everyone back into the nightmare.

The first person she called was Lynn. No answer.

Then she called Betsy. "Another note has arrived. I couldn't get hold of Lynn but I'll try again. Come to my house right after work and ask the others to come with you. It's not over, not even if the person who wrote it thinks so."

"Oh my God! What did it say?" Betsy asked.

Sukie told her. "It could be meant for any of us. Not just Lynn. That's why it's important for us to meet."

"I agree," said Betsy. "It's time for us to make a plan." She hung up without any of her usual joking.

Sukie called Bill Michaels and told him about the latest note. He promised they'd double the swing-by operation he'd set up. Though Sukie was glad for his help, it did little to quell her nerves. Someone, she couldn't guess who, was out to hurt her or her friends.

The evening was unusually dark when the women arrived shortly before six. A storm system had brought much-needed rain to the area most of the day. They were a solemn group as they shook out umbrellas and placed them on Sukie's porch. Sukie ushered them into the living room.

The note lay in the middle of the coffee table like a lit stick of dynamite.

"This is very serious," said Betsy, picking it up and reading it. "Like you said, Sukie, it could be for any of us." She turned to Carol Ann. "Do you think John would do this to you? You know, get back at you for not playing along with him? Reporting him to the police?"

Carol Ann's jaw dropped. "Me? What about you and Sarah?"

Betsy let out a trembling sigh. "Sarah is so upset with me right now I think she's capable of most anything. Look what happened at the school. She wanted me arrested by the FBI, for God's sake."

Sukie couldn't remain quiet. She'd thought about it all day. "I ran into Ted at Bea's the other night and had words with him. After he left our table, Cam warned me to go easy, that Ted is very, very angry. Cam's heard things are not going well between Ted and Emmy Lou. Elizabeth isn't sure the relationship will even last. If looks could kill, I'd be dead right now. Think of what he'd gain with me out of the way—the house, no alimony payments . . ."

"Maybe it's Beau," said Tiffany, cutting in. "Sukie's seen firsthand what he's capable of doing. He's hit me, and those awful words scrawled on the nursery walls . . ."

"Each of us has a reason to be the one," said Carol Ann, white-faced. "I was supposed to give John all my money. Thank God I didn't, but maybe he really does want to get back at me."

"I've made a decision," said Lynn, speaking up. "Tonight I'll contact a safe house and leave town. I won't allow any of you to get hurt because of me."

"But, Lynn," Sukie said. "We don't know for sure you're the one who is being targeted. The notes keep coming to my house. Maybe I'm the one someone's after."

"No. Don't you see? If my ex left me those notes at my apartment, then I'd know for sure he was after me again. This way, I can't go to the police with anything definite. It keeps me on edge. That's how his sick mind works. No, I'm leaving tomorrow."

Sukie could tell from the set of Lynn's jaw and the tears in her eyes, how determined she was. "Let's talk about it with a glass of wine and some refreshments."

"I'm leaving and there will be no discussion about it." Lynn turned to Betsy. "I'll let you handle my departure at the office, explain what my life is like."

At the thought of losing Lynn, Sukie's eyes grew misty. A quiet, no nonsense kind of person, Lynn was a stable part of their group.

She went into the kitchen for refreshments and returned to the living room. "We'll at least send Lynn off with some good memories. And Lynn, we expect to see you again. We'll put an end to this."

A range of emotions crossed Lynn's face, telling of her sorrow and shame. "No matter what happens, I'll always remember our time together and how wonderful you all have been to me."

They were an unusually somber group as they sipped their wine and nibbled on treats. Sukie was sure the others, like she, were thinking of Lynn's strength through the years.

"I'd better go," said Betsy, rising. "Karen will be calling me. She's at an out-of-town meeting." She embraced Lynn one more time. "Think this over, Lynn. Don't be so anxious to leave. I think you're safer here than anywhere else."

Sukie walked Betsy to the front of the house, switched on the porch light, and opened the door.

"Okay, bitch!" a voice cried out from across the lawn. "It's over. No more running."

The menacing figure of a man loomed in the dark.

Sukie froze in the doorway, feeling as if she were trapped in a scene from a violent television show. Light glinted off the barrel of a gun in his hand.

Sukie blocked the entrance to the house as best she could. "Stay back," she warned the women behind her. "He's got a gun."

"You! Get away from the door! Now!" the intruder barked.

Sukie's mouth went dry.

From behind Sukie, someone charged with a roar, shoving her aside. She tumbled to the front-porch stoop with a yelp. A light flashed in front of her eyes as her head hit the brick. Dazed, Sukie heard the deafening report of a gun and a cry of pain.

"Don't move," someone called out in a commanding voice. Another shot rang out.

Sukie lay there, waiting to feel the pain of a bullet piercing her.

CHAPTER FORTY-SEVEN
SUKIE

"Lynn! Lynn!" Betsy screamed, rushing past Sukie.

Trying to clear her head, Sukie sat up.

"Oh my God! Lynn!" shrieked Carol Ann, running out onto the lawn.

Tiffany rushed over to her. "Sukie! Are you all right? Lynn's been shot. That guy must be her ex." Tiffany leaned weakly against the front-porch post. "I think he's dead."

Sirens wailed in the background, becoming louder and louder. Trembling all over, Sukie got to her feet, straining to see in the dark.

"You women, stay out of the way! Don't touch anything!" warned the officer hurrying onto the scene.

"Is Lynn all right?" Sukie's body, which had been so immobile, so frozen, now seemed to melt. Her legs felt so rubbery she had to sit down. She drew in her breath and let it out in shocked, raspy gasps. Tears streamed down Tiffany's cheeks as she patted Sukie's back.

Two patrol cars pulled up, along with another car with official markings.

From the front lawn, Betsy and Carol Ann joined Sukie and Tiffany on the front porch, their faces pale with shock.

Betsy collapsed on the step next to Sukie. "Lynn's hurt real bad," she said brokenly. "The people from the sheriff's office told us to come over here and sit, that they'd take care of her, but I dunno."

"The sheriff's deputy shot the man who tried to kill her. He's dead." Carol Ann's voice shook. "I think I'm going to be sick." She leaned over and vomited in the bushes lining the porch.

"Sukie? Are you all right? Speak to me," commanded Betsy, giving her a troubled look.

"I think she's in shock," said Tiffany, gazing at Sukie with a worried frown.

"She saved my life," Sukie managed to say. The dam of emotions she'd been holding back burst out of her. Sukie cried for everything Lynn had lost. She cried for Lynn's determination to see that none of them were harmed because of her. She cried for fear that Lynn might not make it. She thought Lynn was braver than anyone she'd ever known.

"Sukie! My God, Sukie!"

She looked up to see Cam running toward her. She struggled to her feet and started toward him. He swept her up in his arms and hugged her so tightly she could barely breathe.

"Lynn's hurt, maybe dying," she managed to get out between sobs that racked her body.

"You're okay. You're okay," Cam murmured over and over again as he carried her to the others and set her down. "Lynn's hurt, but what about the guy?"

Betsy blinked back tears. "He's dead. We're pretty sure it's Lynn's ex-husband. She's been running from him for years."

Sukie clasped Betsy's hand. Carol Ann wrapped her arm around Betsy, and Tiffany held onto Sukie in a group hug none of them wanted—not in this way, for this reason.

Sukie turned to Cam. "Where's Chloe?"

"In my car, down the street. One of the sheriff's men is watching her. I've got to go back to her. I don't want her to see any of this."

Sukie broke away from the group and walked a few steps away. She and Cam embraced. With his solid body pressed against hers, deep gratitude filled her. She was alive and it felt so very, very good.

Cam caressed Sukie's cheek, his blue eyes swimming. "Thank God, you're all right. I love you, Sukie."

She'd waited to hear those words. But in these circumstances, they meant much more. She caressed his cheek. "I love you, too—with all my heart."

Cam took off at a run, and Sukie joined her friends sitting on her steps, keeping vigil.

Bill Michaels came over to them and they began telling the sheriff what they knew. As Betsy talked, Sukie gazed out at the chaos in her yard. Yellow tape had been strung around the area and officers were taking care of their duties, gathering evidence and marking spots where the bodies had fallen. Siren wailing, an ambulance pulled into the driveway. Two EMTs emerged and rushed over to where Lynn still lay on the ground. An officer knelt beside her.

Sukie struggled to her feet. "I want to see Lynn before they take her away."

Betsy held her back. "No, hon, you don't. It's gruesome. And she's unconscious. Let them take care of her, like the guy told us they would."

"Yeah, it's awful. A bloody mess. Oh, jeez," said Carol Ann. "I think I'm going to be sick again." She leaned back against the porch railing and closed her eyes.

Sukie's stomach knotted as she watched the EMTs strap Lynn onto a gurney, slide it into the back of the ambulance, and close the door. The flashing red lights atop the ambulance cast eerie, bloody beams into the darkness. Then they were gone.

The sheriff began to question each of the women about what she'd seen and heard. Sukie saw a man approaching them with a camera and she rose.

"Uh-oh. It's the press. Quick! Get inside the house."

Tiffany jumped to her feet and tugged on Carol Ann's arm.

Sukie opened the front door and all three women hurried inside behind her, leaving the sheriff to deal with the press. Inside, they huddled together in the living room.

Betsy shook her head. "I can't believe it. Lynn, I mean Grace, is such a kind woman. It makes you wonder about people, what burdens they really carry."

Bill Michaels rang the doorbell and came inside. "I know how upset all of you women are. You can go now. It's a pretty cut-and-dried case. We're running a check on the guy now, but your story makes sense. There's nothing you can do for her now but pray. Damn shame. The ambulance has taken her down to North Fulton. They've got a level-two trauma center there."

"I think Lynn recognized his voice, which is why she pushed me out of the way." Sukie swallowed hard. "She saved my life."

Bill nodded. "Yeah, she probably did."

Betsy gripped her hand and Sukie squeezed back, trying not to break down again. How do you ever thank someone for saving your life? She thought of her children, of Cam and Chloe.

The sheriff cleared his throat. "I'm leaving now. If anything else comes up, anything at all, please let me know."

After the sheriff left, Sukie turned to the others. "I'm going to the hospital. I can't just stay here, wondering and waiting to know how Lynn is."

"I'm going with you," said Betsy.

"Me too," Carol Ann and Tiffany said in unison.

They grabbed their purses and Sukie walked them to the front door.

As she opened it, a flash of light streamed through the darkness. Sukie screamed and ducked, expecting another gunshot.

"Get out of here, you scum!" Betsy shouted, coming to Sukie's aid.

Sukie straightened, shaking all over.

"It was that damn newspaperman," Betsy explained. "We'll probably make the front page."

"Oh, no," said Tiffany, "my in-laws will be furious if I'm in the paper, associated with a killing."

"Let's go," Sukie said. She felt fine and nobody was going to stop her from being by Lynn's side.

The drive to the hospital was quiet. Memories of Lynn at their lunches and evening gatherings filled Sukie's mind. Lynn had always been the silent one, the mysterious one. Now, they all understood why she'd been on the run to keep her child safe. Her ex was as crazy as she'd said.

Betsy broke into the silence. "If Lynn survives, she's going to need some help. She was shot in the chest right near the shoulder. We're going to have to step in and help her do all sorts of things."

"And what about the expenses? How will she pay for them?" Sukie said. "She lives very frugally."

"Do you think she'll survive all this? It was so bloody," said Carol Ann, gagging.

"Of course she'll survive." Sukie refused to think Lynn might not make it. Lynn had been so strong for so many years, her life couldn't end like this.

They got off Route 400 at the Old Milton exit and Sukie drove west as fast as she dared, over to Route 9 and down to the hospital, following the signs. At that time of night, traffic wasn't bad. Moments later, Sukie swung into the emergency entrance of the hospital and parked the car. They hurried into the emergency room and the four of them grouped together at the information desk, all talking at once.

"Whoa!" said the aide behind the desk. "One at a time, please."

Betsy took over. "Lynn Hodges, I mean Grace Jamison, was brought in with a gunshot wound. Her ex-husband shot her. We're here to make sure she's all right. She has no other family. Just us."

"She'll be in the trauma center, no doubt. Why don't you ladies take seats and I'll see if I can find out some information for you as soon as I can. We don't want to interrupt them now."

Feeling queasy, Sukie went over to a group of chairs and plopped down. This whole scene was surreal. Not that long ago, the women had been chatting together in her house, plotting to save Lynn. Sukie hadn't seen Lynn's wounds up close, but she'd seen enough blood to know it had to be bad.

The waiting period grew longer. First one, then another of them, rose and paced the waiting room.

An endless time later, a doctor appeared, wearing green scrubs. "You here for Lynn Hodges? Grace Jamison?"

Sukie froze in her chair. "Is . . . is . . . she all right?"

"She's got a long road ahead of her, but she's going to make it. She's lost a lot of blood. A bone fragment severed an artery. It's going to take a lot of therapy for her to regain complete use of her shoulder and left arm again. Overall, however, I'd say she's a very lucky woman. Two inches to her right and she'd be dead."

Tears misted Sukie's eyes. "Can we see her?"

The doctor shook his head. "She's in recovery and needs to focus all her energy on herself right now. When she wakes up, I'll ask the nurses to tell her that you were here. Right now, the best you can do for her and yourselves is to go home and get some rest. She'll need you in the coming days. There'll be some major adjustments to her life."

Silently, they went out to the car.

Her thoughts on all that had happened, Sukie headed the car home to Williston. Tiffany fell asleep beside her. Betsy and Carol Ann talked quietly in the back. Her body numb, Sukie turned on light music, anything to keep her mind from replaying the shooting scene over and over.

Pulling into her driveway, Sukie glanced over at the yellow-taped area. As the sounds and images of the struggle came back, she felt the blood leave her face. She groaned and braked to a stop.

"Are you all right?" Betsy asked, giving her a worried look.

Sukie nodded, though she wondered how long she'd always see figures looming at her from the dark and hear the sound of gunshots.

They hugged and murmured good-byes, and Tiffany followed Sukie inside.

Sukie locked the front door and leaned against it, wishing she could shut out memories of the evening's events as easily. She turned to Tiffany. "Are you okay? The baby?"

Tiffany nodded and rubbed her stomach. "We're going to be okay, but I'm going to bed."

Sukie turned out the downstairs lights and followed Tiffany upstairs, hardly able to keep on her feet. The phone rang as she was pulling on her nightgown. She knew who it was before she picked it up.

"Hello, sweetheart. I've been trying to reach you." Cam's low voice was like a soothing hand caressing her body. "How's Lynn?"

"She's going to survive, but it's going to be a long road to recovery." Sukie lay in bed and clutched the phone to her ear, imagining Cam lying beside her. "Cam? Just talk to me. I just need to hear your voice, know you're near."

Cam began talking, calming her. Sometime during his murmurings, Sukie fell asleep, too emotionally drained to stay alert.

The next morning, the sound of the doorbell woke Sukie. Her heart pounding, she jerked upright. It all came back—the shooting, Lynn's struggle to survive.

The doorbell rang again. Sukie went to the window and looked out. Two television trucks were parked in the driveway. Cameramen and crew were milling around.

Tiffany stumbled into Sukie's room. "What's happening?"

Sukie motioned her over to the window. "Word must have gotten out. We're going to be besieged."

Tiffany gasped and put a hand over her mouth. "Oh my God! Regard and Muffy will be furious. I can't go outside."

"I'll call the sheriff's office and see if they can help us. The TV trucks are blocking the driveway and their people are trespassing."

The phone rang. Sukie picked it up. "Sukie? It's Julie. I heard the news. It's all over town. How awful. Are you all right? How's your friend?"

"I'm still trying to get over the shock, but yes, I'm fine. We're praying Lynn will be okay. It's going to take time for her to recover. I need to think of a way to raise funds to help cover her expenses."

"Let me know when you do. We women have to show support for one another. Don't bother to come in to work today. Just take the day off and get some rest."

Relieved, Sukie hung up. There was no way she could concentrate on her job today.

Tiffany called her boss and learned neither Betsy nor Carol Ann was coming into the office.

"I'll get dressed and go downstairs to get rid of the news people," Sukie said. "They'll hang around until someone speaks to them."

Tiffany grabbed her arm. "Sukie? I can't go out there. You understand, don't you?"

Sukie nodded. "Don't worry about it. I know how Beau's family is about publicity—especially something nasty like this. Before I do anything, though, I've got to call my children and let them know I'm all right."

The phone rang. It was Rob. Sukie filled him in on all that had happened.

Rob cleared his throat. "Thank God, you're all right. I love you, Mom."

Tears stung Sukie's eyes. He hadn't said that to her since the divorce. "I love you, too, honey."

Sukie hung up with Rob, dialed Elizabeth's cell, and waited for her to pick up. After four rings, Elizabeth's recorded voice came on, and Sukie was forced to leave a message. She'd call Cam later, after he got Chloe to day care.

Pulling her clothes on, Sukie wondered what she should say to the press. Realizing she had no choice, she went outside to talk to them. Bill Michaels and two of his men had appeared and stood ready on the sidelines.

A female reporter pushed her way to Sukie and held a mic under her nose. "What's your reaction to the attempted murder? How long have you known Lynn Hodges? Did you know that wasn't her real name? Was it your fault that she was almost killed on your property?"

Sukie reeled back on her heels as the reporter's words sunk in. *My God! Was it her fault Lynn was almost killed?* If she hadn't called the meeting, maybe Lynn wouldn't have been shot. The thought made Sukie dizzy. She grabbed onto the porch railing, fighting for balance.

Catching a steadying breath, Sukie spoke as clearly as she could. "Lynn Hodges or Grace Jamison is a wonderful woman who was not allowed to live a normal life because of her ex-husband's stalking. Like so many women in this country, her life was ruined by the violence of a man. I don't wish to say anything more at this time, except to ask you to respect our privacy and to pray for Lynn's full recovery."

"Wait! Tiffany Wright is part of your group. Isn't that Judge Wright's daughter-in-law? There's talk of marital problems there. Why was she here and not at home?" said a man, whose smirk irritated Sukie.

Stunned by his brazen cruelty, Sukie backed away from the reporters. "No further comment."

She turned and hurried back inside the house, feeling as if she'd had her clothes ripped off. *So much for trying to cooperate with the press,*

Sukie thought sourly. They could damn well find all the information they needed in the sheriff's report.

Sukie went into the kitchen, made a fresh pot of coffee, and called Betsy and Carol Ann. They all agreed to meet at Betsy's house for a different kind of Fat Fridays lunch.

After talking to Cam, Sukie phoned the hospital and spoke to the nurse on the surgical floor, hoping to talk to Lynn.

"Grace is still pretty doped up from the medicine, and the doctor is with her now," the nurse informed Sukie. "Hold on and I'll try to get a message to her."

The nurse came back on the phone a few minutes later. "Sorry. She couldn't take the call, but she asked if you all could come see her tomorrow."

Sukie was disappointed, but she understood. "We'll be there tomorrow morning."

"Sure thing," said the nurse. "She just needs a little time."

With the sheriff's help, most of the press left Sukie's yard. A few hours later Betsy greeted Sukie and Tiffany at her door, her expression somber. "Do you realize this is the only time Lynn hasn't shown up for one of our get-togethers? Damn! I still can't get over the whole thing."

When they walked out to the screened porch, Carol Ann was already seated at the table. She gave them a forlorn wave and dabbed at her eyes. "Lynn couldn't take my call."

Sukie took a seat. "I told the nurse we'd be there tomorrow morning."

"Well, I'm glad we're together today," said Betsy, "though I keep imagining Lynn will appear soon. But she's here in spirit, right?"

Sukie nodded and waved her hand for attention. "I have an idea about raising money to cover her expenses. We can set up a fund for her at Citizens' bank and notify the newspapers and the television stations. The story has caught the attention of all of them. I know the chairman of the bank. I'm willing to call him and start it off with a donation of my own."

"Perfect," said Carol Ann. "Lynn's quiet and reserved, but I think she'd appreciate that."

"Me too," said Betsy. "It's a simple sincere outpouring of good wishes."

"We'll keep it very tasteful," agreed Tiffany.

Planning the fund drive seemed to help each of them cope with what they'd experienced. By the time Sukie left Betsy's house midafternoon, she was more at peace. Still, there was something she needed to do for herself.

She drove to Rob and Madeleine's house.

Madeleine greeted her at the door and gave Sukie an extra-long embrace. "I'm so sorry about what happened, Sukie. Is Lynn going to be all right?"

Sukie nodded. "We think so. Can I spend some time with my grandson?"

Madeleine smiled. "I thought you might be by. I've put him in a new outfit, just for you. Come on. He's been fed so he should be ready for a good cuddle." She grinned. "And it will give me time for a shower. I haven't had a chance before now."

Remembering baby-filled days like that, Sukie smiled and followed Madeleine upstairs to the nursery.

Jonathan lay asleep in his crib looking like a miniature version of Rob, his mouth still working as if he were nursing. Sukie picked him up and held him close to her chest. As he nestled against her, a sense of comfort swept through Sukie. Life was unpredictable. Death was a part of it, but so was new life. Sukie clung to that thought as she sat in the rocker and held him, moving back and forth in a soothing rhythm.

Sukie awoke with a start as Madeleine lifted Jonathan out of her arms.

"I'm sorry . . ." Sukie began.

"No, no. I'm glad you got some rest, Sukie. I can't imagine what you've been through."

Madeleine put Jonathan down in his crib and they walked downstairs together, in tune with each other.

That evening, Sukie had dinner at Cam's house. Being with him, hugging Chloe to her, Sukie marveled at how lucky she was. Almost a year ago, she'd been certain her life would never be happy again. Fate had chosen a different future for her and had kept her safe from a bullet.

"Be safe," Cam whispered as he held her before she left to go home. "If anything happened to you . . ."

"Shhh, I love you," Sukie said, silencing his fears with a finger on his lips. Somehow, Sukie knew they'd be given time to enjoy what they had, even if they had to fight for it.

Sukie and Tiffany picked up Betsy and Carol Ann for the trip to Roswell. While driving, Sukie could hardly wait to see Lynn for herself. Her voice had been weak but filled with relief when Sukie had spoken to her earlier that morning.

At the hospital, they were directed to Lynn's room on the second floor. Betsy knocked lightly on the door, and they tiptoed inside.

Lynn lay asleep on the bed, her face almost as white as the sheets. Her shoulder area beneath the hospital gown and extending out from the bandages was bruised and swollen. An IV was taped to the back of one hand, which lay limp atop the sheets. Sensing their movement, Lynn's eyes flashed open. A smile slowly spread across her face, adding needed color to her cheeks.

Sukie rushed to Lynn's side. "You saved my life, Lynn! How can I ever thank you?" She leaned over and kissed Lynn gently on a flushed cheek.

Lynn patted Sukie's hand awkwardly. "Call me Grace. It's over—just like the son of a bitch said." She gave Sukie a weak grin. Relieved to see such spirit, Sukie smiled back.

Carol Ann placed a vase of flowers she'd brought on the nightstand next to Grace's bed. Betsy handed Grace a box of chocolates. Tiffany took hold of Grace's hand and reached out to Carol Ann. They all held hands, surrounding Grace's bed like a circle of protection.

They'd each faced challenges and become stronger. Thinking of herself, Sukie couldn't imagine her life without Cam and Chloe. These women had helped her understand she should simply enjoy the almost magical relationship she shared with Cam, that it was worth striving for and keeping, and that she deserved it.

She gazed with affection at the others. She wasn't sure what the future held for them, but she knew that whatever challenges came their way, the women of the Fat Fridays group would survive—together.

ABOUT THE AUTHOR

Judith Keim has loved stories and reading since she was a young girl. She spent hot summer afternoons lost in novels, traveling from her porch in upstate New York to far-flung fictional destinations. Her writing has been featured in *Chicken Soup to Inspire a Woman's Soul* and *Summer in Mossy Creek*, a Belle Books novel. She has been selected as a finalist in numerous RWA contests. Under the name J.S. Keim, she has also published middle-grade fantasy novels as well as short stories for children in *Highlights*, *Jack and Jill*, and *Children's Playmate*. Keim lives in Boise, Idaho, with her husband and their long-haired dachshund, Winston.